THE TRANSATLANTIC MATERIALS OF AMERICAN LITERATURE

A Volume in the Series

Studies in Print Culture and the History of the Book

Edited by

Greg Barnhisel, Joan Shelley Rubin, and Michael Winship

THE TRANSATLANTIC MATERIALS OF AMERICAN LITERATURE

Publishing US Writing in Britain, 1830–1860

Katie McGettigan

University of Massachusetts Press
Amherst and Boston

Printed in the United States of America

ISBN 978-1-62534-685-8 (paper); 686-5 (hardcover)

Designed by Deste Roosa
Set in Merriweather and Bell Gothic STD
Printed and bound by Books International, Inc.

Cover design and photograph by Rebecca Neimark, Twenty-Six Letters

Library of Congress Cataloging-in-Publication Data
A catalog record for this book is available from the Library of Congress

British Library Cataloguing-in-Publication Data
A catalog record for this book is available from the British Library.

Chapter 1 originally appeared as "Henry Wadsworth Longfellow and the Transatlantic Materials of American Literature," in *American Literature* 89, no. 4 (2017) and appears here by permission of Duke University Press. A portion of chapter 3 appeared as "'Across the Waters of This Disputed Ocean': The Material Production of American Literature in Nineteenth-Century Britain" in *Interventions: Rethinking the Nineteenth Century*, edited by Anna Barton and Andrew Smith (Manchester: Manchester University Press, 2017), reproduced with permission of Manchester University Press. An earlier version of chapter 5 appeared as "Transatlantic Reprinting as National Performance: Staging America in London Magazines, 1839–1852," in *Journal of American Studies* 53, no. 4 (2019). Copyright Cambridge University Press, reprinted with permission.

To my Mum and Dad

CONTENTS

ACKNOWLEDGMENTS

Research for this book was generously supported by a Leverhulme Trust Early Career Fellowship held at the University of Nottingham that gave me time and funds to carry out archival work. Royal Holloway, University of London further supported the project by funding conference attendance and sabbatical leave. While writing this book, I was invited to speak at the University of East Anglia, Keele University, the University of Glasgow, Ruprecht-Karl University Heidelberg, and Nottingham Trent University. At each of these talks, I received feedback that led me to reshape the project in large and small ways, and I warmly thank colleagues for the invitations and for their engagement with my work.

Traces of American literature's transatlantic materials endure in archives on both sides of the Atlantic. This book could not have been written without cooperation from the following institutions, and without generous assistance from their staff: the American Antiquarian Society; the Beinecke Library, Yale University; the Bodleian Library, Oxford University; the British Library; the Connecticut Historical Society; the Firestone Library, Princeton University; the Harriet Beecher Stowe Center; the Historical Society of Pennsylvania; the Houghton Library, Harvard University; the National Library of Scotland; the New York Public Library; Special Collections, the Open University; the Library of the Society of Friends, London; Trinity College, Hartford; University Library, Cambridge University; the University of Birmingham Library; the University of Virginia Special Collections. Special thanks to George Low for permission to quote from the Sampson Low papers deposited at the Open University, and for his generous interest in my research on his ancestors and their firm.

It is impossible to list all the colleagues who have shared their expertise and research, and offered advice and encouragement across the long process of writing this book. The following are among the many who deserve my thanks: Tom Augst, Annika Bautz, Ian Bell, Bridget Bennett, Celeste-Marie Bernier, John

Bryant, Michelle Coghlan, Michael Collins, Thomas Constantinesco, Elena Cooper, Ryan Cordell, Sue Currell, Marcy Dinius, Hilary Emmett, Michael Everton, Duncan Faherty, Chris Gair, Nick Grant, Henning Hansen, Molly Hardy, Tomos Hughes, Leon Jackson, Michael Jonik, Wyn Kelley, Nicola Kirkby, Marie Léger-St-Jean, Tim Lustig, David McClay, Josephine McDonagh, Meredith McGill, Sarah Meer, Hannah Lauren Murray, Hannah-Rose Murray, Jim Mussell, Judie Newman, Stephanie Palmer, Matthew Pethers, Benjamin Pickford, Laura Rattray, Joe Rezek, Peter Riley, Paul Rooney, Cécile Roudeau, Michaël Roy, Thomas Ruys-Smith, Tim Sommer, Mark Storey, Fionnghuala Sweeney, Ed Sugden, Jenny Terry, Zoe Todd, Robin Vandome, Christa Vogelius, James West, Rachel Williams, Michael Winship, and Tom Wright. Tim Armstrong, Ruth Livesey, and Rachel Sykes commented on draft chapters, offering immensely helpful advice. I'd like to extend special thanks to Graham Thompson, whose mentorship was crucial to devising and defining this project, and who has continued to offer advice and support to its completion. The British Association for American Studies, the British Association of Nineteenth-Century Americanists, C19: The Society for Nineteenth-Century Americanists, and the Society for the History of Authorship, Reading and Publishing have all been welcoming scholarly homes, and their conferences have been important venues for developing these ideas.

My former colleagues in the Department of American Studies at the University of Nottingham and my present colleagues in the Department of English and School of Humanities at Royal Holloway have been great supporters of my research and models of collegiality. The undergraduate and postgraduate students at Royal Holloway continue to inspire me with their ideas and enthusiasm. Special thanks to the very first BA English and American Literature graduates of Royal Holloway, who learnt the ropes along with me: Ellen Abernathy, Rachel Farguson, Sally Gibbs, Tamsin Hare, Sarah-Lisa Henning, Rohaan Karim, Cassandra Lau, and Nabilah Shah.

It has been a pleasure to work with Brian Halley, Rachael DeShano, and Courtney Andree at the University of Massachusetts Press: I thank them for their support for the book and their guidance through the publication process. Thanks also to Julie Shilling for her careful copyediting, and to Paula Clarke Bain for producing the wonderful index.

My sincere thanks to Kathryn Crosby, Sandra Hepden, Liza Kouppi, Karen Mullen, Mat Wood, and all the staff at N Family Club Twickenham for the expertise and care they have shown my family.

Finally, my thanks to Maggie Deli, Alex McClellan, Rachel Sykes, Jo Taylor, and Becky Thumpston for their enduring friendship. Thanks to all my family for their love and support, but especially to Ken Knowles, Sheila Probert, Jan Williams, Will McGettigan, Sarah Hines, and Olivia Hines. Thanks to my parents, Jill and Barney McGettigan, whose love and generosity have helped me and my work in so many ways, and to whom this book is dedicated. Thanks to Abelard the pug for the joy he brings.

My mother-in-law, Geraldine Knowles, passed away as I was finishing this book, and I miss her greatly. Her favorite poem, learned in her childhood in rural County Durham, was Longfellow's "The Slave's Dream." She connected her reading of this poem to her desire to help people find freedom, which she pursued through her career as a psychiatrist—thus proving that the transatlantic circulations, receptions, and legacies of antebellum American literature are a more complex, expansive, and marvellous story than I could tell in one book.

Finally, all my thanks and all my love to Chris Knowles—for everything, always—and to Elliot, whose enthusiasm for books is a daily reminder of what amazing objects they are.

THE TRANSATLANTIC MATERIALS OF AMERICAN LITERATURE

INTRODUCTION

The Transatlantic Materials of American Literature

This book returns to two recurring questions in the study of nineteenth-century US literature and print culture: Did a cultural phenomenon called "American literature" emerge in the antebellum era, and, if so, how did it emerge? It approaches those questions through print objects that are almost always excluded from American literary history: editions of US texts that were published in Britain. Through analyzing the networks, exchanges, and print objects that circulated US writing on the other side of the Atlantic, I argue that British publishers and their material texts participated in the production of a national American literary field in the three decades before the Civil War. As they printed and reprinted US texts in an array of forms, British publishers staked out geographical, political, and aesthetic territories for American literature. Their editions championed individual US writers, endowed US texts with different forms of authority and value, and intervened in debates about the nature and future of American writing, authorship, and print culture. In dialogue with US writers and their texts, British print authorized—with both more and less success—competing conceptions of an emergent national tradition and of the terms under which its texts and its writers should be valued in Britain, the United States, and the wider world.

My aim, then, is to tell the story of how British publishers and their print objects defined and authorized American literature in the mid-nineteenth century. To this end, I offer a new history of the multifaceted publication and dissemination of US fiction, poetry, essays, articles, and autobiography in Britain. British publishers issued US texts in cheap paperbacks and in costly illustrated editions, located them alongside British writing in publishers' series and gift books, and reprinted them in "American" magazines. In some cases, American authors collaborated with British firms on these publications, and in others, they did not. Some US texts were distributed by large and prestigious literary firms, and others through social and activist networks outside of the trade. To reconstruct the trajectories of individual authors, texts, and publications, I examine British editions of American books alongside authors' and publishers' correspondence, publishers' archives, trade journals, and literary periodicals. In situating these histories within the wider conditions of textual circulation between the United States and Britain, I restore a thick materiality to transatlantic print culture and recover the role of British print in the emergence of American literature.

The authorization of American literature through British print was heterogenous and speculative, as British books and periodicals materialized different visions of what American literature was and could be, with varying degrees of success. Writers like Herman Melville, Henry Wadsworth Longfellow, and Lydia Huntley Sigourney worked with publishers whose printed books conferred economic and literary value upon their works, and materially reinforced their conceptions of American authorship, readership, and literary aesthetics, even when those editions were not legally authorized. British publications also provided space for US writings that critiqued the making of US nationhood. Longfellow and Sigourney used highly commercialized illustrated volumes to condemn the racialized violence that underpinned the founding and expansion of the United States, although both ultimately stopped short of offering remedies and alternatives. However, British print also participated in the "rhetorics of forgetfulness, [and] strategies for excluding events, meanings, and people who don't fit the myth of community," that Timothy Hampton, Homi Bhabha, and others have identified as counterparts to the positive construction of national narratives and cultures.[1] Black, and to a lesser extent, women writers found it harder to access particular authorizing forms of British print. The authors of US slave narratives used transatlantic print circulation to situate themselves as Atlantic subjects, but their British publishers reinscribed Black bodies as objects of speculation. By examining such tensions and exploring how chance and contingency shaped both successful and unsuccessful attempts to materialize American literature in Britain, I trace the limits of the national traditions that were fashioned and refashioned through British print.

I call the processes and print objects through which British publishers fashioned a US literary tradition the "transatlantic materials of American literature." This term is intentionally capacious, drawing together print materialities of different orders and scales. First, the "transatlantic materials of American literature" refers to the British material texts in which US writings circulated. I pay close attention to covers, prefaces, title pages, editorials, illustrations, appendixes, and adverts to examine where and how British publishers engaged with US writers' conceptions of American authorship, audiences, and aesthetics, and where they did not. Second, it denotes the material processes and relations through which those print objects were produced: methods of publication and dissemination, advertising, financial transactions, the transmission of books and manuscripts across the Atlantic, and trade arrangements between US writers, US and British publishers, and others involved in transatlantic publication. Third, it invokes the wider material conditions under which British editions of US texts were produced: technological developments in book production, an expanding and diversifying reading public in Britain, ever-shifting international copyright laws, and book trade conventions. It is one of the book's central claims that these distinct yet interlinked materialities together produced a fertile transatlantic terrain that could sustain various competing models for American literature. Case studies of different print formats show how multiple iterations of a national American literature emerged from the interplay between various geographies of print, from the transatlantic currents of the mid-century book trade to the hyperlocal spaces of individual volumes, periodicals, and series.[2] By examining British editions of US texts at different scales and from different orientations, and by zooming out and zooming in on these transatlantic materials, this book seeks to make visible the ways in which British print and the transatlantic trade authorized American literature.

These transatlantic authorizing processes involved creative, generative, and reciprocal dialogues between US writers and British publishers, and between US literary texts and British print objects.

The chapters that follow analyze how transatlantic feedback loops incorporating texts, books, authors, editors, publishers, and critics produced overlapping and competing visions of American nationhood, literature, and authorship. I approach British editions as complex acts of reception that engaged with US authors' visions for and disputes over the best models for national American writing and print culture. Authorized and unauthorized British editions intervened in debates about the importance of international copyright to the development of US authorship. They advanced ideas of American cultural nationhood as variously cosmopolitan, polyphonic, and sentimental. They mapped new territories for national writing and located American nationhood in threshold and frontier spaces. These interventions then flowed back into the United States, sometimes in the form of imported British editions, but most often in US writers' imaginative remediations of and responses to their appearances in British print. Furthermore, US critics often turned to the British editions of works and to British publishers when discussing the present state of and possible futures for American literature. To capture these multimedia, transnational conversations, I combine the study of print culture with literary criticism to produce a layered book history that explores the trajectories and legacies of individual texts and books as well as their place in a transatlantic print culture.

The Transatlantic Materials of American Literature thus explores the role of British publishers and their print objects in the emergence of American literature as what literary sociologist Pierre Bourdieu called a "field": a relatively autonomous arena focused on a particular specialized interest, differentiated from other fields, and managed by (official or unofficial) consecrating authorities. A field is formed and unified by struggles for position within it: according to Bourdieu, cultural producers seek to orient their works in relation to others in the field in order to generate for themselves and their works particular forms of value and reception (for example, economic rewards from a bourgeois mass public, or the commendation of their fellow artists). Bourdieu emphasizes that these producers are not only writers and artists but can also include "the critic, the art dealer, the publisher or the theatre manager," all of whom can have "a power to consecrate objects . . .

and therefore to give value [to them]" that might be economic or cultural capital.[3] Traditionally, literary fields have been mapped to national boundaries or linguistic categories, but, as Gisèle Sapiro argues in her global remapping of Bourdieu's field theory, such "anchoring has for a long time concealed the transnational history that underpins the formation of these national fields, as well as the exchanges that have contributed to their evolution."[4]

Britain's place above the United States in what Pascale Casanova has described as "the hierarchy of the literary world" meant that publication in Britain itself had a consecrating power for US writers.[5] As Joseph Rezek observes, London publishers offered US and other "provincial" writers "profit and legitimacy," and so they developed literary strategies to guide their fiction into this vital market.[6] However, rather than focusing on how authors tailored their writing to the expectations of the British market, I analyze how transatlantic circulation, and British publishers' material texts, scaffold US authors' struggles for position in the field of American literature and produce cultural value for particular works, modes of authorship, genres, and aesthetics. Paradoxically, then, British publishers helped to fashion American literature as an autonomous and differentiated field, whose own participants and products were longer reliant upon the British literary field for consecration. In thus authorizing American literature, British publishers were not acting altruistically; they sought financial success and cultural capital in their home field through legitimizing their associations with popular US writers and positioning themselves as gatekeepers of another national field. That is to say, while this study concentrates on the emergence of the American literary field from a transatlantic print culture, there is another story to be told elsewhere about the place of these same transatlantic materials within the British literary field.

Bourdieu's emphasis on the emergence of a field through ever-shifting relations—in which any change in a producer's position reorients all other agents, as well as the field as a whole—helps to explain why transatlantic materials do not produce a single ideal of American authorship, a defining aesthetics for American literature, or a consensus on its proper subjects. The American literature that is produced through British print is always in the process of becoming national; it is characterized by experiments with nationalizing strategies rather than the presence of any one definitive quality or form. British publishers and their heterogenous material texts authorized different visions and values for American literature. Some British print objects sought to fashion a national American literature through reprinting, and others made claims for the centrality of authorship to a truly national literary culture. British publishers materialized both cosmopolitan and domestic visions for American literature and located national literature in threshold spaces. British "American" magazines tried—and failed—to reconcile regional diversity and national unity. Transatlantic print circulation could conjure white national publics united by Anglo-American sympathies, but it could also sustain subjectivities at scales beyond the nation for Black writers.

Indeed, I would argue that British publishers and print did not advance American literary *nationalism*—a phrase that suggests a coherent ideology that links literary production, geographic location, and group identity—but participated in the unfinished business of producing American literary *nationhood*, defined by Hampton as "the struggle to determine language, space, and character, and to define their interaction."[7] In doing so, they echoed antebellum US writing that was characterized by the seeking after, rather than the achievement of, something characteristically American. As Edgar Allan Poe observed in 1845, "Much has been said, of late, about the necessity of maintaining a proper *nationality* in American Letters; but what this nationality *is*, or what is to be gained by it, has never been distinctly understood."[8] British publishers and print sustained and furthered a variety of possibilities for a national American literature at a moment when the shape of US print culture was in flux and the forms and subjects of US writing were insistently debated.

Approaching American literature through its publication in Britain does not resurrect a pantheon of forgotten writers, but it does subtly reconfigure authorial hierarchies and returns attention to figures who have slipped from critical consciousness. Longfellow appears as both an archetypal and exceptional figure in terms of his professional and imaginative navigation of publication in Britain and as an author whose consciously national writings, as well as their complex publication and reception, deserve further study. Melville is the most canonical author I consider, and I reframe his discussions of authorship by restoring the place of British publishers and his British editions within them. While Frederick Douglass remains central to my account of the transatlantic slave narrative trade, I position his engagements with British and Irish print as a precursor of William Wells Brown's more experimental fashioning of authorship and subjectivity through the reprinting of his narrative in Britain. Examining the groupings created by British print forms invites further reflection on how assumed connections between intranational circulation and national literature, following Benedict Anderson's influential yet much critiqued theory of print nationalism, have naturalized certain groupings of writers and obscured other possible connections.[9] Longfellow and Poe, usually on opposite sides of debates, were published in strikingly similar British illustrated editions that championed their status as national American poets. Publishers' series issued Ralph Waldo Emerson's essays alongside novels by Harriet Beecher Stowe and Catharine Maria Sedgwick rather than with Walt Whitman and Henry David Thoreau.[10] And if the field of American literature produced through British print is (unsurprisingly) largely white and Northeastern, analyzing the production of that field shows how Anglo-American print exchanges reframed these ethnic and local identities as national qualities.

This book argues that the period between 1830 and 1860 saw a collision of transformations in British and US literary and print cultures that provided unprecedented conditions for the fashioning of a national American tradition across a transatlantic print economy and in British print objects. In the coda, I address how changes to copyright law, developments in US print infrastructure, and global historical crises beyond the print trade brought this period to an end. However, the process of defining and redefining American literature continues to this day. Readers and scholars are expanding the boundaries of the national tradition and welcoming authors and texts that have been previously excluded on the basis of race, gender, language, and location, transforming the structure of the field accordingly. Including transatlantic materials in American literary histories is, therefore, part of an ongoing critical project to decouple national traditions from the borders of the modern state and map American literature's less familiar print geographies.

The Publication of American Literature in Britain, 1830–1860

The processes by which US texts were published and disseminated in Britain and the material forms in which they appeared have received little scholarly attention. Nineteenth-century Americanists often (implicitly) approach British editions as subordinate to US publications even when they appeared first, or view them as being somehow deficient due to their distance from the author, their unauthorized status, or British publishers' textual interventions, as in, for example, Richard Bentley's edition of Melville's *The Whale* (1851). Moreover, the Greg-Bowers "copy-text" method of scholarly editing positions unauthorized editions outside a work's history in an attempt to reproduce the author's final intentions.[11] It therefore neglects the ways in which reprinting and recirculating create "the iterative structures upon which literariness depends" by preserving a work across time and moving it through space, as Meredith McGill argues.[12] British editions of US texts have also been excluded from scholarship in Victorian studies which, as Caroline Levine argues, selects its objects of study on the basis of the birthplace of the author (in Britain) and the birth-time of the text (in the long, or not-so-long nineteenth century), "obscur[ing] alternative notions of belonging," as well as the networks that texts created as they traveled across geographic boundaries.[13] Most surprisingly, British editions of US texts are rarely discussed within an established and fruitful tradition of transatlantic studies that has largely focused on US authors' imaginative entanglements with British literature and culture, and on the Atlantic as a conduit for the transmission and the transformation of figures, tropes, genres, and structures, rather than texts and books.[14]

For over fifty years, the only study of the circulation of US texts in Britain was Clarence Gohdes's *American Literature in Nineteenth-Century England*, which is impressively broad in its chronological span, but offers less detail about individual publishers, authors, or books, and thus offers a sometimes-immaterial picture of west-east transatlantic circulation.[15] Paul Gilroy's monumental *The Black*

Atlantic, which argues for the transatlantic as the proper scale for understanding Black identity, culture, and "the playful diasporic intimacy that has been a marked feature of transnational black Atlantic creativity," is a key theoretical influence on my chapter 6 especially, but Gilroy pays less attention to the materiality of the exchanges he explores.[16] Aileen Fyfe briefly describes the British trade in American texts and books, but this is within her history of the Scottish publisher W. & R. Chambers's unusual success in commandeering a US market for their cheap, useful knowledge publications.[17] Jessica DeSpain and Joseph Rezek have demonstrated that transatlantic transmission was accompanied by textual and material transformations, but they focus, respectively, on ways that British publishers soften the national identity of US texts, and on authorial textual changes rather than transformations wrought by publishers.[18] Stephanie Palmer illustrates the importance of a set of postbellum American women writers (often marginalized as regional, sentimental, and domestic) to the British reading public, and the importance of British reception to these American writers, but she focuses on reviews and review culture.[19] As such, we know relatively little about the British publication of US writing, and even less about the role of transatlantic materials in the emergence of the American literary field in the years before the Civil War.

The invisibility of American literature's transatlantic materials in academic scholarship contrasts sharply with the visibility of British editions of American books in the mid-nineteenth century. To US and British writers, the circulation of US texts in Britain was substantial in both senses of the word: the increasing circulation of US texts in Britain was inseparable from the diverse, and vividly material print formats in which it circulated. Sometimes American writing was specifically associated with cheap print. An article on Nathaniel Hawthorne suggested that his writings could be found "wherever railways and shilling libraries are on the *qui vive*," and when Frederick Law Olmsted visited Chester, he found a bookstall with "Emerson's 'Representative Men,' and Irving's 'Sketch Book,' on the counter, with newspapers and railway guides, and the proprietor told us he had sold a great many of them," suggesting these texts were packaged as similarly cheap and spontaneous purchases.[20] Elsewhere, however, cheapness combined with material variety: an anonymous *English Review* article noted Emerson's works were "reproduced in every possible form, and at the most tempting prices."[21] Longfellow's writings could be found "every where and in every form,—in complete editions on the counters of the regular booksellers, in stacks of little shilling volumes on railway bookstalls, and in gorgeously-bound and profusely-illustrated volumes on drawing-room tables."[22]

A description of London's bookselling district in 1852 by expat editor and theatrical impresario Henry Howard Paul illustrates the quantity, visibility, and material variety of US writing in Britain. Paul notes that writers from across the literary field can be found on London's bookstalls, from novelists of earlier in the century—"Irving, Cooper, Bird, Paulding"—to poets—"Longfellow, Bryant, . . . Whithier [Whittier], Perceval [Percival], Holmes"—to women writers—"Mrs. Sigourney, Grace Greenwood, Mrs. Kirkland, Margaret Fuller, Miss M'Intosh." Their works circulate in different formats. Paul sees "'Uncle Tom's Cabin!' and the 'Scarlet Letter!'—nine editions of the former, varying in price from three shillings sterling, in muslin, with illustrations, to fourpence, in paper covers, painfully compact," and "multitudinous variations of [George William] Curtis's "Nile Notes," Egar [sic] Poe's Arabesque Tales, and Oliver [Wendell] Holmes's Sparkling Poems." There is also a copy of Noah Webster's dictionary in "pompous maroon binding," while "the magazines, the reviews, the newspapers—metropolitan and provincial—are teeming with extracts from American books," and American titles form a "pile of *tomes* on yonder shelf." And when the paper patching a hole in a window turns out to be "a bit of some exciting American tale, or a funny yarn of Western life," the materiality of US writing subsumes its textuality. When US writers are "reprinted, and extensively read in every part of the United Kingdom," American literature as a national cultural phenomenon exists in and *as* physical printed objects in Britain, as well as in the imaginations of US authors.[23]

Bookended by financial crises, the period between 1830 and 1860 saw sustained and sometimes rapid growth and considerable change for the British book trade. Literacy rates in England and Wales rose from an estimated 57.4 percent of the population (9,131,000) in 1841, to 70.1 percent of the population (14,059,000) in 1861.[24] The end of the Napoleonic Wars and the mechanization of papermaking lowered the costs and increased the speed of print production, as did steam printing, case binding, and stereotyping, although these innovations were adopted unevenly by literary publishers across the 1830s and 1840s.[25] Real wages increased, giving consumers more money to spend on reading. Political revolutions, religious divisions, scientific controversies, and national events like the Great Exhibition all produced flurries of print in the 1840s and 1850s.[26] While there are no government statistics for the mid-nineteenth-century book trade, Simon Eliot's survey of copyright records and literary and book-trade periodicals suggests that there was a steady rise in the number of titles published between 1830 and the mid-1840s. This was followed by a more rapid rise to the mid-1850s, after which growth slowed, then stagnated, and perhaps even declined in the 1860s and early 1870s.[27] At the same time, new books decreased in price. Between 1835 and 1855, "over 10s" moved from the most common to least common price point for a book and "under 3s 6d" moved from least common to most common, as British publishers attempted to meet the demands of an increasingly competitive market.[28] However, new literary books remained more expensive than average, and, as Richard Altick observes, "the provision of cheap books still lagged far behind the spread of literacy" at the mid-century.[29]

As well as issuing more titles at cheaper prices, publishers issued different genres of texts and experimented with novel print formats. Single-author volumes of new poetry declined after the 1820s, and poetry instead became associated with lavishly illustrated annuals, or gift books, produced for the Christmas season and aimed at women readers.[30] An "illustration revolution" made it possible to sell these decorative volumes at middle-class prices. As Michael Twyman argues, popular desires for more and better quality images in books were fed by new technologies, improved printing methods and engraving techniques, and the expansion of illustration from a craft to an "industrial trade."[31] Transport infrastructure reshaped the trade as new railways, built from the 1830s onwards, moved books from London to the country and created new scenes for retail and reading, with W. H. Smith opening its first railway bookstall in 1848. New readers and new places to read increased the market for fiction, especially cheaper and more portable editions. From the early 1830s, publishers began to re-issue relatively contemporary titles as well as older public domain works in cheap editions, often as part of a series or a library, like those that are the focus of chapter 3.[32] While the Stamp Act inflated the price of news periodicals until 1855, publishers offered periodicals containing sensation, entertainment, and useful knowledge at low prices.

Nevertheless, older formats also endured and flourished, including the practice of publishing new fiction in three-volume novels priced at 31s 6d, which was sustained by continuing demand from circulating libraries. As James Raven observes, the mid-century trade was thus characterized by a mixture of tradition and transformation: "Greater productivity resulted from financial and organizational innovation within a trading structure fractured by newcomer booksellers with their cheap reprints and other innovations in salesmanship and product design, but still dominated by large, powerful publishers investing in copyrights."[33] Most important for the purposes of this study, however, is that British publishers of all stripes turned to US texts to win the business of new publics and to fill new print formats, as even older firms began to experiment in efforts to widen their markets.

The best source for data on US writing published in Britain is the *Publishers' Circular* because its proprietor, Sampson Low, was prominent in the transatlantic trade: from 1844, he was the London agent for New York publishers the Harper brothers, and in the early 1850s began publishing London editions of US titles, having secured Harriet Beecher Stowe's business after the success of *Uncle Tom's Cabin* (1852). Low thus attended to information about the latest imports, authorized editions, and reprints of US books, and had a vested interest in announcing them. Between 1839, its first full year of publication, and 1859, *Publishers' Circular* printed at least 1,111 notices of American fiction, poetry, essays, travel writing, and biography aimed at adults that was published by British houses.[34] Importantly, this does not mean 1,111 different titles were announced. Often, more than one publisher would issue an American text that was in the public domain, while the same text might be announced in both an imported edition and one published in London. Additionally, publishers would often announce new, expanded, or illustrated editions of texts in the *Circular* as well as their first publication. Changes to the titles of British editions of American texts, and the often-incomplete announcements in the *Circular*, make it hard to determine if a second announcement of an existing title is a new edition by the same publisher or a reprint by a competitor; this is especially the case before the introduction of annual lists in the early 1850s. As such, adjusting figures for multiple announcements of the same title by the same publisher is likely to introduce errors, so I have not attempted to do so.

Breaking down this number further shows a growth and then decline in the publication of US texts (figure 1). As shown, 83 notices of US books in the categories listed above appeared between 1838 and 1844, 135 between 1845 and 1849, 536 between 1850 and 1854, and 357 between 1855 and 1859. These figures almost certainly underreport the number of British editions of US texts, as Low struggled to get publishers to send information, especially in the *Circular*'s early years. Firms less likely to report their new titles included smaller publishers dealing in cheap books or those whose practices skirted the edges of copyright law—two groups that were especially important for the publishing of US

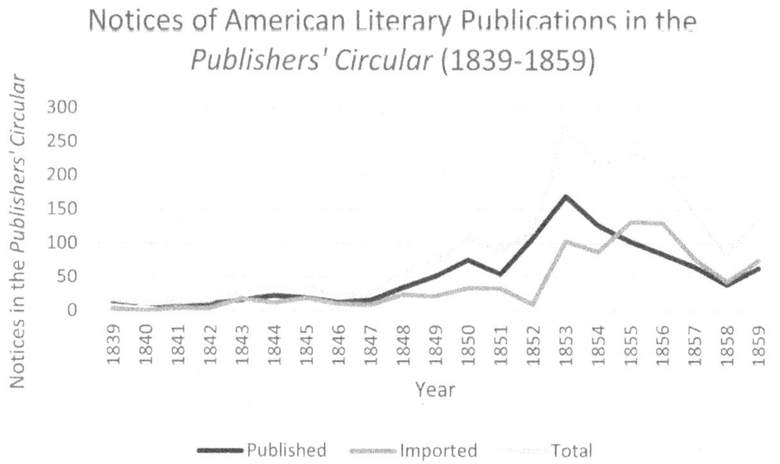

Figure 1. Notices of US literary texts in the *Publishers' Circular*, 1839–59.

texts. Furthermore, it can be difficult to identify US texts from the incomplete publication information listed in the *Circular*, especially if a British publisher suppressed the author's name and changed the title, as was sometimes the case.

Nevertheless, these numbers broadly map onto the publishing trends that Eliot describes, and also the number of publications listed per year in Lyle Wright's *American Fiction*, a bibliography of US fiction between 1850 and 1875. A spike in 1850, when the notices for British-published US texts jumped from 47 in 1849 to 76, can be attributed to the sudden popularity of Longfellow, whose works accounted for 11 of the 76, and to a battle between George Routledge and Henry Bohn in the market for cheap reprints. Further spikes in 1852 and 1853 align with the mania around *Uncle Tom's Cabin*, with an increase in the number of US titles published (1853 is the year with most titles in Wright's), and with British publishers' confidence that the courts would uphold copyright through prior publication. When the House of Lords reached the opposite decision (as I discuss further below) announcements for US titles decreased and announcements for imports increased, although this increase also results from imports becoming a larger part of Low's own business that he promoted through the *Circular*. After 1854, American literature became a specialized product of a group of firms that produced cheap, popular literature: Routledge, Charles Henry Clarke (sometimes in partnership with Samuel O. Beeton), Ward and Lock, Simpkin and Marshall, and Low himself. A plateau sharpened into decline in 1858, after the Panic of 1857 hit the publishing trade on both sides of the Atlantic. Numbers rallied again in 1859, but this revival of trade was to be short lived, as the start of the American Civil War in 1861 reduced US literary outputs.

Why, then, did British publishers turn to American texts to meet the challenges and opportunities of the mid-century marketplace? First, there was more US writing to publish. In 1845, New York publisher George Palmer Putnam noted that the number of "Novels and Tales" by Americans published in the United States had risen from 19 in 1834 to 115 in 1842, although he added that "a large number" of foreign reprints had also appeared in the same year.[35] Still, the proportion of foreign reprints decreased from 70 percent of books published in the US in 1820 to 43 percent in

1850.[36] Second, British copyright law (discussed in more detail below) meant that any US text published first in the United States was in the public domain in Britain. British publishers looking for materials for their cheap series or illustrated books could, therefore, obtain US material with proven popularity abroad but novelty for readers at home, without paying for it. Likewise, cheap periodicals often reprinted American fiction, poetry, articles, and humor. In 1843, *Cleave's Penny Gazette of Variety and Entertainment* "frankly acknowledge[d] that we have at times largely drawn from our American contemporaries."[37] Third, developments outside the book trade increased the attractiveness of US texts for British publishers. The introduction of new steamships from the late 1830s onwards reduced the length of an eastward Atlantic crossing from an average of around thirty days (and sometimes as many as sixty), to less than two weeks. Fortnightly postal packets replaced monthly deliveries. These changes helped British publishers of authorized editions anticipate publication in the United States, and they also helped reprinters who sought speedy intelligence on popular American successes.

Most important was the popularity of US writers during the 1820s; British publishers would not have printed or reprinted any US texts they did not think would sell. Substantial sales and positive reviews of Washington Irving and James Fenimore Cooper's writings showed that American writers could succeed with the British reading public, encouraging British publishers to arrange for authorized editions with Catharine Maria Sedgwick and to reprint texts by James Kirke Paulding and John Neal.[38] It was believed that American democratic institutions, as well as an American book trade based on selling large numbers of cheap books rather than few copies of expensive ones, made American authors particularly capable of producing "popular" literature. An extended British review of *Uncle Tom's Cabin* observed:

> That the popular literature of America is English, and the popular literature of England is American. Reprints of American works of fiction, in which the matter of a large volume is compressed into 400 duodecimo pages of small print on bad, thin paper, cover the railway book stalls, and filter from

> thence into the farmhouses and the back rooms of the village shops. "Uncle Tom," "The Wide, Wide World," "Queechy," and "The White Slave," form now the staple of the reading of the middle classes.[39]

This appeal to the lower and middle classes was important to publishers seeking new markets for cheap print, but cheap books were also purchased by consumers who could afford more expensive editions. Indeed, several US authors had cross-class appeal in Britain. An 1849 review of Emerson's *Essays* playfully proclaimed that an "Emerson Mania" had taken hold, as his essays were read by lower middle-class patrons of provincial mechanics' institutes and also by the "youth of our universities," especially young men of Oxford University in the midst of crises of faith.[40] British editions of Longfellow were available at a variety of prices, generating a working-class readership for the poet as well as an invitation from Queen Victoria in 1868. Chapman & Hall advertised their 1852 edition of Nathaniel Hawthorne's *The Blithedale Romance* at 21s, clearly anticipating that wealthier readers and the circulating libraries would pay more than the 1s for which George Routledge sold his paperback edition of *The Scarlet Letter* in 1851.

British publishers paid careful attention to the US literary scene. A list of "Foreign Subscribers" to the New York literary weekly the *Literary World* from the early 1850s includes reputable houses like Richard Bentley, John Murray, and Longmans, radical periodical publishers Eliza Cook and John Chapman (the latter of whom also traded in imported American books), and publishers that specialized in cheap reprints, like Routledge and Ingram, Cooke & Co. of London, and Simms & McIntyre of Belfast.[41] Bentley and Murray also gained intelligence from their US authors about new works likely to succeed in Britain, although not always soon enough. Both publishers were advised to reprint Richard Henry Dana Jr.'s *Two Years before the Mast* (1840) in early 1841 (Bentley by novelist Richard Burleigh Kimball and Murray by travel writer and geographer Edward Robinson); however, it had already been reprinted in Britain by Edward Moxon, among others.

Eager to see their work published in Britain, many US writers sought relationships with British houses. The editor and writer

Lewis Gaylord Clark, the poet George Colton, and the novelist Catharine Maria Sedgwick all sought Putnam's help to find "a respectable & responsible House" in London, as Sedgwick's brother Charles put it, to publish their works.[42] What US writers wanted from publication in Britain varied, but financial remuneration was not always the primary concern. Some, like Cooper and Melville, carefully negotiated contracts and payments, and others, like Hannah Flagg Gould and Susan Warner, stressed that they wrote from financial necessity and expected British publishers to compensate them. Conversely, Sigourney circulated her works to British writers at her own expense to increase her reputation, and poets Fitz-Greene Halleck and William Cullen Bryant offered to absorb the costs of elegant London editions of their works. Nor did cash payments mean the same thing to all US writers. Leon Jackson's argument that multiple economies were at work in the antebellum US print culture is also true for the transatlantic market.[43] For the authors of slave narratives, for example, payment often came directly from readers, who bought their narratives at lectures and meetings, and was linked—in texts and paratexts of narratives, and reports of their lectures—to their and their families' freedom. For those writers, a publisher's connections to activist networks were more important than what they directly paid.

Across their different motivations for and expectations of publishing in Britain, US authors remained highly cognizant of the cultural work performed by, and the cultural capital embedded in different British print genres. Faced with a home market based on high sales of cheaply produced books and a literary culture centered on reprinting rather than on authorship, many American writers felt better respected and understood by British publishers than by US firms, whom they felt lacked the gentlemanly ethics and fairness that ought to govern the trade, as Michael Everton argues.[44] Sometimes, real friendships developed through the transatlantic trade. Melville's letters to Bentley are far warmer than his letters to the Harpers. Sigourney had a business-like correspondence with American firms, but adopted a "confidential" manner with John Murray II, and shared private griefs with the *Forget Me Not*'s editor.[45] Stowe sent "love" to Sampson Low's family and proclaimed that she felt "safe in entrusting to his hands affairs which I had no means of understanding."[46]

The west-east transatlantic print trade occupied an important place in the literary cultures of Britain and the United States, but the uneven status of those cultures meant that it did not have the same importance in both. Britain had produced the great writers of the Anglophone cannon, it was a net exporter of literary texts (especially to the United States), it boasted superior printers, illustrators, engravers, and binders, and had publishers who, at least according to pro-international copyright Americans, cultivated and rewarded authorship. British publishers thus had the power to authorize not only individual American writers, but also the emergent field of American literature. But British publishers were also struggling for position in their own field, and publishing US texts—with their novelty and popularity–was one way to reposition themselves and to increase sales. Unlike in the late nineteenth-century French literary field on which Bourdieu focuses, cultural and economic capital were not antithetical to one another in the British or American literary fields.[47] Amid fluid international copyright regimes, US anxieties about and hopes for a national culture and British publishers' need to secure shares of a competitive market collided to give British publishers a key role in authorizing American literature.

Copyright, Authority, and Authorization

In arguing that British publishers and their editions of American books *authorized* American literature by championing individual authors and texts and mapping a national literary field, my terminology overlaps with one important way that scholars have traditionally categorized British editions of American books: as "authorized" and "unauthorized" editions. In the US, copyright was restricted to citizens, but at various times until 1854, prior publication in Britain was thought to secure a foreign author copyright, a position that was upheld by Lord Abinger in *D'Almaine v. Boosey* (1835).[48] More important than this legal ruling, Melissa Homestead suggests, were the extra-legal agreements between publishers concerning foreign works printed from advanced sheets—that is, from proof sheets sent in advance of publication in an author's home country. Through the 1820s and 1830s, reputable London publishers treated these works as the exclusive property of the publisher who issued them, creating a copyright in practice if not in law.[49] Publications printed from advanced sheets (or from the author's manuscript if he or she was resident in London) were advertised as "authorized" or "author's" editions. American authors who secured these editions were often paid for these sheets; sums varied from tens of pounds, to hundreds of guineas.

These authorized editions circulated alongside two types of "unauthorized" reprint. First, any text published first in the United States was in the public domain, so any British publisher could reprint it without permission or payment. Second, and especially from the mid-1840s onward, some British publishers began to test the consensus that prior publication secured copyright by reprinting US texts that had been issued in authorized editions. After much back and forth on the legal question throughout the late 1840s and early 1850s, the House of Lords, Britain's highest court of appeal, ruled against foreign authors in *Jeffreys v. Boosey* (1854), establishing that a foreigner could only claim copyright if he or she was resident in British dominion at the time of publication.[50] Publishers continued to issue authorized editions from advanced sheets after 1854. However, unless they could persuade the American author to visit British territory at the time of publication, this only secured priority over the competition and the custom of those readers who were moved by appeals to support the author and buy their "genuine" edition rather than unauthorized reprints.

The division between authorized and unauthorized editions sometimes existed in law and was fiercely policed by publishers like Murray and Bentley, who invested in their production of the former, as I show in chapter 2. But it has been further enforced by narratives of US authors' struggles to secure British copyright and the profits they lost to rapacious unauthorized publishers, which, as I show in the coda, began in international copyright campaigns of the 1870s and 1880s. This narrative positions US writers as helpless victims of a transatlantic imbalance of power, at the mercy of rapacious British publishers and an unfair copyright law. But as Tim Sommer—one of the few scholars to analyze how authors navigated transatlantic print culture—has recently argued of Thomas Carlyle and Ralph Waldo Emerson, writers were not "disenfranchised casualties of the reprint trade," which itself "did not so much do away with authorial agency as reconfigure and diversify the contours of literary authorship."[51] Even authors without the autonomy and cultural capital of Carlyle and Emerson could find agency and authorization through unauthorized or non-copyright editions. Furthermore, US authors sought more than financial gain from publishing in Britain: Longfellow enjoyed the ornate but unauthorized editions that celebrated his aesthetic achievements, Sigourney was proud to find herself in a coterie of British writers in the pages of the *Forget Me Not*, and the authors of slave narratives found publishers connected to abolitionist networks rather than those well versed in transatlantic copyright. Generally, US authors understood the ways in which reprinting and recirculation could create literary value and reputation, even though modern scholarly editing strips canonical antebellum texts of these histories created through unauthorized reprinting.[52]

Maintaining a strict division between authorized and unauthorized editions gives a false impression of practices in the British publication of US books and obscures the myriad of ways that British print could authorize American authors, their works, and the idea of a national tradition. Many publishers dealt in both forms of publication, and individual editions straddled the divide between authorized and unauthorized. To give just two examples, Moxon sent Dana $500 from the profits of his unauthorized reprint of *Two Years before the Mast*—twice what the Harpers paid for the US copyright.[53] In return, Dana sent Moxon advanced sheets for *The Seaman's Friend*, which Moxon issued as *The Seaman's Manual* (1841). Dana's acceptance of Moxon's payment, and subsequent authorized publication with Moxon, does not authorize his edition of *Two Years*, but the relationship sets that reprint apart from the (at least) three other unauthorized reprints that circulated in the 1840s. Similarly, London publisher Thomas Bosworth offered Stowe 3d for every copy sold of his unauthorized edition of *Uncle Tom's Cabin* and was rewarded with an exclusive author's preface that distinguished his edition from the competition, although Bosworth did not become the authorized publisher of Stowe's subsequent works.[54]

The authorized/unauthorized division also works less well outside of single-authored volumes. Texts like magazines, miscellanies, and anthologies had different relationships with authority, authorization, and copyright.[55] Sigourney and Gould were paid for the poems they submitted to *Forget Me Not*, but the gift book's long lead time meant that Sigourney submitted variant versions of the same poems to US periodicals, which published them in advance of the British edition. These poems could not, therefore, be copyrighted, but preserving copyright was probably never Sigourney's intention; she encouraged the simultaneous circulation of her poems in multiple formats—private letters, periodicals, books—and was aware that reprinting built a poet's reputation. Conversely, Frederick Douglass and William Wells Brown maintained control of the authorized, but not copyrighted, British editions of their narratives (which were first published in the United States) by acting as distributers and co-publishers of the texts in Britain. Literary authority could, therefore, be fashioned outside of or alongside copyright. Indeed, the contested status of copyright for foreign authors between 1835 and 1854 created a generative ambiguity around the authority of books and texts in which extra-legal, and, in particular, print-material forms of authorization flourished. Rather than seeing this period as a "copyright window" in which some US authors could protect their texts from reprinting—a phrase that privileges and naturalizes copyright as the only system by which authority can be maintained—I approach it as a time when British publishers and US authors experimented with various ways of authorizing editions, texts, and visions for American literature across various print objects and forms of dissemination.

It is these diverse and dynamic experiments in authorizing and defining American literature through and in dialogue with British print objects that I explore in this book. My conception of unauthorized reprinting as a system and process that enabled new forms of expression and authorization is, of course, indebted to Meredith McGill's transformative work on the culture of reprinting within the antebellum United States. Her directive to examine the conditions of literary production "as a potential site of proliferation as well as a principle of thrift" is at the heart of this project, as is her emphasis on bringing together the rhetorical and the material in considering the "matter of the text." Nevertheless, there are some distinctions between both the culture of reprinting within the United States that she analyzes and the transatlantic reprinting I consider, and between our respective methodologies. While we both argue that reprinting produced impressions of American literary nationhood in unexpected ways, McGill sketches a competition between US authors and printers for cultural authority in the US print market of the 1840s. In contrast, I argue that British publishers like Bentley shored up their authority as cultural gatekeepers by positioning themselves as advocates for US authors and authorship. Moreover, while some British unauthorized editions—like Routledge's cheap series publications—did champion reprinting as a democratizing form of circulation, as did many of the US publishers McGill examines, most of the reprints I examine are attempting to authorize their own production above those of their competitors at the same time as they authorize and give value to American letters. Because I unpick how individual editions materialized these overlapping forms of authority, my study is, in contrast to McGill's, "a study of reprints themselves" as much as a study of "the system of reprinting."[56] Applying sustained critical attention to these texts, I seek to recuperate them and retrieve them for American literary history.

Scope and Structure of the Book

The Transatlantic Materials of American Literature documents the publication of US writing in Britain between 1830 and 1860 and analyses how that publication constructed and authorized American literature as a distinct field and a national tradition. I limit my transatlantic investigations to the publishing of US texts in Britain because of the limits of my own language skills and because Britain was the United States's most important print trade partner, economically and ideologically.[57] Manifestos calling for national literature often pitted American efforts against a British tradition, invoking Britain even as they argued for literary independence. The study's chronology echoes the familiar boundaries of the antebellum period, but it is justified by the particular contours of the west-east transatlantic book trade. Recentering the geography of American literature eastward offers an opportunity to reimagine an historical era that we think we know well through new print objects and at new scales.

The period between 1830 and 1860 was particularly lively and fruitful for American literature's transatlantic materials, as a rise in US authorship coincided with a period of publishing experiments in Britain at the same time as new technologies, changing readerships, and economic growth reshaped print cultures across the Atlantic. The 1820s witnessed the first US bestsellers in Britain, but US writing became truly entangled with developments in popular print in the following decade. Extending slightly beyond the period between legal decisions that established foreign authors' rights via prior publication (1835) and then ended those rights (1854), these thirty years saw publishers and authors experiment with various forms of authorization, many of which were vested in the book object. As I illustrate above, an increase in US authorship coincided with a transformation in the British market that left readers and publishers hungry for more print and new print forms. Yet by the close of the 1850s, due to transformations in the US print market, the emergence of specialist American publishers and booksellers in London, and devasting historical events (the Crimean War, the Panic of 1857, and the US Civil War), the heyday of American literature's authorization through British print was over. I discuss how and why it ended as well as what followed in the coda.

This book makes an argument for recovering and recentering British print in studies of US writing and literary culture. But it will also be of interest to scholars of nineteenth-century British literature and culture. Historians of the British working-classes have observed the importance of particular American texts to this readership, especially Harriet Beecher Stowe's *Uncle Tom's Cabin* and James Fenimore Cooper's historical romances.[58] Jonathan Rose has argued that British Chartists, abolitionists, temperance reformers, and other activists "drew inspiration and support from their American counterparts." By illustrating the embeddedness of the publishers of slave narratives into abolitionist networks in chapter 6, I thread these radical intellectual currents through the material process of the book trade.[59] From a literary critical perspective, Paul Giles and Julia Sun-Joo Lee trace resonances between particular US genres and writers and the mid-century

British novel.[60] But the histories I offer suggest that American texts circulated more widely and more variously in Britain than scholars have recognized. In the wake of Levine's call for Victorianists to move beyond the "logic of autochthony" and instead examine the ways in which cultures emerge from "patterns of circulation rather than rootedness, zigzagging movements rather than stable foundations," I hope Victorianists will take this study as a starting point for new investigations into the place of British editions of US texts in Britain and the Empire.[61] How, for example, did British publishers' decisions about if and how they published US writing impact their position in the British literary field? How did British readers interact with editions of US texts, and how did British writers respond to those material texts as well as to the subjects, language, affects, and literary forms of US writing?

The following chapters offer case studies of different print formats instead of being organized chronologically or by author. Some chapters do foreground particular authors who had creatively fruitful relationships with particular publishers or print formats (Melville with John Murray and Richard Bentley, Longfellow with illustrated editions, Sigourney with gift books). The exception is chapter 6, which explores print diversity within the slave narrative. This structure avoids the exclusive focus on the novel, which is common to transatlantic studies and histories of US literary development, and shows the variety of print and literary genres through which British publishers fashion American literature.[62] Rather than surveying transatlantic bestsellers, from Irving's *Sketch-book* to *Uncle Tom's Cabin*, and *The Last of the Mohicans* to *The Lamplighter*, and presenting the circulation of US texts in Britain as a series of watershed moments, the book examines a variety of authorial voices along with more and less successful publications.[63] Topics and approaches of individual chapters were also determined by the existence of archival sources. Chapter 2, which looks at Murray and Bentley, and the parts of chapter 3 on Bentley's Standard Novels series, are the only sections for which substantial publishers' business archives survive. The archives for key participants in the transatlantic trade, like Sampson Low, as well as most smaller firms, do not survive at all. Chapter 1's deep dive into Longfellow's authorizing illustrated editions is rendered possible by his extensively preserved correspondence; the same is sadly not true for many of the Black abolitionists considered in chapter 6, especially John Brown, whose (probable) illiteracy contributes to the sparsity of evidence about his involvement in the publication of his narrative. Gaps in archival material mean that chapters 3 and 5 give partial portraits of several publications in a genre and, therefore, some discussions of publishers' strategies, marketing plans, and failures are necessarily speculative. These case studies provide the broadest history yet of the British publication of US texts and show the diversity of transatlantic materials through which American literature emerged, but the archival record on which this history is based is, above all, uneven as a result of the impact of racism, sexism, and classism on literary archives.

Chapters 1 and 2 explore how British publishers' prestigious print forms authorized individual writers and models of American literature and authorship. Chapter 1 examines unauthorized reprints of Henry Wadsworth Longfellow by publishers who used illustration to legitimize their own publications, position US authors as important literary voices, and authorize American literature as a valuable and national form. Despite his personal cultural capital and immense popularity, Longfellow struggled to achieve authorized publication in Britain in the 1840s. Nevertheless, David Bogue's unauthorized but lavishly illustrated editions of his works championed Longfellow as a national poet and authorized his vision of a cosmopolitan American literature. In *The Courtship of Miles Standish* (1858), Longfellow then locates the transatlantic circulation of American writing as central to US national culture and exposes the violence against Indigenous people that national founding involved. I end by showing how other London firms reproduced Bogue's model of illustration as authorization in later editions of William Cullen Bryant and Edgar Allan Poe.

Chapter 2 explores authorized editions, arguing that their handsome materiality as well as their copyright status consecrated US authorship. John Murray's and Richard Bentley's imprints were prized by US authors who valued their commitment to copyright editions and their expensive, high-quality material texts, both of which conferred cultural value on American authorship. After exploring how access to these publishers was limited by an authors' race, gender, class, and social connections, I examine Herman

Melville's publications with both Murray and Bentley. The material texts of both legitimized Melville's authorship, but while Murray authenticated Melville as a travel writer, Bentley's authorized editions validate Melville as a cultural producer and argue for the importance of authorship, protected through international copyright, to an emergent national literary culture. Studying the dialogues between Melville's texts and his British editions further shows how his own changing conceptions of authorship, and its place in US print culture, were shaped by and articulated through publication in Britain.

Chapters 3 and 4 consider how British print forms involving a transatlantic range of authors could nationalize and authorize American writing. Chapter 3 explores how US texts shaped the architecture of British publishers' series or libraries at a transitional point in their history, and how the material architecture of those series territorialized American writing. In collecting US texts under titles like "Standard Novels" and "Universal Library," such series authorized the included texts as objects of cultural value. The paratexts that defined the series' boundaries—title pages, prefaces, frontispiece illustrations—situated US texts as national artifacts yet presented American nationality as a phenomenon created by crossings between spaces. In doing so, series' paratexts echoed many of the US texts they published, including works by Charles Brockden Brown, Catharine Maria Sedgwick, James Fenimore Cooper, and Ralph Waldo Emerson that destabilize essential ideas of nationhood.

Chapter 4 investigates the place of the British gift book and the general role of British private space in the making of a sentimental American culture. The *Forget Me Not*, an eminent British yearly gift book, published poems by Lydia Huntley Sigourney and Hannah Flagg Gould from 1837 onward and situated these writers as national American poets within a semi-private coterie of British authors. In their poems for the *Forget Me Not*, both writers explore the relationship between domestic sentiments and national US politics, with Sigourney submitting poems that criticize Indian Removal in stronger terms than in the versions of the same poems she published in the United States. I argue that Sigourney uses transatlantic circulation to continue the political work of the poetess, and, in her travelogue *Pleasant Memories of Pleasant Lands* (1842), to imagine a white, national public whose sympathies have been trained in an Anglo-American print culture. Ultimately, however, this book embroiled Sigourney in controversies about transatlantic circulation that spoke to wider debates about the future of American literature in a culture of reprinting.

As counterpoints to the previous four chapters, chapters 5 and 6 examine transatlantic materials that did not authorize a national American literature and in which British publishers and US authors worked at cross-purposes. Chapter 5 examines three forgotten and short-lived "American" magazines published in London for British readers that contained reprinted texts from US periodicals and books. In dialogue with popular Yankee comedies and through the theatrical form of the magazine, all three periodicals sought to stabilize a national culture that was impossible to establish in the United States, with its regional print cultures and sectional divides over slavery. These fantasies also proved unsustainable in Britain. However, while two publications show the magazine form straining to articulate a cohesive and yet polyvocal national culture, the final magazine shows no clear reason for its untimely end. These artifacts remind us that chance also shaped which British print objects successfully authorized models for American literature, and which publications and conceptions of the tradition faded to silence.

Chapter 6 surveys the publication of US slave narratives by commercial firms, an antislavery organization, and small, abolitionist publishers. Unlike the magazines of chapter 5, which failed to sustain nationalizing visions, Black abolitionists refused to align themselves with a nation that denied their humanity and instead found political power in situating themselves as Atlantic subjects. I argue that Black abolitionists imaginatively employed transatlantic circulation to claim literary authorship in an Anglo-American print market, but that the commercial publication of Solomon Northup's *Twelve Years a Slave* (1853) and the socially embedded dissemination of John Brown's *Slave Life in Georgia* (1855) undermined these claims to subjectivity. Only authors like Frederick Douglass and William Wells Brown, who tightly controlled their publications, could manipulate reprinting in Britain to articulate their subjectivity. British publishers' lack of engagement with these uses of print shows the racial limits of the American literary tradition that transatlantic materials fashioned. This chapter is followed by a short coda that outlines changes in transatlantic print culture in the years immediately before and after 1860 through the partnership of Sampson Low and Harriet Beecher Stowe, and considers the legacies of antebellum American literature's transatlantic materials.

Analyzing the transatlantic production of American literature in the mid-nineteenth century feels strange and urgent in a moment when far-right white supremacist nationalisms, calls for hard borders, and acts of state violence are on the rise in both the United States and the United Kingdom. The COVID-19 pandemic prompted nations to close borders and it restricted international travel in ways that would have been previously unimaginable. For many of us living in and between lockdowns, our worlds became very small, yet reading traveling texts was one important way of enlarging them. This book does not seek to find antecedents of or explanations for twenty-first-century Anglo-American nationalisms in the circulation of literary and material texts of the mid-nineteenth century. But it does intersect with present concerns by showing how national cultures and fields evolve when texts cross borders and when they are materialized and circulated outside of the nation. Because national literature—as a site of pride, affiliation, and belonging, and as a mechanism for exclusion—emerges at scales beyond the nation, scholars of American literary history and print culture need to look outside the United States to understand the role that print played in its emergence. Antebellum US writers understood the various ways in which British publishers and British material texts were vital participants in the ongoing process of making American literature; this study, I hope, will begin to lead readers and scholars of American literature toward that same understanding.

CHAPTER 1

Illustration as Authorization in Longfellow's Reprints

Immensely popular in America and the best-selling poet of any nationality in Victorian Britain, Henry Wadsworth Longfellow was, in many respects, an exceptional figure in the antebellum transatlantic literary marketplace. However, Longfellow initially struggled to arrange for authorized British editions of his works. Richard Bentley offered him "half profits" for an authorized edition of Longfellow's early travelogue *Outre-Mer* in 1835, but when the book lost Bentley £40 10s 3d he did not pursue Longfellow for another.[1] At the same time, Longfellow's various American publishers were uninterested in securing transatlantic copyrights for his works, and friends in England could garner no interest from publishers. Therefore, Longfellow's earlier works circulated in Britain in unauthorized reprints, and continued to do so after Longfellow began to secure authorized editions in 1849.

Appearing in authorized and unauthorized editions, as well as some that straddled the boundary between the two, Longfellow's works were less the exception than the rule among American writings in Britain. Unlike James Fenimore Cooper, Washington Irving, or Herman Melville, who all had sustained relations with particular houses, many American authors—including Nathaniel Hawthorne, Harriet Beecher Stowe, Catharine Maria Sedgwick, and Ralph Waldo Emerson—saw their works issued by several publishers in authorized and unauthorized editions. Similarly, in the 1840s and 1850s, Longfellow's works were published in material formats ranging from cheap penny pamphlets to lavish editions for the Christmas market. Both the variety of Longfellow's dealings with British publishers and the authorizing work performed by unauthorized reprints of his poetry and prose make Longfellow a natural starting point from which to consider the ways British editions beyond copyright publications constructed American literature as a national phenomenon and an object of economic and aesthetic value. Rather than approaching unauthorized editions as sites of failure and loss for American authors, I argue that Longfellow's unauthorized—yet *authorizing*—British editions helped him take a position in the American literary field as a national poet whose works had commercial and cultural value by championing his vision of a cosmopolitan national literary tradition.

After exploring Longfellow's relations with British publishers John Walker, David Bogue, and George Routledge in the late 1840s and 1850s and their editions of his works, I suggest that these publishers employed the materiality of their editions of Longfellow to legitimize their unauthorized reprinting of his works and to negotiate positions as his authorized publishers. At the same time, their material texts championed the commercial and literary value of Longfellow's writing and American literature in general on both sides of the Atlantic, reinforcing Longfellow's bid to be seen as a professional man of letters. When Longfellow made arrangements with British publishers, he considered the benefits of these "embedded economies," as Leon Jackson has termed the non-monetary transactions and social relations that propelled and were created by print circulation, plus any potential financial rewards.[2] Indeed, by examining Longfellow's correspondence with British publishers, the material texts of his transatlantic editions, and Longfellow's poetry itself, I suggest that all parties in these transatlantic arrangements understood how the material forms and circulations of even unauthorized editions could authorize American literature.

Longfellow's British editions, however, challenge the division between authorized and unauthorized editions that structure the study of the transatlantic publication of US writing. Publications existed on the boundaries of this division if they were not protected by copyright through prior publication but were nevertheless produced in collaboration with the author, or for the author's financial or symbolic benefit. In Longfellow's case, the same publishers issued both authorized and unauthorized editions of his works, sometimes in nearly identical formats, showing that a publisher's material strategies for constructing and legitimizing American literature persisted outside of efforts to establish copyrights. Lacking legal instruments, financial transactions, or, indeed, authorial permission, Walker, Bogue, and Routledge all looked to the material text to authorize publications that might otherwise have reeked of piracy, and to regularize their relations with Longfellow, yet they published his work in different forms. Rather than grouping these texts together as unauthorized editions, it is more productive to ask how and under what terms each publisher's material texts sought to authorize both Longfellow and the wider American tradition.

With these questions in mind, I examine in detail one method through which Bogue framed Longfellow as America's leading poet: illustration. Bogue's editions of *Evangeline* (first published 1847, this edition 1850) and *Hyperion* (first published 1839, this edition 1853) featured images from leading Victorian artists that authorized the books' circulation, registered the aesthetic value of Longfellow's verse, and increased his prestige on both sides of the Atlantic. But these illustrations also reinforced Longfellow's cosmopolitan vision for American letters, meaning that Bogue's editions entered into contemporary debates over the thematic scope and future of American writing. Bogue's editions materialized an American literature that became national through its physical and imaginative movements outside the nation. Furthermore, Longfellow's own writing reveals his awareness of the place of British materials and transatlantic circulation in the making of the American tradition. In *The Courtship of Miles Standish* (1858), a poem that narrates the founding of American nationhood via a comic Puritan love triangle, Longfellow suggests that an American form of expression emerges through transatlantic circulation and that British books are central to defining—sometimes violently—the boundaries of American national culture.

The reciprocity between Longfellow's British material texts and his visions for nation-building is unusually extensive. But the conclusion to this chapter examines how this method of illustration as authorization—of the individual reprint, the author, and American writing—was repeated in an edition of Edgar Allan Poe's poems jointly produced by Sampson Low in London and J. S. Redfield in New York in 1858. This edition, like Bogue's editions of Longfellow, was printed with the permission of Poe's US publishers, but not from advanced sheets, and so had no claim to copyright. However, its illustrations authorized its publication and protected it from competing reprints, but also materialized Poe's own reflections on authorship in a transatlantic marketplace. Attending closely to unauthorized, or semi-authorized, editions reveals that these transatlantic reprints, like their authorized counterparts, constructed the terms under which the literature of a new nation might be valued, both in that nation and in the world.

Authorizing Circulations: John Walker and George Routledge

If an American writer did not make arrangements with a British publisher for an authorized edition, their work could still circulate on the other side of the Atlantic in unauthorized reprints. These were printed from American editions, rather than from advanced sheets, and could be produced without the author's permission. Estimating the number of American titles that circulated in this manner, let alone the total number of American reprints that were published and sold in mid-century Britain, is impossible. Announcements in the *Publishers' Circular* did not distinguish between authorized and unauthorized editions, although some firms did mention in their advertisements if theirs was an "author's edition." While some large and successful reprinters of American books, like George Routledge, announced their works and have surviving archival material, many small firms that reprinted American books traded for a few years and then folded, leaving few traces in the print record. Selling from their own bookstalls, such firms may not have announced their works in the trade press, and, with no way of securing copyright, may have forgone the expense of registering a work at Stationers' Hall or the bother of submitting a deposit copy. Sales figures for unauthorized American reprints are equally incomplete. Those quoted in contemporary sources, and thus in subsequent scholarship, tend to focus on runaway best sellers: Routledge was said to have sold twenty thousand of Susan Warner's *Queechy* (1852) in a week, and total sales of *Uncle Tom's Cabin* (1852), available in at least eighteen unauthorized editions, almost certainly topped one million.[3] Yet sources are silent on the hundreds, or perhaps even tens of copies of less popular American works that a small press may have sold.

Before 1854, copyright law distinguished between American books published first in England from advanced sheets and those that appeared after an American edition. A set of lawsuits in 1850, in which Richard Bentley and John Murray III sued George Routledge and Henry Bohn for infringing their copyrights on works by Washington Irving and Herman Melville (that I discuss further in chapter 2), shows that some publishers of authorized editions policed this distinction furiously, even as the law on foreign authors' rights was constantly revised. Bentley and Murray wanted to maintain a division between their firms and products and those of Routledge and Bohn—between respectable authorized publishers who issued copyright editions in expensive prestige formats, and unscrupulous reprinters who traded in pirated paperbacks that sold for a shilling or less. However, authorized and unauthorized transatlantic economies of print were, in reality, not so separate; it was not always a case of reputable firms against unprincipled almost-pirates, or of the bound and blind-stamped authorized edition versus the cheaply printed reprint. Some publishers dealt in both authorized and unauthorized reprints, as Longfellow's own case demonstrates. Some editions that were not printed from advanced sheets, and so had no claim to copyright protection, were nevertheless "authorized" insofar as they were produced in consultation with an American writer, who may or may not have received payment or a share in any profits. Even less-than-respectable publishers could produce editions that used their paratexts and material forms to authorize their own circulation of a US text, an individual writer, and a national US tradition, as an example from the transatlantic materials of Longfellow's contemporary, John Greenleaf Whittier, illustrates.

In 1844, London publisher Henry G. Clarke issued an edition of Whittier's verse, *Ballads and Other Poems*, that was authorizing, though not entirely authorized. All things told, Clarke was one of the less reputable figures in the London trade; he was taken to court and hauled over in the trade press for pirating British works, he ran through business partners in quick succession, and was prosecuted for debt in 1847. He reprinted several American texts in his Cabinet Library series, and there is no evidence he paid for any of them. Nevertheless, Whittier's correspondence shows he at least informally sanctioned Clarke's publication of his poems. In 1844, he wrote to his friend and fellow abolitionist Elizur Wright, who was about to embark for London: "It has been intimated that my poems would be republished in England in Clarke's publications, like Longfellow's etc. Now if the deed is not done when thee arrive will thee take the trouble to see Clarke and let him publish a volume under thy superintendence?"[4] How Whittier heard about Clarke's plans is unclear, but "intimated" suggests that he was not directly asked for permission, but instead sought to intervene in a publication that was already planned. Wright apparently followed Whittier's directions, because Clarke's edition appears with a preface by Wright and also with Whittier's poems in roughly the order the poet proposed in his letter instructing Wright to oversee publication. Clarke's edition also included poems that had not previously appeared in book form, suggesting that Wright may have supplied him with copies from US periodicals.

Wright's preface maps out an American tradition that is both distinct and national, and that has Whittier at its center. Wright assures readers that "Whittier, whatever may be said of other American poets, is of purely republican growth. His poetry borrows nothing from foreign countries or customs."[5] Paradoxically, Britain, and the British material text, is the space in which such claims for Whittier's "pure" Americanism can be made. Wright's framing of Whittier as a national poet contrasts with his reception in the United States in the 1840s, where he was largely perceived as a poet of abolitionist verse and regional themes.[6] Wright further presents this "pure" Americanism as central to the literary value of Whittier's verse. Yet the circularity of his argument—Whittier is valuable because he expresses a national American voice, and American poetry is most valuable when it is like Whittier—shows Wright constructing this tradition at the same time as he places Whittier within it. And, of course, this preface is also valuable to Clarke because it lends authority to a publication—and perhaps also to a publisher—of dubious legitimacy. The preface to Clarke's *Ballads and Other Poems* thus validates that edition in the process of positioning Whittier as a national poet and of constructing a national literature in his image, all of which take place in the borders of a publication that foregrounds its own transatlantic origins.

As Whittier's letter to Wright suggests, Clarke also published Longfellow's poetry in his Cabinet Library. Longfellow was, if anything, more enthusiastic about Clarke's reprint than Whittier. In February 1844, he wrote to the British scholar of Old English, Joseph Bosworth, asking:

> Have you seen the shilling edition of the "Voices of the Night," published by Clarke & Co—old Bailey? It is very pretty, though, I am sorry to see, rather carelessly printed. I am glad to see it in this form being an advocate for cheap editions, which, like light and well trimmed vessels, run far inland up the scarcely navigable streams, where heavier ships of the line cannot follow them.[7]

Longfellow had not authorized this edition and received no money from it. Nevertheless, he expresses pleasure at Clarke's edition; he would later greet a British reprint of *Kavanagh* as "rather piratical, but nevertheless quite flattering."[8] Transforming the pirate publication into a "well trimmed vessel," Longfellow understands that unauthorized reprints could give a writer symbolic capital by introducing his works to new publics, and thus authoring and authorizing literary fame. Moreover, he locates this authorizing ability in the volume's material text. Clarke's edition can increase Longfellow's renown because it is cheap and pretty. Longfellow knew that material texts could manifest authority in multiple ways; indeed, in the US, he issued his works at a variety of price points to take advantage of the authorizing power of both prestigious forms and mass market circulation.[9] Rather than simply classifying Clarke's reprint as authorized or unauthorized, Longfellow's comments show how British reprints drew together distinct but interconnected forms of authorization, and how US authors saw the benefits of, rather than the losses produced by, such publications.

In contrast, Clarence Gohdes concludes his discussion of Longfellow's dealings with British publishers by arguing that Longfellow was much the loser: "Only a desire for extra profits led a few British firms to make agreements with Longfellow, and all of them appear to have cheated him. From the point of view of his popularity abroad, there can be little doubt that the pirates were quite as important as these 'authorized' publishers."[10] Gohdes's focus on monetary loss produces a detailed account of Longfellow's financial transactions with British publishers to which I am indebted, but it fails to account for the embedded economies in these transactions, of which Longfellow himself was clearly aware. Studying the correspondence regarding and the material texts of Longfellow's unauthorized-yet-authorizing editions brings these embedded economies to the fore, showing how those reprints contributed not only to Longfellow's popularity and positioning in the field, but also to his consecration as America's national poet.

British publishers' attempts to license their Longfellow reprints were entangled in these interconnected and materialized discourses of authority. Several used their material texts to claim authorization outside of legal or financial transactions and to position themselves as Longfellow's authorized publisher. John Walker was the first to succeed in this endeavor. While few reprints of Longfellow's writing circulated in Britain before 1848, unauthorized editions began to proliferate after the publication and success of *Evangeline* in the United States. Walker was one of several publishers to reprint *Hyperion*, and he also published an anthology of Longfellow's poetry as *The Poetical Works of Professor Longfellow* in November 1848. Walker distinguished his editions through their superior material texts and paratexts, giving purchasers something more for their money but also attesting to the worth of Longfellow's writing. Walker advertised *Hyperion* as a "new and beautiful reprint," and his *Poetical Works* included a new essay on Longfellow by Rev. George Gilfillan, author of the popular *Gallery of Literary Portraits* (1846).[11]

Walker sent copies of his editions to Longfellow sometime in late 1848 or early 1849.[12] Jackson notes that in nineteenth-century publishing, "gift-giving was not distinct from business . . . it was a way of *doing* business."[13] With this particular gift, Walker aped the business practices of authorized publishers who would arrange for a number of "author's copies" to be sent to the author, and often to some nominated friends. Walker thus acted like an authorized publisher in the hope that Longfellow might consider him as such in the future, but also to imply that his editions were as good as authorized; he circulated his editions privately to Longfellow to sanction his public circulation of Longfellow's texts in Britain—if only between Longfellow and himself. Gifting the books further displayed Walker's gentlemanly conduct, and he continued to send Longfellow presents throughout their business relations, including a game pie, a plum pudding, and some whiskey at Christmas in 1850. But as a strategy for securing Longfellow's future business, Walker's actions were not without risk. These faux-author's copies evoked business arrangements that were absent in this unauthorized publication. Longfellow might have been offended and sought a rival firm who had not tried to pirate his works.

In this case, Walker's tactics worked. Longfellow replied, "I have had the pleasure of receiving the copies of your edition—your very handsome edition—of Hyperion and the Poems, which you were so kind as to send."[14] Longfellow frequently used "handsome" to refer to a book's physical form—in 1867, he described a London edition of his translation of Dante as "not a handsome one, but rather of the cheap kind"—and his vocabulary echoes descriptions of the authorized editions of John Murray and Richard Bentley discussed here in chapter 2.[15] Walker's *Hyperion* was not fine printing, but it had wide margins, large print, and began each chapter on a new page, stretching the novel to two volumes and stopping the book from appearing "cheap." Longfellow's comment was more than an empty platitude, and the edition's materiality helped Walker to secure Longfellow's advanced sheets. Walker's books arrived as *Kavanagh* was being put through the press in Boston by Ticknor, Reed and Fields, and Longfellow offered the sheets to Walker, noting particularly that he would like Walker to "reprint" the book.[16] In response, Walker also emphasized the quality of his books: "Although my editions have been the best & have sold well, yet owing to there being so many editions at a lesser price than mine, I have been obliged to print at a price that can yield nothing more than a mere trades profit."[17] Walker blames his competitors' unauthorized reprinting for his failure to pay Longfellow, implicitly legitimizing his own publication by distinguishing it from theirs.

British publishers did not widely adopt Walker's tactic of sending unauthorized reprints to court American authors in the 1840s and 1850s.[18] However, other publishers tried the same tactic with Longfellow. On September 5, 1851, having heard that Longfellow was preparing *The Golden Legend*, George Routledge & Co. wrote to him, offering twenty pounds for advanced sheets. But rather than sending a quality volume like Walker had done, Routledge sent to William Ticknor, Longfellow's American publisher, a

> small edition . . . issued at a very low price, but at the same time in a manner that we hope you will approve of, it may be also satisfactory for you to learn that this edition has been the means of enabling many to read your works, who could not have procured dearer editions, and caused your name to be as popular, and take as high a rank in England, as any of the greatest & best works of our own countrymen.[19]

As Walker sought legitimacy via privately circulating his "handsome" editions to Longfellow, Routledge sanctioned his cheap reprint by suggesting that its wide circulation had transformed Longfellow into a literary giant. Routledge's letter slips from large sales to literary value, claiming that cheap editions and large audiences, rather than Longfellow's literary merits, make his writings equal to "the greatest & best works of our countrymen." Both publishers, then, legitimized their own reprints by suggesting how their editions would increase Longfellow's cultural capital.

Routledge, like Walker, viewed self-authorizing editions as a step toward exchanges of advanced sheets for cash. Losing out on advanced sheets for *The Golden Legend* (for reasons I will explain shortly) did not stop Routledge using the materiality of his texts to court Longfellow's business. Routledge kept Longfellow informed about an edition of his complete poems that he published in January 1856, which included a portrait of Longfellow that Routledge had commissioned and illustrations by leading Victorian artist John Gilbert, showing that Routledge could legitimize Longfellow with prestigious formats as well as wide circulation. Each update was accompanied by a request for new material from Longfellow that Routledge thought he could use to prevent competitors from reprinting: an offer of £20 for sheets of a projected volume of essays in October 1854, a request for a preface in March 1855, and another for early sheets of new poems that Routledge had seen advertised in August 1855. The material text of the 1856 *Poems* became entangled with (unsuccessful) attempts to publish authorized editions.

Whether or not Routledge's *Poems* was an authorized publication is not a straightforward question. On the one hand, it contained no new material printed first in Britain, and nowhere in the surviving correspondence does Routledge offer Longfellow payment for reprinting this material. On the other hand, the publisher and the author collaborated in its production, with Routledge acquiescing to Longfellow's suggestions about the arrangement of the poems: "We wish to do exactly as you think proper & correct on this subject . . . & if afterwards you think it advisable to alter the arrangement from what it now is in your Ill'd Edition—please to let us have a complete list."[20] Most importantly, Routledge saw the edition as securing future authorized arrangements with Longfellow. He implied that the illustrated *Poems* was an advance of sorts in a disgruntled letter of December 28, 1855, in which he sent two morocco-bound (and thus expensive and prestigious) copies of the illustrated *Poems* to Longfellow, adding that,

> The illustrations alone cost upwards of 1000 guineas—and the portrait is done by one of our best engravers and at considerable expense.
>
> I shall take the liberty of stating that it was a great disappointment to us that we did not get Hiawatha, we should have given quite as much as Mr Bogue—and I flatter myself that we have done more to make your works known than all the publishers in the world put together.[21]

Merry Christmas, indeed. Although Routledge noted that he would have "given as much as Mr Bogue" for the sheets of *Hiawatha*, the mention of the "1000 guineas" for the illustrations suggests that Routledge believed that he had already made part payment. The economic investment in the illustrated *Poems* that validated Longfellow's worth as a cultural producer should also have secured

Routledge's position as the authorized publisher of *Hiawatha* along with the prestige that such a position would bring.

Routledge's and Walker's letters demonstrate that rather than distinguishing between authorized and unauthorized British editions, it is more pertinent to ask how different forms of authority are tied up in any transatlantic edition of a US text. Both publishers argue that the true authority of any English edition comes from its ability to materially manifest the literary value of the US writer, be that through quality printing or wide circulation. Longfellow's continued dealings with Walker and Routledge suggest that he, too, believed that the forms in which his work circulated in England were an important part of his authorization as a cultural producer. However, Longfellow's publications with David Bogue—the publisher who won the advanced sheets of *The Golden Legend*—show that the cultural work of British reprints was more extensive, with Bogue's editions entering debates about the scope and subjects of a national American tradition via their beautiful and extensive illustrations for Longfellow's writing. Alongside authorizing the reprint itself and presenting Longfellow's work as a valuable commodity, Bogue's illustrations visualized Longfellow's literary achievements and championed his concept of a cosmopolitan American literature.

Illustrating an American Tradition: David Bogue's *Evangeline* (1850) and *Hyperion* (1853)

On November 11, 1849, Longfellow invited the German American jurist Francis Lieber to "rejoice with me that an illustrated edition of *Evangeline* is in press in England."[22] That edition was published in late December 1849 (though the title page is dated 1850) by David Bogue, who, initially in partnership with Charles Tilt, specialized in lavish illustrated editions aimed at the Christmas trade. Defying stereotypes of unauthorized reprints, Bogue's *Evangeline* was no cheap paperback. Advertised at the middle-class price of 10s 6d, it was a lovely object, sporting generous margins and a decorated cover and festooned with illustrations by leading Victorian artists Myles Birket Foster, Jane Benham, and John Gilbert. Walker wrote on February 9, 1850, that he had "sent" a copy to Longfellow, adding that it was "a beautiful work & is greatly admired here. I have no property in it."[23] While Walker may have been remarking on the beauty of Longfellow's poem, which was favorably received in Britain, the reference to "property" makes it far more likely that he referred to Bogue's edition, which was praised as especially attractive in reviews.

Longfellow cared deeply about the illustration of his works and had struggled to publish satisfactory illustrated editions in America. He criticized Philadelphia publishers Carey & Hart for proposing to use illustrations from their Christmas book *The Gift* in their luxury edition of *Poems* (1845), arguing that pictures that had "no connection with the subjects in the book—would be to me a deformity and not a beauty."[24] There had been no illustrated edition of *Evangeline* published in America by 1850, making Bogue's *Evangeline* the most extensive testament yet to the aesthetic merits and popularity of Longfellow's poetry. Longfellow wrote in his journal on January 28, 1850, that Bogue's edition was "very beautiful,—the landscapes in particular," although he was less fond of the depiction of his heroine.[25] He chastised his sister, Anne, for failing to admire her copy: "You say nothing of [the] nice English copy of 'Evangeline' I sent you by Chs. S. Daveis some weeks ago;—the handsomest, that has yet been published, with many illustrations."[26] The illustrated *Evangeline* also prompted Longfellow to write to Bogue on February 3, 1850, evidently asking for originals of the illustrations and enquiring about the possibility of an American edition.[27] Bogue responded on February 22 that he had written to Ticknor with a "liberal offer": "This I hope and expect will tempt them to publish the work in America and greatly extend the [amount?] of readers and admirers of your beautiful poem."[28] As well as mirroring Routledge in promising Longfellow more British readers, Bogue proposed that his superior volume would confirm Longfellow as a leading author in America, too.

The material text of Bogue's *Evangeline* helped him to succeed Walker as Longfellow's authorized publisher. Gohdes suggests that when Longfellow came to publish *The Golden Legend* in November 1851, he had tired of Walker's failure to send payment for *The Seaside and the Fireside*.[29] Bogue offered Longfellow £100 for the copyright of *The Golden Legend* before Routledge made an offer of first £20 then £40. Bogue won the authorized edition because he offered more money and secured his deal quickly, but also because he published reasonably priced and prestigious editions, whereas Routledge had thus far only issued cheap editions. After Bogue issued *The Golden Legend* in cloth for 5s in November 1851, he published the collected edition *Voices of the Night, The Seaside and the Fireside and Other Poems* with illustrations for 15s in cloth or 1 guinea in morocco, as well as 6s reprints of Longfellow's prose and poetry, sending these to Longfellow.[30] Even after Bogue became Longfellow's authorized publisher, he continued to publish unauthorized editions of Longfellow's works in both expensive and cheap formats, following the same strategy Longfellow used within the United States.

Not only did Bogue's illustrated *Evangeline* boost him to the status of authorized publisher, the volume authorized its own reprinting. Longfellow appears to have earned nothing from British sales of the illustrated *Evangeline*, Bogue's illustrated *Poems*, his collected *Poems* and *Prose* (1851), or his illustrated *Hyperion* (1853).[31] Although, legally, it occupied the same position as Clarke's shilling edition of *Voices of the Night*, the expense and beauty of Bogue's *Evangeline* meant that it was never perceived as a piracy, even by Longfellow. Furthermore, the illustrations left other publishers unable to produce editions that could compete directly with Bogue's, giving him some of the exclusively of an authorized edition. Bogue was not the first publisher to use illustration as authorization. Hugh Amory describes the expensive plates that London publisher Charles Cooke added to his early-nineteenth-century editions of eighteenth-century novels, which could be protected under the Engraving Copyright Act of 1735 as "proprietary illustration" that worked to "define and legally secure the identity of his edition, like a trademark."[32] By the 1840s, publishers operated under the principle, later upheld by the courts, that wood-engraved illustrations by English artists and engravers that were printed on the same page as letterpress were protected under the copyright acts governing books even if the letterpress text was in the public domain and even if the illustrations did not meet the stricter requirements of the Engraving Act.[33] The time and expense of producing illustrations of a similar quality and number to those included in Bogue's edition were likely the main practical considerations that deterred other publishers from producing a copycat reprint.[34] Routledge issued a rival illustrated edition of the complete poems, but no other British publisher announced an illustrated *Evangeline*. However, this protection had its limits: several publishers still circulated the text of *Evangeline*, and readers who were unable or unwilling to pay Bogue's prices, or who simply preferred a less decorative book, could buy those editions instead.

Illustration also functioned as a site of authorization by offering opportunities for the US author to collaborate with the reprint publisher. The printed texts, illustrations, and photographic images that accompanied the correspondence between Bogue and Longfellow show that Longfellow participated in the reprinting of his works in forms that he admired and that would increase his reputation. Moreover, the materiality of Bogue's edition transformed it more completely than did either Walker or Routledge from unauthorized reprint to authorized edition—albeit authorized in the US, not Britain. Ticknor, Reed and Fields purchased five hundred copies of Bogue's edition with the title page bearing their own imprint and an American copyright statement on the reverse in July 1850.[35] Whereas Longfellow had previously looked to Philadelphia to supply the expensive, illustrated editions that testified to the value and popularity of his works, such testimony came from Britain after 1850.

Newspapers on both sides of the Atlantic agreed that Bogue's *Evangeline* confirmed Longfellow as America's preeminent poet. London reviews suggested that the book would enhance Longfellow's reputation, with *John Bull* observing that Bogue's edition would "make him better known" than the "modest guise" in which the poem first appeared.[36] The *Literary Gazette* added, "How grateful it must be to the honourable pride of Professor Longfellow to find his poetry so admired and appreciated in a distant country, as to induce its reproduction with all the appliances that art and taste can afford."[37] These notices evidence Britain's sense of cultural superiority, but they also celebrate poetry of genuine literary value finding a worthy form. Nor were the British alone in seeing a lavish transatlantic edition as a hallmark for US authors. Advertising the illustrated *Evangeline* in the New York periodical the *Literary World*,

Ticknor, Reed and Fields noted that its illustrations would "be executed by eminent English artists."[38] The attention to nationality reflects the belief that English illustrators, engravers, and printers were more skilled than their US counterparts; the advert sells the quality of the edition and indicates that superior transatlantic craftsmen deemed Longfellow worthy of attention. Despite its literary nationalism, the *Literary World* announced the book as "one of the highest compliments ever paid to any American poet."[39] The *Southern Literary Messenger* similarly noted the "English artists" when labelling the edition "quite a gem in the book way . . . altogether the work is perfect."[40] The Washington newspaper the *Republic* did complain that the publication revealed that "we are a nation of freebooters" who had not progressed in arts and manufacturing since Joel Barlow printed *The Columbiad* in London.[41] But established voices like *Graham's Magazine* applauded the publication even as they struggled to place it, unsure if they were "right in giving it an American origin, as its illustrations are most assuredly English, and its typographical execution is exactly similar to the English edition." Even if the book were English, this showed "Longfellow's popularity abroad," and did not prevent the engravings "so beautiful in themselves" being "true to the spirit and characters they illustrate." "The poem thus illustrated is more beautiful than ever," *Graham's* concluded, still "an American classic" in its English clothes.[42]

The feature of Bogue's *Evangeline* that attracted the most praise was Birket Foster's illustrations of the Acadian wilderness and Evangeline's western travels. Despite Foster having never visited America, the London *Examiner* suggested that Foster's illustrations enhanced the national qualities of Longfellow's poem, noting, with a pun on "engraved," that Foster "gives us, too, in graver touches, the 'forests primæval.'"[43] Although anticipating the chronological period by a decade, Foster's illustrations reflect the shift from decoration to interpretation that characterized the "Sixties" school of Victorian illustration.[44] His landscapes are in such sympathy with the poem as to blur the lines between image and word, text and book. This closeness was furthered by having the engraved illustrations printed on the same pages as the letterpress, unlike Carey & Hart's American illustrated *Poems*, which had separate plates. Rather than simply attributing cultural capital to Longfellow's writing by presenting his work in a prestigious and expensive format, Bogue's layout and Foster's illustrations together register the literary value of *Evangeline*'s representations of American landscape, and locate the poem within an American aesthetic tradition that becomes nationally distinctive through its cosmopolitanism.

In Bogue's edition, the famous opening lines of *Evangeline*—"This is the forest primeval. The murmuring pines and the hemlocks, / Bearded with moss, and in garments green, indistinct in the twilight"—are enveloped by those forests, in an illustration that surrounds the box of text (figure 2).[45] Winding Longfellow's hexameters back on themselves to fit in the reduced space, the page increases the poem's sense of enclosure. Graphically, Bogue's reprint positions Longfellow's text inside the North American landscape. The English illustrations of Bogue's edition thus attempt to render both text and book as American artifacts rather than "divorc[ing] text and image by making a distinction between the American novel and its British illustrations," as Julia Thomas argues is true of the British illustrated editions of *Uncle Tom's Cabin*.[46] In the second half of Longfellow's poem, in which Evangeline travels throughout the United States searching for her beloved Gabriel, there are two sets of facing pages in which Foster's American landscape scenes run vertically alongside the lines of verse. In the first of these (figure 3), a column illustration of the banks of the Mississippi accompanies Longfellow's account of Evangeline's journey on the river, so that the "silvery sand-bars" that "Lay in the stream, and along the wimpling waves of their margin" are made into the margins of the poem. Rather than describing the Mississippi landscape, Longfellow's poem becomes the bank that flanks the river, carved in a channel through the page. Similarly, on the facing page, Longfellow's description of "columns of cypress and cedar sustaining the arches" is positioned next to a column illustration of those trees.[47] The oval frame of the illustration makes the first line appear as though it is completing the arch and making the verse one with the trees. Longfellow's lines seem to grow organically from those landscapes and merge back into them again.

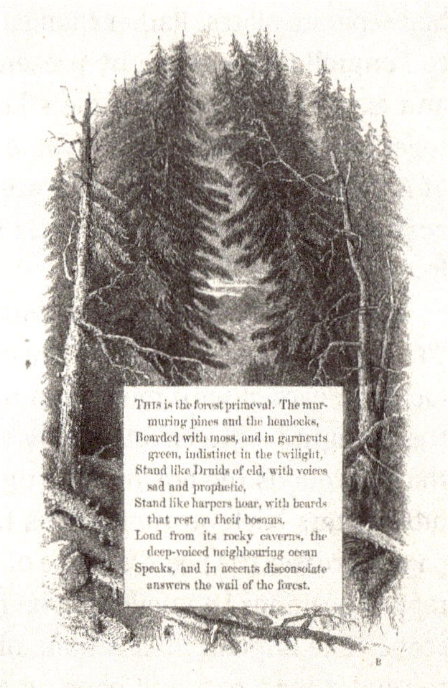

Figure 2. "The Forest Primeval," illustrated by Myles Birket Foster, engraved by Henry Vizetelly. From Henry Wadsworth Longfellow, *Evangeline: A Tale of Acadie* (London: David Bogue, 1850), 1. © The British Library Board, General Reference Collection C.71.d.12.

Bogue's edition of *Evangeline* emphasized that the poem was a product of American geography, but it did so by imagining and reprinting that geography in Europe. This symbiosis between American poem and British book itself articulated Longfellow's cosmopolitan vision for American national culture. Longfellow proposed that literature did not emerge from landscape, as "neither Mexico nor Switzerland has produced any very remarkable poet."[48] The national American tradition would be "a composite one, embracing French, Spanish, Irish, English, Scotch, and German peculiarities. Whoever has within himself most of these is our truly national writer. In other words, whoever is most universal, is also most national."[49] Leslie Eckel finds this cosmopolitan vision in the seemingly nationalist landscapes of *Evangeline*, arguing that they convey Longfellow's vision of a universal American literature by staging "a portrayal of loss [that] is at once intensely personal and immediately universal."[50] Indeed, *Evangeline*'s landscapes are sometimes more transatlantic than American. Longfellow describes the delta streams as "like a network of steel, extended in every direction," above which cypress branches "Waved like banners

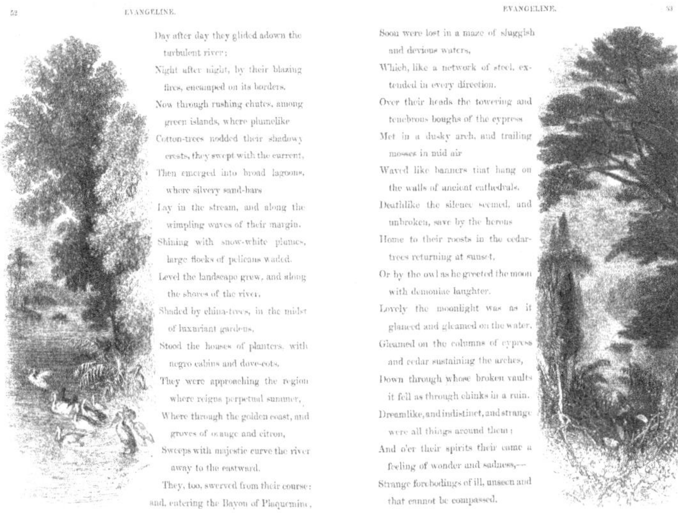

52 EVANGELINE.

Day after day they glided adown the turbulent river;
Night after night, by their blazing fires, encamped on its borders.
Now through rushing chutes, among green islands, where plumelike
Cotton-trees nodded their shadowy crests, they swept with the current,
Then emerged into broad lagoons, where silvery sand-bars
Lay in the stream, and along the wimpling waves of their margin.
Shining with snow-white plumes, large flocks of pelicans waded.
Level the landscape grew, and along the shores of the river,
Shaded by china-trees, in the midst of luxuriant gardens,
Stood the houses of planters, with negro cabins and dove-cots.
They were approaching the region where reigns perpetual summer,
Where through the golden coast, and groves of orange and citron,
Sweeps with majestic curve the river away to the eastward.
They, too, swerved from their course; and, entering the Bayou of Plaquemine,

EVANGELINE. 53

Soon were lost in a maze of sluggish and devious waters,
Which, like a network of steel, extended in every direction.
Over their heads the towering and tenebrous boughs of the cypress
Met in a dusky arch, and trailing mosses in mid air
Waved like banners that hang on the walls of ancient cathedrals.
Deathlike the silence seemed, and unbroken, save by the herons
Home to their roosts in the cedar-trees returning at sunset,
Or by the owl as he greeted the moon with demoniac laughter.
Lovely the moonlight was as it glanced and gleamed on the water,
Gleamed on the columns of cypress and cedar sustaining the arches,
Down through whose broken vaults it fell as through chinks in a ruin.
Dreamlike, and indistinct, and strange were all things around them;
And o'er their spirits there came a feeling of wonder and sadness,—
Strange forebodings of ill, unseen and that cannot be compassed.

Figure 3. "Into the golden stream" and "Now through rushing chutes," illustrated by Myles Birket Foster, engraved by Henry Vizetelly. From Henry Wadsworth Longfellow, *Evangeline: A Tale of Acadie* (London: David Bogue, 1850), 52–53. © The British Library Board, General Reference Collection C.71.d.12.

that hang on the walls of ancient cathedrals."[51] Asynchronously, the Mississippi Delta reaches both backward to European history and architecture and forward to a modern, industrial "network" that dismantles geographic space by entirely overwhelming it.

Such moments indicate that nationhood in *Evangeline* is unstable and mobile, with both Acadia and America depicted as oceanic spaces of circulation. Describing the Acadians arriving in Louisiana as "a band of exiles, a raft, as it were, from the shipwrecked / Nation," Longfellow imagines Acadia as a peripatetic vessel, even before its devastation. Longfellow would extend this image of nation-as-ship in "The Building of the Ship" (1849), but the America of *Evangeline* is also at sea. Evangeline hears the "sound of the sea" as she stands on the prairie: it is an echo of her Acadian homeland and a reminder of the permeable boundary between America and the Atlantic that takes on a threatening aspect when yellow fever enters Philadelphia "as the tides of the sea arise in the month of September." The poem's epilogue connects the graves of Gabriel and Evangeline with their homeland, but also connects two points on the Atlantic coast: Philadelphia, in which "Daily the tides of life go ebbing and flowing," and "the shore of the mournful and misty Atlantic" in Acadia.[52] Bogue's edition echoes Longfellow's Atlantic America by opening the poem's final canto with an image of Philadelphia that foregrounds the Delaware estuary, with the city itself in the background. Yet more than individual images, it is Bogue's attempt to create an autochthonous American book in Britain that truly captures the way in which Longfellow imagines the nation through oceanic circulation. In doing so, *Evangeline* anticipated Bogue's most ambitious Longfellow reprint, his 1853 illustrated edition of the prose romance *Hyperion*, in which the material text articulated Longfellow's vision of himself as a literary professional alongside his vision for a cosmopolitan American literature.

First published in 1839, *Hyperion* follows Paul Flemming, a young American widower and a self-portrait of Longfellow, on a tour of the Rhineland. Flemming experiences sublime landscapes and German student life, has intellectual conversations with fellow travelers, falls in unrequited love with an Englishwoman, Mary Ashburton (based on Fanny Appleton, who became Longfellow's second wife), and finally resolves to move on from his past and return to America to take up "a life of action and reality."[53] However, as scholars have noted, *Hyperion* is less a love story than an exercise in self-justification and self-promotion; William Charvat called it "a campaign by a man who wants to be a poet to make the poet respectable."[54] Matthew Gartner concurs, adding that, through Flemming's return to America, Longfellow frames himself as an expert on Europe's cultivated temptations by showing that he can resist them, enabling Longfellow to "justify his own decision to pursue a life in letters and to construct and confirm his own identity as a man of letters."[55] Through literary allusions, lengthy meditations on arts and philosophy, and knowledge of the German landscape, Longfellow positions himself as a cultural expert who educates his readers. But Longfellow also uses interpolated translations and intertextual references to advocate for a composite and cosmopolitan American literature. Similarly, Bogue's *Hyperion* both supported Longfellow's self-fashioning as a literary professional by testifying to his aesthetic achievements and cultural expertise, and suggested that the nationality of American writing would be achieved through internationalism, authorizing Longfellow's vision for American literature.

Hyperion had been reprinted ten times in the United States by 1852. Although these editions were neatly printed, had generous margins, and, after 1847, bore the literary imprint of Ticknor, they did not offer the prestige and beauty of Bogue's volumes.[56] Bogue never asked for permission to reprint *Hyperion*, but Longfellow was pleased to hear of the plan and especially of Birket Foster's involvement, writing to Bogue in February 1852 that "it could not possibly be in better hands."[57] Furthermore, Bogue attempted to present the illustrated *Hyperion* as an authorized edition. Sending proofs of Foster's illustrations in October 1852, Bogue informed Longfellow that he had discussed with James Fields, who was then traveling in England, whether a new preface would secure the copyright on *Hyperion* (Fields believed it would not). When Longfellow did not take up his offer to write a new preface for *Hyperion*—probably because he did not think it was worth the £10 Bogue offered—Bogue instead printed a publisher's preface claiming that this *Hyperion* "furnishes the first example of a lengthened journey being expressly undertaken to depict from nature all the varied scenes amid which a writer of fiction has laid the incidents of his story."[58] Rather than priority of publication, which would have secured copyright in 1853, Bogue claims a different kind of priority—a publishing first in place of first publication. Moreover, after his legal victory in 1852, Bogue knew that his illustrations were protected by copyright in England, as they were produced by British subjects. Replacing a statement from the author with a description of his illustrations, Bogue implicitly extended their copyright to the text itself. As with *Evangeline*, the illustrations that testified to Longfellow's cultural capital also authorized this British edition.

The "lengthened journey" that Bogue mentioned was a tour of the Rhineland on which Bogue sent Foster and the engraver Henry Vizetelly so that they might "make sketches of the scenery on the spot," as Bogue wrote to Longfellow in January 1852.[59] Vizetelly would later claim that publishing *Hyperion* and traveling to Germany to produce the illustrations was his idea, but it was certainly Bogue who financed it.[60] This economic investment illustrates the market value of Longfellow in Britain. At the same time, the illustrations authorized Longfellow's expertise on European culture by validating *Hyperion*'s depiction of Europe. Discussing Robert Cadell's Abbotsford Edition of Walter Scott's Waverley Novels (1842–47), Richard Maxwell suggests that illustrations can work as an "interconnected multimedia gloss," verifying and explicating a text as well as decorating it. Illustrations had "considerable responsibilities—epistemological as well as aesthetic. Like notes and appendices, images could be considered supplements . . . which by implication should have been there from the beginning even though they probably were not."[61] Bogue's *Hyperion* may have been mimicking Cadell's scholarly impulse, as it also added textual supplements, including an index of places, characters, and artists and authors, suggesting that it could be consulted as a guidebook to landscape or to literature. Bogue's preface emphasizes the edition's educational value, noting that "every local Illustration . . . was sketched on the spot, and is a perfectly faithful representation of the place described or mentioned."[62] As well as supplementing or substituting for a real tour of the Rhine, the correspondences between the book's "faithful representations" and Longfellow's text guaranteed Longfellow's expertise. Vizetelly's appendix, "Notes of a Tour in the Footsteps of Paul Flemming," further evidences Longfellow's knowledge of the Rhineland: "So truthful did we find all the numerous descriptive passages scattered through this work . . . we were fully prepared to see, as we did, the herds of cattle and the herdsman in charge."[63]

Numbering nearly one hundred engraved illustrations, Foster and Vizetelly's supposedly supplementary paratexts occupy considerable space in the book. As in *Evangeline*, the wood-engraved images and the letterpress are printed side by side, and the former frequently dominate the pages, such as when a single verse of one of the Longfellow-Flemming translations is enveloped by an illustration. This reversal of the text-book hierarchy might have subordinated Longfellow's American writing to the English book that contains it, except that it elevated American literature by locating it as the inspiration for such lavish bookwork. "True pilgrims as we were," Vizetelly recounts, "with a reverence for each locality which the genius of our author had invested with peculiar interest in our eyes." The "Notes of a Tour" also bolsters Longfellow's literary credentials. Vizetelly describes visiting a German priest who translated some of the poems featured in *Hyperion*, showing "how admirably Longfellow had rendered them into English verse."[64] Bogue's edition proved that Longfellow was not one of the false scholars who have lost touch with the world, whom Flemming and his friend the Baron criticize while visiting Heidelberg University. Instead, the illustrated *Hyperion* fitted Longfellow as a literary man worthy of the "great importance in a nation's history" that Longfellow—via Flemming—ascribes to them: "Do not these men, in all ages and in all places, emblazon with bright colours the armorial bearings of their country?"[65] Longfellow's knowledge of the world beyond the United States made him the progenitor of a New World literary tradition to match that of the Old.

Most importantly, Bogue's *Hyperion* locates Longfellow as a writer—perhaps even more strongly than does his *Evangeline*—of the international and universal literature that Longfellow himself believed was the most truly American form. The *Literary Gazette* observed that the illustrated *Hyperion* networked the text across space and time: "After reading 'Hyperion' we may often take up the book, and in looking at the illustrations be reminded of other literary and historical associations of which the scenes are suggestive."[66] For this reviewer, Bogue's illustrations furthered Longfellow's efforts to embed his writing and his hero into a diachronic and transnational literary culture; *Hyperion* references Tudor dramatist John Lyly's *Endymion*, Italian poet Matteo Maria Borjado, the legend of Roland, and the German tales of Siegfried in the first chapter alone. Translation is also central to Longfellow's project of a cosmopolitan American literature. Flemming's attempts to woo Mary with improvised translations of German verse are also Longfellow's attempt to convince readers of his poetic skill and persuade them that American literature should be grounded in translation, broadly conceived: a new tradition formed by reworking Old World materials. Longfellow's translations are some of the most extensively illustrated sections of Bogue's *Hyperion*, inviting readers to linger over the kind of literary work that Longfellow believed would be central to American writing.

In particular, Bogue accompanies Longfellow's translation of "The Castle by the Sea" with two elaborate landscapes, visualizing the aesthetic merit of Longfellow's verse. Foster's illustrations also support Longfellow's interpretation of the poem. Flemming agrees with Mary's assessment that the poem's ambiguities mirror "the momentary illusion" of a reflected landscape; and the shimmering quality and reflected light of the illustration aligns Foster and Vizetelly's visual interpretation with Longfellow's textual exegesis, authorizing Longfellow's scholarly credentials. But the visual attention this episode receives is particularly important because Mary's interpretation of the poem is a metaphor for translation itself. The poem conveys the sensation of "beholding a perfect reflection of an old tower in the sea. We look at it as if it were not a mere shadow in the water; and yet the real tower rises far above." Longfellow is convinced that by reflecting the Old World across the Atlantic, American literature can become more than mere shadow and can create the aesthetic sublime that Flemming experiences in response to the poem: "A beautiful cloud landscape, which I comprehend and feel, and yet should have some difficulty perhaps in explaining." While Mary says that such feelings are "quite untranslatable," her comprehension of the poem's emotion has been prompted by translation itself.[67]

In the final book of *Hyperion*, Longfellow demonstrates that his subject is the future of American culture just as much as Europe's history and literature. In Book Four's opening chapter, Longfellow leaves Flemming and relocates the reader to his own "leafy, blossoming, and beautiful Cambridge." Yet the Massachusetts landscape is not solely American. "The broad meadows and the steel-blue river remind me of the meadows of Unterseen and the river Aar; and beyond them rise magnificent snow-white clouds, piled up like Alps. Thus the shades of Washington and William Tell seem to walk together on these Elysian Fields." Anticipating *Evangeline*'s landscapes, where the "steel" delta echoes *Hyperion*'s "steel-blue river," Longfellow provides another asynchronous transatlantic American vista, viewed through a nostalgia that is spatial as well as temporal. On first glance, this episode undermines Flemming's lesson: "Look not mournfully into the Past . . .

[but] Wisely improve the Present. It is thine. Go forth to meet the shadowy Future."[68] However, Longfellow's layering of landscapes avoids the conservative "restorative" nostalgia that Svetlana Boym describes as an attempt to reconstruct the lost home along the "single teleological plot" of national memory.[69] Instead, Longfellow illustrates that "nostalgic longing refuses to privilege the nation," as Jennifer Ladino argues, "and instead imagines belongings at other scales."[70] Longfellow's Cambridge—his center of American literary life—appears more vividly when imagined through—and networked with—a European literary landscape.

Foster and Vizetelly's illustration of Cambridge emphasizes the nostalgic collapse of time and space that creates Longfellow's American landscape (figure 4). The image deviates from Bogue's promise that every scene was drawn on the spot; neither man had visited Cambridge, Massachusetts. A figure that might be Flemming (or Longfellow) sits at a writing slope with his back to the reader and stares out of an open window to the indistinct landscape beyond, which might itself be either Central Europe or Massachusetts. If this scene was indeed drawn in Europe, it mirrors Longfellow's layered landscape. Longfellow uses Cambridge to imagine Europe; Bogue's book employs Europe to depict America. The emergence of the American nation from European landscapes speaks to Longfellow's cosmopolitan national literature and also to the role of Bogue's book in constructing an American literary tradition. While the landscape fades in the distance, a shelf of books remains visible in the foreground. Bogue's *Hyperion* thus imagines an American writer who emerges from material texts as much as from any particular landscape or geography, emphasizing the role of the British book in fashioning American authorship. Longfellow, too, imagines this connection between transatlantic circulation and American literary development in the first major work that he published after Bogue's death in 1856, *The Courtship of Miles Standish*.

America's Transatlantic Origins: *The Courtship of Miles Standish* (1858)

The Courtship of Miles Standish, published in October 1858, is a sequel of sorts to *Evangeline*, echoing the earlier poem's colonial American setting and dactylic hexameters. The poem is a curious mix of

CHAPTER I.

A MISERERE.

In the Orlando Innamorato, Malagigi, the necromancer, puts all the company to sleep by reading to them from a book. Some books have this power of themselves, and need no necromancer. Fearing, Gentle Reader, that mine may be of this kind, I have provided these introductory chapters from time to time, like stalls or Misereres in a church, with flowery canopies and poppy-heads over them, where thou mayest sit down and sleep.

No,—the figure is not a bad one. This book does somewhat resemble a minster, in the Romanesque style, with pinnacles, and flying buttresses, and roofs,—

> "Gargoyled with greyhounds, and with many lions
> Made of fine gold, with divers sundry dragons."

You step into its shade and coolness out of the hot streets of life; a mysterious light streams through the painted glass

Figure 4. "View from the Study Window," illustrated by Myles Birket Foster, engraved by Henry Vizetelly. From Henry Wadsworth Longfellow, *Evangeline: A Tale of Acadie* (London: David Bogue, 1850), 217. © The British Library Board, General Reference Collection 1570/1285.

romantic comedy and reflections on the violence and instability of Early America. Against the backdrop of the Plymouth colony, where wheat is planted over graves lest the Native population see how many have perished, Miles Standish, the Puritan captain in charge of the colony's safety, and his friend, the young and scholarly John Alden, compete for the beautiful orphaned maiden Priscilla Mullins. Despite their age gap, the widowed Standish wants to marry Priscilla and asks John to woo her in his name, not knowing that John is himself in love with Priscilla. John's clumsy wooing goes spectacularly awry when Priscilla asks, "Why don't you speak for yourself, John?" After John confesses his failure, Standish takes offence at what he believes is John's treachery, and the two men quarrel before Standish is called away to defend the colony from Indian attacks. Although John feels guilty, he and Priscilla grow closer and, upon hearing that Standish has been killed, promptly decide to marry. But an armored figure that seems to be "a ghost from the grave" interrupts their wedding feast and reveals himself to be Standish—who is alive, and ready to acknowledge that John is the better man for Priscilla.[71] John and Priscilla then ride off on the back of a bull into an American pastoral, fresh with promise.

Amid such images of national nascence, Longfellow furnishes *Miles Standish* with material trappings of the Old World. In Standish's cabin are his armor and his Bible, which stands between hefty copies of "Bariffe's Artillery Guide" and an English translation of Caesar's *Commentaries*. Longfellow pays special attention to these books: "Prominent three, distinguished alike for bulk and for binding."[72] Moreover, they are not the only texts in the poem's opening. As Robert Ferguson suggests, John is a prototype of the American author, making Priscilla's demand that he speak for himself a call for American literature.[73] For the first canto and a half, John does nothing but write letters, not even stopping when he speaks to Standish. Longfellow renders John's literary capabilities as material production, with Standish proclaiming that John has "skill in the turning of phrases," anticipating fine phrases becoming fine books. But Longfellow also implicitly juxtaposes the haste and ephemerality of John's writing with the solidity of the English books, thrice repeating the line, "Nothing was heard in the room but the hurrying pen of the stripling." While the freshness of "stripling" is positive, the "hurrying pen" could suggest the fast-paced development of American letters or, more pejoratively, a literature that seeks to run before it can walk. Nevertheless, the line perfectly fits Longfellow's dactylic hexameter—a verse form that divided critics but that Longfellow had claimed for his own in America and abroad—aligning John's letters with Longfellow's own. John's writing is not destined for an American audience, however, but for transatlantic circulation, with Longfellow describing the letters as "Homeward bound." While "bound" denotes the direction of circulation, it also connotes the materiality of the book, especially occurring in such close proximity to the description of Standish's English books "distinguished alike for bulk and for binding."[74] Being "Homeward bound" suggests that John's letters might gain the solidity of Standish's books through transatlantic circulation, just as the materialization of Longfellow's own writing in Britain championed his vision for American aesthetics.

Longfellow develops this subtle suggestion that American letters might find solidity in English books in John's courtship of Priscilla, a romance that founds the American nation and produces an American form of expression. John's attempts at conversing with Priscilla after Standish's departure falter, as Priscilla accuses him of repeating his earlier mistake of not speaking in his own voice. She advises him not to "make use of those common and complimentary phrases," signifying John's linguistic failure when "complimentary" wrenches the meter of the line. In contrast, Longfellow strips Priscilla's message back to single syllables to show how far John has deviated from Puritan simplicity and American naturalness: "Let us, then, be what we are, and speak what we think, and in all things / Keep ourselves loyal to truth." When John finally strikes the right note with Priscilla and truly speaks for himself, it is by means of an English book. He woos Priscilla by comparing her spinning to that of Bertha of Swabia, "She whose story I read at a stall in the streets of Southampton."[75] The line is one of Longfellow's more complex, alliterating on stressed syllables and stretching the final word across two feet, but is nevertheless perfectly metrically regular. Around the English book, John and Longfellow construct an American writing that has a complexity that does not threaten its straightforwardness.

As with Bogue's reprints, the English books become a basis for American literature to develop its unique qualities and gain the authority to speak in its own voice.

But *The Courtship of Miles Standish* also uses English books to illustrate that violence accompanies the fashioning of American nationalism. If Standish's Bible and military guides signify the solid forms that John's "stripling" American letters might take once they are "Homeward bound," then they also symbolize Standish's place in the colony. The military books straddle the Bible so that it seems "guarded by these," reflecting how Standish's martial presence ensures the safety of the religious community and illustrating the combination of religious freedom and colonial violence at the heart of the American experiment. Connecting John and Standish through European books as well as through their love triangle with Priscilla, Longfellow suggests that American violence and American literature cannot easily be untangled. Longfellow blames circulations of English blood—"All the hot blood of his race, of Sir Hugh and of Thurston de Standish"—for Standish's violent response to the taunts of the Indian Wattawamat. That is, Standish's transatlantic connections cannot permit forms of expression that he believes threaten the new colony. After Standish kills him, Wattawamat's head is displayed on "the roof of the fort, which at once was a church and a fortress," a description that recalls the arrangement of Standish's books, where the martial tomes prop up the Bible and fashion another fortress-church.[76] In a more brutally honest way than in the vanishing Indians of *Hiawatha*, Longfellow suggests that transatlantic materials define the boundaries of American literature not only by facilitating particular forms of white expression, but also by suppressing Indigenous cultures.

It is important, however, not to overstate the extent to which Longfellow is willing to excavate the violence of cultural nationalism as he imagines an American literature that is fashioned through Atlantic crossings. The European books of *The Courtship of Miles Standish* tie American literary expression to colonial violence, but the triumphs of literary expression also cloak that violence as the pastoral imagery that follows John's successful American authorship obscures the earlier bloodshed. Standish is part of

America's founding, but Longfellow makes clear that John's eloquence and his marriage to Priscilla secure its future. Standish returns for the wedding, but disappears in the final four stanzas of the poem, which focus on the couple alone. In this final scene, when John and Priscilla enter a landscape that "Like a picture it seemed of the primitive, pastoral ages," Longfellow seems to be directing the illustration of the poem.[77] Having imagined an American tradition emerging through transatlantic books, *The Courtship of Miles Standish* concludes by anticipating its circulation in the kind of illustrated edition in which Longfellow's British publishers specialized.

The Courtship of Miles Standish thus demonstrates that the transatlantic material fashioning of American literature was a two-way process in which even unauthorized reprints could be a site of artistic collaboration. Bogue's unauthorized editions of *Evangeline* and *Hyperion* positioned Longfellow as a gifted author and a valuable literary property through the same superior material form that sanctioned their own unauthorized publication. More importantly, however, they championed Longfellow's vision of a distinctive yet cosmopolitan American tradition in which he would take center stage. Nor was Longfellow without agency in this collaboration, imaginatively recirculating the transatlantic print trade in his own poetry. The books in *Miles Standish* are products of a different time, but they are also reflections of Longfellow's own British editions—books that transformed a "stripling" American writing into a literature bound for permanence.

Bogue did not, however, produce an illustrated *Miles Standish*. His death in November 1856 brought his relationship with Longfellow to a close almost two years before the book was published. Writing to Ferdinand Freiligrath, a German friend who was then translating *Hiawatha*, Longfellow noted, "I am afraid Bogue's Illustrated Edition [of *Hiawatha*] will be stopped by his death. This is a great pity."[78] Longfellow's unqualified "this" leaves it unclear as to whether he mourns Bogue's death or the loss of the edition. His comments may seem a blunt response to the sudden death of a man in his forties with whom Longfellow had warm business relations and who left behind young children, as Longfellow would have known from the emotional letter that he received from Bogue's former partner, Charles Tilt. But the merging of Bogue with his illustrated editions and Longfellow's remorse at their ceasing suggest that Longfellow had come to think of these material texts as an integral part of his literary output. While Bogue's death ended one of Longfellow's most important publishing relationships, British publishers continued to use illustration to legitimize and protect their editions of American books and to champion the achievements of American authors on both sides of the Atlantic.

Picturing Poe Posthumously

In the *Publishers' Circular* of July 16, 1857, less than a year after Bogue's death, Sampson Low & Son advertised that they were "Preparing for Publication Early in the Autumn:—Two splendidly Illustrated, PRESENTATION VOLUMES" of poetry: one by Edgar Allan Poe, and one by "Edward Cullen Bryant," whose first name was corrected to William when the volume was announced as being in print that October.[79] Low, formerly the Harper brothers' London agent and Harriet Beecher Stowe's authorized publisher, was experienced in navigating transatlantic publishing, and these editions were semi-authorized. While not printed from advanced sheets, they were produced in conjunction with Poe's and Bryant's US publishers, J. S. Redfield and Appleton respectively, who sold copies of the books in the United States with their imprint on the title page and a copyright statement on the reverse. The archive of Sampson Low is not extant, but the editions themselves suggest that both in format and in publishing process, the firm followed the model that Bogue had established with Longfellow. The illustrations were drawn and engraved by British artists (with the exception of F. O. C. Darley's pictures for the volume of Poe, which must have been sent from America), and the volumes were printed in London by Richard Clay. By producing the illustrations in Britain, parts of the volumes would be protected by copyright in both countries.

As Low's advertisement states, and as the involvement of US firms demonstrates, a transatlantic illustrated edition also confirmed the cultural value of Poe and Bryant: "The names of the Artists engaged on these Works is sufficient guarantee that the peculiar and distinctive merits of each of these distinguished poets of America will be observed, and that an edition of each may be looked for at once characteristic of their opposite style, and worthy of their fame in both countries."[80] The advert locates both men as "poets of America" at the same time as promising that the editions will maintain their individual writerly qualities. However, comparing Low's volumes shows that the books were more similar than otherwise, and that both strongly resembled Bogue's editions of *Evangeline* and *Hyperion*. Large landscapes by Bogue's illustrator Birket Foster dominate particular pages and the volumes as a whole: he produced thirty-four of the seventy-one illustrations for Bryant's poems, and seventeen of the fifty-four illustrations for Poe's. Only the use of gothic ornaments between the poems distinguished Poe's darker subjects. Rather than establishing the writers' "opposite style[s]," Low's editions seem more concerned with establishing that both men resemble Longfellow as national American voices worthy of critical praise and market success.

Contemporary reviews suggest that Low and his co-publishers were largely successful in these aims. The London national *Lloyd's Weekly Newspaper* described the Poe as a "book which we should be glad to find on many drawing-room tables," and the *Southern Literary Messenger* claimed that "luxury in bookmaking can go no further than it has been carried by Mr. Redfield in this really superb volume."[81] The *New York Albion* was particularly taken with the paper of the Poe volume, which it said "resembles Devonshire cream," connecting the volume's transatlantic origins and the luxury format that confirmed Poe's value as a poet.[82] While none of the reviews explicitly mention Longfellow's illustrated editions, they praise Low's books in near identical terms, viewing both as fitting celebrations of US talent and national American writing. Low's editions thus show that Bogue had established both a material form and an aesthetic model through which British publishers could license the circulation of their own editions of US texts, champion individual writers, and envision a national American tradition to which those writers belong.

While these editions mold Poe and Bryant in Longfellow's example, they nevertheless open new vistas onto Poe especially and provide new perspectives on debates over authorship and cultural nationalism. Neither Bryant nor Poe initially seems a likely candidate to have followed in Longfellow's transatlantic footsteps. Unlike Longfellow, who strongly desired illustrated editions of the type that Bogue produced, Bryant confessed to Richard H. Dana Sr. in 1854 that he had a "horror of illustrations"; still, he repeated William Appleton's claim that the illustrations would be "finer than Longfellows" to his wife, Frances.[83] Poe disliked both Longfellow's model of literary nationalism and his illustrated editions. McGill argues that as early as 1839, Poe criticized *Hyperion* for the very cosmopolitanism that Bogue's illustrations enhanced because Poe feared that the text's loose gathering of eclectic materials disguised the work and value of authorial labor.[84] In 1846, Poe further attacked reviewers who gave "to [Longfellow's] morocco binding and gilt edges, flattering portrait of himself, and to the illustrations of his poems by Huntingdon, that amount of indiscriminate approbation which neither could nor would have been given to the poems themselves."[85] The article echoes Poe's other negative judgements on illustrated gift books and periodicals in which the text was a supplement to lavish images.[86] In both cases, Poe bristles at the thought of material texts substituting for the author in a reader's mind, suggesting an anxiety that illustrations, like Longfellow's eclecticism, might displace and devalue the work of writing.

Nevertheless, as Michael Von Cannon demonstrates through a reading of several of Poe's short stories, Poe understood the power of visual culture to shape a writer's reputation; while Poe always "made sure to privilege the literary text in its ability to inspire illustration," he also imagined how writing and illustration "might be used symbiotically to promote the writers and artists who created them."[87] The illustrations in Bogue's Longfellow editions were an example of such a productive, symbiotic relationship between word and image. Those illustrations were produced for the text (rather than vice versa) and engraved on wood so they could appear alongside the text rather than on separate plates, enhancing and illuminating textual meaning rather than distracting from it.[88] Indeed, Poe envisioned such illustrations as integral to his projected periodical *The Stylus*, telling James Russell Lowell in 1844 that the magazine would "be illustrated, not merely embellished, by spirited wood designs in the style of

[French illustrator J. J.] Grandville." For Poe, a magazine with this materiality was as important as an "International Copy-Right Law" in relieving American literature from its present "dreadful" condition.[89] Poe never produced *The Stylus*, but his ambitions for illustration were achieved in Low's edition. Closely examining that book further reveals that its material text is in dialogue with the poems' reflections on US literary culture. If the illustrations' subject and style evoked Longfellow more than Poe, the production and publication of the edition distils Poe's own understanding of a US literary culture that was unfolding in a transatlantic marketplace of reprinting—a relation between text and book that is most visible in "Ulalume."

Even within Poe's strange oeuvre, "Ulalume" is weird. The speaker describes a "night in the lonesome October" walking in conversation with his soul, Psyche, "by the dark tarn of Auber, / In the ghoul-haunted woodland of Weir," when he is suddenly led by a mysterious double-crescented star to a tomb. Upon hearing Psyche read out its inscription—"'Tis the vault of thy lost Ulalume!"—the speaker realizes that he has been here before, precisely a year ago, to bury his lover, which he had apparently forgotten until this point.[90] Despite the poem's textual history demonstrating Poe's strategic orchestration of its reprinting, and its plot pivoting on the exposure of an initially invisible repetition, "Ulalume" has not been read as an engagement with cultures of reprinting.[91] Yet the poem's strange power comes from repetition: from its dense rhyme scheme (each ten line stanza is built around only two different rhyme sounds), to the narrator's initial inability to separate original actions from repetitions, and his sudden realization that everything that seemed new, he has seen before. Poe distils this uncanny relation between event and recurrence into the word "once," which the poem uses first to refer to the walk described in the poem—"Here once, through an alley Titanic, / Of cypress, I roamed with my Soul—"—and then second to refer to the previous, initially forgotten, trip to bury Ulalume: "We noted not the dim lake of Auber—/ (Though once we had journeyed down here)."[92] The repetition of "once" is also a transformation, a moment in which a seemingly singular entity splits into an original and a repetition. Within its text, then,

"Ulalume" resounds the material recursions through which Poe, and the culture of reprinting, established the poem itself.

Furthermore, the culture of reprinting in "Ulalume" is transatlantic. Critics have long acknowledged that Poe named the "lake of Auber" and "woodland of Weir" for people rather than places: the French composer Daniel-François-Esprit Auber, and the Hudson River painter Robert Walter Weir.[93] These references span the transatlantic mid-century print market and also echo the European-American landscape of *Hyperion*'s Cambridge chapter, in which Longfellow has Massachusetts and Central Europe fade into one another. In the version of "Ulalume" that Low and Redfield print, the poem concludes by resketching this transatlantic landscape, suggesting that its contours become newly visible and perhaps even navigable in the moment that the narrator becomes conscious of his repetition: "Well I know, now, this dark tarn of Auber, / This ghoul-haunted woodland of Wier."[94] However, this landscape also manifests the speaker's *unconsciousness* of repetition, because Poe describes both the leaves of the woodland and the speaker's unreliable memories as "sere," thus painting the location as a withered, unredeemable space, like a lost recollection. If the transatlantic landscape and authorial repetitions become jointly visible in "Ulalume," then that same landscape also enacts a kind of spell that so alienates the speaker from his labor—carrying Ulalume to her tomb—that he initially fails to recognize the spot where he placed her body. Read alongside the anxieties over authorship that fueled Poe's campaign to publicize the poem through reprinting, "Ulalume" is a meditation on the fate of authorial labor in a transatlantic print landscape that both facilitates and disguises the reprinting of texts.

The first of two illustrations for "Ulalume" in the Redfield and Low edition of Poe's *Poetical Works* visually reinforces the importance of landscape in the poem. The illustration, by the American artist Jasper Cropsey, shows the speaker's solitary figure on the shore of a lake, which is surrounded by the ruins of trees, while a strange, cross-crescent star hangs in the sky above. Reminiscent of Foster's moonlit scenes for *Hyperion*, the image frames "Ulalume" less as a poem about psychic experience than a poem about landscape. A fellow member of the Hudson River

School, Cropsey may well have recognized Weir's name because his composition echoes that tradition, with a small figure in the foreground illustrating the vastness of the landscape that rises up behind him.[95] Materially, however, the illustration is transatlantic: it was drawn by an American artist who was living in London, engraved by a British engraver, and printed in London. Similarly, the edition itself—co-published by London and New York firms and distributed on both sides of the Atlantic—locates "Ulalume" more firmly than ever in the transatlantic landscape Poe imagines. The illustrated *Poetical Works*' methods of production thus further the transatlantic recursions over which the poem worries. However, its copyright illustrations and text prevent this version of "Ulalume" from being reprinted in either Britain or the US, and celebrate the labor of the author by translating his work into art. Just as repetition in a transatlantic landscape generates both the anxiety in and the power of "Ulalume," the transatlantic *Poetical Works* confirms transatlantic reprinting as a mode of reproduction through which authorial labor and value can be established rather than forgotten.

Redfield and Low's edition of Poe's *Poetical Works* testifies to the legacy of Bogue's illustrated editions of Longfellow. It shows that Bogue created a model for using the materiality of the text to authorize British editions of US texts, the US writer, and the national American tradition, which other publishers imitated. The *Poetical Works* constructs Poe as an important and a national American poet as much by imitating illustrated editions of Longfellow as by visualizing the particular aesthetic qualities of Poe's verse. Understanding these connections between Bogue's edition of Longfellow and Low's edition of Poe further demonstrates that attending to the transatlantic materials of American literature generates unexpected pathways between authors and texts. Rather than placing Poe and Longfellow on opposite sides of debates between cultural nationalists and Brahmin cosmopolitans, approaching these writers through their British editions emphasizes what they both understood about their contemporary publishing moment—that US writers produced their work in a transatlantic print culture, and that it was within that culture that their labors could be recognized.

As I observed in the introduction, Longfellow is an exceptional case in terms of his transatlantic popularity. Such popularity doubtless contributed to the substantial survival of archival materials that make it possible to trace the financial transactions, embedded economies, and authorizing effects that arose from the British publication of his poetry and prose. Yet Longfellow's example invites us to seek out, even if more speculatively, the forms of authorization that other US writers found in British print—for themselves as individual authors and for the national American literature into which British publishers placed their texts. In chapter 3, I show that this work was not limited to expensive editions, but it was also performed by cheap reprints and by the publishers' series and libraries in which they were published. The next chapter, however, remains at the upper end of the market, exploring how the material manifestations of aesthetic value and cultural capital in authorized editions, as well as their copyright status, championed US writers and placed authorship at the center of US literary and print cultures whose structures were still in flux.

CHAPTER 2

Authorized Editions and the Materials of American Authorship

Between November 1854 and January 1855, the *New York Herald* published a series of letters from a London correspondent about the state of Anglo-American literary relations. The correspondent lamented the recent House of Lords decision that prior publication did not establish copyright for foreign authors, and argued that British publishers had done more to help create a national American literature than had their US counterparts. They claimed that London publishers had offered vital support to US writers who were "driven to make [their] reputation in a foreign country" by competition from cheap reprints of British texts, describing an anonymous US author who, having received no interest in his work at home, traveled to Britain, where "he soon found a publisher for his works, the first of which found purchasers for three editions in twelve months."[1] These letters positioned John Murray as the most important publisher of US texts, observing that he disseminated American works in "his very best style," drew them to the attention of press and public, and paid handsomely. In second place was Richard Bentley & Sons, who were not as liberal or as gentlemanly as Murray and were much complained about by English authors, yet "strictly adhered to a legitimate trade" and "tended to elevate the character of American literature abroad." But now that copyright through prior publication was impossible, these "old established and respectable houses, which heretofore did so much to give prominence to American authors and their works, decline to have anything further to do with American works until some protection be afforded them."[2] A vital route for the development of American writing had been closed.

This chapter explores how Murray's and Bentley's authorized publication of US texts contributed to the development of an American literary tradition, paying particular attention to the work performed by their material texts. Rather than seeing these material texts as incidental products of authors' efforts to secure copyright, reputation, or financial reward in Britain, I follow both the commentator from the *Herald* and US writers in paying careful attention to the "style" of Murray's and Bentley's American books. US authors valued these "handsome" or "elegant" books that materialized the worth of individual authors and the centrality of authorship to US print culture at a time when the organization of that culture was in flux. These British editions demonstrated the publishers' investments of time and money in navigating the complex processes of transatlantic publishing as well as an expectation of commercial success. At the same time, they evidenced that an American author had the social and trade connections required to arrange a transatlantic edition—connections that, as Bentley's and Murray's US lists suggest, correlate with privileges of race, gender, and social class. Murray's and Bentley's material texts made these various forms of value visible as literary value. For the *Herald*'s correspondent and others, elegant British editions gave much-needed substance to American authorship when it seemed to be emerging nebulously, if at all.

I begin by exploring how Murray and Bentley established practices for publishing authorized editions of US texts with Washington Irving and James Fenimore Cooper, respectively, and established their imprints as the most desirable for US writers, who sought out these publishers for the material forms of their books as well as for what they paid. One such writer was Herman Melville, who, like Longfellow in the previous chapter, engaged imaginatively with the physical forms and authorizing materials of his British editions. Published by both Murray and Bentley, Melville displays a keen understanding of how British editions offered cultural capital to American authorship. In Melville's British editions, the material texts scaffold Melville's reflections on literary authority that take the form of imaginative "flights": Geoffrey Sanborn's term for the "inessential and resource-rich" digressions, speculations, and meditations that are Melville's stylistic signature.[3] Melville uses the paratextual features of Murray's edition of *Narrative of a Four Months' Residence among the Natives of a Valley of the Marquesas Islands* (1846)—published as *Typee* in the US—that presented the text as a genuine travel narrative to question the authority of both his own text as well as the wider genre. In *The Whale; or, Moby-Dick* (1851), Melville's text and Bentley's book collaborate to champion "the centrality of the author to the production and preservation of national identity," as Meredith McGill argues of antebellum pro-copyright texts.[4] Bentley's material presentation of *The Whale* formed part of his advocacy for international copyright, intervening in wider discussions in the United States over the shape of American and transatlantic print culture that are ludically allegorized in Melville's text. Ultimately, approaching Melville's writing through Murray's *Narrative of a Four Months' Residence* and Bentley's *The Whale* shows how Melville's imaginative treatments of authorship and authority reach their fullest expression in dialogue with his elegant and authorizing British editions.

Publishing Authorized Editions

Authorized British reprints of US fiction began to appear in the very last years of the eighteenth century, with London editions of novels by Susanna Rowson and Charles Brockden Brown published in 1799 and 1800 respectively.[5] But the practice of producing authorized British editions from advanced sheets was established by Washington Irving and James Fenimore Cooper from the 1820s onwards. These editions were protected by trade agreements between reputable publishers, who treated a foreign work published from advanced sheets as the property of its publisher alone, a position that was codified into law by *D'Almaine v. Boosey* (1835). Frequently resident in Britain and Europe, Irving and Cooper were well placed to make arrangements with London firms in advance of their works' appearance in the American market. For his London edition of *The Sketch-Book of Geoffrey Crayon, Gent.* (1819), Irving first partnered with publisher John Miller, a specialist in selling American volumes to English readers and advanced sheets of British works to American publishers, but Miller's financial troubles left him unable to issue the second volume.[6] Thanks to an introduction from Walter Scott, Irving made alternative arrangements for publication with John Murray II, the most fashionable publisher in London, "so famous for his elegant publications," as Irving wrote to an American friend.[7] While Miller's edition of the first volume appeared after the New York edition, Murray's second volume preceded its American counterpart, establishing the process by which Murray produced authorized British editions of almost all of Irving's works until 1851.[8]

The success of *The Sketch-Book*—along with Murray's associations with Lord Byron, his connections to the social and political establishment in Britain, and popular accounts of his gentlemanly conduct and liberal payments—led American authors to seek his imprint above all others for the next three decades.[9] The firm's Manuscript Book—which lists manuscripts submitted and whether they were accepted or rejected—includes entries for Nathaniel Parker Willis's *Papers from the Portfolio of an American Editor* (January 1831), Lydia Maria Child's *Philothea* (April 1836), William Hickling Prescott's *History of Ferdinand and Isabella* (December 1836), Bayard Taylor's poem "The Liberated Titan" (March 1846), and Francis Parkman's *The Oregon Trail* (August 1848).[10] All were declined. Murray, however, did publish several books by American travel writers: in 1841, he issued Edward Robinson's *Biblical Researches in Palestine, Mount Sinai and Arabia Petraea*, missionary physician Asahel Grant's *The Nestorians; or The Lost Tribes*, and travel writer John Lloyd Stephens's *Incidents of Travel in Central America, Chiapas and Yucatán*, having published Stephens's earlier work on the Middle East in 1838. Murray II's selection reflects his move toward nonfiction after 1830, a trend that increased after 1843 under his son and successor, John Murray III, who published histories by George Ticknor and John Lothrop Motley, as well as Herman Melville's *Narrative of a Four Months' Residence* and *Omoo* (1847).

Murray also published *The Pioneers*, Cooper's first novel to have an authorized London edition, in 1823.[11] However, Cooper's more enduring association was with Richard Bentley & Sons. In 1831, Bentley, then a printer, entered into partnership with Henry Colburn, who had been Cooper's authorized publisher since *The*

Prairie in 1827. After the swift and angry dissolution of that partnership in 1832, Cooper stayed with Bentley.[12] Bentley published almost all of Cooper's authorized London editions until the latter's death in 1851, as well as authorized editions of two works by Irving. By far the London publisher most invested in authorized editions, Bentley published more than eighty titles by fifty-seven US writers between 1830 and 1860, including fiction by Charles Fenno Hoffman, John Pendleton Kennedy, Robert Montgomery Bird, Theodore S. Fay, and John Treat Irving.

Bentley's willingness to "push" a book attracted American authors seeking reviews from England to increase their reputation. As Hoffman wrote in 1838 when asking a friend to assist him in arranging an English edition of his "tales & legends" (*Wild Scenes in the Forest and Prairie*, published by Bentley in 1838), "Notoriety there, is reputation here and the circulation of a book over the water has a prodigious effect upon the sales on this side."[13] While Murray waited for US authors to come to him, Bentley approached Abraham Hart in Philadelphia, Ticknor, Reed and Fields in Boston, and Baker and Scribner along with George Palmer Putnam in New York in 1849 and 1850, proposing regular exchanges of titles between their firms.[14] These schemes quickly failed. Bentley complained that Hart did not leave him enough time to secure authorized publication, and that Baker and Scribner sent books that were unsuitable for the British market.[15] But his attempts to secure early access to new American titles shows that by the late 1840s, American literature was a central part of Bentley's business as a publisher of fashionable writing.

Through their sustained relations, Irving and Murray and Cooper and Bentley developed a system for arranging authorized and copyright transatlantic publications. They would agree on the price for a new book—Cooper dealt directly with publishers, while Irving used US diplomat Colonel Thomas Aspinwall as an agent—and then the author would send the manuscript or advanced sheets. The British publisher would then print and publish the work between two weeks and one month before their US counterpart. For copyrights in Britain, Murray and Bentley paid Irving and Cooper handsomely. Murray gave Irving 3,000 guineas for *The History of Columbus* in 1827 and £400 for the copyright of *Abbotsford and Newstead Abbey* in 1835, and Bentley gave Cooper £550 for *The Monikins* in 1835 and £500 for *The Pathfinder* in November 1839.[16]

However, as Melissa Homestead shows in her study of Catharine Maria Sedgwick's negotiations of British copyright, and as I further illustrate below, Cooper's and Irving's experiences were not representative.[17] Even those writers who published with Murray and Bentley rarely saw anything like the sums that Cooper and Irving earned. Bentley paid only £10 for advanced sheets of Robert Montgomery Bird's *Nick of the Woods* in August 1837, and sometimes offered American authors half profits on sales without an advance.[18] Henry Wadsworth Longfellow and Lydia Maria Child published with Bentley under this type of agreement, so when *Outre-Mer* (1835) and *Letters from New York* (1843), respectively, made losses for Bentley, they saw no money at all. Still, these authors had the satisfaction of seeing their work circulate without unauthorized revisions and with their names attached, unlike the editions of US texts that George Palmer Putnam described, which had their origins concealed in Britain by "alteration of the title and preface, or suppression of the author's name . . . Some works of fiction, in their new names and English dress, would scarcely be recognized by their own fathers."[19] As Hoffman's focus on "notoriety" demonstrates, US writers privileged intangible rewards like fame over financial remuneration directly from British houses. US writers approached Murray and Bentley because they believed these firms could make their names, but also because they liked the material texts these firms produced.

American publishers generally made their money by publishing a large edition of a book and selling copies to a book-buying public at low prices. Conversely, British publishers traditionally printed relatively small editions of new titles, selling copies at high prices to the wealthy and the circulating libraries; until the 1840s, British cheap literature tended to be reprints of older or public domain texts. Publishers on each side of the Atlantic produced physically different books: "Just as American reprints of British novels usually squashed three volumes into two, British publishers expanded two-volume American novels to fit their customary three-volume format," Joseph Rezek observes.[20] In meeting the demands of their home market, British editions of

US texts symbolized a work's cultural value and its place within a national American tradition. When a *Blackwood's* review from 1820 that was widely reprinted in Britain and the United States asked that Irving follow *The Sketch-book* with "*An American Tale, in three volumes duodecimo*," it demanded that US writers address topics from their own nation but also confirmed that the most truly American works would appear in a distinctly British print format.[21]

Not all American texts distributed in authorized British editions received this re-materialization. Murray offered to publish US historian William Hickling Prescott's *History of the Conquest of Mexico* "at my own cost & risque & when the Copies are sold to remit one half of the profits to the Author," printing his own edition of the work from proof sheets.[22] He explained that he had published Robinson's *Biblical Researches* this way and had already sent that author half profits of £367. However, in writing to the British theologian Thomas Hartwell Horne on the same day, Murray explained that he could not print the work of Horne's American friend Dr. Jarvis (probably Samuel Farmer Jarvis of Middletown, Connecticut, author of several works of spiritual literature), claiming that "these are not times for Literary Speculations." Murray could, however, offer his services as "an agent." If Jarvis sent copies of the American edition at a fixed price, Murray could bind and disseminate them, adding that he "published the works of Mr. [John Lloyd] Stephens (also an American) on these same terms."[23] Murray's letters make it clear that Prescott is receiving the superior offer and that Murray has far more confidence in his book.

The prestige of an edition that was produced as well as distributed in Britain led US authors to make careful stipulations about the forms in which their works would appear. When Prescott wrote to Aspinwall about the publication of *Ferdinand and Isabella* in January 1837, he was more concerned that a "handsome octavo form may be secured," than about whether a publisher bought the copyright or offered him a share of the profits. Later, Prescott asked Bentley to publish a collection of his periodical essays, lest "they will be caught up and printed in a villainous twopenny pamphlet style, that gives me quite a cold sweat to think of."[24] The "twopenny pamphlet" is a metonym for "villainous" unauthorized publication more broadly, with Prescott playfully expressing fears about losing control over his own works. However, that substitution also demonstrates the importance of the British material text as a signifier of the value and the authority of an edition, and the importance of the author in literary cultures on both sides of the Atlantic.

Some writers were willing to fund a materially superior British edition under a valued imprint. Writing on behalf of Irving and poet Fitz-Greene Halleck in June 1835, Aspinwall explained that Halleck wanted to be "published in London in a small but elegant edition" and was prepared to do so "at his own risk," before asking two weeks later, "What would be the cost of publishing Halleck's collection of poems in an elegant form as Mr W. Irving made that a part of his enquiry."[25] Aspinwall's repeated emphasis on elegance shows that it was not merely the fact of publication in Britain, but also the print form that mattered to American writers. In cases where the edition was printed in the United States and sent to Britain, authors might try to disguise that fact. In 1850, Richard Burleigh Kimball sent "500 copies in sheets and 500 copies title page" of his historical romance *Saint Leger; or, The Threads of Life* to Richard Bentley to issue in advance of the American edition. This edition would have been authorized and protected by copyright, but Kimball was still keen to remove any suspicion of its US origins. He explained to Bentley that he had removed his name from the title page as he preferred "to be in cog & the book to be published as an English book," perhaps because he believed British reviewers would be kinder to a historical romance set in England if it were by a native author.[26] Nevertheless, *Saint Leger* looked different from Bentley's other fiction. It was published in one volume, relatively closely printed, with chapters following one another on the same page, and it retailed for 10s 6d: one-third of the price of a three-volume novel. For comparison, Herman Melville's *White-Jacket*, published in the same year, filled two volumes and sold for double the price at 21s. Melville's book had been materially transformed for the British fiction market; Kimball's book had not, for all that he wanted it "published as an English book."

As well as being elegant objects in their own right, a British-printed authorized edition demonstrated that its publisher had deemed the work valuable enough—culturally, economically, or both—to undertake the complex and sometimes expensive arrangements such editions required. Negotiations, material exchanges, and financial transitions across borders made transatlantic publishing a logistically challenging and often precarious process that required cooperation, efficiency, and trust from all parties involved. Bentley in particular was careful to ensure that his partners knew exactly what to do. Outlining the process to American author John Pendleton Kennedy in a letter of May 14, 1834, Bentley explained the necessity of "forwarding to me the sheets in parcels of 1 volumes at a time, and allow me sufficient time to complete the printing of the concluding volume before you publish in America."[27] Writing to the American firm of Baker and Scribner sixteen years later, his instructions were even more precise:

> I ought to be enabled to publish 4 days at least before you publish, to have any chance of establishing a copyright of the original work; the packet now only goes every fortnight; in April however they will go every week. You will be able by this notice I think to regulate the time when you could publish with safety. I should not require for printing more than . . . 8 clear days.[28]

As the letter demonstrates, "regulating" publication dates required knowing the departures of steamers and estimating the length of the transatlantic crossing. A successful authorized edition required the investment of cash, but also of time—time to collect information, time to develop relations within the trade, and time to wait patiently for ships, and then publish at speed.

To help with these tricky processes, publishers and authors employed agents. Authors usually appointed agents via social connections. As I discuss further below, Melville's brother Gansevoort oversaw the publication of *Narrative of a Four Months' Residence* with Murray; after Gansevoort's death, Melville relied on John Brodhead, Secretary of the American Legation in London, as his replacement. Diplomats were often approached to be agents; as well as acting for Irving, Aspinwall arranged publications for Hoffmann and Sedgwick. American publishers were more likely to use British booksellers as agents, especially those who specialized in purchasing American books for British customers and in sending British books to the United States, because they sent and received transatlantic packages at regular intervals. From 1820, Carey & Lea had an agreement with John Miller, who made arrangements for the publication of their American authors in London and supplied the Philadelphia firm with sheets of new British novels, including those by Walter Scott. Miller also published American authors himself, as did Sampson Low, the London agent for the Harper brothers.[29] Agents were supposed to assist with the complex processes of transatlantic publication, but their presence introduced another opportunity for publication to go awry. Both Bentley and Murray struggled with unscrupulous agents whose actions derailed agreements and disrupted the possibility of a copyright edition. Thomas Delf, who was G. P. Putnam & Sons' agent in London in the late 1840s, undermined Putnam's arrangements with Murray to publish the London editions of Irving's complete works by obtaining copies for Murray's rival, reprinter Henry Bohn. Murray's nephew, Robert Cooke, complained, "This is a dig from what we supposed a friendly quarter as we hardly supposed <u>your</u> agent would directly or indirectly <u>sell a copy of Irving's works</u>"; it was a betrayal of trust that made the already challenging process of coordinating US and British editions to secure prior publication impossible.[30]

A British-printed, authorized edition thus signified that British publishers deemed the book worthy of the higher-than-usual risks of—and the extra effort required for—achieving prior publication. But it also signified that an author had either the financial capital to travel to England, the social capital to have friends in England who could negotiate on their behalf, or an American publisher with the trade knowledge and logistical reach to make arrangements for them. Surveying the US authors that John Murray and Richard Bentley & Sons published suggests a correlation between social privilege and authorized British editions. These writers were exclusively white and predominantly male. John Murray published only one book by a woman from advanced US sheets: *Journal of a Residence in America* (1835) by the immensely popular actor Fanny Kemble, who was born in Britain but resided in the United States after she married wealthy Georgia plantation owner Pierce Butler in 1834. Murray II's letters show concerns that the book would be treated as American for the purposes of copyright law, and he probably only published it because of Kemble's fame: he writes of a "great dilemma" over accepting it, and requested that she wait nearly two months after sending sheets before going to print in the United States.[31] John Murray's lack of American women is, however, consistent with a gender imbalance in the firm's list as a whole that stems from Murray II and III's preference for travel and history. Social restrictions on even upper-class white women in the United States limited their ability to undertake the journeys and research necessary for those genres, and, more importantly, the Murrays' sense that narratives of exploration and encounter were the province of white men further limited their dealings with women writers.[32]

The same is not true of Bentley's list. His specialty was fiction for circulating libraries, a genre that women frequently produced.[33] Ten of the fifty-seven US writers Bentley published between 1830 and 1860 were women, including Lydia Maria Child, Catharine Maria Sedgwick, Ann Sophia Stevens, Grace Greenwood, Maria Jane McIntosh, Susan Warner, and Susan Fenimore Cooper. But aside from Susan Fenimore Cooper, whom Bentley published in part due to loyalty to her father, Bentley published only one book by each of these writers. Perhaps Bentley's success with Cooper Sr. left him unconvinced that the feminine and domestic were the proper topics for American literature even as he published this type of fiction by their British counterparts. Moreover, works by popular American women writers posed practical problems: authors like E.D.E.N. Southworth and Ann Sophia Stephens often serialized their novels in magazines, making copyrighting in England very difficult.[34]

Neither Bentley nor Murray published books by African Americans. This absence of Black writers is reflective of the general publication climate in the United States and Britain. Joanna Brooks, a historian of African American literature, estimates that fewer than thirty "individually authored printed and bound books of more than forty-eight pages" by writers of African descent were published in Great Britain and North America in the late eighteenth and early nineteenth centuries; even into the 1840s, Black-authored books without a connection to an established social movement "rarely succeeded."[35] Eric Gardner argues that "the nascent black periodical press . . . was *the* central publication outlet for many black writers" in nineteenth-century America, and the short and serialized contributions sought by these periodicals were not suited to Murray's and Bentley's publishing economies, especially as authorized publication in London was not built into the Black periodicals' publication timelines.[36] When texts by Black writers were published in Britain, these were almost all slave narratives and were usually circulated by publishers who specialized in reform writings, provincial presses, or charities. The lack of Black authors in Murray's and Bentley's lists certainly reflects the reluctance of large US literary and commercial publishers to publish on the slavery question and the racial gatekeeping in the literary trade on both sides of the Atlantic. But, as I discuss further in chapter 6, smaller publishers who held radical and reforming political views and were embedded in the abolitionist movement offered benefits to Black abolitionists, including access to supportive publics and imprints that may have acted as a guarantor of the narrative's veracity.

Detailing the race and gender of US writers who published with Murray and Bentley does not produce surprising results, but it demonstrates that Murray's and Bentley's expensive books were material manifestations of their authors' social position and cultural power, as well as of the time and money that British publishers invested. Although commentators like the *Herald*'s correspondent argued that elegant British editions recognized the literary worth of American writing, the writers listed invariably displayed extra-textual qualities that Americans had already began to associate with national authorship: they were white, male, and had connections to urban publishing centers in the Northeast. The *Herald*'s list of writers who have been "sought after by English publishers" is as pale, and even more male, than the lists of Murray and Bentley: "Bancroft, Prescott, Washington Irving, Cooper, Emerson, Longfellow, Abbot, Barnes, Dana."[37] Making the British material text a signifier of a genuinely American book seems contradictory, but it ensured that literary prestige would reflect wider social hierarchies of race, gender, and class.

Herman Melville was, then, well placed to follow in Irving's and Cooper's footsteps and publish London editions of his books with both John Murray and Richard Bentley. By the time that Gansevoort Melville took the manuscript of *Typee* with him to London in 1845, the Melville family was no longer wealthy, having found themselves heavily in debt after the collapse of Herman's father's business and his subsequent death in 1832. But they were still well connected. Gansevoort crossed the Atlantic to take up a post as Secretary to the US Legation, a reward for aiding James Polk's successful presidential campaign. This posting gave him the social standing to act as an agent for his younger brother. As a writer of travel and adventure narratives, Melville wrote in genres that echoed successful publications by Irving and Cooper, even if neither of those authors had ventured anywhere as exotic as the Marquesas Islands in life or art. But if Melville's authorized editions followed a beaten track, then the dialogues between his narratives and their British material texts are striking for their complex and playful interrogations of authority through the processes and products of publication in Britain. As well as materially manifesting the value of his authorship and US authorship more widely, Murray's and Bentley's editions facilitated and furthered Melville's imaginative speculations on authorship, authority, and literary value in *Narrative of a Four Months' Residence among the Natives of a Valley of the Marquesas Islands* and *The Whale; or, Moby-Dick*.

Materializing Authority: John Murray, Travel Writing, and Melville's *Four Months' Residence* (1847)

In May 1845, Melville brought the Harper brothers a manuscript that purported to detail four months he spent living among the Indigenous peoples of the Marquesas Islands. The Harpers promptly rejected the book because, as their reader Frederick Saunders later reported, "It was impossible that it could be true and therefore was without real value."[38] Before Melville could take the manuscript to another New York house, journalist and family friend John Nichols read it. He advised Melville to send it to London with his brother and "have it issued there simultaneously with its publication in New York. I felt sure that the reviewers of the English press would make its American success, and I was not at all sure that the process could be reversed."[39] Gansevoort took a sample of the book, then called *Typee*, to John Murray III sometime between his arrival in London in late August and October 17, 1845, when Murray asked to see the rest of the manuscript. On December 3, Murray wrote to Gansevoort, accepting the work for publication in his Home and Colonial Library series and offering Melville £100 for the copyright—a very successful outcome for a novice US writer. Murray, however, shared the Harpers' concerns that the book might be fiction and, upon accepting the manuscript, he began editing the text and packaging it in a material form intended to dispel any doubts about its veracity. Melville, however, engaged with Murray's authorized and authorizing material text to disrupt the conventions and the epistemologies behind travel writing's claims to truth. Murray's authorizing edition did not simply authenticate Melville's tale and materialize its literary value; it also gave Melville a tool with which to deconstruct a genre's formation of authority.

As Sanborn argues, *Typee*'s "eroticization of the already sensitive border between the actual and the imaginary" depends on its presentation as a travel narrative: "If *Typee* had been marketed as a novel, a work of imaginative fiction with an imaginary protagonist, [this] frisson would have entirely disappeared."[40] Yet scholars have not approached *Typee*'s ambivalent relationship to travel writing through the text's materialization within a transatlantic print economy.[41] Publication by the house of Murray was vitally important to the presentation of Melville's book as a genuine account of the Pacific. Therefore, to fully understand the ways that Melville interrogates the authority of travel writing and the travel writer, we must approach this text not only as *Typee* but also as *A Narrative of Four Months' Residence*.

In 1813, John Murray II was appointed official bookseller to the Admiralty and the Board of Longitude, an arrangement that gave him access to writings produced by government expeditions and imperial civil servants. The Murray imprint quickly became associated with new accounts of remote places by authors whose authority and credibility came from their associations with the British establishment—authority and credibility that was transferred to Murray's publications and that Murray could pass to authors who lacked official credentials of their own. Examining the firm's travel writing, Innes Keighren, Charles Withers, and

Bill Bell argue that travel books are "contested objects of reputational and epistemic construction": travel books build credulity for the traveler as an authority and validate the means by which he (for Murray, it was usually a "he") produces knowledge. This production of authority involved rhetorical and material strategies. "Print itself could act as a guarantor of authority," Keighren, Withers, and Bell observe, "not least so when it issued from the house of Murray."[42] By transforming a manuscript into a printed book, a publisher like Murray claimed that its contents merited permanent preservation because they were novel, thorough, and, above all, true. To bolster these assertions, Murray added paratexts, including long, descriptive titles that laid out the exact terrain over which the author claimed expertise, and maps that lent a text cartography's claims to empirical truth.[43]

Murray began the material and textual process of shaping Melville's manuscript into a travel narrative immediately upon accepting it. He informed Gansevoort that the book would require "a few slight omissions—which on the score of taste I have no hesitation in saying will be for the benefit of both Author and book," and he appointed a reader, Henry Milton, to make revisions.[44] Murray's most obvious change was the title. Melville wanted *Typee*, under which the American edition appeared, but Murray preferred the more solid, if less exotic, *Narrative of a Four Months' Residence among the Natives of a Valley of the Marquesas Islands*. The London edition thus substituted a factual statement of time and place for an unfamiliar word that, over the course of the text, becomes an unstable signifier. The narrator and his friend Toby prove themselves unable to distinguish between the supposedly ferocious Typee and the supposedly benevolent Happar, even as they maintain the importance of that distinction, and the question of whether or not "Typee" really "signifies a lover of human flesh" is never completely solved.[45] Murray's change of title attempts to forestall similar misreadings, in particular the misreading of a travel narrative as fiction.

Other changes to Melville's manuscript are harder to locate and to attribute. John Bryant has given extensive attention to revisions in the small portion of the *Typee* manuscript that survives, tracing Melville's shifting intentions and evolving thought, but it remains impossible to say with certainty whether many of the differences between those leaves and the published text of *Four Month's Residence* should be attributed to Melville, to Milton, or to Murray.[46] However, from Gansevoort's letter to Murray of December 6 (three days after Murray accepted the manuscript), we know that Melville sent three new chapters (20, 21 and 27) and some other extra text that would "go far to give a more life-like air to the whole, an[d] parry the incredulity of those who may be disposed to regard the work as an ingenious fiction."[47] Hershel Parker argues that the dates of Gansevoort's letters and of transatlantic crossings make it impossible for Melville to have revised the manuscript in response to doubts that Murray expressed in a letter to Gansevoort of October 17. He proposes that Melville's "own desire to eke out his brief impressions from his four weeks among the Typeeans" inspired the additions.[48] However, Melville could have revised the book in response to the idea of a Murray edition before Murray gave any direct assessment of his work. Gansevoort would very likely have discussed with his brother where he might seek to place *Typee* before he left for London.[49] If Melville knew that Murray was a good fit for an exotic travel narrative like *Typee*, he would have also known that Murray would raise the same questions as the Harpers about its authenticity. In a letter to his mother, Maria, of September 16, Gansevoort explains that he has written to Herman with "information" about *Typee*, providing an opportunity for Melville to learn about the kind of changes that Murray might later demand.[50]

In this timeline, Melville's changes can be understood as a variant form of the "transatlantic revision" identified and theorized by Rezek. Rezek defines "transatlantic revision" as changes an American author made to tailor their works for the London market. Such revision was rare—so rare, in fact, that Irving and Cooper provide the only examples in American texts published in London before 1832. However, by expanding transatlantic revision to include changes to an American text that emerge in the process of its transatlantic production, we can include Melville's changes to *Typee*. Without access to *Typee*'s variant texts, it is impossible to trace individually small changes that become meaningful en masse, as Rezek does when demonstrating how Irving and Cooper reframed the literary as a sphere of Anglo-American communion.[51] Melville's transatlantic revisions are messier in terms of evidence and in terms of the results they produce. Nevertheless, they show Melville using Murray's authorization as an opportunity to demonstrate his own authority and interrogate how authority might be established and unraveled, expanding Rezek's definition of transatlantic revision and his sense of the purposes to which authors could employ it.

Rather than completely acquiescing to Murray's expectations, Melville used the revisions he made in autumn 1845 to introduce uncertainty into the sources and nature of authority in travel writing. The sections that Melville added introduce factual detail that satisfied Murray's idea of what a travel book should contain and that might offset a reader's incredulity: precise information about the customs, beliefs, daily life, and dwellings of the Typee, and discussions of the natural history of the Marquesas Islands. But these sections also make space for set pieces in which Melville questions whether such empirical observations produce authoritative accounts, as we see in chapter 21's account of the island's "vast terraces of stone." The narrator's Indigenous guide, Kory-Kory—"my authority in all matters of scientific research"—explains that the structures are "coeval with the creation of the world; that the great gods themselves were the builders; and that they would endure until time shall be no more." The narrator immediately dismisses this local knowledge: Kory-Kory's "attributing the work to a divine origin, at once convinced me that neither he nor the rest of his countrymen knew anything about them." Yet the narrator cannot summon a better evidenced explanation. While proclaiming that the terraces are "doubtless the work of an extinct and forgotten race," he also admits that they have "no inscriptions, no sculpture, no clue by which to conjecture its history; nothing but the dumb stones." The narrator claims an authority to interpret the scene, but admits his interpretations have no basis in empirical observation. More particularly, by lacking "inscription," the stones resist one of nineteenth-century travel writing's basic assumptions: that lands, peoples, and experiences can be fully articulated in and by printed texts.[52]

Existing outside the written record, the terraces prompt the narrator to turn to natural history and to speculate on the geographical formation of the island:

> The origin of the island of Nukuheva cannot be imputed to the coral insect; for indefatigable as that wonderful creature is, it would hardly be muscular enough to pile rocks one upon the other more than three thousand feet above the level of the sea. That the land may have been thrown up by a submarine volcano is as possible as anything else. No one can make an affidavit to the contrary.[53]

The "coral insect" is a reference to Charles Darwin's theory, proposed in 1836, that coral islands formed when the Pacific seabed subsided, submerging volcanoes that had once been above sea level and thus encouraging coral growth.[54] Darwin's theory emerged from his and others' observations of coral islands, but, because island formation took place over thousands of years, the theory could not be tested through experimentation. Michelle Elleray, in her study of coral insect metaphors in Victorian culture, argues that the coral reef problem was both part of the mid-Victorian zeitgeist and "the testing ground for tensions between theoretically- and empirically-based modes of scientific inquiry, as science fashioned its disciplinary bases."[55] It was also a site of conflict between science and religion, as the ongoing formation of coral islands contradicted the Biblical account of a Creation complete in seven days.

Melville, therefore, takes up a subject that pitted forms of knowledge against one another; the narrator of *Typee* is not simply debating how Nukuhiva was formed, but which methods and disciplines are legitimate routes to truth. The "coral insect" passage and the new segment thus introduce factual discourse of natural history that Murray expected in travel books and reinforce the epistemological uncertainty at *Typee*'s core. These sections seek to bolster the book's credibility as travel writing while also dismantling the epistemic systems on which travel writing relied. It is tempting to read such deliberate challenges to the forms of knowledge in which Murray traded as evidence of Melville's hostility toward both Murray in particular and the book trade in general, especially considering the critical commonplaces of Melville's distaste for the publishing trade and his later disavowal of *Typee* and *Omoo*.[56] However, Melville is writing as much with Murray and his material texts as he is against them: Murray places Melville and his book in a position of authority from which Melville's narrator can deconstruct authority itself.

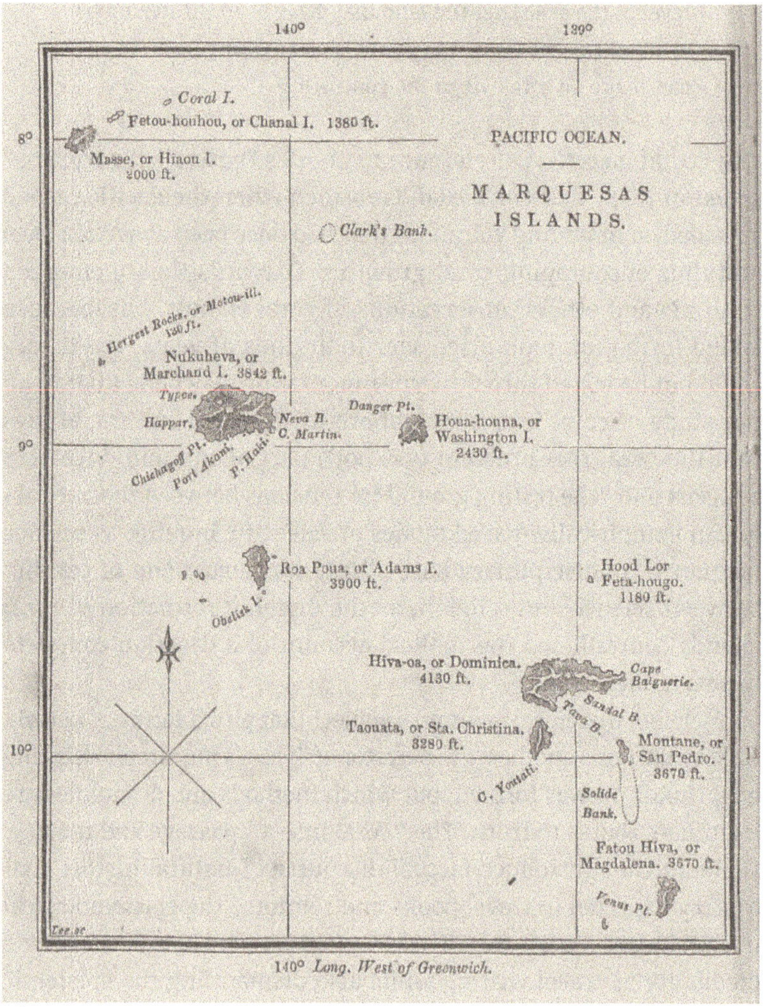

Figure 5. Map from Herman Melville, *Narrative of a Four Months' Residence among the Natives of a Valley of the Marquesas Islands; or, A Peep at Polynesian Life* (London: John Murray, 1846) [xviii]. Wellcome Collection, London. Public Domain Mark.

Melville's deconstruction of authority employs Murray's material additions to his book as well as the textual changes that Murray demanded. Murray's edition of *Narrative of a Four Month's Residence* included a map of the Marquesas on the verso facing the beginning of the book's first chapter. Sanford Marovitz, the only scholar to pay sustained attention to the provenance of the map, suggests that Melville copied a detail from a map that he owned.[57] But Marovitz does not consider Murray's accounts for *Typee*. These accounts list a 10 shilling payment for "Drawing plan p Walker:" likely J & C Walker, the father-son mapmakers whom Murray employed to produce the maps for the firm's popular guidebooks, and who drew the map that Marovitz suggests is the source for the map in *Typee*.[58] While "drawing" could mean drawing the map from scratch or making a copy of a map that Melville supplied, this entry differs from Murray's accounts for *Omoo* (1847), for which Melville definitely drew the map. There, Murray lists a payment to "L. C. Martin," likely the engraver Leopold Martin, for £2 5s for "Map-Tahiti," and to the printers Spottiswoode and Shaw for "Printing Round Robin" for £1 12s 6d (an illustration that Melville also drew), but nothing for "drawing." Publishers' account books do not use terms consistently, but the fact that *Omoo*'s entry uses different terms and the difference in price suggests that Murray commissioned Walker for a different kind of work, perhaps supplying an illustration from one of their maps. As Melville had little money and little experience with the trade, it seems likely that Murray commissioned the map to bolster the text's authenticity.

Melville's narrator, however, is skeptical about the authority of maps. He describes a ship called the *Perseverance* that was thought lost, having been last reported as wandering around those "unstable islands in the far Pacific, whose eccentric wanderings are carefully noted in each new edition of the South-Sea charts." Satirically juxtaposing the mapmakers "careful" drawing with their inability to pin down the location of the islands, Melville reminds readers that precision is not the same as accuracy, and that a map is an interpretation that can change over time. No map should, therefore, be read as absolutely authoritative. The *Perseverance*, furthermore, offers a different kind of travel experience than those in which Murray traded. Never returning home, the ship cannot publish an authoritative account of itself and its journey. Instead, it is known by "shadowy report" while it traverses obviously fictitious ground "somewhere off Buggerry Island, or the Devil's-Tail Peak."[59] Crossing into fictional territory, the *Perseverance* transgresses the generic boundaries that Murray's map sought to impose on Melville's text.[60] By reinforcing the text's location in the real world, Murray's map pulls into relief the genre-blurring voyages of the *Perseverance* and Melville's commentary on the shortcomings of maps, calling attention to moments where Melville's narrative steps beyond that map's geographic and epistemic bounds.

As well as enabling Melville's play with authority, Murray's authorizing edition shepherded Melville's book into a national American publication. With Washington Irving's encouragement, Gansevoort took a copy of Murray's early proof sheets to the London branch house of Wiley and Putnam, where George Palmer Putnam received them enthusiastically. Putnam sent copies of those sheets to the firm's New York headquarters, where they were set in type and published in their Library of American Books. That edition thus incorporated Melville's additional Murray-oriented material, Henry Milton's revisions, and Murray's map, meaning that the textual and material changes that made the manuscript into an authorized edition and an authentic travel narrative were duplicated in the American book. However, it also reproduced, even if inadvertently, Melville's interrogation of travel writing's authorities. Wiley and Putnam's American edition reprinted Murray's map, but the edition's less-than-precise printing created dots that appear to be islands, the edition thus materializing the "eccentric wanderings" that Melville had observed in maps of the Pacific. This was not the only way that Wiley and Putnam located *Typee* geographically. By publishing Melville in the Library of American Books, an open attempt to encourage literary nationalism that was advertised as a "valuable and popular series of the writings of American authors," Wiley and Putnam suggest that this narrative of the Pacific is also a quintessentially American book.[61] What their publication disguises, however, is that the "value" of Melville's book was established through its publication in London.

The forms of authorization offered by Murray and his Home and Colonial Library were well suited to Melville's interrogations of travel writing's authorities and epistemologies. However, they were less suited for supporting Melville's authorship once he turned away from (ostensible) nonfiction and toward romance. As Melville explained to Murray, his new work, *Mardi*, required a different form of publication than had his first two books, and so he made a series of blunt demands, beginning with 200 guineas and half profits after expenses, and ending with:

> Your edition is to be an exact transcript of the copy forwarded you . . . I would here beg to remind you of your own suggestion:—that it would be advisable to publish the book in handsome style, & independently of any series.—Unless you should deem it *very* desirable do not put me down on the title page as "the author of Typee & Omoo". I wish to separate "*Mardi*" as much as possible from those books.[62]

For *Mardi*, Melville wanted a different kind of authority than Murray's maps and Home and Colonial Library: the authority that came from a "handsome style." Did Melville really think that Murray—who had never paid more than £150 outright for one of Melville's books, who revised all of Melville's texts, who disliked fiction, and who had until now published Melville in a cheap series—would agree? Perhaps Melville thought he was now a successful author who could dictate terms. Alternatively, Melville may have anticipated that Murray would refuse these terms and believed that breaking with Murray was no bad thing, especially as Murray's interest in American letters was waning. As Melville sought to reposition himself in the American literary field, he needed a publisher who could market him as a romancer while defending American authors' rights to and profits from their works.

Luckily, there was such a publisher to whom Melville could turn if—or perhaps, when—Murray refused *Mardi*. Richard Bentley had written to Melville, probably in May 1847, suggesting that he would offer good terms if Melville had a new book to sell. Melville responded that he was not, at present, able to entertain any offer from Bentley—"a partial understanding with another publisher forbidding"—but he kept Bentley in mind and turned to him after Murray rejected *Mardi*.[63] Bentley offered everything that Melville had demanded from Murray: light editing, 200 guineas, and "handsome publication." But while Bentley's three-volume edition of *Mardi* celebrated Melville as a writer of fiction, it was Bentley's edition of *The Whale* in 1851 that combined the authorization of Melville as an imaginative genius with the promotion of American authorship. As an intervention in a transatlantic debate about the impact of international copyright on American letters, *The Whale* championed a model of American national literary culture with native authorship at its core.

"For Unless You Own the Whale": Championing Copyright in Richard Bentley's *The Whale*

Melville's trade relations with Bentley coincided with a turbulent time for London publishers that dealt in authorized editions of American books. By the late 1840s, the trade convention that publishing an American book from advanced sheets gave the publisher of that book exclusive rights was being attacked by a new generation of reprint publishers, including George Routledge and Henry Bohn, who produced popular and cheap series targeted at the emerging market of railway readers. Encouraged by *Boosey v. Purday* (1849), in which the courts decided that prior publication did not secure foreign authors copyright, Routledge and Bohn reprinted works by Irving and Melville to which Bentley and Murray claimed copyright. Bentley was incensed at the prospect of losing profits on works he had paid for and this flouting of the trade's gentlemanly standards. Never one to miss an opportunity for litigation, Bentley issued proceedings against Bohn and Routledge and persuaded Murray to do the same. The reprinters held out, forcing Bentley and Murray to spend money on obtaining evidence that their editions had anticipated the American publications. This uncertainty over the copyright law made British publishers anxious about investing in authorized editions of American texts and thus affected the ability of US authors to obtain both the handsome material texts that connoted their works' literary value and the desired "handsome sums from London publishers," as the pro-copyright *Literary World* observed. The *World* hoped that now this "plank" holding up American authorship had "gone by the board," more US authors would join the agitation for a comprehensive international copyright law at home.[64]

The unsettled state of copyright law had a material impact on Melville, who, while never receiving the sums that Irving and Cooper did, relied on payments from London for a substantial part of his literary income. When Melville traveled to London in November 1849, planning to sell *White-Jacket*, publisher after publisher declined the book on the grounds that American books were too risky. Although Bentley did eventually offer £200 for the book, the story of Melville's struggle made it into the press through articles in the London *Times* that were reprinted in the *Literary World* in February and March 1850.[65] In the first article, an anonymous "importer of foreign books" described how "the author of *Typee*, &c . . . wearily hawked his book from Piccadilly to Whitechapel . . . and could find no one rash enough to buy his 'protected right.'"[66] In the second article, Bentley responded that far from Melville hawking the book: "The work was in the first instance offered to me by the author himself, and I have become the purchaser of what I firmly believe to be the copyright, for a considerable sum: quite sufficient to make me in earnest to defend that right." To this exchange, the *World* added a further letter from "K," who was almost certainly Richard Burleigh Kimball. Kimball was the author of *Saint Leger*, a novel that Bentley had published, and the two men continued to correspond to Bentley's death. Kimball was friends with the Duyckinck brothers, editors of the *Literary World*. While agreeing that "Mr Melville had not the slightest difficulty in making an arrangement for the publication of *White Jacket* with Mr. Bentley," "K" also adds that "Mr Bentley [is] not the publisher to allow so capital a book to escape him . . . his liberality to authors is proverbial . . . we can say with truth that no English publisher is so well and so favorably known here." The *World* further noted that "Mr Bentley . . . is still disposed to try the issue whether a book purchased from a foreign author and first published in England is not protected by the law."[67] Here Melville is representative of US authors' struggles at home and in the transatlantic marketplace, and Bentley is a guardian of US authors' rights, and, more importantly, of American authorship and American literature.

The publicity around *White-Jacket* and debates over copyright contextualize Melville and Bentley's negotiations for *The Whale*. Melville offered *The Whale* to Bentley in June 1850, a year before it was completed. In a letter that attempted to reassure Bentley about the copyright situation, he observed that Bentley's publication of *White-Jacket* had not "been interfeared with" and assured Bentley that he "shall, of course, put you in early & certain possession of the proof sheets, as in previous cases."[68] When Melville proposed the book again, probably in June 1851, Bentley replied, offering "£150 on account of half profits . . . as we shall all be in the same boat, this mode of publication is the most suitable to meet all contingencies of the case."[69] Bentley's reference to "contingencies" suggests that Melville raised the issue of copyright again, perhaps hoping that Bentley would be in a more optimistic mood than the previous year. Indeed, by the time he published *The Whale* that autumn, Bentley did have more reason to be confident that its copyright could be secured. Overruling *Boosey v. Purday*, the Court of Exchequer upheld foreign authors' rights in *Boosey v. Jeffreys* (1851). Sensing the tide turning against them, Routledge and Bohn promptly settled out of court with Bentley and Murray in the latters' favor.[70] This change in the law and in Bentley's mood between spring and autumn 1851 illuminates the dialogues about international copyright that take place between *The Whale*'s literary and material texts.

Both Melville's text and Bentley's book intervened in debates taking place in the United States and Britain, debates that encompassed not only the rights of authors but also the place of authorship within a emergent national print culture in the United States. As Adam Gordon has recently argued, the antebellum United States saw the expansion of a self-reflexive literary criticism that was less concerned with blunt debates over literary nationalism than with the ways in which "specific print media . . . gave material shape to abstract political contests."[71] Such a criticism was aware of the role played by British authorized editions in the struggle to promote American authorship within the United States. Pro-international copyright campaigners in the United States referred to Bentley's efforts to promote and protect the works of American authors in Britain in their arguments about the damage that foreign reprints inflicted on American literary culture. In March 1850 Lewis Gaylord Clark, the fiercely pro-copyright editor of the *Knickerbocker Magazine*, observed that "although many of our own [publishing] establishments may rival the English ones in the number of their publications, yet as we Americans have the opportunity of taking up the best English works for the mere price of the copy to print from, it follows that in amount of capital invested, the English publishers are largely in advance of our own." Clark gave Bentley as an example of such investment, beginning with his payment of "one thousand guineas" to Irving for *The Alhambra*, and ending with the observation that "the liberality of Mr Bentley toward American authors is well known, and he is now identified with the literature of this country."[72] Until American publishers paid for foreign works as Bentley did, Clark implies, they and American literary culture would always be behind London. In July 1851, Clark further congratulated Bentley on his legal triumph over Bohn and Routledge, observing that he "'held on' like a brave 'BULL'-dog as he is," and affirmed Bentley's demand for Congress to pass an international copyright law: "Such an act is demanded at our hands as a matter of justice and right, and therefore of national good faith and honor."[73] As Michael Everton argues, debates over international copyright framed it as an "ethical as well as an economic question," with the pro-copyright lobby employing a "moral vernacular" in their submissions, which we see in Clark's discussion of "good faith and honor."[74] Clark thus marshalled Bentley's payments to, support for, and presentation of American authors to evidence a moral superiority in the British trade, but also a moral lacunae in the publishing trade at home.

Melville takes up similar questions of where US authorship and authors' rights might be located, risked, and articulated in *The Whale*, although Melville is far more ludic than Clark and far less sycophantic to his British publisher. Writing *The Whale* in copyright limbo, Melville playfully links the London print market as a site for generating financial and cultural value for US authorship with his creative project by refracting copyright debates through his novel's central symbol and object: the whale. In one of the texts' imaginatively rich digressions, chapter 3 of the third volume of *The Whale*, "Fast-Fish and Loose-Fish," Ishmael addresses the legal question of who owns harpooned and beached whales, explaining that the entire question can be summarized in two laws:

> I. A Fast-Fish belongs to the party fast to it.
> II. A Loose-Fish is fair game for anybody who can soonest catch it.

Ishmael quickly admits that the "brevity" of this code disguises the "vast volume of commentaries" needed to interpret it. Deciding which fish are "fast" and which are "loose" is far from simple. These statements are an accurate summary of English whaling law, but they are also a version of the English Courts' position on foreigners' copyright in *D'Almaine v. Boosey* and later in *Boosey v. Jeffreys*. American books that entered the British marketplace attached to a British publisher—"connected with an occupied ship" or bearing a "recognized symbol of possession," as Melville describes the Fast-Fish—belonged to that publisher. Those that floated over from America after being published were, like Loose-Fish, "fair game" for any publisher to issue. And, as with the laws of whaling, this apparently simple distinction was, throughout 1850 and 1851, the subject of extensive legal argument.[75]

Melville develops this account of copyright law into a critique on its shortcomings through Ishmael's ironic examples of Loose-Fish, which are tied up with the violence of conquest and colonialism: "What was America in 1492 but a Loose-Fish, in which Columbus struck the Spanish standard by way of waifing it for his royal master and mistress? . . . What India to England? What at last will Mexico be to the United States? All Loose-Fish."[76] America and India seemed "Loose-Fish" to white colonialists who disregarded the Indigenous populations; the United States could claim that Mexico's northern regions, home to fewer Europeans, were "Loose," but the Mexicans violently disagreed. Ishmael's question "What all men's minds and opinions but Loose-Fish?" thus becomes an ironic parody of anti-copyrighters' arguments for the democratic necessity of a free commerce in texts, an echo of Melville's earlier critique of the anti-copyright faction in his review "Hawthorne and His Mosses."[77] There, Ida Rothschild argues, Melville adopts the persona of the "Virginian" to satirize the arguments against international copyright that his authorial construct parrots: the Virginian declares the literary independence of the United States, but Melville expresses a "desire for greater cultural communcation and sharing between England and America" from which American literature would arise.[78] Similarly, Ishmael's ironic listing suggests that the law, often and unfairly, deems things to be Loose that are actually Fast, allowing them to be appropriated by those who have no real claim. Melville suggests that protection through prior publication is far from satisfactory.

The subsequent chapter, "Heads or Tails," locates such unfair appropriations on English shores, as Ishmael dives into another quirk of English whaling law. Of "all whales captured by anybody on the coast of that land, the King, as Honorary Grand Harpooneer, must have the head, and the Queen be respectfully presented with the tail." However, "all royal emoluments incident to the Cinque Port territories" pass to the Lord Warden of the Cinque Ports. Ishmael describes a case in which "honest mariners of Dover, or Sandwich" worked hard to bring in a whale, only to see it, and the "150*l*." they would have made from the "precious oil and bone," slip from their fingers as the Warden's factotum—"a very learned and most Christian and charitable gentleman, with a copy of Blackstone under his arm"—claims his master's prize. Melville thus envisions a scenario in which those who bring a whale to the English shore at "great trouble and peril, and some expense" are cheated out of £150 by a peculiarity of law.[79] Like the mariners, Melville had experience of his property being seized by customs authorities: the sheets of his second book, *Omoo*, were held on suspicion that they were a piracy of an British book. Now, having labored to land his books in Britain, Melville faced his income being eaten away by disputes over copyright law. Indeed, the mariners are cheated of the very sum that Bentley offered for *The Whale*, £150, a sum that is not mentioned in other accounts of the case, including the *Literary World* article from June 1850 that James Barbour argues was Melville's source for the chapter.[80] Within a broader attack on the legal system favoring the wealthy and powerful, "Heads or Tails" allegorizes the precarious position in which British copyright law placed Melville and American authors.

These two chapters of *The Whale* critique the apparent capriciousness of British legal rulings on foreigners' rights and illustrate the negative effects of this instability on US authors. However, Melville's satire is more playful than bitter. Even as he allegorizes his genuine disappointment in the London market, the chapters are full of ribald humor: observations about a wife being compared to a loose-fish in a "crim. con" (divorce) case, and the whale's tail going to the Queen. Melville was also poking fun at the moralizing tone in which copyright reform was discussed by men like Clark and even by Bentley, who claimed, rather sententiously to George Palmer Putnam, that Bohn, "being a man of education," should "know better than to pass a course so contrary to fair dealing."[81] Everton argues that, to many, the pro-copyright campaigners "came off as overzealous protectionists, or, more to the point, as selfish pedagogues," arguing a moral case for a reform that would, according to opponents of reform, make books more expensive and put money in these authors' pockets.[82] Having already been mocked in the press for hawking his books in England, Melville must have been wary of appearing so blindly sententious; real dispossessed mariners rarely got dinners with John Murray and friends. Moreover, this episode embeds the production processes of transatlantic authorized editions—their legal frameworks, complex logistics and financial risks—into the imaginative project of the text. The problem of copyright in a transatlantic marketplace becomes entangled with Melville's attempt to make poetry from blubber. While this episode of *The Whale* does, on balance, come down on the side of international copyright reform, that it remains a question of balance shows that Melville is more interested in how transatlantic print circulation creates conditions for imaginative play than with castigating the uncertainty over copyright, however poorly it affected him personally.

This fusion of creativity and copyright was also visible in the material text of *The Whale*. Through his lavish and beautiful presentation of Melville's text, Bentley asserted US authors' rights to authorized and copyright editions. Bentley chose *The Whale* to make such a statement partly due to coincidences of timing. *The Whale* was the first American novel that Bentley published after *Boosey v. Jeffreys* and the settling of his suit against Bohn and Routledge. *The Whale* further presented an opportunity for Bentley to advertise these legal victories because Melville was well known in Britain after the success of *Typee* (even if his most recent books had not sold well) and because his struggles under copyright uncertainty had been publicly documented. However, the claim that Bentley made through *The Whale* went beyond the copyright of Melville's book alone. He used *The Whale* to proclaim the soundness of his American copyrights in general, and, by extension, the propriety and necessity of international copyright itself. In doing so, he followed a tradition of copyright campaigners on both sides of the Atlantic employing the material text within their arguments. On January 26, 1850, the London *Athenaeum* published an article speculating on the impact of the withdrawing of foreign authors' rights on the materiality of texts, which was then reprinted by the *Literary World* in New York on March 9, 1850. The article observed that "a publisher who has a right of property in the book which he sells consults his own interests as well as the tastes of a high class of readers by issuing it in the form most appropriate to the subject of which it treats; but where there is no security against cheap reprints, who will have the hardihood to spend money in ornament?"[83] Removing copyright protection for foreign authors, the correspondent argued, would put an end to the elegant British editions that manifested the value of American texts; instead, readers would be left with the cheap paperbacks of Bohn and Routledge.

Bentley's American titles were always handsomely published, but *The Whale* was decorative on another scale entirely. Bound by the large and successful London binders Remnant and Edmonds, each of its three volumes featured blue cloth on the face and white on the spine. Along with the title, volume number, the names of author and publisher, and the place of publication, the spines of each volume were decorated in gold with an image of a right whale swimming downward—the wrong species of whale, as at least one reviewer noted. Melville scholars have long struggled to understand why Bentley commissioned such an expensive binding, especially considering that he had lost money on *Mardi*, *Redburn*, and *White-Jacket*. While it is possible that Bentley intended the binding to encourage sales of a book whose mixed genre and encyclopedic style did not fit expectations of a three-volume novel, this would have been an expensive way to go about it.[84] But reading the material text of *The Whale* as advertising its copyright status and the validity of foreign authors' rights explains Bentley's decision; "spending money in ornament"—the phrase used in the *Athenaeum*—enabled Bentley to advertise his "right of property" in *The Whale*.

Moreover, by embossing a gold whale on the spine Bentley layered the material text and the whale in a way that echoed both Ishmael's "bibliographical system" for the classification of whales and Melville's layering of whaling and copyright law.[85] Bentley's elaborate design ensured that *The Whale* bore a "recognized symbol of possession," claiming the text as a "fast-fish." For Bentley to have read "Heads or Tails" as copyright allegory would have required close and imaginative engagement with Melville's text, but Bentley's letters to Melville strongly suggest that he read and enjoyed the latter's writing.[86] To translate this veiled discussion of copyright onto the book's binding was, certainly, a substantial step, and one that did not make particularly good business sense. But, for Bentley, copyright was always an issue of principle more than of profit.

In claiming US authors' rights to copyright in Britain, Bentley's material text for *The Whale* also intervened in debates over whether the United States should allow foreigners to copyright their works, and, by extension, over the place of authorship in US literary culture. As Meredith McGill demonstrates in her study of US cultures of reprinting, debates over international copyright in the United States evoked the wider question of whether a national American literary culture would emerge from authorship or print circulation. British and American pro-copyright petitions to the US government construct a vision of national print culture that is centered on US authorship: if an international copyright law protected US authors by ending the unauthorized reprinting of British books, American literature could flourish. In contrast, anti-copyright petitions claimed that the United States could prove its cultural independence by constructing a radically different kind of marketplace based in reprinting and mass circulation, and that "the author was largely irrelevant to republican publishing." In such anti-copyright petitions, McGill observes, "the resetting of type becomes a powerful point of re-origination, the most important stage in the adaptation of the foreign text for American uses."[87] The physical transformation of a British three-decker into a closely printed, one volume American reprint was a sign that America was developing its own distinct literary culture through reprinting. Conversely, by materializing *The Whale* as an expensive and beautiful print object, Bentley validated a copyright system in which foreign authors had rights, and a literary culture that centered on authorship. More than simply a defense of his own property, Bentley's authorized edition of Melville's book championed a particular vision of American print culture at a time when the shape of that culture was far from settled—and following the attention given to his dealings with Melville and copyright battles in US periodicals, he may well have expected it to be received as such.

This, however, was not to be. Although far from an absolute critical failure, *Moby-Dick* was not widely received as an American classic within the United States until the early twentieth century.[88] Yet Bentley's lack of success at consecrating Melville as a national author in his own lifetime was not because Bentley backed the wrong horse. *The Whale*'s reception was mixed but some early reviews were very positive, including one in *John Bull* that described the book as "far beyond the level of an ordinary work of fiction" and "a whole philosophy of life."[89] Instead, Bentley and Melville fell foul of the uncertainties of transatlantic circulation, which could defeat even two skilled navigators of the trade. The only two British reviews reprinted in the United States before the publication of *Moby-Dick* were two of the most damning, from the *Athenaeum* and the *Spectator*. The increasing independence of US critics meant that these reviews did not absolutely taint the reception of *Moby-Dick*, but they did not help it, either. In his biography of Melville, Hershel Parker is implicitly critical of Bentley for not sending Melville a "kit of reviews" with which he might have countered these accusations, as Melville did when he placed anonymous notices guaranteeing *Typee*'s legitimacy in Massachusetts newspapers.[90] Bentley, who was used to having his dealings with Melville reported transatlantically, may have believed it unnecessary to send notices that he thought would be reprinted anyway, or he may have sent packets that—like many bundles of transatlantic sheets—went astray or were delayed at sea. Ultimately, *The Whale*'s reception was shaped both by a British publisher's efforts to materially fashion American authorship and by the contingencies of the transatlantic print sphere.

Jeffreys v. Boosey (1854) and the End of the Authorizing Publisher

Bentley's edition of *The Whale* was the high point of attempts to consecrate American authorship through authorized British editions in the mid-nineteenth century. While *The Whale*'s materiality signified Bentley's investment in Melville, those investments failed to show financial returns. Melville followed the commercial failure of *The Whale* with *Pierre; or, The Ambiguities* (1852), a work that Bentley refused to publish without permission to "make or have made by a judicious literary friend such alterations are as absolutely necessary to 'Pierre' being properly appreciated here."[91] No reply from Melville exists, but as Bentley did not publish *Pierre*, it seems that his proposal was unacceptable and their partnership ended. Melville's last two fiction volumes—the short story collection *The Piazza Tales* (1856) and the novel *The Confidence-Man* (1857)—were issued in Britain by Sampson Low, but these consisted of imported US sheets bound with a cancel title page bearing the London firm's name.

Bentley's break with Melville coincided with a decline in the publisher's position in the transatlantic trade. Tracing Bentley's relations—or lack thereof—with Melville's contemporary and sometimes close friend Nathaniel Hawthorne illustrates changing US attitudes toward Bentley and the changing values of an authorized British edition. At the time that he published *The Scarlet Letter* in spring 1850, Hawthorne ought to have been a prime candidate for a Bentley edition (publishing fiction, he would not have been in Murray's line). Hawthorne was a middle-class white man, not especially wealthy but well connected through his Bowdoin education, and he had some reputation in Britain after positive reviews of *Twice-Told Tales* (1837, 1842). His Boston publisher, Ticknor, Reed and Fields had been approached by Bentley, who suggested exchanging titles. On February 28, 1850, Ticknor, Reed, and Fields sent sheets of the first half of *The Scarlet Letter* via a trusted agent, describing the book as being "of remarkable spirit and interest" and noting that Hawthorne's earlier works had already been reprinted in England. By adding that Hawthorne "ranks here with Irving and Cooper," and that the novel "gives a better impression of the early days of Massachusetts than any other work ever published," the Boston firm appealed to Bentley's previous successes with US historical romances. They also noted: "We do not know as it could be advisable to include the introductory chapter called The Custom House, but of this you can best decide."[92] However, Ticknor, Reed and Fields had made a mistake in their timing. When they sent the second half of the sheets in mid-March, the book was already published in the US, and Bentley was not pleased. "It is not the slightest use to send me anything in which I cannot be assured of priority of publication here," he replied tersely.[93] After circulating in imported editions in 1850, the first edition of *The Scarlet Letter* printed in Britain was an unauthorized reprint by George Routledge published in June 1851.

The never-published Bentley edition of *The Scarlet Letter* is fascinating not least because it could apparently do without "The Custom-House." There were practical reasons for Ticknor, Reed and Fields to suggest that it could be dropped, including fears that its discussions of US politics would bore or alienate Bentley and lead him to refuse the book. Indeed, Bentley may well have been responsible for moving *Moby-Dick*'s "Etymology" and "Extracts" to the end of *The Whale* to give the book a more conventional beginning. But Ticknor, Reed and Fields's suggestion also implies that the preface's work would not be necessary once the book was materialized in Bentley's edition, perhaps because both preface and handsome London edition shared the work of navigating the relationship between American literature and American nationhood and between authorship and citizenship. "The Custom-House" is famously ambivalent about these relations. It paints 1850 as a moment at which an American can, for the first time, be a "writer of story-books," but also as a moment in which authors are still negotiating their "personal relation with the public." In terms of the relationship between national culture and the nation's body politic, the civic space of the Salem custom house and Hawthorne's political appointment as its surveyor furnish the "substantial materials" from which he weaves his romance. Yet Hawthorne cannot write his romance until he is forced out of office: there, "I had ceased to be a writer of tolerably poor tales and essays, and had become a tolerably good Surveyor of the Customs. That was all."[94] The preface thus occupies a political-national space and is occupied with Hawthorne's removal from that space, an act that, as Lauren Berlant argues, locates national culture away from state power and moves it into literary and cultural memory.[95] To apprehend the state's use of the national symbolic and alternative sites for the formation of a national collective, Hawthorne must step outside the custom house, a process that he famously renders in terms of national identity: "I am a citizen of some-where else."[96]

"The Custom-House" thus imagines how psychic deterritorializations can create national narratives and examines the necessity of mentally placing oneself outside the political machinery of governance to analyze and understand the ways in which the collective fantasies of nationhood and national culture emerge and can be sustained. A similar, but material, deterritorialization occurred when US texts were remade into handsome English books. Bound in and bound for the British market, these books became "citizen[s] of some-where else." Simultaneously, however, they became representatives of a national and valuable American authorship because they manifested a culture of authorship that did not yet exist in the United States but that might one day be possible—if only US publishers would agree to international copyright and would furnish the (similarly fine) materials that Richard Bentley & Sons could supply.

But only two years later, it was no longer clear that Bentley was able to furnish the materials for American authorship. In 1852, Hawthorne's US publisher, James Fields, visited London and, while there, negotiated for the English copyright of *The Blithedale Romance*. He wrote to Hawthorne:

> I find on investigation that the London Publ. who deal in cheap issues (Routledge & others) are determined to get this book at £50 and they will not offer more. I have been round among the upper tens of the Trade and altho Bentley says he will publish it at ½ profits I do not think it politic to let him have it because his [illegible] plan is to take all himself and say the expenses have eaten up the author's share. This I hear from literary men in England who have dealt with him on these terms. He only prints 750 copies of a Romance & you may judge what the author's share may be.

Fields's ill-feeling toward Bentley suggests that he was perhaps still smarting at the latter's rejection of *The Scarlet Letter*. However, Fields is clear that Bentley's expensive editions and advertising are not what Hawthorne requires, although neither is the potentially wide circulation offered by those who "deal in cheap issues." Instead, for Fields, Britain is somewhere to make financial profits rather than to materialize less tangible forms of literary worth. "I want you to make a fortune as fast as possible," Fields told Hawthorne, explaining that he had offered the copyright to Chapman & Hall, a firm without much experience in American books, for £200.[97] The arrangements for *The Blithedale Romance* suggest that even before the success of *Uncle Tom's Cabin* later in 1852, American authors who had made a name for themselves were seeking different forms of authorization from publishers in London. It was no longer as simple as Hoffman's "notoriety there, is reputation here"; American writers knew that different London firms offered different rewards—generous payments, handsome editions, large circulations—and some authors could pick and choose between them. But Fields's letter also shows that American publishers were learning to navigate the British book trade, creating markets for their authors' books and also performing the moral duty of protecting their authors' income and copyrights.

At the same time, Murray and Bentley were retreating from the transatlantic trade. Murray's interest in American books waned after his legal struggles with Bohn and Routledge. In 1851, he divested of Irving's works—his most valuable American properties—by selling his rights to Bohn. Bentley, however, kept investing in authorized editions of American books until 1854, when the House of Lords ruled that foreign authors could only have copyright in Britain if they were resident in British territory at the time of publication. Suddenly, Bentley found that he had paid tens of thousands of pounds for copyrights that, in law, had never existed. "The present value of the copyright seems to be exactly the same as the value of an estate without any title. It is the value of a nonentity," he told historian George Bancroft, explaining that he would no longer be paying Bancroft £300 per volume for a copyright that "has no existence."[98] The loss of these properties coincided with a general downturn in the London trade around the Crimean War, creating particular financial troubles for Bentley. Unable to service its debts, his firm was forced to operate under the oversight of inspectors, who drastically curtailed new publications. While Bentley continued to publish Prescott and Susan Fenimore Cooper and approached Nathaniel Hawthorne and Susan Warner with offers for prospective new works, he never again published as many US texts.[99]

Melville scholars have often dismissed Murray's edition of *Four Months' Residence* and Bentley's edition of *The Whale* as regrettable bowdlerizations. In concentrating as much on how they materialized Melville's writing as on how they altered his texts, I have argued that Murray and Bentley instead offered—and materialized—forms of authority that Melville could not get in the United States, but that resonated with his own reflections on genre, authorship, and the production of knowledge. Bentley's contribution to the authorization of American literature between 1830 and 1860 was not, however, limited to expensive, multivolume editions of new works. His pioneering experiment with reissuing recent fiction in relatively cheap editions in his Standard Novels series paved the way for one of the most important formats in which US texts circulated in Britain: the publisher's series or library. The next chapter traces the mutually beneficial relationships between American texts and the British series in which they were published, and how series' transatlantic architecture made an American literary tradition at thresholds and in the crossing of spatial boundaries.

CHAPTER 3

The Transatlantic Architecture of the Publisher's Series

On May 1, 1852, an editorial in the British book trade magazine *Publishers' Circular* announced:

> Publication of the Works of American Authors continues to form an important feature in the literature of the day—their popular character and general adaptability to the requirements of our own public being evidenced by the avidity with which unprotected works are pressed into the various cheap series of "Readable Books," "Railway Libraries," &c.; and the readiness with which the publication of new or forthcoming works is undertaken in advance of their appearance on the other side, securing their copyright in this country.[1]

US texts had regularly featured in British publishers' "cheap series" since the early 1830s. Seeking material that they could issue at low prices for large audiences, British publishers were drawn to US texts' lack of copyright protection and their "popular character." While sometimes they were the site of first publication for US titles—as in John Murray III's publication of Herman Melville's *Narrative of a Four Months' Residence among the Natives of a Valley of the Marquesas Islands* in his Home and Colonial Library, discussed in chapter 2—publishers' series more often reprinted texts that had already been issued in either Britain or the US, sometimes with revisions and often with new prefaces and illustrations. Between 1830 and 1860, British cheap series issued a range of US writings, from fiction by Nathaniel Hawthorne and Harriet Beecher Stowe to poetry by William Cullen Bryant and John Greenleaf Whittier and travelogues by John Lloyd Stephens and George William Curtis.

The *Circular* implies an opposition between "unprotected" series reprints and "copyright" editions from advanced sheets but, as this chapter shows, even unauthorized series reprints authorized American literature and framed it as nationally distinctive and culturally valuable.

British cheap series materialized the nationality of American literature as a transnational phenomenon. They mapped geographies for American literature that challenged the idea of America as an autonomous national space and suggested that nationhood was, as Laura Doyle describes it, "dialectical and dyadic, yet also multiple and circumferential and horizonal." Furthermore, "nations do exist," Doyle notes, "but as transnations or internations."[2] British cheap series suggested that American nationhood and culture came into being through the layering of, and at the intersections between, spaces of different scales—from the transatlantic span of the literary marketplace, to the hyper-local interior of a single printed volume—a view also articulated in texts that those series published. Through the architectures of their series and of individual series volumes, British series located and fashioned American literature in the paratexts of books, domestic thresholds, geographic borders, and transnational spaces, and in movements across and between these liminal zones.

I use the term *architecture* because it encompasses two distinct but interrelated features of the series. First, architecture relates to the structure of the series itself. The mid-century series existed both as an actual collection of printed books and as an ideal, coherent whole projected by publishers' marketing strategies. By printing US titles in series, publishers frequently placed them alongside "classic" British and European texts that were also in the public domain, which gave American books cultural capital. Second, architecture refers to the paratexts that linked together titles in a series and gave coherence to the whole. Covers, prefaces, frontispiece illustrations, and lists of titles bounded individual volumes and scaffolded the series-as-ideal, giving it a uniform identity. Acting, as Gérard Genette observed, as "a zone not only of transition but of *transaction*," these paratexts located US texts geographically at the same time as they relocated those texts into series.[3] British series' prefaces and illustrations coded texts as American while also approaching America itself as a product of spatial relations rather than an autonomous entity. In doing so, individual paratexts illustrated that placing a text within a series both located a text (within a category, in relation to other texts) and rendered its location contingent, because the boundaries of a series could always expand and its contents could always be reconfigured.

The essential logic of placing and replacing at the core of publishers' series made the geographies and the "Americanness" of US texts hypervisible. More specifically, series mapped America as a relational, rather than essential, space and suggested that nationhood, like the series itself, was subject to continual remaking. The contingent nationhood materialized by publishers' series amplifies ideas of nationhood in the US texts they reprinted, which imagine America as most visible and comprehensible at its borders, from outside those borders, and at moments when the nation intersects with other local and transnational spaces. In the margins of their series volumes, British publishers enter into conversation with writers like Charles Brockden Brown, Catharine Maria Sedgwick, James Fenimore Cooper, and Ralph Waldo Emerson, who approach the problem of fashioning a national culture through domestic spaces, unstable coasts and frontiers, and transatlantic comparisons.

Tracing dialogues between US writers and their British series reprints requires the close reading of material and literary texts in tandem. As such, it is impossible to discuss all of the many British series that reprinted American titles. The first section of the chapter does chart the wider presence of American books in series between 1830 and 1860, exploring why US titles came to be published in series and why contemporary commentators overstated their presence. But the rest of the chapter focuses on four series publishers. Richard Bentley's Standard Novels (1831–55) and the various libraries of George Routledge and Co. (1848–99) were some of the most successful and long-running series of the mid-century. William Smith's Standard Library (c.1838–46) and Ingram, Cooke & Co.'s Universal Library (1852–53), which reprinted several of its titles from Smith's plates, were less influential and less exceptional than Routledge's or Bentley's publications. But Smith's series is representative of the "classic" series type, whereas the series of Ingram, Cooke & Co. bridged the classic and the popular, offering actual value: the Universal Library gave readers a well-printed work with at least two illustrations for only a shilling. These case studies give a cross section of the format while also creating a smaller corpus in which it is possible to analyze in detail how any one series and its volumes could have authorized a US text and also materially manifested the imaginative movements and material exchanges across local, national, and transatlantic spaces that made American literature.

The Transatlantic Turn in the British Cheap Series

The mid-century cheap series consisted of a set of (often numbered) volumes issued by a single publisher at more-or-less regular intervals under a general title. Publishers usually issued these volumes in a uniform style, reinforcing the series identity though identical bindings, the consistent style of title pages and use of illustrations, and the catalogues of the series that frequently appeared at the front or rear of volumes. Although some publishers issued single-author series—for example, Robert Cadell's Waverley Novels series (1827) of Walter Scott's novels—most cheap series featured a number of different authors, allowing publishers to take materials from wherever they could find them and offering range to potential purchasers. The publisher's series was thus a physical collection of books *and* a metaphorical space into which a potentially limitless number of titles could be deposited. Grouping together what could be widely varied contents, the series name operated as a brand and marketing tool in three important ways, as Richard Altick observed: a series capitalized on readers wishing to complete a set, it suggested to readers who enjoyed one title that the rest would be as good, and it proclaimed its cultural importance through the idea of the "library."[4] Although Leslie Howsam argues that not all of these points held true for every series, she agrees that series suggested that "the sum of the collected books was greater than their original parts," and that publishers viewed series as commodities, proving themselves adept at repackaging the same titles—and even the same printed sheets—in different, sometimes increasingly elaborate formats.[5] The possibility for marketing existing texts to new audiences—be that the lower classes, or railway travelers—made the series one of the most popular publishing vehicles of the nineteenth century. Most British literary publishing houses attempted at least one series, with varying degrees of success.[6]

In the late eighteenth and early nineteenth centuries, series like John Bell's Poets of Great Britain (1777–83), Barbauld's British Novelists (1810), and Ballantyne's Novelists Library (1821–24) reprinted the "classic" works of British and European literature from the eighteenth century and before.[7] Publishers could offer these works cheaply because they were out of copyright, but they justified this commercial strategy by claiming that they were making the most important works of literature available to the widest possible public. The relationship between series publication and canonicity was, therefore, mutually constitutive. Canonical works were published in series, and publication in a series denoted a work as canonical; as John Spiers suggests, series "usually seek to fix texts by giving them the authority of permanence."[8]

The role of the cheap series began to change when, in March 1831, the short-lived partnership of Richard Bentley and Henry Colburn commenced the Standard Novels series with an unauthorized reprint of James Fenimore Cooper's *The Pilot*, first published in Britain and the United States in 1824.[9] As its adverts emphasized, the Standard Novels offered something entirely new, with editions of "such Novels and Romances, written subsequently to the time of Fielding and Smollett, as have, like the productions of those great delineators of nature and manners, taken their rank among English Classics." In other words, Bentley and Colburn combined the public recognition of a series as an arbiter of culture with the tempting prospect of relatively recent fiction at relatively low prices. Titles were revised for republication, accompanied by two illustrations and a new preface, and were sold at a price that would, the publishers claimed, "enable the great mass of the public to enjoy these Works."[10] In reality, many people did not have a disposable income high enough to spend 6s on a book, but a Standard Novels volume was certainly value for money in the 1830s, and it was an offering other publishers quickly began to imitate.[11]

Why did Bentley and Colburn start their series with a reprint of a US text? In 1831, Cooper was at the peak of his popularity and *The Pilot* had been exceptionally successful on both sides of the Atlantic, so the publishers could expect public interest and strong sales of the reprint. A US text also harmonized with the democratizing sentiments in their announcement. As illustrated by Low's comment on the "popular character" of American writing, British publishers and reviewers thought US writers had a particular talent for pleasing mass audiences due to the higher numbers of book-buyers in the United States. However, there is some evidence that *The Pilot* was not Bentley and Colburn's first choice to commence the Standard Novels. Adverts between February 12 and 19, 1831, announced that the first volume would be William Godwin's *Caleb Williams* (1794), which became volume two.[12] Godwin's Gothic tale of the inequities of the law would have appeared more "standard" than Cooper's Revolutionary adventure, not least because it was thirty years older. These adverts may, of course, be erroneous, but they could also suggest that Colburn and Bentley's plan for the series changed only a month before it commenced. An advert in the *Literary Gazette* of February 12 might explain such a late change. The magazine, part-owned by Colburn, noticed a new edition of *The Spy* for 5s, projected as the first in a series of Cooper's novels by Liverpool publisher A. C. Baynes.[13] A prospectus in that edition announced that *The Pilot* would be the next in an "elegant Series" of "the exquisite novels of Mr. Cooper."[14] Bentley and Colburn may have switched their publication schedule to beat the competition, rushing out *The Pilot* before they had time to organize revisions or a new preface. For all of the other Standard Novel's editions of Cooper's texts, Bentley paid Cooper for revisions and new introductions.[15]

If Bentley and Colburn did change the order of titles, this reveals how much they wanted to claim Cooper's works for their series of contemporary fiction. Indeed, their insistence that *The Spy* be the third volume of the series, even when postal delays slowed Cooper's revisions and threatened timely publication, illustrates the central position of his novels to their venture.[16] As Joseph Rezek observes, "Cooper's inclusion in the Standard Novels not only elevated and canonized him, it also legitimized and added star power to the series." He adds, "It might seem implausible today that the stature of *Pride and Prejudice* [a later inclusion in the Standard Novels] could have been bolstered by its proximity to a novel like *The Last of the Mohicans*, but that is exactly the conclusion we must draw if we consider the Standard Novels in the spirit of their age."[17] While not all publishers were as scrupulous as Bentley, and not all American writers had Cooper's popularity, his importance to the Standard Novels shows that English publishers did not always hold all the power. Cooper was certainly not afraid to suggest that they needed him more than he needed them, writing on March 14, 1831, that he expected "a London publisher to deal en grand, or I would send you the letter of your Liverpool rival [Baynes]."[18]

The messy beginnings of the Standard Novels series suggest that its publishers knew that American texts would be central to transforming series from repositories for classics into forums for contemporary writing. American texts were also very profitable for Bentley and Colburn. In his house history of Richard Bentley & Sons, Royal Gettmann notes that in the first eighteen months of publication, the three novels by Cooper brought in £656 of profit, over £100 more than the combined profits of the other eight volumes published in 1831.[19] Gettmann also suggests that the desire to create a new copyright for Cooper's works prompted Bentley and Colburn's decision to revise all the texts published in the series and commission new prefaces. Because later series copied the Standard Novel's stylings, Cooper's texts thus shaped the paratextual architecture of the cheap series as well as giving it a transatlantic scope. Furthermore, Cooper's revised texts for the Standard Novels formed the basis of the collected edition of his works published by George Palmer Putnam in New York, which themselves became the basis for future editions of Cooper's works. The mutual standardization of author and series thus rippled outwards from Bentley and Colburn's editions, shaping Cooper's legacy on the other side of the Atlantic.

Over the next twenty years, publishers followed their example by including modern literature and American books in their cheap series. John Green, an early specialist in the American trade, went further and began the Standard American Literature series in 1839, which showcased texts that are no longer standard in any sense, including didactic fiction by Hannah Lee and Eliza Lee Cabot Follen, historical novels by William Ware, and biographies by Elizabeth F. Ellet. Arguing that the publication of American texts in series grew steadily until the 1850s, declined during the Civil War, and then increased sharply from the 1870s onward, Clarence

Gohdes concludes that "almost every very popular American book not protected by copyright found its way into one or more of the series."[20] But conclusively establishing the number and titles of American texts included in British publishers' series is a challenging task. The series was a fluid entity, with publishers rebranding and renumbering titles to increase sales, selling their series to one another, and producing additional numbers that sometimes constituted series in their own right.[21] Many series, especially at the cheaper end of the genre, were short-lived and produced by small publishers whose records do not survive. Series lists in advertisements must be treated with caution, as they often excluded out-of-print titles and included projected titles that might never have been printed. As cheaply produced reprints of existing titles, series volumes are less likely to have survived in the holdings of libraries and collectors. Catalogues produced by scholars and collectors are framed around individual publishers or collections, and give greater attention to fiction and less to the essays, poetry, and travel writing that were also published in cheap series.[22] The appearance of a title in a series list gives no sense of the size of its edition or its sales, although it does indicate the works that publishers thought would be successful.

Two contemporary sources for mid-century series publications are Sampson Low's *English Catalogue of Books* for 1858 and 1864, which, respectively, attempt to catalogue all books published in England between 1837 and 1857 inclusive, and 1835 to 1862 inclusive. The index to each catalogue lists libraries, or publisher's series. These lists are not comprehensive. For example, George Palmer Putnam's Library of American Books (1845–47) appears in neither, and, despite the cumulative nature of the catalogues, some series listed in 1858 disappear in 1864, such as Henry G. Clarke's Home Library and Cabinet Series.[23] But in the absence of a complete enumerative bibliography, they provide useful snapshots of the genre in the mid-century, although figures drawn from them can only be indicative rather than conclusive.

The 1858 catalogue lists 179 series in total, of which 32 are aimed at an adult readership and feature at least one work of fiction or poetry published after 1830, and the 1864 catalogue lists 164 series, of which 46 fulfil those criteria. This increase in contemporary literature series indicates that series were changing from homes for classic texts to a places where readers could find popular, newer writing. In the 1858 catalogue, 20 of the 32 contemporary literature series contained at least one title by a US author. Two series—Bohn's Shilling Series and Routledge's Cheap Series—contained more American works than British ones, as did the two series dedicated solely to American authors (John Green's Standard American Literature and Routledge's American Poets). In the 1864 catalogue, 24 of 46 literary series feature American texts. Only one of these 24 series—Henry Bohn's Cheap Series—had more American titles than British, besides the series labeled as American (Beadle's Sixpenny American Library and Routledge's American Poets). For comparison, in the 33 series of contemporary fiction published between 1820 and 1865 listed in Michael Sadleir's catalogue of Victorian fiction, 16 contain American titles. We might cautiously suggest, then, that American literature featured in around half of all series that reprinted contemporary literature for adults in the mid-nineteenth century.

US texts were not the only foreign works to be published in British series. They frequently included French, German, and other European texts in translation. In her study of cheaper serial fiction published in weekly parts, Marie Léger-St-Jean argues for a triangle of reprinting in the cheapest of reprint series, as the transmission of texts between English penny-bloods, French *roman-feuilletons*, and American pamphlet novels between 1835 and 1860 created the first transnational mass media culture.[24] Data from Low's catalogue suggests that although European fiction remained important in the more expensive cheap series, these series reprinted more titles from the United States than from any other single nation. Léger-St Jean's research also shows that British publishers often reprinted American translations of European works that were, like all other American books, not subject to English copyright if published first in the US. I have not attempted to include these in my figures but it is likely that some translations of European titles in the series Low catalogued were by Americans.

Within series that reprinted US texts, the number of US titles in series varied widely. Some only included one American work, while by 1864, Routledge's Cheap Series contained 75 American titles by 27 different authors in its 259 volumes. Cooper and Irving were easily the most popular authors in terms of the number of their titles published and the numbers of series in which they appeared, both aided by their extensive outputs. Emerson's essays and Longfellow's prose and verse were also popular, with the latter being published in Routledge's American Poets and British Poets series. The runaway success of *Uncle Tom's Cabin* (1852) led to Harriet Beecher Stowe's novels frequently appearing in series; other female writers who appeared in three or more different series by 1864 included Susan Warner, Catharine Maria Sedgwick, and Maria Cummins. Within the contents of publishers' series across the period of this study, there is a general shift in the genres of their US texts from mostly male-authored history, travel writing, poetry, and essays, with some fiction in the 1830s and early 1840s, to mostly fiction and poetry with more female authors in the later 1840s and 1850s. If, as I argued in the previous chapter, women writers found it harder to secure authorized publications, their texts still circulated in other formats.

Changes in the types of books published in cheap series between 1830 and 1860 meant that the relationship between the architecture of the series and the US texts within them also changed. Reflecting on mid-century publishing in 1854, writer and publisher Charles Knight distinguished between libraries of "established literature" and the newer phenomenon of railway libraries devoted to "novels, old and new, and to American reprints."[25] But US titles appeared in a library that Knight placed within the first sort of series: William Smith's Standard Library, also described by the *Monthly Chronicle* as "one of the cheapest and most comprehensive" of the series that "recur to the sterling literature of the past."[26] Reprints of classic texts did indeed form the bulk of Smith's series, which included essays by Oliver Goldsmith, Milton's poetry and Sheridan's drama, and more modern classics like the essays of Charles Lamb and the poems of Walter Scott. But Smith also included American reprints in his series, issuing editions of Bryant's poems, Emerson's essays, two novels by Sedgwick, two travelogues by John Lloyd Stephens, and George Colton's poem *Tecumseh; or, the West Thirty Years Since* (1842), between 1841 and 1844.

Smith's Library illustrates how unauthorized reprinting in a series could offer authority to a US text. This authority did not come from an expensive material form as in Bentley's edition of

Melville or Bogue's editions of Longfellow; Smith's volumes were cheaply, if not badly, printed in two columns and issued in paper covers for between 9d and 6s (the price depended on the length of the work). But his library suggested an equivalence between American and classic works by issuing them in identical formats. Furthermore, the series severed the link between copyright and authority that publishers like Bentley emphasized. American texts and classic texts could enter the series because their respective spatial and temporal distances from mid-century London placed them in the public domain. Within the series, those distances create equivalences in cultural value, according to the advertisement on the back cover of each volume:

> Classics of this country, and others which deserve to be so, will, enriched by the productions of our French, German, and American brethren, be placed, in a handsome form within the reach of all classes of the community. They will appear in no specified order, but, being protected by a Wrapper, may be preserved and arranged in volumes, according to the taste of the purchaser.[27]

As well as equalizing the authors of Britain, Europe, and America as "brethren," Smith's advert claims that the presence of American titles will "enrich" the native British productions. Of course, Smith's advertisement is a justification for using potentially non-standard works to fill his Standard Library, but it shows how the absence of copyright protection could generate forms of authority and value by giving US texts proximity to older works.

In addition to placing US authors within a carefully selected canon, Smith's cheap reprints promised wide circulation. Smith's argument that his standard works should, and now could, be within reach of "all classes of the community" implicitly connects cheapness and wide circulation with lasting value and textual authority: everyone should read these works because they are the best. In the absence of publishing records, we cannot know whether Smith's American offerings sold as well as his classic titles (although he issued two editions of Bryant's poems, which suggests it was popular enough to bear reprinting), let alone whether readers did approach the titles as equals. Nevertheless, the reprinting of American texts did not seem to reduce the cultural value of Smith's Standard Library to writers like Knight, nor did the cheap format reduce the prestige of his series to US audiences. On the contrary, the *Southern Literary Messenger* acclaimed the publication of Bryant's poems in the series, adding, "We are gratified to learn that the works of Richard H. Dana and Henry W. Longfellow will soon appear in the same series."[28]

Publication in series canonized US authors but US authors could also canonize series. The presence of Cooper in Routledge's Railway Library marked the series as a valuable collection. By beginning the series with *The Red Rover* in 1848, Routledge selected a work by an author whose popularity was assured and who was closely associated with one of the most successful and well-known series projects of the previous two decades, Bentley's Standard Novels. A subsequent renumbering of the series made Cooper's *The Pilot* the first volume, in direct imitation of the Standard Novels. Routledge was almost certainly goading Bentley, whose claims to Cooper's copyrights had recently been imperiled by the courts in *Boosey v. Purday*, but he was also using Cooper's works to implicitly position his series as the successor to the Standard Novels and the next game-changer in the literary marketplace.[29] Whereas Bentley had used the series format to suggest that modern novels like Cooper's could be standard works, Routledge employed Cooper's novel to give his series cultural capital. US titles, therefore, shaped the architecture of the series as well as being shaped by the series.

To commentators in mid-century Britain, American literature seemed to have a uniquely intimate relationship with the cheap series, which led them to overstate its actual presence. Figures from Low's catalogues suggest that American literature was never ubiquitous in British series. It formed a notable part of their contents, but the majority of series volumes listed by Low were not US books. Yet commentators consistently remarked on the presence of American literature in series, while saying little about European texts that were published alongside them, perhaps because European titles had always featured in classic series whilst the inclusion of US texts was novel and suggested a change in the medium. Knight wondered whether "the cheapest supply of reading for these kingdoms is to be kept up by piracies from America or republications of expired copyrights?" although he also noted that "the fashion of American novels is now somewhat stale."[30] In the preface to the first of his Readable Books series, Henry Vizetelly promised that it would differ from those produced by "buccaneers of the book trade—those gentry who treat the public to three separate editions of every work they see cried up on the other side of the Atlantic, no matter how dull it may be," but still used a reprint of Edgar Allan Poe's tales and poems as his first volume.[31] Rezek has demonstrated that Cooper's revisions to *The Pioneers* for the Standard Novels emphasized the remoteness of the US text from its British readers, for example, when the revision of "our nation" to "the nation" means that the British audience "watch Natty from a greater distance—now, indeed, from across the Atlantic."[32] Occasionally, the American identity of a series' titles bled into the identity of the series itself. Bentley's Standard Novels, originally labeled a National Library, were advertised in September 1832 as a "Cheap and Uniform Edition of Cooper's Novels."[33] Transformed into an edition of Cooper, the whole series takes on an American identity that its contents, in fact, belied.

These examples show that, for all their claims to offer permanent homes for standard volumes, publishers' series were highly contingent spaces. The location and identity of a text and of the series itself were subject to change every time a new title was added: at different moments, and to different readers (who perhaps owned different selections of its volumes), a series and the books within it could be more or less British or transatlantic or American. It was this contingency of the series form—the Standard Novels shifting into an edition of Cooper's Novels, Routledge's renumbering of his series, and Smith's instruction that readers might rearrange the Standard Library "according to [their] taste"—that made it such a powerful arena for establishing and questioning what American literature was and could be. The series was a tool for (re)positioning and (re)orienting texts through their relations with other titles and to the series as whole. By relocating texts as they reprinted them, series assumed that texts were inherently locatable—that they belonged *somewhere*. But the contingency of any text's position in the series and of the borders and limits of the series itself illustrated that locations and spaces were relational and not essential. That is, if texts belonged *somewhere*, then that somewhere needed *elsewhere* to establish and reestablish its borders.

Transatlantic British series both Americanized US texts and interrogated the geographic and cultural coherency of America itself, which explains why US texts in series became hyper-visible and why commentators exaggerated their ubiquity. Drilling down into individual series volumes further illustrates how British series took up questions about where and how US texts and American literature could be located. Through the spatializing material and paratextual features, British publishers sought to define American literature not by rooting it in US soil, but by routing it through thresholds, boundaries, borders, and oceans. In doing so, they entered into dialogue with texts in which American nationhood and culture are as shifting and contingent as the space of the series itself.

Mapping America through Series' Architecture

All writing and printing has a spatial dimension: the directionality of the text from left to right (or right to left), the space occupied by the words on the page, and the room that the physical print or manuscript object takes up in the world. Charles Lock argues that it is this spatial dimension that "makes the printed word, the written discourse, finally irreducible to the temporal directionality of speech . . . [Instead,] writing endures by occupying space."[34] The shared vocabulary of publishing and architecture furthers this connection between print and physical space. William Sherman observes that publishing terms like frontispiece, gutter, and sill (the latter two of which date from the nineteenth century) have their roots in architecture.[35] American author Oliver Wendell Holmes articulated this relationship between book space and built space when he wrote to Sampson Low about the transatlantic reprinting of his novel *The Guardian Angel* in 1867. Holmes implored Low to retain his author's preface, asserting that "it is a part of the book as much as the porch is a part of a house," and that it would assist readers in comprehending the text's overall design.[36]

Publishers' series foregrounded the spatial dimension of writing and print. Publishers' marketing encouraged readers to view series as occupying space in the world and to map them onto physical and geographic space. The word "library" appears frequently in series' titles, connoting prestige but also suggesting a room devoted to the housing of books, even as such a room would have been beyond the reach of many purchasers. Others projected themselves onto domestic spaces, such as Henry G. Clarke's Home Library and Cabinet Series and Simms and M'Intyre's Parlour Library of the 1840s. Routledge's Railway Library associated the series with its place of sale, but also with spatial mobility. Publishers reinforced these spatial identities through the features of the book that allow a text to take up space in the world—its paratexts. Gérard Genette proposes that paratexts "surround . . . and extend [the text], precisely in order to *present* it, in the usual sense of the verb but also in the strongest sense: to *make present*, to ensure the text's presence in the world, its 'reception' and consumption in the form (nowadays, at least) of a book."[37] Within series, these paratexts took on particular importance, as they fashioned the identity of the series as a whole and also framed individual volumes. The intellectual undertaking, cultural work, or commercial project of any series was manifest in the material boundaries of book-space.

As well as defining the series' boundaries, paratexts also mapped series onto geographic space. In an announcement for the Railway Library published in 1849, Routledge described its contents in some detail:

> The splendid and spirited painting of COOPER tells its eloquent tales of oceans and prairies; and in a fine and fiery novel, like the *Romance of War*, by [Scottish author James] Grant, we recognize the work of genius glowing with boldness and power. But turn aside, and on the same shelf of entertainment you read of the genuine country life of England, which fixed a nationality upon Jane Austen's plume; you catch the vigorous solider-histories of Gleig; the scintillations of strong Scotch sense and shrewdness illuminating the pages of MacKay.[38]

Here, Routledge maps his series onto spaces of widely different scales. The series occupies a single "shelf of entertainment" yet it also stretches across the entire Atlantic. Within the boundaries of the series, simply by moving from one volume to another, the reader can travel from Britain to America as the series brings together "the fresh genius of the New World" and "some of the imperishable charms of our own dear native literature." This imaginative mobility surpasses the mobility of the library's anticipated scene of reading: the railway can take a person between towns, but the Railway Library could take them across continents. But amid this transatlantic span, each text's individual American, English, and Scottish identities stay intact, and are perhaps even enhanced in being juxtaposed with one another.

Ingram, Cooke & Co.'s Universal Library exemplified the mapping of the British mid-century series as a global and transnational entity and as a space for the fashioning of national literary canons. Published from 1852 until 1853, the series was mostly printed from the stereotype plates of Smith's Standard Library with added frontispiece illustrations and, eventually, some new titles. Its paper covers made grand claims for the series' scope and substance, transforming the commercial decision to reprint public domain works by British, French, Swedish, German, and American writers into an intellectual virtue and a public service. An advertisement that appeared on the rear paper cover of each number promised to bring works that had "so completely gained universal approbation as to have become an indispensable part of the world's literature; such works as ought to be found in every public library . . . [and] within reach of the inmates of every house where English is spoken."[39] As in Routledge's traveling shelf, the Universal Library claims to be a site at which the global and local converge, placing the entire world's literature within a single home. Such claims were echoed by the imposing illustration of a spinning globe on the back, and the classical columns on the front of each number, which implied the works were universal in the sense of being global and timeless. Yet the nation as a framing construct does not disappear within the transnational space and asynchronous time of the series. Whereas the numbering of the series organizes titles generically (into essays, travel, fiction, etc.), the advertisement on the back cover lists authors by nationality. In its "universal" scope the series crosses national boundaries but also enables those boundaries to be constructed around national literary traditions insofar as they exist alongside and in relation to one another.

Other series used different material methods to simultaneously denote the specifically national identity of their US texts and relocate those texts within the boundaries of the series. The paper covers of Smith's Standard Library editions of Bryant's *Poems* and Colton's *Tecumseh* both bear the phrase "AMERICAN POETRY" underneath the British royal coat of arms, framing the texts as representative of an American national tradition at the same time as stamping them with a symbol of British monarchical authority. Moreover, Smith's covers suggest that the transatlantic transmission of these texts produces their American national identity; it is the reprinting in Britain (symbolized by the coat of arms) that makes it necessary to label Bryant and Colton's poetry as American. More explicitly and more specifically than the Universal Library, Smith's Standard Library claims the British reprint series is the space where a distinct and geographically specific American literary identity is realized through the transatlantic relocation and juxtaposition of texts.

This claim takes on particular resonance in relation to Catharine Maria Sedgwick's *Home* (originally published in Boston in 1835), which appeared in both Smith's Standard Library and the Universal Library. Melissa Homestead notes that although scholars often view Sedgwick's shorter, didactic fictions of the 1830s as inferior to her more complex earlier novels, contemporary responses on both sides of the Atlantic praised these simple, domestic tales for their use of uniquely American materials and their articulation of Republican values. Reviewers perceived her "shift to a 'lower' form of literature as an embrace of a *higher* ambition for her literary works, an ambition exactly suited to the condition of American society."[40] Sedgwick herself stakes a claim for *Home* as a domestic fiction in both senses of the word, explicitly connecting the happy home life of the Barclay family with their location in the United States. She claims that the Barclays' domestic bliss would be impossible in "what *was* 'merry England,'" where "the working man, be he 'capable, diligent, and frugal' has an alms-house in his perspective, or the joyless alternative, a life of safe and pining singleness."[41] Later in the text, this particularly American domesticity serves national expansion as the Barclays' son Charles exports his home life to a new settlement on the Western frontier. *Home* thus performs the "manifest domesticity" that Amy Kaplan identifies as a central facet of American imperialism, and in which home acts as a "mobile and mobilizing outpost that transformed conquered foreign lands into the domestic sphere of the family and nation," a process that also "efface[s] all traces of violent conflict."[42]

Central to both the Barclays' all-American abode and Charles's frontier domesticity is a shelf of transatlantic books. Along with "'Marshall's Washington'" and "'American Revolution'," the Barclays display "'Shakespeare,'—'Milton,'—'Pope,'—'Addison,'—'Goldsmith,'—'Fenelon,'" and a "capital Atlas!" as Mrs. Barclay describes it.[43] Homestead reads the Barclays' bookshelf within Sedgwick's own sophisticated negotiation of debates over copyright in mid-century America. Observing that "many of the books on the Barclay's bookshelf are by authors long dead, their works by definition public property and thus financially accessible even for a barely middle-class family," she suggests that Sedgwick proposes a model in which the rights of the author do not restrict the circulation of texts—ironically, within a text that would prove to be one of her most valuable literary properties.[44] It is later implied that these books—or books very much like them—travel with Charles to the frontier, where they are central to his domesticating project. He writes home that he has "made a circulating library of the books father gave me" and has founded a reading-room, creating a "barter trade of our ideas."[45] As well as ensuring the stability of the existing American domestic, the unrestricted circulation of uncopyrighted texts expands that domesticity westward.

Sedgwick implicitly positions *Home* alongside the books on the Barclays' shelf as she envisions model Republican authorship, but Smith's Standard Novels and the Universal Library actually situated her book alongside the poetry of Milton and the essays of Goldsmith. These series created an "Atlas" of world literature that was mirrored by the illustration of a globe on the wrappers of the Universal Library. These publishers were probably not consciously fulfilling Sedgwick's ideals, but the presence of the bookcase in the frontispiece illustration of the Barclays' home in the Universal Library edition suggests that Ingram, Cooke & Co., at least, attended to this detail of the text. Moreover, in a preface to an American translation of Swedish writer Fredrika Bremer's *The H——Family* that he reprinted in the Standard Library in 1843, Smith defended his unauthorized publication of American texts by arguing that he was replicating the conditions of the American market. Smith "offers no remark on the state of the law," but contends that, "What benefit may exist to counteract the evil of that law, [the publisher] has, in every case, given to the public. He has never placed a copyright price on works in which no copyright existed." Arguing that the British book trade model of printing small, expensive first editions ill-served the reading public, Smith positioned himself as righting this wrong: "He has in no instance followed the example of houses, whose acknowledged respectability might have seemed to sanction such a course, in reprinting at a high rate, works which original publishers and writers had been content to issue cheaply."[46] Here, Smith parrots the arguments of the anti-copyright faction, who argued that keeping foreign works in the public domain helped to create a truly republican print culture in which knowledge could circulate cheaply and freely.

Unlike the Universal Library and the Standard Library that produced American literary identity by mapping their series onto a global scale, Routledge's American Poets (1852–54) constructed an American literary geography by contracting the US's national borders. American Poets claimed to offer the most authoritative and the most up-to-date texts of American verse. Like the Standard Novels, several of the volumes boasted new introductory material. Other adverts boasted that texts were set from "the last American edition" (in the case of John Greenleaf Whittier) or the "last revised American edition" (in the case of Nathaniel Parker Willis). Unauthorized reprinting here becomes a virtue and an authorizing process in that it gives British readers the most recent texts and registers the US texts as authoritative by circulating them in Britain. Routledge's advertisement notes that "many of these writers are but little known in England" but that several "bear the unmistakable stamp of genius, and render them deserving a place beside our own Campbell and Wordsworth's."[47] Here, Routledge briefly imagines relocating these writers into a British canon, an idea reinforced through the series itself when he added an edition of the Scottish poet Thomas Campbell, "Uniform with the above [American Poets], in Size, Price and Binding" that also included poems by Thomas Gray and William Collins. However, rather than colonizing American poets into a British canon, Routledge seems instead to be questioning where the borders of American poetry might lie. Perhaps Campbell's account of the "woods and wilderness" of Wyoming in *Gertrude of Wyoming* (even with its somewhat inaccurate promise of "the flamingo . . . /Disporting like a meteor on the lake") rendered him an "American Poet," even as the same British publisher could claim him as "our own."[48]

Routledge's claim that these US poets were "little known" was untrue. Several of them were discussed in the best-selling British author Mary Russell Mitford's *Recollections of a Literary Life: or, Books, Places and People* (1852), and her selections almost certainly influenced Routledge's. Josephine McDonagh has argued that Mitford's own selections were influenced by her friendship with James Fields, who had encouraged further friendships between Mitford and the US writers that he published.[49] Routledge's series thus drew similar borders for American literature around New England that Fields's firm undertook by publishing New England authors in their prestigious brown cloth volumes, which were themselves modeled on English books.[50] Routledge's advertisement for the series on the back cover of its edition of Oliver Wendell Holmes's poems similarly drew the borders of American literary geography. It claims that the poets in the series "possess an originality that is becoming more and more apparent in the imaginative literature of the New World: and they breathe a spirit of freedom and a sense of humanity that is becoming more and more apparent which will ere long tend to obliterate the stain from New England's fame,—THE FUGITIVE SLAVE LAW."[51] Mentioning the Fugitive Slave Law was a mercenary attempt to capitalize on the success of *Uncle Tom's Cabin*, published the previous year. But the America of Routledge's American Poets is one without enslaved persons, only fugitive slaves, with the effect that the series could point the finger at the US's national shame (and affirm British superiority in abolitionism) while still framing New England as a haven of "humanity." The series did not feature Southern poets like William Gilmore Simms or Edgar Allan Poe, nor any from outside New York and New England. By making the "imaginative literature of the New World" consummate with "New England's fame," Routledge's series staked out a territory for what could truly be called American literature, and that territory was Northeastern, white, and mostly male.[52]

British publishers display a good deal of cultural superiority when they draw the geographic boundaries of American literature, and when they suggest, however implicitly, that American literature emerges and becomes fully national through its republication in Britain. Nevertheless, in suggesting that an American literary identity arises outside of the nation and from relations between spaces, British publishers echoed American writers' own efforts to determine how national literature might be formed. Even Sedgwick's *Home* requires the liminal space of the frontier to shore up the Barclays' national domesticity, even as it portrays their home domesticating that frontier. Charles's stint on the frontier is precipitated by a fracture in domestic bliss that arises when he and his brother fall in love with the same woman, and which is only truly healed when Charles returns from the frontier with a fever that eventually kills him. In Sedgwick's text, the nation emerges from the interpolation of a local space (the home) with a transnational one (the frontier), and through movements between these differently scaled spaces. By imagining America in the margins of their volumes, British series publishers enter into dialogues with American writers about how a national literary voice might be achieved through relations between spaces.

America in the Margins

The illustrations in series volumes were not as skilled and ornate as those in the books analyzed in chapter 1, but they and the prefaces performed the similar work of authorizing and geographically locating American literature. Two series in particular—Bentley's Standard Novels and Ingram, Cooke and Co.'s Universal Library—featured prefaces and illustrations that map the US texts they reprint onto geographical spaces that are distinctly, but not essentially, American: spaces that become American against, alongside, and between other spaces of different scales. The material boundaries of these British books present America itself as a threshold space that can only be realized in relation to the intersections of other geographies, including the hyper-local space of the bound volume and the transatlantic literary market. In imagining American literary identity as contingent and interdependent, these series speak to ideas and concerns within US texts themselves, raised by US authors such as James Fenimore Cooper, Charles Brockden Brown, and Ralph Waldo Emerson.

The first ten volumes of Bentley's Standard Novels emphasize the role of the frontispiece and title-page vignette illustrations as thresholds to the text. Illustrations for Cooper's *The Pilot* and *The Last of the Mohicans* (numbers 1 and 6), William Godwin's *Caleb Williams* (2), Jane Porter's *Thaddeus of Warsaw* and *The Scottish Chiefs* (4 and 8), Mary Shelley's *Frankenstein* (9), and Friedrich Schiller's *The Ghost-Seer* and Charles Brockden Brown's *Edgar Huntly* (10) all feature windows, doors, or gates. The repetition of thresholds implies that boundaries are porous and suggests that readers can move between volumes in the series and, in the process, make connections across national borders. In particular, the spatial dynamics of the illustrations for *The Pilot* call attention to Cooper's American nationality and the transatlantic circulation of the text while establishing the parameters of the new series. The frontispiece of *The Pilot* (figure 6) features the two female leads of the novel, Katherine Plowden and her cousin Cecilia Howard—young American women who are effectively held prisoner in England by Cecilia's Loyalist uncle, Colonel Howard, who has returned following Republican victory in the Revolutionary War. On the left-hand side, as the reader views it, Katherine looks out of a window and, to her right, Cecilia sits in a chair with a book on her lap. Opposite, the title-page vignette displays a ship sailing toward the left-hand border of the picture. Both of these illustrations point left, and so westward on a typical compass—a geographical import that is augmented by the map that hangs on the wall behind Katherine and Cecilia.

The threshold illustrations of *The Pilot* thus direct the assumed British reader toward Cooper's country of origin, which would have been common knowledge for readers of this reprint of a popular work. Their spatial import sends the reader in the opposite direction from Cooper's own geographical introduction to the novel, which promises to transport the assumed American reader eastward: "A single glance at the map will make the reader acquainted with the position of the eastern coast of the Island of Great Britain."[53] But this apparent misdirection works in harmony with the text. The westward-pointing illustrations anticipate the text, directing the British reader where Cooper has assumed his American audience will

Figure 6. Frontispiece and title page, James Fenimore Cooper, *The Pilot*, Standard Novels (London: Colburn and Bentley, 1831). Robarts Library, University of Toronto. Digitized for the Internet Archive: https://archive.org/details/pilotstandard00coopuoft.

be so that Cooper can then relocate them to England. At the same time, the frontispiece illustration functions as a response to Sydney Smith's infamous question, "Who reads an American book?"[54] On Cecilia's lap is a signal book that Katherine has created in order to secretly communicate with her American fiancé, Lieutenant Barnstable. Cooper specifically codes this book as American through reference to contemporary debates over the need for an American form of English, with Katherine announcing, "It's a fine thing to be able to invent names and make dictionaries."[55] In Bentley and Colburn's edition, then, the reader is presented with an image of someone reading an American book—an image that also mirrors the actions of the real-life reader of the Standard Novels volume.

The construction of American identity in *The Pilot*, however, is not as straightforward as Katherine suggests, as Cooper's anxieties about America's path to nationhood run alongside his celebratory maritime nationalism. Jason Berger argues that Cooper's Republican patriotism is compromised by a fear of the masses that requires "writing out a romantic lower-class constituent who had risen too far for comfort," and Cynthia Schoolar Williams suggests that the liminal coastal setting of *The Pilot* "resist[s] the trope of the nation as organic" and presents US nationhood as contingent.[56] The novel's characters have transatlantic identities rather than British or American nationality. The pilot, based on John Paul Jones, is a British subject who allies himself with the American navy. The Loyalist Colonel Howard lives in England as "a stranger . . . in the land whose rule he upholds so blindly." On his deathbed, Howard partially converts back to America—"perhaps I may have also mistaken my duty to America—but I was too old to change my politics or my religion"—although he then blesses the British monarch. Symbolically, he dies while in the fluid space of the ocean and is buried in Holland, not England. His American estates "had never been confiscated," and are claimed by Cecilia and Lieutenant Griffith, the hero of the novel, when they marry, transplanting a hereditary lineage into the newly Republican landscape. Even Katherine's "American book" is a transatlantic production because it is engendered by her entrapment in England, and Cecilia implicitly dissevers Katherine's sign system from the American landscape when she mistakes Barnstable's flags for English leaves, claiming they "want the vivid tints which grace the autumn of our own dear America!" Most importantly, the transatlantic production of American culture persists beyond the conflict with Britain. In the novel's conclusion, Griffith, domesticated by marriage and a return to America, learns the pilot's true identity by reading "English prints": American national histories arise from a transatlantic circulation of print that prefigures *The Pilot*'s own course.[57]

Similarly, Bentley and Colburn's illustrations suggest that transatlantic circulation is integral to the production of American literature. The westward import of the illustrations only gestures toward America from a British starting point, foregrounding Cooper's national identity through processes of relation rather than fashioning it as an essential situation. As in *The Pilot* itself, America emerges in dialogue with British territory and British print. The illustrations also encourage a misreading of Cooper's promise to "conduct" his reader "across the waters of this disputed ocean," dropping readers of the Standard Novels edition somewhere in the middle of the Atlantic rather than the North Sea. In doing so, the illustrations emphasize that Cooper's "disputed ocean" might easily be mapped onto the Atlantic, especially as the novel details a conflict between America and Britain. Toward the end of the novel, Katherine substitutes the North Sea for the Atlantic Ocean, imagined as an American space, proclaiming that its air seems "as if it were wafted from our own distant America."[58] Pairing a domestic scene, albeit one set in England, with an image of a ship on the ocean, the illustrations enhance the symbolic possibilities of Cooper's maritime setting by implying connection, as well as opposition, between the liminal space of the ocean and the idea of home. Imagining the North Sea as America reinforces Cooper's commitment to the nascent American navy as an instrument of nation-building. But Katherine's comment also renders America a fluid, in-between space and a site of crossings. Relocating this overlap between American national spaces and fluid border regions to the threshold of their volume, Bentley and Colburn integrate the space of the book and its transatlantic circulations within this complex discourse of national fashioning. The paratextual elements that construct the boundaries of the Standard Novels series and relocate Cooper into a canon of contemporary fiction also locate American literature both as distinctly national and transatlantically fashioned.

The same interplay between transatlantic relations and American national culture features in the Standard Novels preface to Charles Brockden Brown's *Edgar Huntly*, which appeared as the first half of number 10. This edition omitted Brown's brief original preface that presents his romance as an attempt to create native literature by finding gothic elements in the American landscape and "calling forth the passions and engaging the sympathy of the reader" through "the perils of the western wilderness."[59] That preface was missing from the first British Minerva Press edition, so Colburn and Bentley may not have known of it, or they may have omitted it because of its potentially confusing references to Brown's previous novel *Arthur Mervyn* (1799). Instead, Bentley included a new, longer introduction, attributed to "O. C.," who introduces Brown as "one of the earliest American novelists, and inferior to none of his countrymen who succeeded him." However, he quickly adds that "it might truly be said, that in *originality* he has not been surpassed by any inventor of story of whatever age or country," resituating Brown within a global community.[60]

The introduction then draws together the transnational and the local by inventing an alternate history for Brown. While Brown was actually born in Philadelphia, as the introduction eventually notes, O. C. first quotes from "a forgotten journal" (in fact, volume 1 of the *Attic Miscellany* from 1824), which suggested that Brown "probably passed his early youth in the house of a settler." Leaving its untruth aside, the preface figures domestic (national) spaces through domestic (household) spaces, an interaction between national and local space that anticipates its mapping of American landscape onto the volume itself: "we know not where could be found such striking and grand descriptions of American forests, wildernesses, and caverns, and such fearful pictures of savage life and desperate adventure, as occur in the pages before us."[61] The preface locates Brown and his text at a frontier space similar to the setting of *Edgar Huntly*, an environment that is both distinctly American and a place in which identities—including national identity—are never properly secure.

The position of Brown's novel within the series as whole ensures that the novel is presented as more than an autochthonous curiosity and reinforces the introduction's efforts to situate Brown transatlantically. The passage from the *Attic Miscellany* that O. C. quotes also connects Brown to Godwin, suggesting that the two writers formed a "community of thought," a view shared by later scholarship on the two writers.[62] The publication of *Edgar Huntly* in the same series as *Caleb Williams* materially reinforced this connection between them. More specifically, *Edgar Huntly* was published in the same volume as the second half of Schiller's *The Ghost-Seer*, the first half of which had been published in the same volume as *Frankenstein* by Mary Shelley, Godwin's daughter, who was herself influenced by Brown. In effect, *The Ghost-Seer* and *Frankenstein* act as both intertexts and paratexts for *Edgar Huntly*, inviting readers to approach Brown's novel through a transatlantic frame.

In fashioning American literature from within a transatlantic nexus, the Standard Novels mirrors Brown's own construction of a frontier that is distinctly American, but also shaped by dialogues with the Old World. Brown's preface frames *Edgar Huntly* as "a series of adventures, growing out of the condition of our country," but the narrative's complex events reach back to familial, platonic, and romantic connections formed in Ireland, and one of its subplots concerns mercantile trade between America and Europe.[63] Counterintuitively, transatlantic images enter the novel when its settings and subjects are apparently most autochthonous—that is, during Edgar's traumatic stay in the wilderness and his violent encounters with Indigenous Americans. In the untouched American forests, Edgar laments that he "scarcely knew in what region of the globe I was placed" or whether he is separated from home by "a river or an ocean." Lacking the means of establishing geographic relations, Edgar loses his sense of national location. Furthermore, Edgar mediates his wilderness experiences through the history of the Old World rather than the landscape of the New. Having sleepwalked into a cavern and then slain a panther and eaten its raw meat, Edgar decides to drink his own sweat after "remembering the history of certain English prisoners in Bengal, whom their merciless enemy imprisoned in a small room."[64] Comparing himself to an English subject, Edgar requires Old World frameworks to understand Indigenous North American persons and experiences. He nicknames an elderly Native woman "Queen Mab" as "there appeared to me some rude analogy between this personage and her whom the poets of old-time have delighted to celebrate."[65] Although writing two decades before Cooper, Brown's America similarly emerges through transnational connections—connections that were articulated in *Edgar Huntly*'s publication in the Standard Novels.

A similar framing of America as a national and a relationally constructed space emerges in the paratexts of the Universal Library. Two decades separated the Universal Library from the Standard Novels, and while the latter was an innovative venture, the former trod the well-worn path of the cheap series so deeply that it was printed from another publisher's plates. However, there were material similarities between the series. In imitation of the Standard Novels, each number of the Universal Library opened with two illustrations. These, its advertisements claimed, gave the series value for money and cultural value: "Beautifully and uniformly printed in royal octavo, with two or more first-class illustrations to each number, and a handsome cover."[66]

In contrast to the broad parameters projected by the series title, the Universal Library's reprint of Emerson's *Essays and Orations* opened with an image that was highly local but also entirely foreign to its British readership. Accompanying a frontispiece portrait of a youthful-looking Emerson is a title page vignette of a building that is captioned "Emerson's House" (figure 7). These pictorial choices are unusual for nineteenth-century editions of Emerson's works. Emerson kept a great deal of control over his publications within the United States, financing the costs of the plates and retaining ownership of them, and he did not include pictures of himself or his house in any first US edition. The vignette of the house is also relatively unusual among the illustrations in the Universal Library. Catharine Maria Sedgwick's *Home* is illustrated with domestic interiors, but these belong to the Barclay family of the story rather than Sedgwick herself. The editions of Francis Bacon's and John Locke's essays, Robert Burns's poems, and John Bunyan's *Pilgrim's Progress* do open with vignettes of the authors' residences or birthplaces, but those buildings appear as uninhabited memorials, their doors shielded from view. Emerson's house appears occupied—children are in the front garden, an empty chair sits under the tree perhaps awaiting Emerson himself—and almost inviting. The front door is open, emphasizing the location of the illustration at the threshold of the volumes by aligning it with the threshold of the house.

Emerson did, indeed, do much of his writing from his Concord home, although this is rarely mentioned in his writings.[67] Instead, the illustration invokes the house metaphors that Emerson weaves through *Essays: First Series*, the collection Ingram, Cooke & Co. reprinted. Emerson articulates the need for native literature with architectural metaphors: "why need we copy the Doric or the Gothic model?" He laments that "our houses are built with foreign taste; our shelves are garnished with foreign ornaments," and suggests that if the American artist will only consider "the climate, the soil, the length of the day, the wants of the people, the habit and form of the government, he will create a house in which all these will find themselves fitted, and taste and sentiment will be satisfied also."[68] In introducing Emerson's American writing with a picture of his

ESSAYS AND ORATIONS.

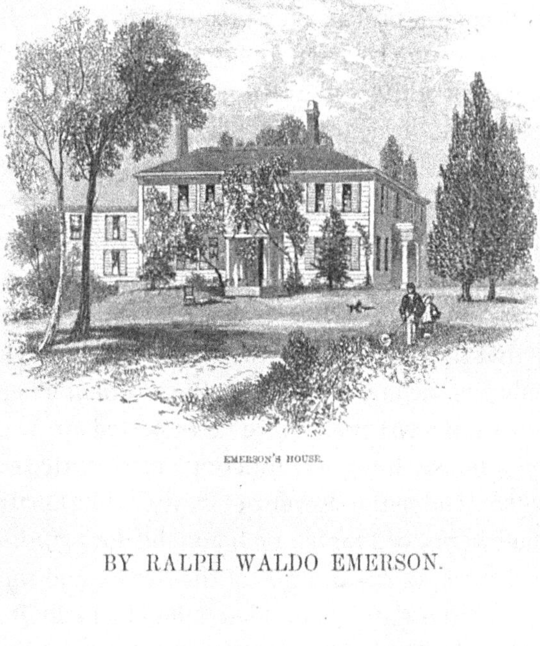

EMERSON'S HOUSE.

BY RALPH WALDO EMERSON.

Figure 7. Title Page "Emerson's House," Ralph Waldo Emerson, *Essays and Orations*. Universal Library. (London: Ingram, Cooke & Co., 1853) © The British Library Board, General Reference Collection 12204.e.5/2.

American house, Ingram, Cooke & Co.'s volume implicitly frames Emerson as the American artist for whom Emerson himself calls.

The origins of the illustration further develop this transatlantic nationalism. A comparison of the Universal Library's illustration with the engraving of Emerson's house included in *Homes of American Authors* (figure 8)—an anthology of descriptive accounts published by George Palmer Putnam and distributed in Britain by Sampson Low three months before Ingram, Cooke & Co. published their volume of Emerson—suggests that the latter engraving was the source of the former.[69] Putnam's introduction claims that the volume demonstrates the prosperity of American letters, with "comfortably housed" writers evidencing that American authorship "has at last become a profession which men live by."[70] But it also argues for a connection between American literature and American land, placing even authors like George Bancroft and Cooper, who spent large amounts of their writing lives outside of America, firmly within the nation. The volume implicitly, and sometimes explicitly, amalgamates the domestic-as-home and the domestic-as-not-foreign. Indeed, George William Curtis, who wrote the chapter on Emerson in Putnam's volume, spends far more time on Concord than on Emerson's house, which he admits is of no great interest, concluding that the readers "will easily see [Concord's] landscape on Emerson's pages," and that despite their "oriental" and "tropical" influences, his writings "have no imported air."[71]

Emerson's house, however, functions differently in *Homes of American Authors* and in the Universal Library. While Curtis does not dwell on the interior of Emerson's home, he does go through the front door, describing the interior of the library and the Monday night literary parties that he attended. Like American literature in Putnam's cultural nationalist vision, Emerson's house is a structure in its own right, each building of the cluster to which it belongs "standing liberally apart."[72] In the Universal Library, the reader never makes it inside the building. The house is situated not only on a threshold at the opening of the book, but *as* a threshold. A liminal space between the text and the outside world, Emerson's house is something that the reader passes through rather than something to be inhabited. Reprinting the illustration thus disrupts Putnam's literary nationalist project because it renders the American domestic as a space that emerges through crossings between spaces and that is always constructed relative to something else.

Transforming the house into a liminal space speaks to Emerson's own disruptions of his architectural metaphors across *Essays: First Series*. While the house-nation in "Self-Reliance" is a relatively stable space that must be built and occupied by truly American writers, this is not the case for the houses in "Circles." The essay "Circles" emphasizes the impermanence and instability of all architecture in the face of the forces of history: "a rich estate appears to women and children, a firm and lasting fact; to a merchant, one easily created out of any materials, and easily lost." In "Circles," houses are important not so much as spaces to inhabit, but as thresholds from which to perceive other houses. "We fill ourselves with ancient learning; instal [sic] ourselves the best we can in Greek, in Punic, in Roman houses, only that we may wiselier see French, English and American houses and modes of living. . . . The field

Figure 8. "Residence of R. W. Emerson, Concord, Mass.," *Homes of American Authors* (New York: G. P. Putnam & Co., 1853), 244. Robarts Library, University of Toronto. Digitized for the Internet hive: https://archive.org/details/homesofamericana00newyuoft/page/244/mode/2up?q=emerson.

cannot be well seen from within the field."[73] Emerson's sentiment here appears antithetical to those in "Self-Reliance": rather than eschewing the Gothic and Doric, by inhabiting "Greek . . . Punic . . . Roman houses," American dwellings become visible. As houses become places to see from—thresholds from which other spaces become visible—rather than spaces to occupy, Emerson's metaphor suggests that literary traditions can only be apprehended from outside of themselves. American writers need to fashion a national house, but there needs to be something beyond that house for it to be realized. The process of American literature becoming national involves realizing that the nation itself is a relational space.

Despite their differences in price and prestige, the Standard Novels and the Universal Library achieved similar effects in their framing of American texts. The architecture of both series' volumes—the illustrations and prefaces that formed the thresholds of the books—drew national boundaries around the texts, framing those texts as national American products, wedded to a distinct geographic area. But those paratexts also disrupt the autonomy of American national space. In their material texts and in dialogue with the US texts they publish, the British publishers of transatlantic series champion a literary nationalism that imagines the nation—geographically, politically, and culturally—as continually refashioning itself in contested borderlands, liminal landscapes, and places far from home. Moreover, the version of America and of American literature articulated by a series and its volumes was always contingent and could change with the addition of the new volumes or the rearrangement of the series as a whole. This contingency echoes the way that British series publishers and their material texts engaged selectively with ongoing discussions about literary nationalism, trying out arguments rather than seeking to conclude them.

In doing so, these British books reflected a body of US writing that itself offered conflicting pronouncements on what it meant for a person or a cultural object to be truly American and suggested that the most truly American spaces of all were to be found at or reinforced by contested borderlands, in landscapes that were both indigenous and elsewhere, or in the middle of oceans, far away from home. Writing in different genres and at different moments, Sedgwick, Brown, Cooper, and Emerson do not sit alongside one another in most discussions of American literature. Yet cheap series created strange bedfellows, and studying the reprints of these texts in British series amplifies similar notes within them and resonances between them that might otherwise have remained silent. All four authors map Americas that are constructed, transformed, and released through intersections with other spaces and places—including the space of the British book itself. Studying the transatlantic architecture of the British publishers' series thus illuminates a persistent strand of relational nationalism that is woven through antebellum US writing.

Transatlantic architecture was a feature of British publishers' cheap series throughout the nineteenth century, and, to this day, publishers use series to construct canons and negotiate the formation and reformation of regional, national, and transnational affiliations and identities. British publishers' mapping of American literature through series and their volumes are antecedents for literary nationalist series in the US like Wiley and Putnam's Library of American Books (1845–48). They were also antecedents for late nineteenth-century uses of series to form British colonial identities and for those series published from the former imperial power and the newly independent nation that sought to establish and define post-colonial literary traditions in the second half of the twentieth century. The next two chapters continue to explore how publishers established the value of US writing through multi-author formats, by examining gift books, and reviewing "American" magazines published in London. These formats had neither the longevity of the transatlantic publisher's series, nor the prestige and cultural legacy of a series like the Standard Novels. But they show how polyvocal print formats provided space to navigate the shifting geographies and complex spatial relations that arose as the United States pursued violent imperial expansion and became entrenched in an ever-deepening sectional conflict over slavery.

CHAPTER 4

The *Forget Me Not*, the American Poetess, and Sentimental Nationalisms

In the preface to its 1838 edition, the *Forget Me Not*, a British gift book, announced that its latest volume offered poems by "some whose names are new to our pages," and directed "particular attention to those of Mrs. Sigourney and Miss Gould, who hold a distinguished rank in the literature of the United States."[1] Lydia Huntley Sigourney's name was new to the pages of the *Forget Me Not*, but she may have been known to its readers. In 1834, the New York *Knickerbocker* proudly professed that the "ablest reviews of England and Scotland, have yielded willing testimony to the excellence of her verse."[2] Her poetry circulated in Britain in reprints of her American volumes, and also in periodicals, anthologies, and edited collections produced by British publishers. Like the *Forget Me Not*'s other new American contributor, Hannah Flagg Gould (who was less well known, but also regularly published in Britain), Sigourney worked in the "poetess" tradition, writing poems that addressed domestic and religious subjects through an aesthetic of the beautiful and the affects of the middle-class home. But the two women also applied those aesthetics and affects to national and political subjects. Sigourney's poetry in particular celebrated and interrogated US nation-building, exploring US history and mapping American landscapes, but also addressing the violent displacement and deaths of Indigenous Americans caused by Indian Removal and westward expansion.

Sigourney employed publication in Britain and transatlantic circulation in her experiments with a sentimental rhetoric that was both celebratory and critical of US nationhood. Scholars have analyzed the public work of the private sphere since Jane Tompkins's now-classic study of sentimental fiction, but little attention has been paid to the place of transatlantic print culture in sentimentalism's public work outside of the success of *Uncle Tom's Cabin* in Britain.[3] I examine this relationship between British middle-class print objects and sentimentalism's national modes of address through the *Forget Me Not*'s publication of Gould's and Sigourney's poetry, and Sigourney's travelogue *Pleasant Memories of Pleasant Lands* (1842). Scholarship on her writing has traditionally argued that during the later 1830s and 1840s, Sigourney turned away from the political work of her early verse and toward more conservative celebrations of domesticity and motherhood.[4] I instead argue that, at the intersection of transatlantic circulation and the charged boundary between public and private space, Sigourney found room to cultivate a sentimental nationalism through which she critiqued westward expansion while also investing in sympathy as the foundation of a national reading public.

I begin by examining Sigourney's and Gould's unusually long relationships with *Forget Me Not*, which printed their poetry between 1838 and 1846, when it ceased publication.[5] Their correspondence with the gift book's editors shows that both writers gained financial remuneration, cultural capital, and creative freedom from this British publication. The material form and paratexts of the *Forget Me Not* situated Gould and Sigourney both as trusted intimates of its genteel coterie of British writers and as national American poets, categories that reflect the gift book's ability to work across and between private and public modes. Its public-and-private space further allowed Gould and Sigourney to experiment with a sentimental rhetoric that praised and attacked US nation-building and to work through the political role of the poetess to quite different ends. Gould's contributions employed the values and emotional bonds of the domestic sphere to define republican citizenship at a transatlantic scale. Sigourney's poems, however, denounced racialized violence against Indigenous Americans at a safe distance from the United States itself. But Sigourney and Gould also used their transatlantic circulations to image how such circulations and British print could cultivate a national, white sentimental public for their own works. Sigourney drew on her publication in the *Forget Me Not* in the pages of *Pleasant Memories of*

Pleasant Lands, which moves between domestic and transnational scales to cultivate and gather sentimental readers at the national scale. In *Pleasant Memories*, Sigourney uses the American reprinting of British texts and her own circulation of British letters to train US readers in sympathy before asking for the same responses to her own writing and an imagined national tradition. However, when *Pleasant Memories* itself circulated in Britain, British periodicals attacked Sigourney's transatlantic print strategies, with her travelogue becoming fuel for debates about the development of American literature within a culture of reprinting.

Like Longfellow, whose material and imaginative negotiations of transatlantic print I examined in chapter 1, Sigourney's experiences with publication in Britain were both exceptional and typical. Before the successes of Susan Warner and Harriet Beecher Stowe in the early 1850s, Sigourney was one of the best-known female US writers in Britain. However, aside from her twelve-year connection with *Forget Me Not*, she had no sustained relations with British publishers and often circulated copies of her works in Britain at her own expense. Her authorization as a national American writer in Britain came through publications that straddled the boundary between authorized and unauthorized, and she ultimately invested in unauthorized reprinting as the foundation of an American literary culture and a national reading public. Unravelling Sigourney's strategies invites us to re-situate the American poetess as a fundamentally transatlantic figure. More than simply taking inspiration from British counterparts, both Sigourney and Gould found space for political uses of privacy in British print objects and in transatlantic circulations that occupy, transgress, and pull into relief the charged boundary between public and private space. Analyzing how this boundary provided terrain for political and public uses of privacy that both critique and cultivate white US nationhood moves us closer to answering questions about whether the poetess's sentimental writings always serve the state or whether they can critique the state's racialized and gendered definitions of citizenship and its uses of violence. Sigourney's example in particular suggests that while British material texts and transatlantic circulation created space for such a critique, its ultimate purpose was to create white, transatlantic communities of sympathy, from which a national reading public for American literature might emerge.

Locating the American Poetess in *Forget Me Not*

As chapter 2 illustrated, US women writers found it harder than their male counterparts to access the handsome authorized editions that materially championed American authorship. In 1843, Sigourney sent John Murray II copies of *Pleasant Memories of Pleasant Lands* to sell, but his son, who took over the firm that year, seems to have made little effort to push them; all remained on hand a year later, leading Murray III to advise that they "be offered to sell for what they would fetch."[6] Such failures did not necessarily mean that Sigourney had "a smaller, narrower, and more downmarket presence in Britain" than British writers like Felicia Hemans had in the United States, as Gary Kelly argues.[7] Instead, Sigourney and Gould found publication, audiences, and prestige in *Forget Me Not*, a text that, like those discussed in chapters 1 and 3, complicates distinctions between authorized and unauthorized editions.

The *Forget Me Not* was the oldest and arguably the most prestigious of Britain's gift books. It was the brainchild of Rudolph Ackermann, a German publisher living in London and specializing in art prints, who drew upon European pocketbooks to create a new annual publication for the Christmas trade. A combination of its novelty, its high-quality illustrations, and its contributions from popular authors like Felicia Hemans, James Hogg, Letitia Elizabeth Landon, and Mary Russell Mitford made *Forget Me Not* an immediate success when it first appeared in 1823. Its pairings of steel engravings and short literary contributions became the signature of the annual or gift book. The engravings usually depicted picturesque landscapes, beautiful women, or sentimental scenes, and the accompanying poetry and prose—often commissioned to match the illustrations, rather than vice versa—likewise favored sentimental, domestic, and picturesque subjects. As a beautiful, highly commodified object for feminine consumption, the *Forget Me Not* circulated in the affective economies of the middle-class home and the market economies of the book trade. Its texts and paratexts projected intimate bonds between its contributors and between contributors and readers, mirroring how purchasing, gifting, and reading a gift book could create, signify, and strengthen attachments between friends and family members.

Although gendered as female and associated with the middle-class home, gift books like the *Forget Me Not* were not entirely private objects. As Lorraine Kooistra argues in her study of the mid-century gift book, "In its ornate architecture, the book symbolically represented the middle-class home itself, and its most cherished values, while also marking boundaries of inside and outside, public and private, female and male, individual and community, nation and world."[8] Margaret Linley further suggests that purchasers' inscriptions in gift books translated "the purchase of a beautiful commodity . . . socially and symbolically from a commercial transaction into a communal act," so that gift books uniquely encouraged purchasers to merge the mercantile transactions of the book trade with the social economies of home and family.[9] Gift books were displayed in semi-public domestic spaces, such as drawing rooms, where they would be admired by visitors to the home. Katherine Harris observes that annuals further straddled the boundary between public and private by presenting themselves as "repositories of memories," both collective and individual.[10] As periodical publications, they recorded the passing of time, allowing owners to connect public events with their personal memories, which could be recorded on the pages intended for inscriptions. Gift books took seriously their role in commemorating public figures and celebrating public events, and also in preserving white, middle-class identity and values at a time of rapid urbanization, industrialization, and social change on both sides of the Atlantic.[11]

For authors, publication in a gift book was an invitation into the coterie of the volume itself and the home of the reader, but one that also meant participating in a highly commodified form of publishing that foregrounded the book-as-object over the book-as-text—which was why many, especially male, writers complained about writing for annuals even as they enjoyed the generous payments. Mid-nineteenth-century gift books, therefore, operated at and across the boundaries between private and public spheres, familial bonds and market exchanges, sentimental affects and political rhetoric, and domestic values and state regimes.

Its situation at the intersections of multiple loci of power and authority is what made the British gift book such a fertile space for American poetesses seeking to forge a national poetics that was both political and sentimental.

In 1836, writer and editor Robert Shelton Mackenzie, who was an admirer of American culture (he was a foreign correspondent for the New York *Evening Star*) and a contributor to *Forget Me Not*, wrote to Sigourney and Gould asking for contributions to the annual. It is unclear whether these approaches were Mackenzie's own idea or a plan developed by the editor of *Forget Me Not*, Frederic Shoberl. Nor do we know how Gould and Sigourney were selected as potential contributors, but they would have been obvious choices for a British gift book seeking new US voices. While Sigourney's popularity outstripped Gould's, both women were sought-after contributors to US gift books, some of which were imported into and sold in Britain. They both appeared in the unauthorized *Selections from the American Poets* published in London by Simpkin and Marshall in 1834, and, in 1835, they were the subject of a paired review in the *North American Review*, an American periodical that circulated in Britain.[12] Mackenzie had also been in contact with Gould since at least 1835, when she asked him about publishing a copyright edition of her poetry in England.[13]

Why, then, did the *Forget Me Not* seek out American contributors? There are three possible reasons. First, by publishing Sigourney and Gould's poetry, the *Forget Me Not* could offer British readers something novel while not straying from their expectations for the genre. Sigourney and Gould's poems contained the exotic allure of foreign climes and American Indians, and familiar religious piety and domestic relations. The *Forget Me Not* solicited Gould and Sigourney at a moment when many of its original star authors had died or ceased to contribute, and the popularity of the form was waning; once "especial favourites," annuals were now "regarded almost with indifference," as the *Forget Me Not for 1842* mourned.[14] By publishing American writers, especially those who already had some literary fame in Britain, the *Forget Me Not* could claim much-desired novelty and differentiate itself from its competitors. Second, the editors may have included US writers to appeal to the *Forget Me Not*'s US readers. In the preface to the 1838 edition,

Shoberl suggests that the "kindness" of Sigourney and Gould's contributions is "a token of the warm interest we know to be felt by the kindred population of America for the annual publications of the mother-country in general."[15] During the 1830s and 1840s, Shoberl made arrangements for US distribution of *The Forget Me Not* with Daniel Appleton of New York, and either Appleton or Shoberl may have believed that including American poets would increase sales in the United States.[16] Third, Shoberl may have included US poets as an attempt to halt unauthorized reprints of his annual in the United States; his reference to Americans' "warm interest" may have been a coded dig at such reprints.[17] He or Appleton may have hoped that including US authors (whose poems were always followed by their place of residence), would deter US publishers who did not want to violate copyright law from reprinting the entire *Forget Me Not*.[18] However, I have found no copies of the *Forget Me Not* with a US copyright statement, and if including US poems was a strategy to prevent unauthorized reprints, there is no evidence that it worked.

In any case, reprinters were unlikely to have been deterred from using poems by Americans that had already been republished elsewhere in the United States. Ten of Sigourney's eighteen poems for the *Forget Me Not* had appeared in the United States by the time the annual published them in Britain. Sigourney habitually circulated her poetry through a variety of channels. Her manuscript poems often bear two dates at the top: the first, marking when she sent the poem to a friend, and the second, when she sent it to a magazine. She might later include the poem in a book of her verse. The *Forget Me Not* required Sigourney to send material in late spring for October publication, so it was possible for her to submit an original poem to the *Forget Me Not* and later send it to a weekly or monthly American periodical; this periodical would publish it before it appeared in Britain, and others would reprint it. Gould frankly admitted to Mackenzie that she sent the *Forget Me Not* poems that had previously appeared elsewhere:

> Did you let [Shoberl] know that the "Bubbles" had before appeared in print? I was glad to see it in the Annual, for I think it appeared <u>better</u> there, & thank you for giving it the

> place. But I should be sorry to have Mr Shoberl think that I sent him as original what another had used, or the editor of the paper, who had paid me once for the article suppose that I afterwards sent it abroad as original.[19]

While Shoberl sought permission from Sigourney and Gould, and paid them for their contributions, these poems were not always prior publications that could be protected by copyright. Nevertheless, Gould's observation that that the poem appeared "better" in the *Forget Me Not* than in an American periodical suggests that the British gift book was a handsomer print object but also that it gave her poem cultural capital, authority, and perhaps even improved its aesthetics. Like Bogue's semi-authorized editions of Longfellow and unauthorized series volumes, the *Forget Me Not* was an authorizing material form even if it did not print copyright editions of US texts.

Gould, however, would not write for cultural capital alone. In April 1840, she informed Mackenzie that she had explained to Shoberl that she was "under the necessity of turning my writings to pecuniary account" and must "candidly" inform the publishers that "if the[y] wish the continuance of my contributions, and are in the habit of paying for the matter inserted, I shall gratefully receive such pay as my articles may be esteemed worth to their annual."[20] Publication in Britain was a source of additional income for Gould, who was supporting herself and her family. Sigourney appears to have been less concerned with financial rewards from the *Forget Me Not*, even though her literary income funded her household while her husband's business failed to prosper. Shoberl wrote in August 1839 that he had instructed his American agent, Appleton, to pay her five guineas for her contributions, as he "cannot expect them to be always gratuitous."[21] But she did not make explicit demands for payment, and Shoberl's letter implies that she may have initially gone unpaid. Her correspondence with Shoberl and Mackenzie lacks the attention to the details of business and the competitive nature of the literary marketplace that Melissa Ladd Teed finds in her letters to American publishers, instead favoring the sociable tone of the private sphere.[22] Writing to Mackenzie and Shoberl, Sigourney seems more concerned with the prestige and positioning that came with publishing in the *Forget Me Not*, which she called "the 'parent Annual,' of my father-land."[23] A committed Anglophile, Sigourney was delighted to appear in a volume that had previously featured Felicia Hemans, Letitia Elizabeth Landon, and Mary Russell Mitford, some of the authors whom Sigourney called "the rulers of the lyre in that father-land, which from earliest recollection, I have revered and gloried in."[24]

The *Forget Me Not* imparted cultural capital by inducting Sigourney and Gould into a coterie of genteel British writers. Its paratexts painted its stable of writers as a social circle, "friends" of the *Forget Me Not*, and intimates with whom readers could share their homes and their emotions.[25] Sigourney seems to have especially valued this suggestion of social intimacy with British writers, an intimacy that she furthered through her material dealings with Mackenzie, who acted as her editor. Their correspondence intermingled the business of publication with the affective landscape of the private sphere. Upon receiving one of the poems Sigourney first sent to the *Forget Me Not*, "God Loveth a Cheerful Giver" (retitled "The Mother's Sacrifice" when published), Mackenzie responded with an emotional account of how the poem resonated with his own experience of the death of his daughter and brought comfort to his grieving wife. He also included a poem of his own on the subject of reading Sigourney's poem, to which Sigourney replied describing her own grief upon hearing of the Mackenzies' loss, and including a more personal elegy for their daughter.[26] Publication alongside Mackenzie in the *Forget Me Not* symbolically reinforced this real intimacy, but also extended that intimacy to the other writers in the gift book. The *Forget Me Not* thus became a material manifestation of connections to British writers that Sigourney felt when reading their books, and that she tried to cultivate by sending them copies of her US publications.

At the same time as it introduced them into a private gathering of British intimates, the *Forget Me Not* also presented Sigourney and Gould as part of a national American tradition. Forming such canons and traditions was as much a part of the *Forget Me Not*'s cultural work as generating intimate and private bonds. The preface to the edition for 1840, which sorrowfully considered how many of the gift book's original contributors had died in recent years, proposed that "the page which they inspired when living—when dead should be their monument," rendering the material text itself as a public site for commemoration.[27] Public commemorations continue in the first poem of the volume, a response to the coronation of Queen Victoria in 1838 by Sheffield poet James Montgomery; an image of Victoria also appeared as the volume's frontispiece. Yet while Montgomery's poem begins by depicting Victoria metonymically through the state attire that transforms her into a public figure—her "orb and sceptre," "crown of gold," and "purple robe," it ends by imagining her as a private figure, in her "closet," praying to God for guidance.[28] Similarly, the *Forget Me Not*'s 1844 elegy for the poet laureate Robert Southey mourned a public figure and invited readers to share the publication's personal connection to Southey: the elegy is written by Southey's son-in-law, Edward Quillinan. The elegy considers Southey's position as public poet and private man, asking "what avails it now / That the laurel graced thy brow?," noting Southey's public honors even as it dismisses their importance.[29] It is not simply that the *Forget Me Not* was equally adept at forging private attachments and fulfilling public functions, but that its ability to produce the former increased its capacity to perform the latter.

Likewise, the *Forget Me Not* was both a "friend" of Sigourney and Gould and an authorizing material text that could canonize and nationalize their writing. The preface of the *Forget Me Not for 1838*, the first volume in which their works appeared, explained that both poets "hold a distinguished rank in the literature of the United States," adding that their "compositions in this volume any of our native poets might be proud to own."[30] There is a strong sense of British cultural superiority here when the highest compliment that can be paid to US writing is that it matches up to British productions. Yet the preface acknowledges a distinct US tradition that is broad enough to have its own "ranks," and developed enough to merit the attention of readers in the Old World. Indeed, by suggesting that Sigourney and Gould have been selected because of their "distinguished rank" in the United States, the *Forget Me Not* accepts and further legitimizes the validity of the aesthetic judgements through which that tradition has been formed, insofar as they reflect the *Forget Me Not*'s own. The *Forget*

Me Not continued to identify Sigourney and Gould's contributors as American by appending the location of composition to most of their poems published over the next nine years; in contrast, place of publication was only listed for British contributions when it had a strong connection to the poem's subject. Although several of Sigourney's poems addressed Indigenous American subjects and both poets depicted picturesque American landscapes, even poems like Sigourney's "The Constant Friends"—a lyric that praises flowers as a reminder of God's beauty, and has no particular affinity to place—is labeled "Hartford, Connecticut, U.S.A."[31]

The emphasis on Gould and Sigourney's nationality in the *Forget Me Not* contrasted with the presentation of their works in the US. When Gould's "American Wild Flowers for Queen Victoria" first appeared in the *Forget Me Not for 1842*, it was located in "Newburyport, Mass., U.S."[32] But reprinted in Gould's 1850 *New Poems*, it bore the note, "Written for and published in Ackermann & Co's 'Forget me Not,' London, 1842."[33] The London gift book presented Gould's poem as a specimen of American writing uprooted from its place of origin; the US collection marked it as the product of a transatlantic trade in texts. This transatlantic framing was commonplace in US anthologies which, Paraic Finnerty argues, frequently grouped American and British women poets together: "National designation, even when mentioned, is generally less important than shared gender identity."[34] US anthologies sometimes even de-nationalized Sigourney and Gould's verse. Both were among the fourteen female poets that Rufus Griswold included in his *Poets and Poetry of America* (1842). But the 1849 eleventh edition removed all female writers with the explanation that they now appeared in *The Female Poets of America* (1849). Although Griswold's preface to *The Female Poets* observed that some will find "more decided indications of the infusion of our domestic spirit and temper into literature, in the poetry of our female authors than in that of our men," the reorganization was predicated on the logic that poetry by American women was defined primarily by the author's gender, leaving the national poetic tradition as the preserve of men.[35] In the *Forget Me Not*, however, Sigourney and Gould consistently appeared in mixed gender company, with their nationality as the defining feature of their writing. It was undoubtedly a typo in the *Forget Me Not* for 1841 that located Sigourney's "The Benefactress" in "Hertford, Connecticut (U.S.)," but by spelling the American town like its British namesake the gift book encapsulated how Sigourney and Gould's status as national poets was fashioned transatlantically through their publication in British books.[36]

However, the *Forget Me Not* was not alone in locating a national American tradition within its exclusive and intimate but also public-facing textual space. Gould and Sigourney's poems for the annual explored US nationhood and identity through transatlantic circulation and at the boundary between public and private space. In the poems they submitted to the *Forget Me Not* and in their letters, Gould and Sigourney show that they, too, understood the British private and domestic spaces that the *Forget Me Not* embodied and into which it circulated as places for fashioning an American poetry that used sentimentalism and sympathy to address public issues of citizenship, republicanism, and the shape of the nation itself. As such, the *Forget Me Not* functioned as a space for Gould and Sigourney to experiment with sentimental nationalism to celebrate and critique the development of the United States.

Writing America: Gould's and Sigourney's Sentimental Nationalism

At the core of sentimental literature is a belief that emotional identification with an other, in particular with an other's pain and suffering, can create affinities between individuals and groups. While these empathetic responses are generated between individuals and cultivated in the private sphere, scholars have argued that they did not remain there. Glenn Hendler observes that in the antebellum US, "the experience of sympathetic identification characteristic of the sentimental novel, an act that often took place in the intimate realm of the nuclear family, functioned as psychological preparation for readers' participation not only in the reading public, but also in the political public."[37] Both Mary Louise Kete and Shirley Samuels agree that sentimentalism was a mode for imagining and reinforcing national as well as individual identities.[38]

Nor was this work limited to fiction. In the first half of the nineteenth century, when the reading and writing of poetry was commonplace, sentimental poetry could equally provoke private feelings and transform them into social and national bonds.

Scholars disagree, however, as to the outcome of sentimental literatures' political work: Did it necessarily serve the state's agenda, or could it identify and challenge state violence and speak out for those whom the state disenfranchises, excludes, and harms?[39] Gould and Sigourney's poems for the *Forget Me Not* show the potential for sentimentalism do both of these types of national political work. Gould's "American Wild Flowers for Queen Victoria" uses transatlantic attachments to imagine democratic and liberal citizenship, both reinforcing the state's power to shape individual identity and, as Tricia Lootens has argued of poetess poetry, "elaborating visions of the intimate, personal implications of international affairs."[40] In contrast, Sigourney's poems for the *Forget Me Not* challenge racialized state violence against Indigenous Americans to a greater degree than do the versions of those same poems that were published in the United States. In both cases, British print allowed Gould and Sigourney to explore the potential of sentimentalism and sympathy as a public discourse through which they could interrogate individual and group relations with, and the power of, the state.

"American Wild Flowers for Queen Victoria" illustrates what Elizabeth Maddock Dillon has termed American sentimentalism's "concern with establishing the freedom (the autonomy and constraint) of the liberal subject."[41] In "American Wild Flowers," Gould explores what it means to feel American and claims American citizenship through constructing sympathetic affinities between America and Britain, and especially between herself and the young Queen. These sympathies rely on transatlantic circulations of print, both those imagined in the poem and the poems' own publication in the *Forget Me Not*. The speaker, whose biographical details suggest is Gould herself, argues that there is no conflict between her hereditary ties to Britain and her democratic fervor as an American, suggesting instead that "what, perhaps, inspirits me, / Is British blood that warms my veins." Even the speaker's father, who fought in the Revolutionary War, "loves of England's Queen to hear."[42] The poem makes the case that private, emotional sympathies with Victoria (as opposed to the relation of subject to sovereign experienced by Britons) evidence one's public role as an American citizen.

Gould's admiration of Queen Victoria's domestic conduct facilitates her expression of republican values. The poem begins:

> Fair Sovereign, whose young maiden brow
> With Britain's crown so lately shone—
> A bride so soon—a mother now,
> I bow to thee, but not thy throne.

Gould must symbolically remove the crown that "lately shone," rendering Victoria as only "bride" and "mother," before "bow[ing]" to her personal strengths and not her office. Such personal admiration for Victoria removes her from the political realm, but this is itself an intensely political gesture through which Gould rejects any lingering claim by Britain over her former colonial subjects. Gould captures the entanglement of her sympathetic relation to Victoria and her American citizenship in the second stanza:

> Not drawn by state or titles forth,
> My liberal heart would homage pay ;
> But at the sign of moral worth
> I bring these fresh wild-flowers to lay.

Gould's "liberal heart" suggests both an overflow of sentiment and a republican politics, both of which encourage her to commend Victoria's "moral worth" but not her "state" rank. Gould concludes her poem by framing its "simple wreath" as "A free-will offering of the free," reconfiguring a private gift between two women as demonstration of an idealized American politics that is seemingly performed by Gould as an individual and by a national polis, "the free." In the process of creating sympathetic bonds between the speaker and Victoria as young mother and devoted wife (much is made of her promise to "*Obey!*" Albert), Gould's poem claims her own position as a republican citizen; the forms of affinity that she can offer both produce and are produced by her public and political identity.[43]

"American Wild Flowers" thus runs alongside, although does not entirely join, a tradition of American responses to Queen Victoria identified by Elisa Tamarkin in which Americans are uniquely positioned to appreciate the symbolism and spectacle of monarchy "because they will never be its subjects"; Victoria's lack of political power over Americans makes her resonate all the more fully as a symbol, and so that symbolic resonance becomes indicative of their republican identity. Gould's poem registers the monarch-love that Tamarkin identifies as, paradoxically, an index of feeling American. However, Gould is clear that she is not won over by the symbolic trappings of monarchy, but by an imagined interpersonal relationship with Victoria that springs from the empathy between two women. Nevertheless, this feeling "returns to politics," as Tamarkin argues of other responses to Victoria.[44] Gould can relate to Victoria as one private individual to another because of her American citizenship, just as other Americans could admire the symbolic power of monarchy because they were not subject to Victoria's political power. Moreover, "American Wild Flowers" places print circulation between Britain and the United States at the heart of this transatlantic imagining of national belonging. Gould and her aging father feel the sentimental connection to Victoria and Albert that furthers their republican politics because they have seen the British monarchs' likenesses in print: "aided by the artist's skill, / We've looked upon his form and thine."[45] Transatlantic print culture fosters the intimate and private sentiments toward Britain that help Gould articulate the political experience of being American, and Gould herself participates in that print culture by publishing "Wild Flowers" in the *Forget Me Not*. The gift book and Gould's poem perform the same cultural work, using the British domestic to host a distinctly American tradition of women's poetry in which republican values are expressed through structures of feeling from the private sphere.

Sigourney likewise saw the *Forget Me Not as* a space from which she could speak to the public, political, and national concerns of the United States while also cultivating private sympathies in Britain. Writing to Mackenzie, she imagined the gift book both as a restricted social circle and a site of international relations. Lamenting their failure to meet during her trip to Europe in 1841, Sigourney took comfort in the fact she could "meet you in your own [country], on the 'field of the cloth of gold,' which the beautiful 'Forget Me Not,' spreads; for an introduction to which I forget not, that I am indebted to you."[46] While observing that publishing in the gift book needed an "introduction" similar to those needed for entrance into polite society, Sigourney compares the book to the site of the historic meeting between Henry VIII and Francis I. Her poetry for the *Forget Me Not* exhibited the same blend of private and public spheres, using sentimental tropes and sympathetic affects to celebrate the expansion of national space but also to critique the white violence and displacement of Indigenous people that were intrinsic to US settler-colonialism.

Nina Baym established Sigourney as a "republican public mother" whose early poetry in particular is deeply concerned with patriotism and history even when it espouses domestic ideology.[47] Recently, Elizabeth Petrino has observed that this is particularly true of Sigourney's US gift book poems of the early 1830s, such as "The Indian's Burial of the Child," published in *The Token for 1831*, which offers a "counter-national narrative" that "encouraged her middle-class readers to immerse themselves in a contested political debate about Indian removal and connect with the fate of Native Americans."[48] Critics generally agree that Sigourney's verse became less political toward the end of the 1830s, with Lootens remarking on "Sigourney's progression (or regression) from the public, republican activism of *Traits* [*of the Aborigines of America* (1822)] to the politically resigned, domesticated philanthropic writing of her later years."[49] I want to instead suggest that, rather than suppressing her criticisms of state violence against Indigenous Americans in the 1840s, Sigourney found a new home for it in British print.

Of the twenty-one poems that Sigourney submitted to the *Forget Me Not*, four discussed the violent displacement of Indigenous Americans. While this is fewer than she submitted on domestic or European subjects, the same number of Indian poems appeared in her *Selected Poems* (1839), which contained over one hundred poems, meaning that a much higher proportion of Sigourney's output for the *Forget Me Not* concerned Indian Removal. It seems to have been Sigourney's choice to submit these poems for publication. The very first poem she sent in response to Mackenzie's request for contributions was "The American Indians" (published in the United States as "Our Aborigines"), which contains a visceral image of a white farmer plowing up the bones of an Indian warrior whose ghost then emerges from the soil to invoke "the vengeance of the sky."[50] She may have been encouraged to send further Indian poems by Mackenzie's comment that this poem was an especial favorite of William Wordsworth.[51] Sigourney also likely believed that Indigenous subjects would be welcomed by a British reading public that had embraced Cooper's Leatherstocking Tales. However, it was not only that Removal poetry remained prominent in her *Forget Me Not* contributions even as it diminished in her US collections. In two cases, Sigourney sent variant versions of Indian poems to the *Forget Me Not* that contained stronger criticisms of Removal than did the versions published in the United States and unpacked the ways in which sentimental domesticity was made to prop up national expansion at the expense of Indigenous homes and families.

The first of these two examples, "The Grave of Osceola," is an elegy for the Seminole leader who was captured as he traveled to peace talks near Charleston, South Carolina, in October 1837, and died four months later. Osceola's capture and death became a national and international scandal, although the outrage did not halt the removal of the Seminole from Florida. Two versions of Sigourney's poem exist. She submitted the first to the *Forget Me Not for 1845*, probably in late spring 1844, and it was published there in October of the same year. It subsequently appeared in some US periodicals that probably reprinted it from the British volume.[52] The second version, retitled "Osceola's Grave," circulated in a few US periodicals in 1847 and was also reprinted in the *Illustrated London News* on January 29, 1848.[53]

The poem is a graveside lament, a common genre in which a white observer watches the burial of an Indian, praises their personal nobility and that of the race, and mourns the passing of the race while presenting that passing as inevitable. As Kate Flint observes, in the 1830s and 1840s—at the height of Indian Removal and violent westward expansion—these laments were attacks on Removal, and "an acknowledgement, and celebration, of [white poets'] capacity for compassionate feeling."[54] In Sigourney's poem, however, the absence of white mourning for Osceola mutes any celebration of white compassion:

> Thy pale-fac'd brother knows the tale,
> But renders no reply.
> Why breathes he not some dirge of woe,
> Beside thy resting-place;
> Some lay thy murmuring shade to soothe,
> Thou noblest of thy race?[55]

In a twist on the genre and an unusual restructuring of sentimental bonds, Sigourney engages the readers' sympathy for the non-white Other through the white observer's failure to extend an empathetic response. This creates tension between the poem's content and the expectations of its genre, within which it creates space for a more radical critique of Indian Removal and racialized violence. Moreover, this critique is present to a greater degree in the version of the poem Sigourney published in *Forget Me Not* than in the version she circulated in the United States.

Sigourney habitually revised her poems, but her small yet significant revisions between "The Grave of Osceola" and "Osceola's Grave" work consistently to transform Osceola from the leader of a militant uprising against a conquering force, as he appears in *Forget Me Not*, to a tragically doomed Indian, as he appears in the 1847 American periodicals. The first stanza of the British text calls Osceola "strong heart and bold!" and describe his "fearless bosom," while the second stanza asks, "what spell hath made thy spirit quail? / And dimm'd thy dauntless eye?"[56] The American text instead refers to Osceola as "high heart and brave!" and notes his "heaving bosom," before asking, "what check'd thy pinion's soaring flight? / What dimm'd thy piercing eye?"[57] These changes mute Osceola's rebellious qualities and emphasize his tragic fate. At the same time, the *Forget Me Not* version positions Osceola's death as part of recent and ongoing acts of white violence rather than past actions and inevitable historical processes. In the British printing, Sigourney's use of the perfect tense "hath made" suggests that the betrayal of Osceola continues into the poem's present, against the past tense "check'd" of the American text.

The 1847 US text also omits the entire final stanza of the *Forget Me Not* text. It ends with a restorative stanza in which nature pays

Osceola the funeral tribute that the whites deny him: nature quietly atones for the white people's failure to mourn, although not for their crimes against the Indians, which go without redress. The British version, however, continues by describing a ghostly procession of Indians—"a shadowy train, / The buried chiefs of old"—that gather by the grave, but are eventually "lost in evening's shade."[58] This ending, too, risks muting Sigourney's critique of Indian Removal by recruiting Osceola into a pantheon of vanishing Indians, all of whom disappear as the sun symbolically sets on their race. Yet before they disappear, these Indians cast "a stern, upbraiding eye" on Osceola's grave and, implicitly, on those who dug it, before pointing to "the avenging sky." As well as echoing "The American Indians," "avenging sky" appears in Sigourney's earlier poem "Death of a Father" (1841) where it suggests future punishment for those who commit excessive and repressive violence; after British soldiers kill eight colonists, "the blood soaked earth at Lexington / Invoked the avenging sky."[59] By transferring that phrase into "The Grave of Osceola," Sigourney aligns white settlers with the repressive and unjust British regime and suggests that as these settlers move further West toward "evening's shade," they, too, risk righteous vengeance from the Indians they displace. The *Forget Me Not*'s text thus ends with a threat of violent Indian responses to white settlement that is entirely absent from the poem's American version. It is important not to overstate the radicalism of "The Grave of Osceola," which still trades in stereotypes of the noble Indian and attributes Osceola's death to "a broken heart" rather than to the less romantic reality of chronic malaria. But the British version is more attuned to and critical of the white violence inherent to US nation-building, suggesting that the *Forget Me Not* gave Sigourney space to develop a critical sentimental nationalism.

Sigourney further mourns the displacement and genocide of Indigenous peoples in "Welcome to Wisconsin." Composed three years later for the imminent accession of Wisconsin to statehood, the poem celebrates national expansion. It imagines the nation as a household of sister-states, held together by affective bonds. But in the version apparently intended for the *Forget Me Not*, Sigourney also uses the vocabulary, emotions, and architecture of the private sphere to interrogate the violence of nation-building.[60] Like "The Grave of Osceola," "Welcome to Wisconsin" exists in two versions: a version first printed in the *Hartford Courant* on January 7, 1847, and a manuscript version with the composition date of January 7, 1847, that also notes that the poem was sent to the *Forget Me Not* on March 27, 1847.[61] However, the poem was never published there, as the gift book issued its final volume in autumn 1846. The manuscript Sigourney sent to the *Forget Me Not* does not survive, but her March dating at the top of the surviving manuscript version suggests that she worked from it when writing a fair copy to send to London.[62] In both versions, modeling the nation as a family enables Sigourney, the conduct writer, to advise on political questions by approaching them through the relations and emotions of the private sphere. But, like "The Grave of Osceola," the version marked for the *Forget Me Not* is more critical than the text published in US newspapers about the effects of national expansion on Indigenous Americans.

In the manuscript version, Sigourney refers to Indians as the "exil'd forest-race," creating a stronger image of their mass displacement than the *Courant*'s "forgotten forest son."[63] She also details acts of violence against the Indigenous population, describing how they "left naught behind / Not the echoing heart-wail, when his babes, / And women from the flaming wigwams fled."[64] These lines are absent from the *Courant*'s text. The poem as it circulated in America loses Sigourney's acknowledgement that the national family of sister states expands through a more brutal intersection of public and private spheres: the systematic, state-sanctioned destruction of Indigenous homes. The middle-class British home—the *Forget Me Not*'s intended destination—acts as a space where Sigourney can illustrate the contradictory roles of private space in a national politics that is sustained by the sanctification of the white home as a pure and apolitical sphere, and by dismissing Indigenous homes as expendable impediments to national expansion. In doing so, "Welcome to Wisconsin" exposes the racialized construction of private space in the antebellum US, puncturing the fiction of its separateness from the political realm.

The version of "Welcome to Wisconsin" labeled for the *Forget Me Not* also navigates the tension between the continued presences of

Indigenous names in US cartography and the absence of Indigenous peoples from their former lands. In a stanza that is missing entirely from the *Courant*'s version of the poem, Sigourney observes that America's "streams and mountains" "bear / His baptism from Ontario's thunder-lake / To where the Talulua [Tallulah] leaps its rocky verge." White Americans, however,

> declare the names
> He seal'd upon them, and we learn their lore,
> Repeating daily, like a lesson'd child,
> His dialect, but not revering him.[65]

In this stanza, Sigourney almost rewrites her 1834 poem "Indian Names," which juxtaposed the persistence of Indian nomenclature with the disappearance of Indians themselves: "But their memory liveth on your hills, / Their baptism on your shore, / Your everlasting rivers speak / Their dialect of yore." "Indian Names" refuses to frame the disappearance of Indians as an inevitable vanishing, instead charging its white audience with complicity in violent displacement—"Ye drive them from their father's lands, / Ye break of faith the seal"—and suggesting that divine judgement may follow—"Think ye the *soul's blood* may not cry / From that far land to him?"[66] Neither version of "Welcome to Wisconsin" is as damning of colonial violence as this earlier poem. Unlike in "The Grave of Osceola," there is no suggestion of vengeance. But rather than simply noting that white Americans are "uttering his names, / Speaking his words, but not remembering him," as in the *Courant*'s text, the manuscript for the *Forget Me Not*, like "Indian Names" before it, invites the reader to articulate those names: "Ontario," "Wyalusing," "Oregon."[67] Moreover, the manuscript poem inverts the expected hierarchy of civilized whites and backward Indians by comparing the settlers to "a lesson'd child." Here, Sigourney uses the familial relations that underpin the sister-states metaphor to challenge the logic of national expansion. In doing so, the version of "Welcome to Wisconsin" marked for the *Forget Me Not* exposes contradictions in the sentimental nationalism that it also employs.

However, both versions of "Welcome to Wisconsin" finally retreat from their criticisms of settler-colonialism and end with near-identical assertions that Indigenous Americans should convert to Christianity and assimilate with the white settlers. The version for the *Forget Me Not* concludes by papering over the violent chasms it has exposed, imagining the "brighter day" that will follow for "civilized Indians."[68] Joining the national polity requires that Indigenous Americans conform to Christianity and middle-class domesticity. Though Sigourney criticizes white violence against Indigenous people, the whiteness of the American nation cannot be compromised. Attacks on white nationalism and settler-colonialism are, therefore, limited in the British texts of "Welcome to Wisconsin" and "The Grave of Osceola."

Nevertheless, Sigourney's poetry for the *Forget Me Not* is certainly more critical of the policy of Indian Removal as state-sanctioned violence than the poetry she published in the United States, especially in comparison to her collections of verse.[69] For Sigourney, the British gift book was therefore another kind of semi-private space in which she could continue the political work of the poetess that she seems to have felt was incompatible with her lasting place as a woman poet. But whether or not her poetry for *Forget Me Not* is more politically radical is a complex question. In her discussions of the cultural work of Indian Removal poetry in Britain, Flint observes that it functioned as a site for depoliticized sympathy. She argues that, "Locating loss in a foreign land that is no longer the responsibility of one's nation is a way of sharing the sentiment of nostalgia with . . . readers while sidestepping the need to engage with any kind of responsibility for having brought such change about."[70] Similarly, Sigourney could invite British readers to sympathize with the plight of Indigenous peoples while knowing that it was not their responsibility to effect change. Unlike the Black abolitionists I discuss in the final chapter who wanted to enlist British support in the fight against slavery, Sigourney did not seek to inspire the *Forget Me Not*'s readers to act or protest on behalf of the Indigenous peoples she depicted. Instead, the cultural work performed by these poems is to generate an Anglo-American community of sympathy around Indigenous Americans in the absence of such a community in the United States. If private sympathies could encompass national politics, then national political issues also engendered a reading community of sympathetic strangers.

Publication in the *Forget Me Not*, therefore, furthered both Sigourney's and Gould's performances as American poetesses:

figures whose strategic deployment of private sentiments and spaces produced national verse. The overlapping geographies of the gift book—its public and private orientations, its spanning of household, national, and transatlantic scales—created a terrain for transforming empathy between individuals into national sentiments that was also set comfortably apart from the United States. The *Forget Me Not*'s physical publication outside the US, and its claims over the imagined, supranational territory of "home" gave Gould a focal distance that sharpened her vision of American character and gave Sigourney a vantage point from which to survey the racialized violence that accompanied US expansion. But for both poets, the geographies of *Forget Me Not* also made the national sentimental mode a means of securing communities defined by shared sympathy and shared whiteness. For Gould, the Anglo-American sympathies through which she defined American identity were predicated on the common "blood" of a shared racial lineage. And while Sigourney's poems critiqued national politics through encouraging sympathy for a non-white Other, that sympathy does not alter the fundamental whiteness of America itself: her poems offer Indigenous Americans no alternatives to death or assimilation.

Understanding how Sigourney in particular used the *Forget Me Not* to fashion national sentiments that aligned US nationhood with an Anglo-American whiteness is important for understanding how and why she attempted to continue this strategy in publications elsewhere. Her 1842 travelogue, *Pleasant Memories of Pleasant Lands*, draws on her visit to Britain and Europe in 1840 and 1841 and on her experiences publishing with the *Forget Me Not*. Sharing material and textual qualities with the *Forget Me Not*, *Pleasant Memories* uses semi-private domestic and textual spaces alongside the transatlantic circulation of British texts as training grounds for US readers to learn the sympathetic responses and bonds necessary for a national culture of sentiment and a national American literature.

Transatlantic Circulation and Sentimental American Publics in *Pleasant Memories of Pleasant Lands*

Pleasant Memories of Pleasant Lands is not an annual, although its structure, content, affects, and material form echo that genre.

Rather than a continuous travel narrative, the book is a series of poems, each followed by short prose sections that extrapolate on details in the verse, creating a similar miscellaneous structure to that of *Forget Me Not* and the US gift books Sigourney edited. Sigourney's preface for *Pleasant Memories* aims for the same domestic intimacy as *Forget Me Not*. She locates the book's origins in "notes of a Journal regularly kept" and proclaims that her readers are as "a brother and a sister unto me," suggesting that, by publishing the book, she has expanded a private audience rather placing the book in the public sphere. Yet she also acknowledges the book's public character by observing that she would not "embarrass and embroil God's creatures" by exposing Britain's faults.[71] Sigourney wanted her travelogue to mimic gift book materiality as well as gift book rhetoric. She was disappointed that the book's American publisher, James Munroe of Boston, did not include the steel-engraved plates, characteristic of annuals, that appeared in the British edition published by Tilt and Bogue, and "which seem to be so much liked."[72] As in Bogue's illustrated editions of Longfellow, the British publisher placed Sigourney's work in a desired and prestigious format, and perhaps relied on the engraved plates to secure protection from reprinting (Tilt and Bogue's edition appeared two months after the US publication, when imported editions were already being announced in the *Publishers' Circular*). Sigourney was then pleased when Munroe changed his mind and decided to add more plates to two hundred copies of the book's 1844 second edition, and "furnish them for gift books."[73]

In *Pleasant Memories*, Sigourney included accounts of public sights of historic interest, but also of her visits to the homes of British writers. For some years before she traveled to Britain, Sigourney attempted to cultivate transatlantic literary relations by sending editions of her works as gifts: British recipients of her verse included the poet laureates Robert Southey and William Wordsworth, and the popular novelists Anna Maria Hall (Mrs. S. C. Hall) and Maria Edgeworth. Sometimes she added an invitation to contribute to one of the many American gift books she edited, which was usually declined. Sigourney's earliest—and rather hostile—biographer, Gordon Haight, implies that she was imposing herself upon these writers by "collecting letters of introduction" and regarding anyone who had politely replied to her letters "as acquaintances with whom no further formalities were necessary," but his charges of vulgarity are unfair.[74] It was common for American writers to correspond with British writers whom they admired, and to arrange visits if they traveled across the Atlantic. While British writers made snide jokes about streams of Americans turning up with letters of introduction in hand, they generally welcomed those visitors all the same. Having also published alongside several of these writers (or members of their circles) in the *Forget Me Not*, Sigourney had more reason than most to think she would be warmly received, especially as Mackenzie also told her in March 1838 that Wordsworth and Southey were both "Sigourneyites."[75]

By the mid-nineteenth century, the homes of writers like Wordsworth and Southey functioned as extensions of those writers' published works rather than as entirely private spaces; Samantha Matthews argues that they "had a complex public significance as homes of the major poets, shrines to 'genius' connoting a spirit of place that went far beyond bricks, mortar and family life."[76] Sigourney suggests that her visits to British writers fell somewhere between personal encounters and public events by merging these writers' persons with their published works. She notes that Wordsworth has "the same, full, expanded brow, which we see in his busts and engravings" and Maria Edgeworth is "Truthful and tender as thy pictured page."[77] By implying that these authors are already public property because they have circulated themselves in print, Sigourney justifies publishing accounts of what some might have taken to be private visits. *Pleasant Memories* thus operates at the same fluid boundary between public and private as did the *Forget Me Not*, and likewise entwines that boundary with the transatlantic print economy.

By writing about her visits, Sigourney portrays herself as a trusted friend of the British literati, which she hoped would increase her literary standing at home. But Sigourney also circulates semi-private British texts in *Pleasant Memories* to cultivate a sympathetic audience for her own works in the United States. Central to these efforts was Sigourney's account of her attempt to visit Southey, a writer whose role as poet laureate made him a public figure as well as a private individual. Sigourney had requested a visit with Southey, but by 1840, his advanced dementia made this impossible. His wife, poet Caroline Bowles, wrote to Sigourney to explain, and reflected on the personal strain of caring for her husband: "Scarcely can I keep hold of the last poor comfort of believing that he still knows me," Bowles wrote, adding, "The last three years have done on me the work of twenty." Without a visit to include, Sigourney instead chose to print sections of Bowles's letter, adding that she could "trust to be forgiven for selecting from one of her recent letters, a few passages for the friends, who in this western world have admired, in almost every department of literature, the inventive genius of Dr. Southey."[78] By referring to Bowles's "recent letters," Sigourney projects an extended intimate friendship that she then expands to include all "friends" who have read and admired Southey. If the transatlantic circulation of Sigourney's poetry in *Forget Me Not* located her as a trusted friend of her fellow contributors and of the gift book's readers, then Sigourney here imagines similar intimacies between US readers of British reprints. The public domain status of Southey's writing in the United States produces a community whose members are united by their shared British reading.

Sigourney further ties this community together through encouraging a common emotional response to Southey and Bowles's suffering: the sympathetic identification at the core of sentimental literature. Sigourney observes that she expects this news of Southey's decline to "awaken deep sympathy here, as well as in Europe." She even models this sympathy for her readers, ending her sonnet to Southey with her own emotional response to the news of his decline: "They told me, and I wept, / As on my pilgrim way o'er England's vales I kept."[79] In imaging the American mourning for Southey, Sigourney creates a fantasy of collectivity in which a mass of American readers connect with one another through a shared reading experience that is also a shared emotional experience. Most importantly, this experience connects these readers with Sigourney herself. What remains unsaid is that the "friends" who read and weep for Southey are also readers—and likely purchasers—of *Pleasant Memories*. In cultivating sympathy for Southey, Sigourney produces what Lauren Berlant called an "intimate public" for her own work. Berlant defines intimate publics as consumer communities whose purchase of "texts and things" that seem to express their "core interests and desires" confirms a sense that, before this market existed, there was "a world of strangers who would be emotionally literate in each other's experience of power, intimacy, desire, and discontent."[80] By sympathetically identifying with Southey, Bowles, and Sigourney, these readers become a public who share emotional attachments to each other. But they also become ideal purchasers of Sigourney's travelogue and her other sentimental writings. Sigourney, therefore, uses the transatlantic circulation of print to create empathetic bonds that produce a reading public for herself at home.

As *Pleasant Memories* continues, Sigourney transfers the sympathy she encourages for the Southeys onto herself by imagining herself in the location between life and death that Southey occupies, as Bowles describes it: "the dull cold ear of death is not more insensible than his." While traveling, Sigourney spends a considerable time visiting liminal spaces between the living and the dead: the Necropolis at Glasgow, Abbotsford House (where Walter Scott's writing lamp is still "partially filled with oil" though Scott himself is "closed in the darkness of the grave"), and the cemetery of Litchfield Cathedral. She transcribes epitaphs into the text, echoing the pairing of intimate sociability and public commemoration that was the trademark of *Forget Me Not*. Her occupation of a space between living and dead reaches its peak during a visit to Westminster Abbey, in which Sigourney follows a visit to the graves of famous Britons by imagining a lack of commemoration for her own death overseas. Moving from the city of the dead to the city of the living, Sigourney is overcome with a "suffocating fear" of dying in the crush of London's streets: "You might never get clear of them, and breathe freely in your native woods again; and then comes a deep feeling, that you are as nothing among them; that you might fall in the streets and die, unnoticed or trodden down."[81] The sympathetic response that Sigourney encourages towards Southey has prepared readers for the sympathetic bonds that she now seeks to create between them and herself. Slipping into the second person, she asks them to share her "deep feeling," and to thus forestall the abandonment she fears.

At the same time, this scene of affiliation between author and reader evokes an archetypally American landscape—the "native woods"—in the middle of the British metropolis. In reaching across the Atlantic, the familiar bond between American reader and American author also generates national feeling and belonging. Not only does "weeping" and "sympathy" for Southey train Sigourney's American "friends" to respond to her own authorship, but it prepares them to participate in a national mourning that Sigourney anticipates will await her on her return to the United States. In the final poem of *Pleasant Memories*, she asks:

> Since I last these scenes surveyed,
> Who have in the tomb been laid?
> Who the bitter tear have shed
> O'er the bosom of the dead?
> Who beneath the sable pall
> Hath the poet's lyre let fall?
> Who, that won a nation's trust,
> Sleep in silence and in dust?[82]

Having cultivated their skills in sentimental affinities through their responses to British authors, American readers are now ready to propagate the "culture of true feeling" that Berlant argues characterized American public discourse and popular literature from the 1840s onwards, and that would make them ideal recipients of Sigourney's own sentimental republican poetry.[83]

The sentimental nationalism of *Pleasant Memories*—its use of transatlantic emotional bonds to create an American reading public held together by shared empathy—is less overtly political than "The Grave of Osceola" and "Welcome to Wisconsin." Moreover, it lacks even their limited critique of US nation-building. *Pleasant Memories* places emotional affinities between Anglo-Saxon nations at the heart of the American reading public. Although never overtly stated, the whiteness of the American public that Sigourney cultivates is assumed and assured—she calls the British settlers that landed in Massachusetts "our ancestors," a phrase that blurs the political work of nation-building with hereditary descent and projects whiteness onto her readers.[84] The whiteness of the sentimental national public that Sigourney fashioned through transatlantic circulation reminds us that such movements of print are not inherently radical. If transatlantic circulation gave Sigourney the opportunity to reflect on the dispossession and murder of Indigenous populations, then it also provided space for her to construct white publics in the absence of any such criticism. *Pleasant Memories* shows that the US national politics articulated at the boundaries of public and private space in Britain could reinforce the whiteness of public power and private emotion in the antebellum United States.

Sigourney's print strategies in *Pleasant Memories* produced a largely conservative sentimental nationalism, but this did not stop her uses of circulation being highly controversial. After *Pleasant Memories* began to circulate in Britain, Sigourney found herself at the center of a transatlantic scandal concerning her decision to publish Bowles's letter in her book. Like the travelogue itself and the *Forget Me Not*, this scandal illustrates how the boundary between private and public space in Britain provided terrain for mapping American literary culture. But British critics' attempts to police Sigourney's uses of transatlantic print circulation and her violations of unspoken covenants of polite society show the heated responses that could be directed at a poetess deemed to have stepped outside the private sphere. The backlash against Sigourney's use of supposedly private materials reveals anxieties about what might happen if the American poetess instead decided to commandeer the public domain and place unrestricted circulation, rather than the liberal subject and the private property of copyright, at the heart of American literature.

Sigourney's Scandal, and the Future of American Literary Culture

The British press were not as quick to forgive Sigourney for sharing Bowles's letter in her travelogue as she had hoped. A new London periodical called the *Story-Teller*, edited by Robert Bell (who would go on to publish the series "Bell's English Poets"), attacked Sigourney for several violations of confidence. The magazine charged her with doctoring Bowles's letter, claiming she had added "phrases implying intimacy" to the letter, and with "pretend[ing] an intimacy with a distinguished writer only for the base purpose of publishing a scrap of a letter to the world at a moment of domestic affliction."[85] In other words, the *Story-Teller* accused Sigourney of exposing a private letter containing private feelings to the public gaze, and of obtaining Bowles's letter with precisely that intention. These accusations were picked up by more prominent publications like the *Athenaeum*, *Tait's Edinburgh Magazine*, and the *Eclectic Magazine*, which led to aggrieved responses from American magazines like *Brother Jonathan*, which called the episode "a disgraceful hoax" that sought to profit "at the expense of a woman and a stranger."[86] Sigourney could prove that she did not adulterate the letter relatively easily; trusted famous friends with transatlantic reputations, like the chemist Benjamin Silliman, testified that they had seen the original letter and that the printed version was a true copy. But Sigourney found it harder to shake off the charge of putting a familial letter into print. The question remained: Was this a violation of private confidence and social rules, as the *Story-Teller* claimed, or a difference in understanding between Sigourney and her British readers over what it meant for a letter to be private and whether her readership was truly public?

Sigourney was not the first American writer to fall foul of ambiguous divisions between public and private in British literary society. In 1835, Nathaniel Parker Willis was similarly charged with violating the privacy of his British hosts. A gifted writer of light sketches, Willis penned descriptions of the literary soirees of the Countess of Blessington and others for the *New York Mirror*. When these columns were reprinted in the *Liverpool Journal*, Willis was denounced by the *Quarterly Review*'s John Lockhart for working as a journalist when he had been invited as a guest, ignoring the expectations of discretion that accompanied offers of hospitality and placing his own self-publicizing above his hosts' privacy. "As far as we are acquainted with either English or American literature," Lockhart raged, "this is the first example of a man creeping into your home, and forthwith printing—accurately or inaccurately, no matter which—before your claret is dry on his lips—unrestrained *table-talk on delicate subjects, and capable of compromising individuals*."[87] British periodicals situated Sigourney's alleged transgressions in relation to Willis's, with the *Story-Teller* drawing a direct comparison between the two writers, and the *Athenaeum* referring to Sigourney's writings as "pencillings," recalling *Pencillings by the Way* (1835), the volume of his European and British columns that Willis published.[88]

At the center of Willis's and Sigourney's scandals were contested and unstable categorizations of domestic and textual spaces. As Hendler observes, by describing Blessington's salon as a "home," Lockhart presented these gatherings as more private than they were.[89] Blessington's guests were expected to share details and guest lists orally with others in the same social circles. Willis's error was putting such information into print, where it might circulate to a wider public and where others could reprint it. Likewise, in the mid-nineteenth century, letters were at best semi-private. Matthew Pethers and Kate Thomas have discussed how, in America and Britain respectively, newly modernized postal services brought private individuals into contact with the public mechanisms of state bureaucracy; "When it came to correspondence," Thomas argues, "public and private were intermixed, intermediated."[90] Letter writers, especially well-known authors like Bowles, might expect their missives to be shared with anyone invited into the recipient's house, just as Sigourney would have expected the manuscript poems she sent to friends and neighbors on the occasions of births, marriages, and, most often, deaths, to be shared with others in the recipients' social circles. Sigourney herself engaged with the complex status of the letter in her conduct books *Letters to Young Ladies* (1833) and *Letters to Mothers* (1838), which used the epistolary form to "unite the public and private spheres," offering the illusion of intimate personal advice within the mass reproduction of print.[91]

In *Pleasant Memories*, too, Sigourney uses Bowles's letter to create intimate bonds with the sentimental public that she addresses and constructs. By styling her readers as "friends," Sigourney frames her publication of the letter as an extension of the established social ritual of sharing correspondence with one's acquaintances. Held together by bonds of empathy, the national public that she cultivates is no different from a familial audience except in terms of its scale. But other writers saw a clear distinction between sharing a letter socially and putting it in print, however intimate the writerly address. Writing to Sigourney after the publication of, and controversy around *Pleasant Memories*, Maria Edgeworth emphasized that "I only request that my letters should not be published—you are quite at liberty to show whatever I send or say to any friends you may wish to show it to."[92] Edgeworth's distinction suggests that the true problem with Sigourney's publication of her letter was not her sharing its content *en masse*, but the possibility of the letter being reprinted, placing the question of who read the text and in what context beyond either the author's or the recipient's control.

The uncontrollable circulation of Bowles's letter was central to *The Story-Teller*'s criticism of Sigourney. The periodical suggested that, once in print, the letter would be "copied, and read, and circulated with avidity," and explicitly linked Sigourney's supposed "violations of domestic confidence, these shreds and patches of literary tailoring" with the unauthorized reprinting of British literature in America: "They have no literature of their own, and so they must come to us for a supply."[93] There is, then, far more at stake here than one woman's violation of another's "domestic confidence." The *Story-Teller* made Sigourney's publication of Bowles's letter a proxy for the American reprinting of British literary works in general; Sigourney's alleged violation of privacy is equated with the American publishing industry's supposed violation of English authors' private literary property. The timing of *Pleasant Memories*'s publication in Britain in 1843 certainly helped this analogy. The previous year had seen Charles Dickens's tour of the United States in which he spoke out against the American reprinting of his works, and British MP Thomas Noon Talfourd's Copyright Amendment Act (1842), which allowed Britain to make bilateral international copyright treaties with other nations. Ironically, by associating Sigourney's alleged violation of social rules with American copyright law's treatment of British authors, the *Story-Teller* performed the same overlapping of private and public spheres that Sigourney employed in *Pleasant Memories*, and encouraged the very reprintings of Bowles's letter that it condemned and allegedly feared. *Tait*'s magazine reprinted the supposedly offending passage, and while the *Athenaeum* claimed to notice the passage "with reluctance" it nevertheless published more than one article about the controversy.[94]

Ultimately, Sigourney and the *Story-Teller* both use *Pleasant Memories* to make contrasting arguments about how American literature and authorship can emerge from a transatlantic economy of reprinting. For Sigourney, the circulation of reprinted British texts, like Southey's poetry and Bowles's letter, do not present a barrier to the development of American authorship, as writers like Willis and Cornelius Mathews vocally argued. Instead, this reprinting creates conditions through which Americans might train themselves as sentimental readers and learn to become the type of public that could support native authorship like Sigourney's. This investment in reprinting between Britain and the United States echoes Sigourney's authorial practice within the United States, where she circulated her own poems in multiple formats—public and private—and relied on periodicals reprinting them from one another to build her reputation. For the *Story-Teller*, however, it was impossible for American print culture to become a mature national culture when it relied on these forms of recirculation rather than cultivating US authors through international copyright. So while the *Story-Teller* was ostensibly accusing Sigourney of a private transgression, her real crime was to suggest that systems of reprinting, rather than author-centric markets, offered opportunities for writers to claim positions of autonomy and legitimacy and to address, and even to form, national publics.

It is difficult to say which side won the debate over *Pleasant Memories*. Sigourney felt compelled to remove the section on Southey, including Bowles's letter, from the book's second edition, even asking Monroe if he could contact a British reprinter and "enter into an arrangement with him, to have the same literary alterations made in his next edition, which we shall make. . . . I am particularly desirous that this should be done."[95] When she sent this "improved" edition to her friend British author Mrs. S. C. Hall, she remarked that "'I must be a dull scholar if some of the criticisms from your side of the Ocean had failed to instruct me. Give my old volume of the "Memories" to your pretty dogs to nibble on and tear, if you choose."[96] But in the United States, the scandal prompted exactly the extension of sympathy she had imagined in her travelogue. *Brother Jonathan* refuted the charge that Sigourney had attempted to claim intimacies with Bowles to increase her reputation by contending that such a move was unnecessary because there were already "some millions of people who know Mrs. Sigourney through her writings." The same article also located Sigourney as a national writer, claiming that "women of genius" like her were "the stars of our national banner, the plumage that glitters upon the breast of our American eagle."[97] In the United States, the transatlantic circulation of texts in *Pleasant Memories* and the ensuing scandal gave Sigourney what she had envisioned in the book: a leading place in a sentimental national literary culture.

The scandal around *Pleasant Memories* showed that the intersection of the transatlantic materials of American literature and the fluid boundary between British public and private space was a perilous yet productive terrain for American women writers. When Gould and Sigourney were backed by the consecrating power of the *Forget Me Not*, they could reap its financial, reputational, and creative benefits. The gift book gave them space to explore the potential and the limits of sentimentalism as a public form through which to address US expansion, nationhood, and citizenship. However, the backlash from British periodicals when Sigourney conducted her own transatlantic circulation of texts in *Pleasant Memories* suggests that the British literary establishment was not willing to allow US women to manipulate a transatlantic culture of reprinting in order to fashion themselves as national writers. Above all, the scandal over *Pleasant Memories* distilled the ways in which a mid-century transatlantic print culture made British private spaces and the print forms that evoked them powerful arenas for debating very public questions about the shape and mechanisms of a national print culture and the violent means by which the US nation itself was expanding. In Sigourney's transatlantic authorial self-fashioning, as in *Forget Me Not*, British domestic spaces and American nationhood as well as private sympathies and public modes of address prove to be mutually constitutive. Sigourney's transatlantic practices also show how systems of reprinting that transmitted texts across the Atlantic could be a means of imagining a national literary culture within the United States. As the next chapter shows, she was not alone in attempting to forge a national culture through transatlantic reprinting; that tactic was also used by Britain's "American" magazines.

CHAPTER 5

"American" Magazines and the Failures of Transatlantic Reprinting

Between 1830 and 1860, three "American" magazines appeared in London: the *American Miscellany* (1839–1840), the *Great Western Magazine* (1842), and the *American Magazine* (1851–52).[1] Each claimed to be pioneering the transmission of US periodical literature to British readers and, implicitly through their titles and explicitly in their editorials, each promised to showcase a national American literature. Despite opening with confident predictions of success, all three magazines folded within a year of their first issues. Having neither influential literary figures among their staff nor any discernable impact on periodicals that followed, these "American" magazines have been almost entirely forgotten. Yet this chapter argues that these magazines are worth recovering both for the ways in which they tried to use the formal and material qualities of the periodical to authorize a national American literature and for their failures to do so. Examining the nationalizing strategies of these magazines illuminates how and why Britain emerged as a space for staging a unifying white national culture in a period where regional print markets structured the US print landscape and sectional tensions over slavery threatened to split the nation apart. Examining their rapid collapses illustrates that there were limits to the material forms through which British print could authorize American literature and limits to models for a national literature that could be authorized through British print.

In Britain and the United States, periodicals' physical forms, publication rhythms, and material circulations created different authorizing discourses from those manifested by the material forms of printed books. The Christmas books, handsome authorized editions, and gift books that previous chapters examined associated the value of US authorship and writing with the endurance of the individual volume. The illustrations, bindings, adverts, and other paratexts that authorized that publisher's edition, championed the US author and text, and consecrated a national American tradition also claimed for the volume a permanent position on purchasers' shelves. Periodicals, on the other hand, have a contradictory relationship to endurance. Individual issues claim authority through their contemporaneity, with a magazine's date-stamped cover materializing the title's and the form's ability to speak to the times. Yet the ideal periodical also seems to have always existed, its rhythms of production marking time in its readers' lives. Serial releases and the repetition of formal elements across issues create a sense of a periodical's endurance in the past and what Matthew Levay has called "the promise of futurity and continuation upon which some periodicals can never deliver, but to which they almost always aspire."[2] Yet, James Mussell argues, because the ideal periodical can never end, it "can only offer a kind of perpetual middle, a precarious vantage point from which to view the past, neatly lined up and numbered in the form of archived back issues, and the future, also lined up, if only in virtual form."[3] These temporal tensions and precarities contribute to the essential instability of the periodical form.[4]

Such tensions and instabilities are amplified in the three London "American" magazines this chapter discusses. Their limited lifespans mean that the magazines' stabilizing serial pasts and futures are purely projections; for the twenty-first century scholar, who knows the magazine's fate, they sit almost at odds with the few numbers bound in library volumes. These magazines remind us that stabilizing pasts and futures are continuously created and recreated by each number from a "precarious" middle: like the series discussed in chapter 3, periodicals redraw, and often shift, the qualities and forms that define the whole in every successive issue. This perpetual (re)production of the whole by its constituent parts echoes how each of these magazines brought into being the national American literary culture they claimed to display: a tradition that a decentralized print culture and sectional tensions over slavery made impossible to sustain within the United States.

To different degrees and ends, all three magazines argued that the defining characteristic of American literature was its polyphony, yet this chorus of disparate voices could only be realized in a British magazine. At a geographical distance from the slavery debate and under their unifying "American" titles, these magazines pulled together materials that may never have circulated alongside one another in the United States, and they offered either space to safely stage and resolve conflicts over slavery or the possibility of side-stepping those conflicts entirely. The problem, however, was that this chorus of voices that unified a white citizenry by respecting its regional and sectional differences proved as impossible to sustain in Britain as in the United States, as evinced by the magazines' rapid ends.

Although their tones vary and they seek different readerships, the three magazines shared strategies for attracting readers, signaling "Americanness" through the corporate form of the magazine, and producing their nationalizing polyphony. All three magazines understood both the importance of the theater as a space for making national culture and their position within what Peter Reed, discussing theater culture in the Early Republic, has called a "print-performance culture." In such a culture, stage and print overlap and printed and verbal forms "produce and record traces of performance," but also "reshape performance through their respective aesthetic conventions and production practices."[5] In particular, the magazines traded on the popularity of the Yankee comedy: a dramatic form that centered on the humorous antics of the archetypal New Englander, Brother Jonathan, and that had itself emerged as distinctly American through its staging on either side of the Atlantic. "American" magazines sought to piggyback on the success of Yankee comedies, reprinting sketches that showcased the genre's trademark humor and mirrored its plot lines in which aimable (and not-so-aimable) confusion and factional division among white US citizens resolve to harmony and unity.

I begin by situating the magazines within a transatlantic, urban popular culture in which periodicals and the stage were overlapping and mutually sustaining forms, before detailing how the Yankee's transatlantic theatrical circulations transformed him from regional archetype to national icon. I then examine how these magazines replicated these circulations in their own reprinting of US texts. All three magazines drew the majority of their contexts from US periodicals and gift books. In her landmark study of the culture of reprinting within the antebellum United States, Meredith McGill sketches a complex relationship between that reprinting and literary nationalism, arguing that US reprint periodicals like the *New World* and *Little's Living Age* registered cultural ties to and dependence on British print while also radically decontextualizing and recontextualizing their selections, creating miscellanies that cut across the political and class divisions that divided the British periodicals from which they reprinted.[6] Similar remapping took place when US texts were reprinted in London "American" magazines. In the recombining of US materials, the magazines created regionally and, in some cases, politically diverse selections of texts that would have not appeared alongside one another in US periodicals. Variously, the magazines used Britain as a space to transcend regional difference and project a national culture, and to stage and resolve sectional conflicts at a safe distance from the United States. Repositioned under the nationalizing banner of the *American Miscellany*, texts from New England and even Old England become emblems of national culture. The *Great Western* attempted to give voice to different perspectives on slavery, but its reprintings also transformed intranational differences within texts—between regions, country and city, and social classes—into contrasts between Britain and the United State that muted the polyphonic chorus for which the magazine aimed. The *American Magazine*'s reprintings restaged romantic comedics, whose plots resembled the Yankee comedies, as stories of national reunion, using British print to imagine the healing of sectional tensions that were, in reality, growing ever deeper.

The swift failures of these magazines suggest that the national American traditions they projected were untenable. The *American Miscellany*'s nationalizing theatricality, the *Great Western*'s representative polyphony, and the *American Magazine*'s recurring romances of reconciliation all came under strain shortly before each magazine ceased production. In the absence of archival material about the production and circulation of these magazines, precisely why each of them failed remains impossible to confirm. But the necessarily speculative nature of my histories of these magazines suits their essentially speculative mode. Each sought to project a present and future for American literature that could only be realized in print forms that were assembled and circulated elsewhere, and that relied on contingency and chance for their production. The brief lives and ideological tensions of these magazines remind us that British print and transatlantic circulation did not always successfully map geographies, aesthetics, and subjects for competing models of American literature. Instead, the transatlantic materials also produced Other American literatures that did not survive to contest the terrain of a national tradition, but only sounded briefly in Britain before sputtering into silence.

Making the Yankee in Britain: The Transatlantic Stage and the Reprint Magazine

In both Britain and the United States in the first half of the nineteenth century, the periodical press and the stage were closely connected. Writers like Cornelius Mathews and Nathaniel Parker Willis in the United States and George Augustus Sala and Douglas Jerrold in Britain wrote both for the stage and for periodicals like the *New York Mirror* and *Punch,* which themselves reported on theater news and reviewed the latest productions. Furthermore, theater historian Jeffrey Richards suggests that in post-Revolution America, periodicals acted as a surrogate for the stage for those removed from urban centers, even sometimes printing real or mock playscripts; print was not a retreat from performance so much as "a stimulus to observe or at least imagine performance."[7] Periodical reading could also be a social performance. As Michael Collins observes in his study of performance and the nineteenth-century short story, coffeehouse periodical reading embodied and made visible the print public sphere, and, in antebellum New York particularly, confirmed one's membership of a politically engaged, largely male audience who were also frequent patrons of the theater.[8] Collins, Jenna Gibbs, and Amy Hughes have all argued that print and theater need to be understood as "parallel mediums" that worked together to shape the politics and aesthetics of mid-century transatlantic culture.[9]

The material texts and formats of periodicals also operated in dialogue with theatrical trends and genres. Antebellum American magazines presented themselves as spectacles, mirroring one of the era's most popular dramatic techniques.[10] The 1830s and early 1840s witnessed a fad for "mammoth sheets," cheap periodicals whose standard dimensions were two feet by three feet, but could reach over one thousand square inches per sheet.[11] While British publishers did not adopt this trend, other aspects of their periodicals evoked theatrical performance, including cover illustrations that resembled *tableaux-vivants*, and banner headlines that resembled playbills. Anne Horn suggests that both Victorian stage performances and magazine forms were characterized by "variety and interruption rather than by focus and continuity"; the typical Victorian theatrical evening offered several performances, aligning with the composite contents a magazine presented to its readers.[12] These shared features alerted magazine readers that they were engaging with what Josette Féral describes as a "framed theatrical space," that is, a space with which one interacts as a spectator, rendering the objects within that space as representations and enabling "the construction of a fiction."[13]

These theatrical features were particularly prominent in US reprint magazines. The two most famous mammoth weeklies, *Brother Jonathan* and the *New World*, both offered entire unauthorized editions of British novels as "extras." In her study of "pirate fictions"—short stories, novels and plays that address literary piracy through maritime piracy—Monica Cohen further argues that such texts both critique literary piracy and celebrate it as "a creativity that is appropriative, recombinative, collective, and pointedly theatrical," through borrowing a set of "histrionic codes" from an illegitimate theater that itself relied on unauthorized adaptations and "visually arresting gestures, poses, and tableaux."[14] The *Corsair*, a New York journal of literature and arts edited by Willis and Timothy O. Porter, exemplified this overlap between unauthorized reprinting, maritime piracy, and theatricality in the United States. As its title suggests, the *Corsair* was a pirate publication, although its ultimate aim was to attack the system that it exploited: Adrian Johns observes that "the very egregiousness of the *Corsair* was supposed to prove how morally irredeemable American practice was. . . . [Willis's] paper existed to prove the need for its own destruction."[15] Pressing the shared nomenclature between literary and maritime piracy to its limits, the *Corsair* opened with a dialogue called "The Quarter Deck," in which American, French, and German writers unite and promise to promised to take full advantage of American copyright laws that allowed the unrestricted reprinting of European works, and "overhaul every craft on the literary seas—ransack her landing—take out of her what is valuable, and send her on her voyage." Both the dialogue format and the pirate clichés ("hark'ye," "scuttle all who sail under false colors") create a staginess that suggests literary production under such conditions must always be a theatrical performance: an American author can either play pirate, like Willis and Porter, or "strip his works of all suspicions of Americanism, and write anonymously as an Englishman!"[16] In either scenario, American literature echoes the New York theater culture to which the *Corsair*'s articles devoted considerable attention.

Although less ostentatious in their presentation than the mammoth weeklies, the British "American" magazines positioned themselves at the same intersection of reprinting and theatricality. The *American Magazine by Brother Jonathan* evoked a leading mammoth weekly in its full title, and *Brother Jonathan* itself noticed the *Great Western*, praising the idea of "*Americans* furnishing the matter for a foreign magazine" as a novel reversal of its own and its competitors' practice.[17] The *American Miscellany* reprinted extensively from the *Corsair*, and all three magazines echoed that periodical's interweaving of transatlantic reprinting and theater culture. Indeed, at least two of the three magazines' editors were theater men.[18] An obituary for Isaac Clarke Pray, the editor of the *Great Western*, described him as a "gentleman, well known in literary and theatrical circles" who "won conspicuousness as a journalist, a playwright, an elocutionist and an actor."[19] Similarly, the editor of the *American Magazine*, Henry Howard Paul, whose description of American reprints in London bookstalls I quoted in the introduction, had a successful career in England as a theater impresario, playwright, and actor after the *Magazine* folded, gaining particular fame for performing in a comic duo with his first wife.[20]

All three magazines also frequently included articles and fiction about the theater. At the start of its run, the *American Miscellany* reprinted reports of the earnings of star American performers like Edwin Forrest, and of the American reception of British singer and actress Madame (Lucia Elizabeth) Vestris. The *Great Western* reviewed London performances. It praised tragedian William Charles Macready's Drury Lane Theatre for its subtle and sophisticated performances aimed at true "lovers of the drama," and criticized its populist melodramas and spectacular stagings in ways that anticipate the class-inflected positions of Macready and his US rival Forrest that prompted the Astor Place Riot in 1849.[21] The *American Magazine*'s monthly Chit Chat column included anecdotes about the successes of American performers Charlotte Cushman and Edward Davenport in Britain, and a snippet about Irish singer Catherine "Katty" Hayes's tour of America.

In aligning themselves with the theater and claiming to embody national cultures, London's "American" magazines showed that they understood the power of theatrical performance to create and sustain such cultures and affiliations. Theater historians have demonstrated that the theater was a crucial site for constructing, negotiating, and testing the nature and limits of American national identity in the first half of the nineteenth century.[22] But while early American theater historians have largely restricted their investigations to performance within the nation, performance studies scholar Joseph Roach argues that the nationalizing performances of US culture emerged within a "circum-Altanic world" in which various cultures "perform[ed] their pasts in the presence of others" and "performed themselves" by also performing "what and who they thought they were not." These extra-national nationalizing performances, Roach suggests, occur through "displaced transmission," a process in which performances cross boundaries through surrogation, a performance by a substitute that generates deficits and surpluses of meaning through its differences from the original. Such surrogate performances provoke strong emotions that Roach argues can transform "improvised narratives of authenticity and priority" into "full-blown myths of legitimacy and origin."[23] Unravelling these processes reveals how apparently stable and fixed cultural forms emerge through messy, disparate, and ongoing processes of transmission and transformation across geographic boundaries and in far-away places.

Contemporaneously with these magazines, London theaters were places in which and through which one of the era's most popular American types was formed. Appearing in comic dramas of courtship and marriage, the stage Yankee was characterized by his rustic birth, verbal comedy, democratic and independent mindset, keenness in financial dealings, distinctive costume, and exaggerated New England dialect.[24] The Yankee, usually known as "Jonathan," embodied the essentially performative nature of culture, relationships, and identity in antebellum America that Karen Halttunen and Stephen Mihm identify, especially after 1820, when the character shifted away from the rustic bumpkin and toward the shrewd dealer who plays the fool to get the better of his social superiors.[25] The stage Yankee was therefore one of a "surprising range of racial and ethnic characters" in the early nineteenth century that "helped Americans think through questions of identity and belonging," as Heather Nathans observes, but he became this national American figure through his restaging in Britain.[26]

Although audiences on both sides of the Atlantic understood the Yankee as an American original, transatlantic circuits of performance fashioned both the character and the forms of national identity he came to embody, as Matthew Pethers has shown. After the American Revolution, playwrights increasingly juxtaposed the Yankee with "Old World rivals," and this change coincided with the Yankee's shift from rustic naïve to shrewd dealer. Furthermore, when the Yankee was juxtaposed with a British other, rather than with other Americans, his regional idiosyncrasies became national traits. Pethers argues that British actors and playwrights were influential in this shift in Yankee comedy. He gives the example of Charles Mathews's *A Trip to America* (1824), in which Mathews's British narrator "served as a familiar, normative standard against which the linguistic and social peculiarities" of the Yankee, and other satirical American types were measured. Yet the Yankee was redefined through transatlantic amalgamations as much as oppositions. Even though Mathews's satirical swipes offended Americans, US dramatists and actors incorporated aspects of his slick trickster Yankee into their plays. Indeed, by the mid-century, this national character was transatlantically fashioned, as British actors' and playwrights' Yankees influenced American renditions of the character, and American actors sought approval for their Yankee performances in Britain.[27]

The career of American Yankee comedian George Handel Hill illustrates how transatlantic performance circuits produced the

Yankee as an authentic American. Before his first London tour in 1836, critics in New York and the provinces praised Hill's Yankee as an accurate presentation of a regional type. Yet Hill knew that changes would be needed for London audiences, who "don't take all the Yankeeisms as readily as my audiences in the States."[28] Indeed, English reviewers praised Hill's premier of London playwright William Bayle Bernard's *The Yankee Pedlar* as authentically American rather than authentically regional. In doing so, they were actually celebrating Hill for fulfilling a British idea of the American. The London *Chronicle* commended Hill for "completely realiz[ing] the conceptions we had previously formed of the singular race whose representative he is." The phrase "singular race" suggested that Americans were both unique and unified, and aligned US national identity and citizenship with whiteness. *John Bull* went further, applauding Hill's performance of a character that had already been "rendered familiar" to London audiences by British comedians like Mathews.[29] Hill's own London version of the Yankee did not remain in England, but traveled back with him to New York. When Hill returned to the Park Theatre—then arguably New York and the United States' most prestigious venue—he performed a version of *The Yankee Pedlar* as adapted by US playwright Morris Barnett that became his signature piece.[30]

Importantly, especially for the nationalizing projects of the three "American" magazines, transatlantic Yankee plays and performances worked to align whiteness and US nationhood by producing the Yankee as a national figure who was also indisputably white. As Dale Cockrell observes, Yankee plays assisted in "the maintenance of racial distinction," with critics such as Sean Goudie and Nathans also analyzing how pairings of the Yankee and Black Americans and West Indians reinforced racial differences and solidified ideas of white nationhood.[31] For example, in *The Yankee Pedlar*—performed in London in 1851 by another celebrated US Yankee comedian, Joshua Silsbee, as well as by Hill in 1836—one trick played by the Yankee Hiram Dodge involves Dodge taking payment for labor that is performed by enslaved Black people, effectively demonstrating that his signature shrewdness not only lampoons those at the top of the social ladder, but also functions to keep the Yankee himself above those Black people at its bottom. In Silsbee's other great success, an 1851 revision of

Samuel Woodworth's *The Forest Rose* (1825), the Yankee Jonathan Ploughboy's catchphrase is "I would not serve a negro so," a phrase that, Jeffrey Richards notes, is "meant as a statement of humanity," but actually reinscribes the hierarchical relation between the "decent white person" and the Black person as the habitual subject of abuse.[32] Moreover, the play's comic denouement involves Jonathan tricking the white villain Bellamy into kissing Rose, a Black woman. This act, which all the characters in the play regard as a humiliation for Bellamy, reinforces Rose's subjection and her place outside the citizenry proper. The positive reception of these Yankee performances suggests that the British were a willing audience for this fashioning of US national identity as whiteness: a review in the *Examiner*, which was reprinted in the United States in the *Living Age*, describes Silsbee's effect on the audience as "immense," and recounted how Silsbee was called back to the stage for a short speech, "in which he still retained his Yankee manner" and "expressed his gratitude for the warm reception he had met."[33]

The timing of two of the three London "American" magazines suggests that they were directly inspired by the popularity of the stage Yankee. The *American Miscellany*'s first edition appeared just after Hill completed his second British tour. Likewise, the *American Magazine* frequently reported on Yankee comedian Silsbee, who was conducting a highly successful British tour when that magazine commenced in 1851. Both these magazines and the *Great Western* reprinted Yankee sketches and "notions" that, in the context of London's popular culture, signified authentic Americanness. But more than simply inserting the Yankee into their own theatrical spaces, the reprinting practices of London's "American" magazines also echoed the transatlantic circulations that made the Yankee into a national icon. The magazines transformed regional and, in at least one case, non-American texts into the materials of a national culture by reprinting them in Britain, and in doing so either side-stepped sectional divisions within the United States or staged those divisions in order to heal them. While all three magazines claimed to showcase the polyphony of US culture through the corporate form of the magazine, their nationalizing work was in fact sustained by the strategic silencing of intra-national differences, the anxious containment of debates over slavery, and the omission of Black and Indigenous voices. The magazines thus constructed an American literature that, like the Yankee comedies, aligned nationality with whiteness by staging that culture in and against Britain.

But these magazines also reproduced the transatlantic (re)circulations that transformed the Yankee from a regional type into a national icon. Each of the magazines invented the American tradition that it claimed to be showcasing, transforming regional texts into exemplary artifacts of national culture through the process of transatlantic reprinting. While all three magazines claimed that their corporate authorship would reflect the diversity of voices within the United States, they largely excluded Black voices even when ventriloquized through racist caricatures. On the issue of slavery they took divergent tactics, with the *American Miscellany* and *American Magazine* remaining largely silent on the issue and the *Great Western* attempting to play out sectional debates from safely across the Atlantic. Ultimately, neither strategy worked, and the magazines' performances of unified white American nationhood proved unsustainable. In running out of nationalizing material, stretching the magazine form to its limits, and prematurely collapsing, the *American Miscellany*, *Great Western*, and *American Magazines* registered the limits of the visions of American literature that could be authorized through British print and the limits of magazine reprinting as an authorizing material practice.

The *American Miscellany* (September 1839–August 1840)

The American Miscellany of Popular Tales, Essays, Sketches of Character, Poetry and Jeux d'Espirit was published by George Berger of Holywell Street near the Strand from September 21, 1839. Berger specialized in cheap print, publishing inexpensive periodicals on a variety of subjects, few of which lasted long. He was likely attracted to publishing American writing both because of Hill's recent success on stage (several of Berger's periodicals focused on humor and light entertainment) and because he could reprint it for free, thus selling his magazine at a low price.[34] The *Miscellany* was issued weekly and cost 2d for sixteen pages of double-column, closely printed prose, with a half-page illustration on the front cover.

It promised readers "a selection from the literary productions of our Transatlantic brethren," that were "quite new to the English public."[35] As its name suggests, the *Miscellany* offered a range of writing, including fiction (ranging from Western adventures to domestic romances), poetry, factual articles on history and science, and snippets of American humor. Berger achieved this generic variety with a slender selection of source materials by reprinting from American newspapers, magazines, and gift books. In the *Miscellany*'s first four months, it reprinted articles from Willis's *The Corsair*, and the *New York Mirror*, for which Willis was a foreign correspondent, both of which combined light and sentimental verse and prose with witty commentary on the culture, theater, and fashions of New York and abroad.[36] These periodicals appealed to women readers, as did some of Berger's other sources, the monthly periodical the *Ladies' Companion* (1834–43) (a New York rival to the Philadelphia *Godey's Lady's Book* that similarly published sentimental literature and fashion), and the gift books *The Token* and *The Atlantic Souvenir*.[37]

As well as reprinting American texts, Berger's periodical echoed the theatrical and carnivalesque qualities that Isabelle Lehuu argues characterized antebellum American print.[38] The arrangement of the *Miscellany*—a showpiece illustrated tale supported by a selection of shorter texts—mirrored the arrangement of a mid-century entertainment in which the main theatrical event was followed by one or more supporting dramas. A substantial number of articles on the theater reinforced this interplay between stage and magazine. The *Miscellany*'s fourth number featured an article on "Things Theatrical, and the Star System in America," and its eighth contained an anecdote about the manager of the Bowery Theatre. The theater was the subject of Emma C. Embury's story "The Play and the Afterpiece," reprinted in January 1840, in the same number as an essay detailing the decline of the Park Theatre in New York. On October 26, 1839, the magazine reprinted a report on a large fire at New York's National Theater as its illustrated story, transforming the blazing theater itself into an object of spectacle. The *Miscellany*'s cover illustrations often resembled *tableaux-vivants*, with figures frozen in an arrangement that encouraged the reader to interpret the image as a scene in process.

The theatrical qualities of the magazine form supported the *Miscellany*'s vison of an American culture characterized by orality and performance. The *Miscellany* featured dialect fiction, such as an extract from James Kirke Paulding's *Swallow Barn* (December 28, 1839) and the short tale, "Management: A Yankee Story" (April 11, 1840). Also popular were jokes, a form that Bob Nicholson argues would become "America's most successful cultural export" and a "staple feature of Britain's bestselling newspapers and magazines" later in the century.[39] Writing these jokes out in a question-answer format encouraged readers to imagine them being performed, especially as they mirrored the wordplay and verbal trickery that was a staple of Yankee comedies. Yet this performative reprinting did not simply import an autochthonous American form into Britain. Tracing the reprinting of two jokes from the *Corsair* that appeared at the end the *Miscellany*'s second issue illustrates how transatlantic reprinting, as much as US origins, made the *Miscellany*'s content American. The following jokes were labelled as being "From the American Papers":

> Why are London females unhappy at three quarters past seven? Because the *mails* leave at eight.
>
> At the feast of animals, who sits at the head of the table? The cow—because she *calves*.[40]

Although these jokes seem to be straightforward examples of "racy" Yankee humor—especially the first, with its sexual suggestiveness and satire of British social mores—they are not, in fact, American. In the *Corsair*, both jokes feature in Willis's dispatches from London and are introduced as "conundrums" he heard when "a grave old Professor gave them to the ladies *for new*."[41] In the *Corsair*, these are British jests, but reprinted in the *Miscellany*, they are American humor. The *American Miscellany*, therefore, re-clothes the *Corsair*'s New York and transnational contents in national American costume through reprinting in Britain.

The Yankee was a frequent presence in the *American Miscellany*. As well as "Management: A Yankee Story," the Yankee appeared in "Deacon Marvel" (July 4, 1840) and "Adventure with a Bear"

(July 18, 1840). One of the *Miscellany*'s sources shows a particularly strong link between the theatrical Yankee, transatlantic reprinting, and the magazine's national performance. In its first four months of publication, the *Miscellany* reprinted five sketches from a volume of humor, *Yankee Notions: A Medley* by Timothy Titterwell (a pseudonym of Samuel Kettell, a Massachusetts magazine writer and editor) published in Boston in 1838. Although reviews of *Yankee Notions* in New York, Philadelphia, and Cincinnati magazines suggest that the volume found a national readership, it roots itself firmly in a local New England setting. Titterwell signs his preface from "Merry Go-Nimble Court—No. 2, round the corner, Next door to the fat man's," giving a street address that situates the volume in relation to a neighborhood rather than a place that can be mapped.[42] Much of the humor in *Yankee Notions* is local, in one case relying on the reader's knowledge of the social geographies of Boston. Titterwell's preface also distances his work from those he ironically calls "our great American authors," whose productions are too dour and didactic for his taste, suggesting that he has no interest in joining the quest for a national literature.[43] Titterwell's book, therefore, displays an expectation of the kind of regional readership that Trish Loughran argues was the defining feature of early American print culture in spite of the nationalizing rhetoric of some of its texts.[44]

When reprinted in the *Miscellany*, these "notions" lose their Boston regionalism. The magazine reprinted neither Titterwell's localizing preface nor the sketches that rely more strongly on Boston knowledge for their humor. Instead, it selected the book's more general lampoons of, for example, Germanic metaphysics and Useful Knowledge Societies, removing these sketches from their localizing context by interspersing them with other materials and labelling them as "American" writing. Heeding, if unconsciously, Hill's advice that London audiences needed a less localized Yankee, the *Miscellany* tailored its contents to a British readership in ways that also nationalized the texts it reprinted by removing them from the local print cultures for which they were intended by their US writers.

However, in its second volume, the *Miscellany*'s tone changed, to the extent that it informed readers that it would now be publishing a "series of papers illustrative of the Geography, Biography, Institutions, and Government of the United States," and "Historical and Topographical illustrations," and that "in subsequent Numbers we shall print the Constitutions of the various States." While it promised that this would not "materially abridge the entertaining reading that has hitherto graced the *American Miscellany*," this was precisely what happened.[45] The magazine's interest in the theater as an important location for the making of American culture decreased, with the last article on the subject being a notice of the "Low State of Theatricals" in New York in January 1840.

This change in tone and content meant that the light, comic variety that the *Miscellany* had previous identified as distinctly American fell away from the magazine. Even the Yankee slipped from his pedestal as national icon. In February 1840, the *Miscellany* reprinted John Neal's "Traits of the New-Englanders, Otherwise the Yankees," which warned against believing that "the portraitures of Mathews, and Hackett, and Hill, were delineations of national character," and instead argued for the Yankee as a regional type specific to the Northeast.[46] By reprinting this piece, the *Miscellany* back-tracked on the nationalizing work it had performed on Yankee stories until then, especially as other reprints also emphasized regional and political divisions, like "The Southern States" or the "Log Cabin Song" composed in support of 1840 Whig presidential candidate William Henry Harrison. Similarly, articles about geography and state constitutions fragmented the nation rather than voicing a cohesive American identity.

It is not clear why the *Miscellany* changed so much after its first volume. A new editor may have been installed, but a call for "contributions in furtherance of [its] objects"—a phrase that might have referred to either articles or cash—suggests that it was running out of subscribers, articles to reprint, or both.[47] If reprinting and the magazine form allowed the *American Miscellany* to fashion an American cultural identity distinguished by orality and humor, sustaining this national mode seems to have been beyond the publication's best efforts. It ended its second volume by announcing a move from weekly to monthly publication; while it promised this would provide "an increased volume of letter press," it may have been an attempt to reduce the amount of material required, or at least the frequency with which it needed to be obtained.[48] Perhaps its editor even envisioned the *Miscellany* reprinting longer extracts from novels and histories, a move that would also have shifted

American national literature away from the insistently contemporaneous, fugitive pieces offered in publications like the *Corsair*. In the end, a third volume never appeared. Nevertheless, it would be only two years before another publisher and editor experimented with using the magazine's polyvocality and material fluidity to articulate Americanness—but that magazine would also find itself struggle to balance reprinting, sectional politics, and national identity.

The *Great Western Magazine* (April 1842–October 1842)

It is unclear what brought the Boston-born author, theater manager, and actor Isaac Clarke Pray to London. Arriving sometime after April 1839 and staying until at least March 1843, Pray edited the *Great Western Magazine and Anglo-American Journal of Literature, Science, Art, Commercial and Political Economy, Statistics &c*, published by Simpkin, Marshall, and Co., for the seven months between April and October 1842.[49] His opening editorial justifies the project by locating Britain as an ideal space for performing and establishing American national culture: Britain and America "though divided, in many respects are one—one in sentiment, thought and feeling," making Britain "as open a field" for American literature as "had the colonies never been separated from the 'Mother Country.'" Although describing itself as Anglo-American, the magazine consisted entirely of what Pray described as "the best thoughts and opinions, the highest and most delicate fancies, the most pleasing and lofty sentiments in poetry, which emanate from the minds of Americans."[50] While Pray contributed several original pieces, most of the *Great Western*'s articles were reprints. These included texts by authors who would subsequently become canonical, such as Edgar Allan Poe's "Eleonora," two stories by Nathaniel Hawthorne, and "The Tomb Blossoms," a short story by one "Walter Whitman."

Pray's periodical struck a more highbrow tone than the *Miscellany*, containing literary reviews and longer articles on politics, philosophy, and the arts. Published monthly at 2s 6d, its single-column layout mirrored the form of the prestigious quarterlies. But the magazine also traded in Yankee humor, joining the *Miscellany* in reprinting sketches from Titterwell's *Yankee Notions*, even as Pray promised to give authentic American voices to replace the false "stage-Yankee." Indeed, Pray argued that his magazine would avoid reducing America to a stereotypical figure by showing the diversity of voices within US writing. A magazine was best fitted for this task because its composite form could encompass the United States' "characteristic" polyphony and showcase several of the "styles of expression peculiar to some portions of the United States" in each issue: "it will be Yankee, but not limitedly."[51] Pray admitted that such polyvocality would inevitably generate conflict: "A magazine which claims to give the thoughts of American writers, without partiality, must necessarily introduce in the course of its progress, ideas that will clash with one another."[52] The most common cause of these clashes in the *Great Western* was sectional divisions over slavery. True to his word, Pray printed both "Moral and Political Freedom" by the staunchly unionist Henry W. Bellows (later president of the United States Sanitary Commission) and Virginia politician Abel P. Upshur's defense of states' rights and the three-fifth's compromise in the same number.[53] As such, the *Great Western* used transatlantic reprinting to rehearse intra-national debates, mitigating their ferocity by distancing them from the union.

At other times, however, Pray seemed less than comfortable with letting such divisions play out, attempting to downplay certain opinions even as he gave them space. In the first issue, Pray published an essay called "War with America: An Examination of the Instigations and Probable Effects, by a Kentuckian." This lengthy article combined a defense of slavery with claims that Britain's policing of the North Atlantic slave trade was a veiled attempt to increase the might of the British Empire. The article was so vituperative that Pray felt compelled to add an editorial note observing that "he does not enter into the spirit of some passages," and that "there are opinions in the article which are considered by many as wholly local, or, at least confined to statesmen in the southern part of the United States."[54] Indeed, by attributing the article to "a Kentuckian," Pray marked such views as a regional sentiment rather than a national mood. Therefore, at the same time as he argued that a magazine could offer the polyphony of voices of a truly national literature, Pray proscribes which voices should be allowed to speak for America as a whole. The magazine's corporate authorship was useful, then, but only when under the strict control of Pray's editorship.

Pray's discomfort with sectional conflict is also visible in his magazine's title, which emphasizes the West over the more fraught cartography of North and South. The West is, furthermore, established as the site of an unproblematically white future nation in the periodical's first article, "North American Indians," a review of George Catlin's book on the subject, written by Pray himself. While sympathetic to the suffering that national expansion inflicted on the Indians, Pray, like Catlin, was convinced that "the total destruction of the original owners of the soil seems certain."[55] While setting up the battle for the West as a conflict between the Indian and the white man, which the former would inevitably lose, Pray erases the debates over Black bodies and their freedom that were at the root of sectional divides in the United States. Indeed, unlike the *American Miscellany* and the *American Magazine*, the *Great Western* did not print Black voices—even racist dialect sketches that caricatured African Americans were entirely absent from its pages. The dual meanings of the magazine's title presented transatlantic circulation of US literature as a step toward this white nationhood. Pray noted that the phrase "Great Western" evoked the United States as a whole—"the United States of America and the *Great West* being in many instances synonymous"—but also suggested the British railway of the same name or "the progress of a steam-ship ploughing the waves against a head-wind."[56]

Within the *Great Western*, the theater shares the magazine's role as a site of Anglo-American communion and a place to stage national American culture. Pray noticed an American actor performing in London, and he reprinted an extract from British American author Henry William Herbert's translation of Greek choruses and reviews of British performers from the Young America periodical *Arcturus*, founded by Cornelius Mathews and Evert Duyckinck.[57] On another occasion, the magazine's reprinting of a short story about the theater transformed the original's exploration of geographic and class difference within the United States into a comparison between Britain and the United States. In the comic story "The Drama at Tinnecum, or Mr. Chipp in the 'Provinces,'" reprinted in the magazine's second number, Mr. Chipp's mediocre theatrical troupe visits a small, rural town and creates joyful chaos as the excited residents learn how to attend a play. As published in New York periodical the *Knickerbocker*, "The Drama at Tinnecum" uses stage and quotidian performances to make fun from divisions between urban and rural life and between social classes. The town's aldermen have a lively discussion about the merits and morality of the theater before allowing the actors to perform. Their meeting reads like a stage dialogue, with dialect speech, interruptions, and misunderstandings: speeches are met with "uproarious applause" or "a volley of groans and hisses." Having constructed a stage especially for the play, complete with curtains made from horses' blankets, the townspeople are anxious to perform correctly as an audience, with the newspaper foreman giving instructions on how to "cry out *brayvo* or *oncore*." Boundaries between performed and sincere emotion further collapse in Mr Chipp's supposedly impromptu speech of thanks, in which actions styled as stage directions, with brackets and italics, suggest it is rehearsed: "[*His voice falters. Mrs. Chipp leans upon his shoulder, and weeps.*]."[58] The story ends with successful performances on both sides of the proscenium arch, with townsfolk believing they have displayed cultural nous by applauding a troop whose work clearly falls below the standard of the metropolitan stage.

The comic ironies of these performances would have been obvious to the story's original audience, the urbane and cultured readers of the *Knickerbocker*. Founded in 1833, the *Knickerbocker* began to flourish a year later under the editorship of Lewis Gaylord Clark, who drew on his friends in the New England, New York, and Philadelphia literati for contributions. The magazine was aimed at the urban middle classes, who would have been aware of the shortcomings of the Chipps' performance and felt themselves distinct from—and probably superior to—the provincial inhabitants of Tinnecum.[59] In laughing at the story, those readers reassured themselves that they inhabited a cultured, sophisticated, and non-performative America away from the "Provinces." However, when restaged in the *Great Western* and for a British audience, the contrast between metropolitan readers and rural characters is replaced by a contrast between an Old World readership, implicitly positioned as superior, and a rough-and-ready New World. If the original publication confirmed American progress toward culture, because *Knickerbocker*-reading New Yorkers could distinguish bad acting from good, when reprinted in Britain, the international contrast between the tale's subjects and audience threatened to return America to a pre-Revolutionary past in which even the best theaters relied on "second-tier performers who played supporting roles in London and enjoyed occasional starring opportunities in the provinces."[60] Pray promised "distinguished writers of America," yet printed stories that, for British readers, presented American culture as backward. The Chipps' lack of sincerity may also have reinforced a British idea of all Americans as consistently engaging in deceptive performances, even as Pray claimed to be refuting the stereotype of the slick-talking, double-dealing stage Yankee.

Elsewhere in the *Great Western*, the transatlantic fashioning of US nationhood was far more fraught. Its sixth number was entirely given over to a series of letters titled "The United States and England" that had been printed earlier in 1842 in the London *Times*, and that attacked England's policing of the slave trade as a calculated effort to ensure the economic supremacy of the British Empire. The article begins by observing that "so far as it relates to their domestic concerns, they are twenty-six distinct episodes [in the United States]," but "in what relates to foreign nations . . . the United States are one people." It then argues that England's efforts to turn the "public opinion of the North" against the South would fail, as US citizens would defend the rights of "American" slave holders (never referred to as Southerners) against foreign interference.[61] Regional divisions that threaten national unity pale in comparison to differences between the United States and Britain, thus creating national unity by proxy. Although very different in origin, subject, and genre, in the pages of the *Great Western*, the story "The Drama at Tinnecum" and the series "The United States and England" perform the same cultural work, subsuming regional differences into a broader American identity that is defined both in and against Britain.

However, the cost of this national unity was the corporate authorship that Pray had originally argued would characterize his national magazine. Containing only this one article, the sixth issue of the *Great Western* swapped its desired American polyphony for the single voice of "an American" speaking for the nation, something that Pray had originally argued was impossible. Moreover, while the anonymous author of "The United States and England" identified themselves as American, the series' prior publication in the *Times* meant that *Great Western* was not fulfilling its stated task of publishing "valuable information [from the United States], such as in no other shape would reach the press."[62] This strain on the magazine form illustrates the difficulties inherent in Pray's project of creating a national magazine. The *Great Western* could not be both "characteristic" and "American" because a unified nationhood was not a characteristic of the United States in 1842. The *Great Western* revealed this contradiction by printing a "Skeleton Map of the United States" to accompany "The United States and England" that marked both actual and "proposed" railroads, to show how these improvements "will bind the parts of the Union together by cementing their interests."[63] The map actually shows how much of this work was still to be completed, with proposed railroads far outnumbering completed ones. A connected US nation, like a unified, white US nationhood, could be projected in and against Britain, but did not exist on the ground.

The *Great Western* did return to its habitual form of generically diverse contents reprinted from US periodicals, but only for one more issue before the magazine folded. As with the *American Miscellany*, there was no announcement of the magazine's imminent demise: an eighth issue simply never appeared. Yet its failure is not entirely surprising. Even as its reprints of "The Drama at Tinnecum" and "The United States and England" performed similar nationalizing work—uniting a politically, geographically, and socially disparate white citizenry against a British other—they are tonally worlds apart. Indeed, unlike the trains and ships that its name evoked, the *Great Western* always seemed to be pulling in two different directions rather than steaming straight ahead. The *Great Western* staged sectional conflict at a safe distance but it also subsumed regional tensions within transatlantic difference. Pray also invoked the magazine form's corporate authority while interfering with its polyphony. Further still, he began by asserting the similarities between Britain and the United States before proceeding to construct US national identity against Britain, as well as through transatlantic reprinting. Even the fluid form of the magazine could not hold such contradictory impulses together. While the last of the London "American" magazines was more successful in creating a stable tone and identity, it, too, struggled to celebrate white US nationhood in the midst of tensions over slavery.

The *American Magazine* (October 1851–February 1852)

The *American Magazine by Brother Jonathan* was a shilling monthly published by William Spencer Johnson from October 1852. Its editor was Henry Howard Paul, a Philadelphian who came to Britain in 1850, initially lecturing on the Gold Rush before turning his attentions to print. Paul seems to have devoted considerable time to promoting his magazine; over forty metropolitan and provincial publications in Britain gave the *Magazine* favorable reviews, and at least twenty-six reprinted its articles. The New York *Literary World* noticed the publication, and *Sartain's Union Magazine* of Philadelphia reprinted a positive review from the London *Daily News*. Paul collected his British reviews in a column that closed three of the *Magazine*'s five issues, titled "What the Press of the United Kingdom Say of Us!" in which long lists of reviews implied the periodical's wide circulation. Creating this impression of popularity and reach gave Paul's magazine authority as an organ of American culture overseas.

The *Magazine*'s tone and contents were closer to the *Miscellany* than the *Great Western*; it reprinted humorous sketches and jokes along with sentimental and romantic fiction. But, like Pray, Paul suggested that his magazine could create "a perfect harmony and good understanding between the two great communities of Great Britain and the United States," and saw the magazine's composite form as a means to stage the "varied" talents of his "widely extended country," claiming we "shall choose from all quarters, confident that there are many great minds in the young country that only require a proper introduction at the firesides of this realm, to be read and appreciated."[64] Throughout the *Magazine*'s very short life, Paul consistently presented his periodical as a "national enterprise" while also inviting its nationality to be judged from outside the US.[65] For example, he sent a copy of what he called "my National Work," to exiled Hungarian nationalist

Louis Kossuth along with a letter setting out his aim of "establish[ing], in England, a medium for the more direct promulgation of American sentiments and literature," a statement that suggested "England" might be the place where such national sentiments could be most directly promulgated.[66]

The *Magazine*'s concern with fashioning an American national literature through reprinting US texts in Britain was evident from its front cover, which featured a jaunty stars and stripes (figure 9). However, this particular flag had seventeen stars and thirteen stripes, and was never an official flag of the United States. It thus inadvertently signified that the *American Magazine* offered a fantasy of a unified national culture at a time when sectional tensions were increasing after the Compromise of 1850 and its controversial Fugitive Slave Law. Like its predecessors, the *Magazine* staged this fantasy by combining transatlantic reprinting with transatlantic theater culture, drawing on transatlantic Yankee theatricals and fashioning itself as an extension of the theater.

Of all the London "American" magazines, the *American Magazine* located its own national performance most strongly within a transatlantic theater culture. Its full title positioned the magazine as the creation of "Brother Jonathan," the archetypal stage Yankee, and also recalled the spectacular US mammoth weekly of the same name. Paul's Chit Chat column reported on American performers in Britain, including the Bateman children, whom Paul described as "wonderful little specimens of 'Young America,'" using the pun to blur the transatlantic circulation of performers with US cultural nationalism.[67] The most prominent performer in the *Magazine* was the Yankee comedian Joshua Silsbee, who became a friend of Paul's while the two men were in England. Silsbee's act generated a substantial amount of the magazine's contents, with Paul even writing a flattering review of Silsbee's performance in Yankee dialect: "I say ur this is my favurit resort, an' I tell yeou wi . . . uncle Josh. Silsbee's down-east yarns (which remind me so much uv hum)."[68] The magazine here becomes another stage on which Silsbee's act could be performed, and Silsbee's act becomes part of the nationalizing work of the magazine. Silsbee even acted as a spokesman for national unity. Reprinting "A Chunk of Fun from the 'New York

Figure 9. Front cover, *American Magazine by Brother Jonathan*, vol. 1, no. 1, October 1851. © The British Library Board, General Reference Collection P.P.6393.a.

Dutchman,'" Paul included the joke, "Yankee Silsbee says, the idea of dissolving the Union is one of the impossibilities. In his opinion it would be easier to lap up the Pacific with a two-pound terrier. Silsbee is right."[69] Silsbee may never have told such a joke, although its combination of absurdity and home-spun wisdom is characteristic of the Yankee characters he played. But even if he didn't, the reprinted joke reinforced an aspect of the Yankee plays he performed in London that was itself echoed in the stories that the *Magazine* reprinted: the importance of overcoming sectional differences to achieve national (re)union.

Paul's attention to Silsbee and his use of the Brother Jonathan persona was a good promotional tactic in the autumn of 1851 when Silsbee was in the middle of a run of 123 performances of a revised version of Woodworth's *The Forest Rose* at the Adelphi Theatre. More than simply recreating a familiar and by now national American type, Silsbee's Yankee plays both exposed and healed contemporary sectional tensions in the United States. The version of *The Forest Rose* licensed for performance in London in 1851 transformed the villain, Bellamy, from an Englishman into a New Yorker. The change was made to please London audiences, but it had the further effect of replacing differences between the United States and Britain with differences within the United States at a time when internal sectional tensions were rising.[70] In contrast to "The Drama at Tinnecum," where transatlantic reprinting muted internal conflicts by transforming them into a contrast between the United States and Britain, *The Forest Rose* employed Britain as a space to work through such internal conflicts. Silsbee also revived Hill's hit *The Yankee Pedlar*, in which the villain, Colonel Bantam, is a slave-holding Virginian with an ingrained hatred of Yankees. Yankee Hiram Dodge heals this sectional conflict by orchestrating the marriage of the Northern hero Moreland to Bantam's daughter Nancy, softening Bantam's attitude to Northerners in the process. In his final metatheatrical monologue, Dodge—played by Silsbee—aligns his success with the Southerners with acceptance from his British audience when he proclaims "perhaps they won't altogether object to another visit from a Yankee Pedlar," the pronoun encompassing Dodge's Southern and Silsbee's British hosts.[71]

Paul also chose stories for the *American Magazine* in which pseudo-theatrical performances work to reunify romantic divisions that can, in the context of the magazine, be read as national allegories. Much of the magazine's fiction was reprinted from what Cynthia Lee Patterson has called "Philadelphia Pictorials": magazines like *Godey's Lady's Book* (1840–98), *Graham's Magazine* (1841–58), and *Sartain's Union Magazine* (1849–52), which were "the first to target a national reading audience of moderate means."[72] The *American Magazine* reprints several stories about couples who misunderstand each other and become estranged, only to reconcile through performing roles that, ironically, help them see each others' true selves more clearly. In Clara Moreton's "The Estranged Hearts," originally published in *Sartain's*, Margaret's marriage to Howard crumbles when she attends a *tableaux-vivants* party against his will, but performance then helps the couple reconcile after Margaret dons a disguise and faithfully nurses her own children while posing as a hired nanny. In Caroline Lee Hentz's "The Mob Cap," the rich young widow Gertrude dresses up as an old woman to coax a confession of love from the poor but honest Edward Stanley. And in Moreton's "Meeta Clifton's First and Second Loves," the titular young woman turns down Clarence Grenville because she is not his first love, before Grenville apparently dies in a shipwreck. Meeta then falls in love with the exotic Signor Manfredi, only for it to be revealed that Manfredi is Grenville in disguise.

Reprinted outside of the domestic realm of *Sartain's* and *Godey's*, in a magazine that claimed to be truly American and which identified so strongly with Silsbee's performance of a national icon, these re-unions of divided couples resonated at a national scale. In the *American Magazine*, these stories imagine how America's divided regions might learn to understand one another and come together once more. "The Estranged Hearts" ends with a plea for compromise and understanding that resonates with contemporary political tensions:

> For very seldom is it when pride, and jealousy, and suspicion creep in to separate two hearts, that any after reconciliation can entirely root out the weeds which have sprung up . . .

> More frequently, the breach widens with years; each grows to think the other the aggressor, and that complete isolation takes place which is so terrible to contemplate.[73]

Anne Norton observes that by the 1850s, "it had become commonplace . . . to liken the Union to a marriage," but Moreton's story gives a marriage that seems like the Union.[74] The word "aggressor" in particular suggests more martial than marital tensions, and the stakes of an isolation "so terrible to contemplate" seem particularly high.

The *American Magazine*'s performances of national (re)union are most visible in Paul's reprinting of Hentz's "The Pedlar," a sequel to "The Mob Cap," originally published in the Philadelphia *Saturday Courier* in 1841 and reprinted in the *American Magazine*'s third issue in December 1851. This story focuses on Edward Stanley's sister Clara, who, in "The Mob Cap," accidentally gave a peddler valuable papers when she was induced by her own vanity to trade an old trunk for a gaudy necklace. Clara has been left with a violent aversion to peddlers, but nevertheless, she strikes up a friendship with one named Rover who appears in the village at the same time that her sister-in-law Gertrude's handsome, rich, Southern cousin, Washington Graham, arrives for a visit. Washington courts Clara, but she grows closer to Rover despite the class barrier separating them. Matters come to a head when Rover is wrongfully arrested and Clara breaks him out of jail using Gertrude's old woman disguise from "The Mob Cap" before publicly declaring her love. But on Clara and Rover's wedding day, Washington reveals that he disguised himself as Rover to be sure that Clara was not marrying him for his wealth alone, and Clara is rewarded with riches as well as a man she loves.

Reprinting "The Pedlar" alongside notices of Silsbee's performances brings out the story's similarities to *The Forest Rose* and *The Yankee Pedlar*: all three feature confused lovers in rural America, class prejudice being overcome, and a marriage at the end. That theatrical context and the heightened tensions of the early 1850s gives Hentz's tale a deeper political hue when reprinted in the *American Magazine*, and encourages reading of the climactic marriage as an allegory for sectional reconciliation. Ostensibly,

Washington dons a disguise to test whether Clara truly loves him for himself and not his riches. But his peddler performance actually enables Clara to look past his Southern-ness, which is a barrier to their marriage. Washington is described as a "southern stranger" who is perpetually "attended by a negro," and, at one point, the thought of Washington looking at her "filled [Clara] with dread." But Washington's pretending allows the "unpretending" Clara to see their true compatibility beyond sectional difference. As in *The Yankee Pedlar*, the climatic marriage unites North and South, but "The Pedlar" more forcefully suggests the indivisibility of the Union by having the peddler, the traditional occupation of the stage Yankee, and the Southerner be the same person. As Clara daydreams of "the blending images of Washington Graham and the pedlar," a shared whiteness literally dissolves sectional difference.[75]

Yet Black figures haunt and produce the white national (re) union of Clara and Washington, and the white national figure of the Yankee. "The Pedlar" contrasts the "unsunned whiteness" of Washington's forehead and Rover's "dark complexion," a comparison that disrupts the Yankee peddler's assumed whiteness. Both Rover's racial ambiguity and the revelation that the exceptionally white Washington has been disguising himself as Rover suggest that we might be in a blackface minstrel show rather than a Yankee comedy. Rover functions as something like a tragic mulatto in the text, a seductive and racially ambiguous Other whose—in this case metaphorical—death secures the continuation of white America. Nor is he the only Black character on whose presence and exclusion the romance of Union relies. Clara is able to find Rover in the prison, thus releasing Washington, because she has already been there to visit a "poor black woman" who was wrongly "accused of an attempt to poison a white family." Clara observes that this "poor creature" died in the very cell Rover occupies and fears he will share her fate: "your innocence will serve you nothing when the law is in its strength."[76] The presence of both Rover and the unnamed Black woman, therefore, is necessary to bring about the union of Clara and Washington, but both have to be removed from the text before the union can be finally enacted, and white nationhood secured.

These fleeting Black presences in "The Pedlar" inadvertently echo the *American Magazine*'s treatment of Black Americans. The *Magazine* repeatedly stresses the need to sustain the union, but spends almost no time at all on the issue that was putting the union at risk: slavery. When it does reprint texts that approach the slavery question, these do so obliquely. The February issue reprints extracts from an 1848 speech by Speaker of the House of Representatives, Robert C. Winthrop, who observes that, "The extension of our boundaries, and the multiplication of our territories are producing, directly and indirectly, among the different members of our political system, so many marked and mournful centrifugal tendencies"—an "indirect" description of the problems arising from new slave states being admitted to the Union, which itself never uses the word "slavery."[77] Indeed, the few references to slavery in the *American Magazine* are distanced from the contemporary United States in time (an anecdote, intended to be humorous, about an enslaved Black man "a great many years ago when there was slavery in Massachusetts") or space (references to Brazilian slavery in a narrative of the whale fisheries there).[78] More references to slavery appeared in the *Magazines*'s collections of its British reviews than in the US texts it reprinted. Like the absent-present Black woman in "The Pedlar," slavery was the topic that the *American Magazine* could not mention, even as the divisions that slavery caused within the US states prompted the *Magazine*'s nationalizing work.

At only five issues, the *American Magazine* had the briefest lifespan of all three British reprint periodicals, and yet its failure is the hardest to explain. It commenced publication at a moment in which US writing in Britain was more popular than ever before: the previous two years had seen a flurry of editions of Longfellow's works alongside George Routledge's and Henry Bohn's unauthorized reprints of Herman Melville, Washington Irving, and James Fenimore Cooper. Moreover, the *American Magazine* was more successful than its predecessors at capturing the humor, romance, and popular (in both the democratic and the attractive senses of the word) tone of Yankee theatricals, while also reprinting high-quality articles. Unlike the *Miscellany*'s editor(s), Paul does not seem to have run out of appealing material, and unlike the *Great Western*, Paul did not break the magazine form to articulate national unity. During its short life, the *American Magazine* received warm reviews, and its reprints were themselves reprinted in national and provincial British and Irish periodicals. While this attention would not necessarily have converted into strong sales or profitability, it would have been harsh for the publisher to end so positively reviewed a publication so quickly. It is hard not to agree with the *Dundee, Perth and Cupar Advertiser*, who lamented its sudden disappearance in March 1852: "But what has become of the 'American Magazine?' It had far too much vitality in it to now be defunct."[79]

One possible explanation is that Paul simply tired of magazine editing. A month after the *Magazine*'s final issue, Paul journeyed with Silsbee to Europe, and upon his return he turned his literary and promotional talents to other formats while still maintaining his American niche. He published two volumes of his own comic "Yankee" sketches in Britain—*Dashes of American Humour* (1852) and *"Patchwork": Embroidered with Wit, Whim and Fancy* (1858)—and edited *The Book of American Songs* (1857), published by Ward and Lock in an edition that also advertised their reprints of Robert Montgomery Bird's *Nick of the Woods* and Ann Sophia Stephens's *Zana; or, the Heiress of Clair Hall.* Most of his attention, however, was directed at the theater itself, especially after his marriage to the popular actress and comic opera singer Isabella Featherstone. That Paul's decision to realign his career may have caused the demise of the most promising of London's "American" magazines is a reminder that American literature's transatlantic materials were forged by chance as much as by design, and by individuals' aims and desires for themselves as much as by any author's or publisher's vision for a national literature or print culture.

Within this necessarily speculative history of the *American Magazine* and its premature end, it is interesting to imagine what might have happened if Paul had still been editing his *Magazine* when Harriet Beecher Stowe's *Uncle Tom's Cabin* reached Britain. Stowe's novel—which had its own print-performance culture in London, through its many stage adaptations—took the British literary marketplace by storm in the summer of 1852, only a few months after the *American Magazine* ended. As I discuss further in the coda, the success of *Uncle Tom's Cabin* threatened to shift American literature from a field defined by contests over its proper subjects, aesthetics, and models of authorship, to one defined as feminine, sentimental, and antislavery. On the one hand, had the *American Magazine* continued to reprint feminine fictions, it would have been ideally placed to capitalize on the immense popularity of Stowe's novel. On the other hand, the *Magazine*'s emphasis on national (re)union and its relative silence around slavery itself may have sat oddly in a transatlantic print culture in which the United States' representative novel devoted itself to the moral wrongs of slavery and proposed that its readers align their sentiments with the cause of immediate abolition. As an astute observer of popular culture and a skilled publicist, Paul was almost certainly capable of transforming and remarketing his periodical to better fit any post-*Tom* sense of American writing held by his British reading public. On the question of whether his own politics would have encouraged him to adopt or resist a more explicitly anti-slavery position, the surviving evidence remains unclear.

Perhaps surprisingly, I can find no attempts to revive the British "American" reprint magazine in the wake of *Uncle Tom*'s success. This may have been because literary and light periodicals with majority British contributors had begun to reprint American fiction more frequently, often without attribution and often changing details to make the stories seem British in origin. The *American Magazine* accused the London *Family Herald* of doing just this in its December issue, adding that the *Family Companion* at least credited the American authors whose work it reprinted.[80] The first number of the *Englishwoman's Domestic Magazine*—published by Samuel O. Beeton, previous partner of the first British publisher of *Uncle Tom's Cabin*—serialized an abridged version of Hawthorne's *The Scarlet Letter* in 1855 with accompanying illustrations by Myles Birket Foster, who had illustrated David Bogue's editions of Longfellow, discussed in chapter 1.[81] It may have been that, as in the series of chapter 3 and the gift books of chapter 4, publishers found that transatlantic composites proved more suitable and more sustainable ways to attract British readers with popular American texts.

However, there may also have been ideological reasons why the genre was not revived in the wake of *Uncle Tom's Cabin*. These American magazines sought to either diffuse or to sidestep sectional tensions between North and South—either by ignoring divisions over slavery, or by creating a space in which those divisions could be aired, or a space in which anticipatory reunions could be imagined—even before the United States had severed itself in two. Those aims no longer made sense when slavery itself was the subject of America's most famous book, and the print and theatrical markets were becoming saturated not only with versions of *Uncle Tom* itself, but also with various "Tomitudes" and "Anti-Tom" texts and performances that riffed on and responded to Stowe's novel. *Uncle Tom* may have changed the publishing landscape and British perceptions of the United States so drastically that it was no longer possible to conceive of American culture as a polyphony of voices that could appear alongside one another in a composite text, even if that text was published far from home. It is ironic, then, that the popularity of Stowe's novel left less space for competing visions of Americanness—even unstable and untenable visions—to exist alongside it. I will return to this idea in the coda.

The genre of the London "American" magazine did have a last gasp in October 1861, in the form of the *American Scrap Book and Magazine of United States Literature*, the sister weekly publication of the daily *London American* newspaper, edited by John Adams Knight, an American expatriate.[82] The *Scrap Book* lacked the editorials celebrating transatlantic cultural connections and the appeals for the British recognition of US writing that appeared in previous "American" magazines. Although it had a column called "Yankee Notions" that traded in the stage Yankee's performative verbal comedy, it did not use Yankee humor as a national mode. Instead, the *Scrap Book* turned Yankee wordplay against the South in jokes like "Louisiana Sugar—*Slave groan!*" and "What the Southern Confeds want—The Capitol. What they can't get to take it with—The Capital."[83] While this sectional loyalty is to be expected from a Civil War publication, it shows that the "American" magazine in Britain had shifted from a means of overcoming or sidestepping sectional conflict in the 1850s to a means by which one side could gain an ideological—and perhaps also material—advantage in that conflict. However, the *American Scrap Book* was no more successful than its predecessors: its final issue appeared almost a year after it was first published, on September 20, 1862.

Trying to explain the failures of the *American Miscellany*, *Great Western*, and *American Magazine* risks placing undue weight on those failures. The periodical form is predicated on perpetuity—that there will always be another issue tomorrow, next week, next month—and so all periodicals end in failure, because to end is to cease fulfilling an integral element of the form. Furthermore, most nineteenth-century periodicals failed quickly: their short lives make London's "American" magazines the rule and not the exception. But attending to these failures reminds us that the process of authorizing American literature through British print materiality was not uniformly successful, either in terms of producing profitable publications or in generating print objects that sustained particular visions of a national tradition. These "American" magazines not only failed as publishing concerns, but also in constructing a national tradition according to the theatrical, polyphonic, and unifying terms by which they defined it. Their national fantasies do not shatter so much as they struggle to stabilize, and they end not with bangs but with whimpers. Their failures mark a limit for the visions for American literature that transatlantic materials could sustain and they show that Britain was not a space in which American literature could neatly escape from sectional tensions within the nation itself.

CHAPTER 6

The Transatlantic Slave Narrative Trade

In September 1852, British abolitionist George Thompson told the president of the American Anti-Slavery Society, William Lloyd Garrison, that in Britain, "There is just now an unprecedented demand for Anti-Slavery Literature." Thompson was referring to excitement around Harriet Beecher Stowe's *Uncle Tom's Cabin*, which had arrived in London that spring and was by then a best-seller. But Thompson also told Garrison that this demand was "the fruit of your labors," suggesting that British abolitionists at least attributed the increase in antislavery interest to the work by US abolitionists to cultivate British audiences.[1] From the 1830s onward, Black Americans visited Britain to further their self-education, to garner British support for immediate abolition, and, after 1850, to escape the Fugitive Slave Law. Historian Hannah-Rose Murray has recently argued that these visits forged a distinct "Black American protest tradition in Britain" of "adaptive resistance" that consisted of performative strategies through which Black abolitionists "exploit[ed] their position as outsiders to American citizenship *and* their position abroad to challenge America's artificial freedom and national ideology."[2] Successful adaptive resistance involved the abolitionist's engagement with British print culture to reinforce his or her public performances, and while Murray focuses on the newspaper press, many Black abolitionists also circulated narratives of their lives and experiences in slavery in British editions.

Between 1830 and 1860, at least twenty book- or pamphlet-length slave narratives were published in Britain.[3] Some were published there first, including the *Narrative of the Life of Moses Grandy* (1843), *Autobiography of a Fugitive Negro* (1855) by Samuel Ringgold Ward, and *Running a Thousand Miles for Freedom; or, The Escape of William and Ellen Craft from Slavery* (1860). Others, like the *Narrative of the Life of Frederick Douglass* (1845), the *Narrative of William Wells*

Brown (1847), and the *Narrative of the Life of Henry Box Brown* (1849 and 1851), were republished in Britain, sometimes in edited versions. Extracts and abridged narratives also appeared in newspapers, magazines, and anthologies like John Passmore Edwards's *Uncle Tom's Companions: Facts Stranger than Fiction. A Supplement to "Uncle Tom's Cabin"* (1852).[4] Eight slave narratives appeared before *Uncle Tom's Cabin*, and sales suggest that their popularity paved the way for Stowe's bestseller. In 1844, Black American lecturer Moses Roper claimed that his *Narrative of the Adventures and Escape of Moses Roper from American Slavery*, first published in 1837, had sold "twenty-five thousand English, and five thousand Welsh copies."[5] Frederick Douglass sold two thousand copies of his *Narrative* between September 1845 and March the following year, and between August 1849 and August 1850, six thousand copies of James W. C. Pennington's *The Fugitive Blacksmith* (1849) were printed in London.[6]

The transatlantic publication histories of these narratives have largely been neglected in the rich scholarship on African American print that has emerged over the past twenty years.[7] Material histories of slave narratives have thus far followed the nation-centric frameworks common in book history rather than building on Paul Gilroy's theorization of how Black cultural production draws on "the successive displacements, migrations, and journeys (forced and otherwise)" that are centered on the Atlantic Ocean and that "have come to constitute these black cultures' special conditions of existence."[8] Like the white authors considered in previous chapters, the authors of slave narratives understood themselves and their texts as participants in a transatlantic print economy. However, they imaginatively remediate transatlantic print circulation and use printing and reprinting in Britain to locate themselves as Atlantic subjects and not as national American writers. As Fionnghuala Sweeney observes, "For slave narrators in particular, the politics of resistance was early linked to the politics of location."[9] By situating themselves in transnational spaces, slave narrators claim authorial positions they were denied in the United States by the dehumanizing logic and practices of slavery and by white abolitionists' presentation of self-emancipated Black Americans and their texts as bodies of evidence.

This chapter asks if and how the materialization and circulation of slave narratives in Britain furthered the locational politics of those narratives and of Black antislavery more widely. Michaël Roy argues that acknowledging the material diversity encourages a "defamiliarization of the genre," and challenges perceptions of slave narratives as "homogenous."[10] The same diversity characterized their publication in Britain. Many slave narratives entered Britain through anti-slavery channels rather than book trade networks. These were issued by smaller, reform-minded publishers whose imprints, material texts, and dissemination practices offered different forms of authorization to the literary firms considered in chapters 1 to 4. Others were issued by anti-slavery organizations and by literary houses. Two important works stand at opposite ends of this commercial-charitable spectrum of Black abolitionist publications: Solomon Northup's *Twelve Years a Slave* (1852), published by the well-connected London literary publisher Sampson Low, and John Brown's *Slave Life in Georgia* (1855), disseminated by the British and Foreign Anti-Slavery Society (BFASS). Recovering the histories of these publications reveals tensions between their authors' imaginative use of transatlantic print and print culture and the materialization and circulation of their texts in Britain. While authors Northup and Brown use transatlantic circulation to claim agency and subjectivity, their publishers framed the Black authors as objects for the white gaze: Low by transforming Northup's narrative into a commodity of the popular literary marketplace, and the BFASS through a "socially embedded" dissemination of Brown's text.[11] It was only by controlling the transatlantic production and circulation of their narratives that authors such as Frederick Douglass and William Wells Brown created material texts that embodied the new forms of mobility and subjectivity they found in Britain. Through the paratexts of their British editions and the process of republishing their narratives, Douglass and Brown re-presented themselves as literary authors rather than slave narrators, escaping the identities and modes of authorship to which their US publications confined them.

This chapter, then, seeks to expand the histories of transatlantic abolitionism and its print cultures in the mid-nineteenth century. But it also plots new transatlantic geographies of Black print, sounding a counterpoint to studies by Eric Gardner and Derrick Spires that explore how Black Americans theorized personhood, citizenship, and belonging through the materiality of print beyond the slave narrative.[12] Understanding the transatlantic dynamics and print materials of early Black American authorship reconfigures its canons. If Douglass remains a lynchpin of my discussions, his writing and publishing sit alongside John Brown's less-studied yet exemplary imaginative engagements with and material navigations of the abolitionist Atlantic and appear as precursors to William Wells Brown's more expansive experiments with the expressive materiality of print.

In moving from confining modes of publication and dissemination to print practices through which Black Americans created space for mobility and subjectivity, this chapter risks presenting an over-simplified arc of the evolution of British print into a space for successful resistance to the logic of slavery. In fact, Black abolitionists' radical uses of transatlantic circulation were coterminous with print forms that situated them as objects to be read rather than as authorial subjects. If it is important to recover the agency that Black writers, editors, publishers, and artists found in British print, then, as Brigitte Fielder and Jonathan Senchyne observe, we must also consider how "print and the infrastructures surrounding it might more often be constricting than freeing."[13] Analyzing how British publishers of slave narratives failed to materially reinforce their authors' self-fashioning as Atlantic subjects demonstrates that productive dialogues between US texts and British print were not an inevitable feature of west-east transatlantic circulation. The heterogeneous British print formats that sustained competing conceptions of what American literature was and could be also drew racial boundaries around the literary field that they co-produced.

Publishing Slave Narratives in Britain

As in the United States, the publication arrangements for slave narratives in Britain were diverse.[14] While it is beyond the scope of this chapter to provide a complete history of the slave narrative's publication in Britain, outlining some of the ways that slave narratives were published and circulated calls attention to the variety of their physical forms and the unevenness of their circulation. Literary historians and historians of abolitionism use slave narratives' high sales figures to argue for their absorption into literary and popular culture in Britain and for their importance to the transatlantic abolition movement.[15] But simply comparing sales figures disguises differences between the publication and dissemination of individual narratives and between the ways in which white-authored texts and texts by Black abolitionists entered into and circulated in Britain. It was quite a different thing for Moses Roper to sell twenty thousand copies of his narrative than for Sampson Low to sell twenty thousand copies of Solomon Northup's *Twelve Years a Slave*. Moreover, quoting sales figures for best-selling narratives suggests a false fluidity, rapidity, and regularity to their circulation. Whereas some slave narratives sold quickly in particular parts of the country, in other cases, even committed British abolitionists could struggle to obtain copies of key US texts. Leeds abolitionist Wilson Armistead, who corresponded with US abolitionists and founded an antislavery library and pamphlet series, complained that "some American works we have difficulty in getting," noting the particular challenge of obtaining editions of *American Slavery as It Is* (the antislavery miscellany produced by Angelina Grimké, Sarah Moore Grimké, and Theodore Dwight Weld) and "Douglas's [sic] Orations & his Lectures in Corinthian Hall."[16] Indeed, temporal delays, geographical variation, and formal variety characterized the circulation of slave narratives in Britain.

Although most British editions of slave narratives were published in collaboration with their authors, it was not until after the success of *Uncle Tom's Cabin* in 1852 that London literary publishers issued texts by self-emancipated African Americans. Solomon Northup's *Twelve Years a Slave*, published in 1853, followed a trajectory closer to those of white-authored texts, entering British print culture via an arrangement between US and British publishers, as I explain below. Even then, the most reputable London firms, like John Murray or Richard Bentley & Sons, did not publish slave narratives, and nor did the publishers of unauthorized cheap reprints, although the latter did dabble in antislavery fictions like Richard Hildreth's *The White Slave* and anti-Tom novels in the wake of Stowe's success. After 1852, Black abolitionists instead published with literary firms that had interests in American writing, like

Sampson Low, who published *Twelve Years a Slave*, or in religious writing, like Partridge & Oakey, who published Charles Freeman's *The Escaped Slave* (1853) as well as William Wells Brown's novel *Clotel* (1853).

Racial discrimination in the United States and Britain and US publishers' desires to avoid abolitionist politics prevented Black authors from publishing with the British firms most invested in authorizing an American literary tradition. As Michaël Roy has shown, commercial US publishers like the Harper Brothers in New York and Phillips, Sampson in Boston—those most likely to seek authorized British editions or to be approached by publishers like Bentley—routinely declined works that expressed abolitionist sentiments.[17] The hostility of the commercial trade led the American Anti-Slavery Society (AAS) to devote significant resources to publishing and dissemination infrastructure, although when funds became tighter after the schism in the US movement in 1840, abolitionists instead turned to "forms of dissemination that were more artisanal, but also more embodied—and not necessarily less efficient."[18] The activist networks that abolitionists used to disseminate texts were transatlantic; as shown by the letter between Thompson and Garrison with which this chapter opened, antislavery activists on both sides of the Atlantic corresponded and collaborated frequently. Between the 1830s and 1860s, Black abolitionists looked to these networks to print and circulate their narratives in Britain.

Whereas American antislavery societies grew in numbers and developed complex national infrastructures during the 1830s and 1840s that enabled them to circulate antislavery texts, this was not true of Britain, where the membership of antislavery societies declined after emancipation in the Empire in 1838.[19] As such, British antislavery societies did not routinely publish US slave narratives; instead, antislavery activists directed these narratives toward smaller publishers who had personal connections with and strong sympathies toward the antislavery cause. John Scoble, the secretary of the British and Foreign Anti-Slavery Society, orchestrated the publication of Moses Grandy's *Narrative of the Life of Moses Grandy* with a Quaker publisher, Charles Gilpin, in 1843. Gilpin was the nephew of Joseph Sturge, the organizer of the 1840 World

Anti-Slavery Convention, and was himself described as a "determined enemy to slavery" in his *Publishers' Circular* obituary. He would go on to publish William Wells Brown's *Narrative* and James W. C. Pennington's *The Fugitive Blacksmith* in 1849.[20] Douglass's Dublin publisher, Richard Davis Webb, was also a Quaker and a friend of the Estlin family, Garrison, Thompson, and many other prominent antislavery activists in Britain and the United States.

Embedded within the British and Irish antislavery movement, publishers like Webb and Gilpin understood the audiences that would be most interested in US slave narratives. If Douglass implored Webb to send more copies of his *Narrative* for him to sell at lectures—"All my Books went last night at one blow," he wrote on December 6, 1845, "I want more[.] I want more"—then he also relied on Webb to circulate his books to prominent antislavery activists who distributed it among their own networks.[21] Roy notes that "well-connected [antislavery] families such as the Estlins in Bristol and the Jenningses in Cork bought copies in bulk from Richard D. Webb and redistributed them locally."[22] Gilpin and Pennington also seem to have strategically sought reviews for the *Fugitive Blacksmith* in nonconformist, antislavery, and temperance publications.[23] In the second edition of the book, Pennington's preface attributed its strong sales to the "favorable reviews" that brought the book "before the notice of the public"—that is, before particular publics that Gilpin, with a knowledge of reform campaigns, targeted.[24] By the third edition, Pennington also acknowledged the role of what Ronald and Mary Zboray term "social dissemination" in circulating his book: readers who lent or gave away books to establish or strengthen bonds between friends, relatives, or those who shared values and purposes.[25] Pennington describes how "in almost every instance where I have gone into a place, I have found the way prepared by the book. In some cases a single copy had been handed from one to another in the town, and some minister or leading gentleman has been prepared to speak of it at my meeting."[26] While this social dissemination involved people lending or giving away copies as much as buying books, Pennington's and Gilpin's shared political commitments meant that both men would have characterized success as both the spread of abolitionist ideas as well as financial profits from sales. In any case, Gilpin almost certainly understood that by building audiences at lectures, social dissemination could also build a market for the text.

Gilpin and Webb materialized slave narratives in formats that aided social dissemination. Gilpin's edition of *The Life of Josiah Henson* (1851) was printed on cheap paper with paper covers, small type, and in a small format to keep costs low. The pamphlet-like book suggests an ephemeral urgency and could be carried in a pocket. It was advertised at 1s, and an advert for Gilpin's edition of Pennington's *The Fugitive Blacksmith* on the back cover similarly notes that text was sold for a "mere trifle" in order to raise money to purchase Pennington's family's freedom.[27] Webb seems to have made similar calculations in the presentation of Douglass's *Narrative*. Writing to American abolitionist Maria Weston Chapman, his wife, Hannah Webb, observed that in comparison to the compendium *Slavery as It Is*, "Frederick's [book] is in a more popular form & will catch more readers."[28] In his Bordieuan analysis of Gilpin's, Pennington's, and Brown's relations and positions within the literary field, Michael Drescher proposes that these authors and their publisher shared an understanding of the need to realize strong sales and to "legitimiz[e] the generation of high economic profits with the demands of the abolitionist project."[29]

Without surviving copies of their accounting books or other business records, the precise financial arrangements that British publishers made with the authors of slave narratives remain unclear. While many published narratives claimed to be sold for the benefit of the author or to manumit their family members, it is hard to know how much authors actually earned. Evidence in correspondence and in the material texts themselves suggests that author-funded publication was common. By the 1846 "thirty-third thousand" edition of his narrative, Roper was certainly self-publishing, and the degree of control he appears to have exercised over his narrative in terms of changes between editions suggests that he may always have been absorbing the financial risk.[30] When Webb printed William Wells Brown's *Narrative of William W. Brown* in 1849, Brown was responsible for the costs.[31] Douglass, who collaborated closely with Webb on the format, materials, and paratexts of his Dublin editions, may also have borne some of the costs of publication.

This type of commission publishing—in which authors paid the cost of publication plus a sum to cover the publisher's time and labor, and was then (usually) responsible for distributing the book—was more common in Britain than in the US. It suited authors and organizations whose works had a well-defined and immediate audience (institutional reports and catalogues, occasional lectures, sermons), or who sought to publish literary, religious, or medical works for which sales would likely be limited.[32] Michael Winship notes that for the Boston firm of Ticknor and Fields, publishing on commission was a means of furthering organizations, activities, and causes the partners supported while also making a small profit.[33] Publishing slave narratives on commission would have made sense for reformers like Webb and Gilpin, who were, nevertheless, running businesses. There were also advantages of this model for Black abolitionists. Once they had paid the costs and publisher's commission, all profits on sales were their own, and, in the case of sales they made personally at lectures, cash came immediately to hand. Paying publication costs also allowed abolitionists to maintain their independence from antislavery societies, which was particularly helpful for US abolitionists who sought to rise above factional divisions in the antislavery movement at home while they were in Britain. But such independence was only possible for abolitionists like Douglass and Brown, who arrived with funds, as illustrated by John Brown's entanglement with the BFASS, discussed below.

The imprints of these smaller, reform-minded publishers may have acted as a guarantee of a narrative's antislavery politics and, more importantly, its legitimacy.[34] British reviewers praised the literary talents displayed in slave narratives, but, in doing so, they often questioned either the veracity or the authorship of the text. For example, the *Spectator* commended the "natural force and fluency of language" in Douglass's narrative, but concluded by wondering whether the narrative was "of the nature of true stories by De Foe," questioning whether Douglass's narrative was, like *Robinson Crusoe*, largely an exciting fiction.[35] Similarly, the *Athenaeum* said of Northup's *Twelve Years a Slave*, "This book of adventure is well written," a compliment that nevertheless positioned the book alongside fictional "adventure" narratives, before adding, "but how far the skill displayed is to be credited to the Negro, how far to the sensible and humane editor, we have no means of ascertaining."[36] Realizing that their narratives risked being read as inventive fictions, the authors of slave narratives and their supporters may have chosen to keep them away from the publishers who specialized in American fiction and poetry, even as doing so reduced their chances of a literary reputation.

To summarize, then, it is not simply that racial discrimination kept Black abolitionist authors from accessing the publishers and print objects that authorized white US authors, their texts, and their particular visions for American literature: handsome editions, legitimizing series and anthologies, and authorizing illustrations. Black authors of slave narratives also had good reason for seeking out British publishers who shared their political convictions and who presented their texts in formats that echoed and sustained the mobility that men like Brown, Douglass, Pennington, and Roper embodied in their transatlantic travels and itinerant lecturing. Indeed, by not situating slave narratives as part of an emergent national American literature, these publishers echoed the political position adopted by their authors, who saw themselves as Atlantic subjects rather than belonging to a nation that continued to deny them the basic rights of citizenship. Where white American authors engaged with British print culture to further the fashioning of a national literature, Black abolitionists used a different sphere of that culture to situate themselves within and to expand an Atlantic reform culture in which radical social change was possible. However, there were also ideological tensions between slave narratives' imaginative uses of transatlantic print culture and their print presentation in Britain. Even publishers with antislavery convictions still published and disseminated those narratives in ways that reinscribed Black bodies as objects for speculation, though the texts of those narratives use transatlantic circulation to express Black subjectivity. Case studies of Solomon Northup's *Twelve Years a Slave* and John Brown's *Slave Life in Georgia* illustrate that these frictions emerge in publications by commercial firms and antislavery organizations in which print materials reinforced the logic of slavery that the narratives themselves exploded.

"Graphically Illustrated": *Twelve Years a Slave* and the Violence of Commercial Print

Michaël Roy observes that *Twelve Years a Slave* was the "first slave narrative to be published [in the United States] under the imprint of a commercial publishing house."[37] Although the division between commercial and abolitionist publishing in Britain was not so stark, *Twelve Years a Slave* was also the first narrative to reach Britain via the networks of the transatlantic book trade rather than those of transatlantic abolitionism. Northup's American publishers, Derby and Miller of Auburn, New York, arranged with Sampson Low for its simultaneous publication, securing copyright on both sides of the Atlantic. Neither firms' archives survive, so the details of the arrangement are lost, making it impossible to know which firm first suggested the collaboration. In his autobiography, James Derby mentions having dealt with Low Sr. in his capacity as the Harpers' agent since 1838, and he may have met Low Jr., who traveled to New York in 1852 to further the firm's American interests, or seen the *Literary World*'s glowing recommendation for the firm as a transatlantic partner for American houses.[38] Alternatively, Low may have seen may have seen the announcement of a "A Thrilling Narrative of Slavery!!" in the April 15, 1853, edition of *Norton's Literary Gazette*, which was advertised in Low's own *Publishers' Circular* from 1852 onward, and then approached Derby and Miller.[39] What Low paid for the British rights—and whether it was a fixed sum or a royalty on sales—is unknown, as is how much, if anything, Northup received from the twenty thousand copies Low claimed to sell in Britain in the six months after publication.[40]

Materially, the British edition of Northup's narrative was very different from previous British editions of slave narratives, as a comparison with Charles Gilpin's edition of Josiah Henson's *Life of Josiah Henson* demonstrates. Gilpin published Henson's book in a small, pamphlet-like format, bound in paper covers and priced at 1s. Low printed *Twelve Years a Slave* in octavo format—a size associated with novels—with an embossed cloth binding and it retailed for 6s. Gilpin's book suggests an ephemeral urgency and could be easily carried in a pocket, while Low's cloth volume belongs on a shelf and demands permanent preservation. While committed abolitionists may likely still have purchased Northup's book (it was reviewed in the *Anti-Slavery Reporter* and the *Anti-Slavery Advocate*), obtaining the book required no engagement with abolitionist politics, and it may have appealed to those who enjoyed *Uncle Tom* for its romance and adventure as much as its antislavery message. Furthermore, in producing a product for this middle-class literary market, Low created a material text that undermined Northup's challenge to the objectification and enforced embodiment of Black subjects and his articulation of that subjectivity at a transatlantic scale.

Unlike most slave narratives, which begin with the narrator's birth into slavery in the South and end with an escape to freedom in the North, Northup's life as a free person of color in New York is shattered when he is lured to Washington, DC, kidnapped, and sold into slavery in Louisiana. Within this North–South trajectory, *Twelve Years a Slave* also constructs transatlantic geographies through quotations from British poetry, which begin after Northup is bought by the cruel Edward Epps.[41] Through these quotations, Northup presents himself as an active agent in the transatlantic circulation of texts. Like an editor or publisher, Northup-the-narrator reprints texts from across the transatlantic print culture in which his narrative itself would later circulate. *Twelve Years a Slave* is therefore both a local account of slavery in a specific US region and a transatlantic artifact for which the publication arrangements echo Northup's use of Anglo-American literary circulation to establish his cultural literacy and creative powers.

While the narrative's epigraph comes from the antislavery favorite *The Task* by William Cowper (1785), the British poetry recirculated in *Twelve Years a Slave* itself is not from the antislavery canon. The narrator seeks to capture the limits of Epps's sympathy in lines from "A Destiny" (1840) by writer and divorce law campaigner Caroline Norton, a narrative poem in which a cruel and rash husband ensures an unhappy life and early death for his wife. The enslaved woman Patsey's "idea of the joy of heaven" is expressed by (slightly variant) lines from "Byron's Prayer" (1831) by Scottish author, colonial administrator, and friend of Lord Byron, John Malcolm. Finally, Northup describes Bass, the white Canadian who helps facilitate his rescue, through lines from Alfred, Lord Tennyson's 1842 conclusion to *The May Queen*. Daniel Hack has recently argued that the nineteenth century saw the development of an "African American tradition of citation" from Victorian poetry, to which Tennyson, especially, was central.[42] Hack's reading of this tradition—as a claim to cultural literacy and a demonstration of creative agency that emphasizes gaps between two literary traditions as well as creating convergences—illuminates Northup's citational practice. *Twelve Years a Slave* internally echoes a print culture in which Tennyson's poetry and slave narratives can appear side by side—a proximity that was materialized in Low's cloth-bound, octavo edition, which implied that Northup's book belonged on the shelf of a home or library. However, these quotations from British texts also create distance between white writers and Northup and others enslaved on the plantation.

The quotation from "Byron's Prayer" is particularly complex, as Northup transforms its meaning in order to assert Patsey's subjectivity as well as his own. Though Patsey has been "reared no better than her master's beast," Northup affirms that she still understands the idea of freedom, as do all enslaved people: "The most ignorant of them generally know full well its meaning." Applying a quotation from a poem that ventriloquizes Byron's dying thoughts to Patsey suggests that she has the same capacity for feeling as a great poet. However, the emotions that Byron and Patsey express are not identical. In the original poem, the lines express Byron's melancholy and his dissatisfaction with life and fame. For Patsey, however, the lines follow Northup explaining that "her idea of the joy of heaven was simply *rest*":

> I ask no paradise on high,
> With cares on earth oppressed,
> The only heaven for which I sigh,
> Is rest, eternal rest.[43]

Applying these lines to Patsey emphasizes the differences in hers and Byron's struggles, as well as their shared capacity for emotion; the quotation suggests cross-racial similarity and encourages cross-racial sympathy, but it also illustrates the distance between its original subject and Patsey. Malcolm's poem participates in a public commemoration of Byron's death, while Patsey's brutal existence—and the existences of millions like her—would remain unknown and unmourned if not for Northup's narrative. Northup thus uses the transatlantic circulation of texts to contrast the transatlantic culture of feeling around the death of one white man with the collective refusal to acknowledge the transatlantic traumas of slavery.

Northup's use of transatlantic print circulation to generate bonds of empathy between feeling subjects—Patsey and Byron, and Patsey and the reader—resonates with Lydia Huntley Sigourney's uses of transatlantic materials, discussed in chapter 4. But while Sigourney seems confident that a transatlantic print economy can train the kind of sympathetic readership she requires, Northup questions whether the sympathies generated through these circulations are either equally applied or politically effective. By showing that Patsey can feel like a white man—and like Byron, no less—Northup illustrates that she is deserving of feeling at the same time that he probes the inequities in sympathy itself. Moreover, does recognizing Patsey as a feeling subject actually help her? This question was even more pressing after the unprecedented transatlantic success of *Uncle Tom's Cabin*, a text that *Twelve Years a Slave* referenced in its dedication, and that Low consciously echoed and evoked in his publication and advertising. Patsey feels, and readers feel for Patsey, even at a transatlantic distance, but at the end of the text, she remains trapped on the Red River plantation. By expanding the geography of his narrative through quotations, Northup suggests that slavery is not simply a Southern, or even an American, problem, but a problem in which a transatlantic reading community is implicated, and which their feelings alone cannot solve.

Low's adverts for *Twelve Years a Slave* also situate the text within a transatlantic print economy. They suggest that its Anglo-American publication proves the book's commercial value and authenticity without locating either in Northup's authorial skills. For Low, the agreement with Derby and Miller was not just a means of securing copyright, it was also a tool for promotion. As chapter 2 demonstrated, organizing authorized editions required professional connections, logistical experience, and financial investment that was beyond the reach of many authors; simultaneous publication, therefore, testified to a text's cultural and market value. When announcing *Twelve Years a Slave*, Low drew attention to its publication arrangements: "'Solomon Northup,' published in London this week, in advance of its publication in New York, is a genuine slave narrative, and its mere announcement on the other side of the Atlantic had led to orders for above 10,000 copies."[44] Low also prominently displayed these "International Arrangement[s] with the American Publishers and Authors" in an advert in the London *Literary Gazette* for his "NEW WORKS" that included Northup's narrative.[45] By placing the simultaneous publishing agreements next to the description of *Twelve Years* as a "genuine slave narrative," the advert suggests that Low's authorized edition, as much as Northup's authorship, authenticates the narrative. Low's edition thus becomes part of the "white envelope" of institutional power that enclosed Black testimony and validated it according to white standards of the "truth" about slavery.[46] Indeed, by calling the book "Solomon Northup," Low's advert renders Northup as a text to be read rather than an authorial subject.

Commercial imperatives also led Low to produce a material text for *Twelve Years a Slave* that conflicted with its antislavery politics and especially with its assertions of Black subjectivity. The British Library deposit copy of *Twelve Years a Slave* has a note pasted to its front inside cover that reads: "The plates to Solomon Northope [sic] are not yet ready the book is published without them Low & Son Jun 3."[47] The note indicates that either stereotype plates or printed copies of the illustrations had not arrived from the United States when Low needed to go to press to secure copyright; the illustrations are listed in the contents but do not appear in this copy. These illustrations were commissioned by Derby and Miller from a local artist and engraver, and were specific to the details of the text.[48] They formed an important part of the book's appeal, but Low could not risk losing his copyright by waiting for them. Therefore, the first British readers did not see the striking frontispiece image of Northup in his plantation suit, a calm and dignified figure staring up to the sky, his expression hard to decipher (figure 10). This image employs what Martha Cutter calls "parallel empathy," a mode of visual rhetoric that could generate a connection with, rather than pity for, the enslaved, but could also "lead to a sense of the ambiguity of the lifeworld of the enslaved—a consciousness that some aspects of enslaved experience cannot in fact be represented or comprehended, and remain outside of the viewer's realm of understanding."[49] The frontispiece illustration resists both easy legibility and the reduction of Northup to familiar iconography of enslavement. It thus preserves Northup's subjectivity even as it presents him to the reader, and that subjectivity is emphasized further by the facsimile signature underneath the image, which signifies Northup as an author even if *Twelve Years* is not precisely "Written by Himself."

Instead, the only image with which *Twelve Years a Slave*'s first British readers were presented was the one embossed on the book's spine (figure 11). This depicts a scene that is not in Northup's narrative in which a white man raises a whip over a chained and kneeling Black man in front of a large plantation house; it was likely a stock antislavery image.[50] The positioning of the Black man recalls Josiah Wedgwood's "Am I Not a Man and a Brother?" medallion, one of Cutter's examples of the "hierarchical empathy" produced by images in which the enslaved is an "inferior entity that needs the help and mediation of the white viewer" and "possesses only an unfinished and open selfhood, rather than the finished and closed selfhood of the viewer."[51] This image associated *Twelve Years* with an established antislavery canon, but it also presented Northup as a legible symbol rather than an agential subject. Moreover, the positioning on the spine—unique to the British edition—creates a troubling correspondence between the body of the slave and the body of the book. As Andrew Piper observes, books, like human bodies, are "essentially vertebral," and in the book trade and the slave trade, potential purchasers used the spine to decide whether or not to buy.[52] Northup observes that "scars upon a slave's back were considered evidence of a rebellious or unruly spirit, and hurt his sale," but Low placed traumatic marks on the spine to encourage sales of his "genuine slave narrative."[53] The binding of Low's first edition of *Twelve Years a Slave* presented the book as an enslaved Black body that "bears abundant marks of authenticity," as the London *Eclectic Review* said of Northup's narrative; that is, it bore the kind of marks that white abolitionists had made into circulating signifiers of slavery.[54]

Even when the original illustrations were restored, Low's textual production continued to situate the enslaved body as an

Figure 10. Frontispiece: "Solomon Northup in his Plantation Suit," from Solomon Northup, *Twelve Years a Slave* (Auburn: Derby and Miller, 1853). University of North Carolina. Digitized for the Internet Archive: https://archive.org/details/twelveyearsslavenort/page/n9/mode/2up.

Figure 11. Spine showing a gilt anti-slavery image of a white man about to whip an enslaved Black man. From Solomon Northup, *Twelve Years a Slave. London* (London: Sampson Low & Son & Co, 1853). Cadbury Research Library: Special Collections, University of Birmingham. r E449.N67.

object for white speculation. Like any good publisher, Low turned the original absence of the illustrations into a marketing opportunity. In August, he advertised a "re-issue" that drew attention to the new images: "Just ready, price 6s., graphically illustrated."[55] Low's phrase "graphically illustrated" is unsettling, promoting the artistic skill of the images but also gesturing toward their explicit depictions of violence. While Low's advertisement promised a material text consummate with Northup's unflinching testimony, by placing "graphically illustrated" immediately after "price 6 shillings," it also commodified those horrors. In doing so, Low's advertisements inadvertently mirror the slave market's commodification of bodies and persons, against which Northup's narrative protests. The publisher risks becoming, like Northup's description of the slave-trader, "a speculator in human flesh," with "speculator" echoing the intersection of the visual and the commodity present in Low's advert.[56] The British edition of *Twelve Years a Slave* therefore reinforced both the authenticity of the text and horrors of slavery, but also affirmed what Saidiya Hartman calls "the fungibility of the commodity [that] makes the captive body an abstract and empty vessel vulnerable to the projection of others' feelings, ideas, desires, and values."[57] Low's material text made Northup a legible and saleable object rather than an authorial subject.

In observing how Low's edition echoed the logic of slavery, I do not mean to suggest that Low was not supportive of the antislavery cause. While I have found no evidence of his involvement in antislavery activism, Low was a committed Anglican who was dedicated to charitable work; his business partner Edward Marston, noted that Low's "zeal and energy took a less selfish and more philanthropic turn than is generally characteristic of mere business men."[58] It therefore is likely that both financial and moral concerns influenced his decision to publish *Twelve Years a Slave*. Moreover, by presenting Black bodies as fungible objects, Low's edition succinctly analyses the status of the enslaved, calling for the empathy of potential readers as well their cash. Yet this demand for an emotional transaction shows the limits of empathy to which Northup himself draws attention. If Low's "graphically illustrated" spectacles of slavery call for empathy, this does not negate the fact that they also commodify the enslaved. Just as the empathy that Northup generates through the transatlantic circulation of texts does not save Patsey, any empathy that Low's edition creates does not ameliorate the situation of the enslaved. At best, Low's edition confirms Northup's suspicions about the failure of transatlantic white sympathy to effect change; at worst, it emulates the logic of slavery by making the enslaved into a spectacle for purchase. Nevertheless, commercial publishers like Low were not alone in exposing and exploiting enslaved bodies to sell slave narratives. The circulation of John Brown's *Slave Life in Georgia* by the British and Foreign Anti-Slavery Society demonstrates how charitable organizations and social dissemination also relied on the Black body as an object of white speculation.

Slave Life in Georgia and the Speculations of Socially Embedded Distribution

By his own account, John Brown (who had no connection to his Harpers Ferry namesake) arrived in England in August 1850. He had escaped from slavery around three years earlier and found work in Michigan before staying briefly at the Dawn Institute in Canada. Brown had come to England intending to join a Cornish miner who had offered him work, but he arrived in Cornwall to find the man had died in Boston. After working in Bristol and Lancashire, where he also experienced racial prejudice, Brown traveled to London in April 1851 to seek work. There, he quickly made contact with the British and Foreign Anti-Slavery Society (BFASS).[59] Five years later, he published a narrative of his enslavement and escape, *Slave Life in Georgia*, which was dictated to and edited by Louis Alexander Chamerovzow, Secretary of the BFASS, printed by W. M. Watts of Temple Bar, London, and distributed by the BFASS. No American edition appeared in Brown's lifetime.

Unlike *Twelve Years a Slave*, which was the product of a collaboration between experienced commercial publishers that followed an established process for copyright editions, Brown's narrative was printed with the assistance of abolitionists who knew little about publishing and was circulated through the networks of the BFASS and networks created through Brown's lecture tours. While *Twelve Years a Slave* was aimed at the middle-class reading public who had been thrilled by *Uncle Tom's Cabin*, active abolitionists were the primary audience for *Slave Life in Georgia*. The two books were also materially very different objects. *Slave Life in Georgia* was no octavo volume with a gilded cloth binding; it was printed in a small and portable format on thin paper, and was advertised in the BFASS's paper, the *Anti-Slavery Reporter*, at 1s.

Despite these material differences, both texts use transatlantic circulation to articulate Black subjectivity. The localizing title of Brown's narrative belies the mobility within the text; his various escape attempts take him to Tennessee and New Orleans as well as Michigan and Canada. However, Brown's aim is always to reach England, having heard from John Glasgow, a Black British subject, that Black men can find freedom there. In a chapter that was first published in the *Anti-Slavery Reporter*, Brown explains that Glasgow had served on a Liverpool ship that docked at Savannah, where he was imprisoned under Georgia's Negro Seamen Act: a law under which free Black seamen were jailed for fear they would incite uprisings among the enslaved.[60] When Glasgow's white

English captain failed to redeem him, due to the "enormously high" gaol fees, Glasgow was sold to Thomas Stevens, Brown's second enslaver.[61] Glasgow tells Brown that in England, "folks would respect me as much as they did a white man," and this, Brown explains, "inspired me with a longing to get to England, which I made up my mind I would try and do some day."[62] For the rest of the text, Brown is determined to reach England even if he does not know always know where England is.

The few scholars who have studied Brown's narrative agree that he introduces this praise of England to aid the circulation of his text therein. Audrey Fisch argues that the contrast between Glasgow's experiences in England and the United States would have appealed to a British public that read slave narratives to confirm their superiority over Americans and shore up a "fragile and contested" English identity, even as the cruel behavior of Glasgow's captain disrupts this opposition between bad Americans and good Brits.[63] Ikuko Asaka suggests that Brown changes key details in the Glasgow story and perhaps invents the story altogether to better "advance a major concern in 19th-century British abolitionism [the Seamen Acts]," thus showing his ability to craft his text in response to popular issues.[64] Both scholars argue that Brown's introduction of transatlantic circulation shows his authorial control; he could tailor the facts of his life and control the meaning of his narrative even as it was edited and packaged by white abolitionists. However, I would argue that Brown also uses transatlantic circulations in *Slave Life in Georgia* to fashion himself as an Atlantic subject.

For Brown, transatlantic circulation is characterized by friction and delay, rather than the fluidity and hybridity that Gilroy attributes to the Black Atlantic. Nevertheless, Brown's attempts to reach England provide him with opportunities to invert the logic of slavery and become a scrutinizing subject rather than a legible object, even as these attempts fail. In his second escape attempt, Brown tries to reach England via New Orleans, believing that it is "only just across the water"; however, once in New Orleans, he realizes that he is "in the very heart of slavery, and further off from England than when I was in Georgia." Brown therefore decides to re-enslave himself and attempt another escape at a later date.

Paradoxically, in choosing to relinquish his tenuous freedom, Brown makes the transition from enslaved object to authorial subject that is usually associated with the slave narrator's climactic escape north. Seeking a white man who will pose as his enslaver, Brown inverts the gaze of the slave auction as he categorizes and evaluates white bodies. The white target's "blood-shotten and puffy eyes" make him legible as a "gambler and a drunkard" who "might want money" from the deal that Brown proposes.[65] Although Brown fails to reach British soil this time, he demonstrates the personhood that he believes the British will recognize, relocating himself as an Atlantic subject while still on US soil. Within the text, friction in circulation, as much as fluid transatlantic crossings, enables the articulation of Black personhood.

Like Brown's efforts to reach Britain, the circulation of *Slave Life in Georgia* in Britain seems to have been halting and not always successful. Letters between BFASS members show the circuitous route that brought Brown's narrative to print.[66] On October 26, 1853, Edinburgh abolitionist and BFASS supporter John Wigham wrote to Chamerovzow, explaining that Brown had "orders for one thousand copies of his narrative, and a few have paid in advance," suggesting that Brown had been planning to publish his life for some time. Wigham proposed contracting with a printer for two thousand copies and stereotyping the plates in case further editions were required, and offered to "be security to the printer for the first 2000 which when sold [at 1s each, a standard price for a slave narrative] would yield 100 pounds."[67] On October 31, Wigham wrote again, explaining that Brown had found a printer who would contract for two thousand copies and stereotype the plates on the security of Brown's subscription list. This letter also indicates that Brown and Chamerovzow had been preparing a manuscript for a narrative, but that preparation had been interrupted by Chamerovzow's ill health. Wigham writes that Brown has found a "learned man (rather poor) who offers to put the manuscript in the best form he can, for a small sum," adding that this man will not be the equal of Chamerovzow, an erstwhile historical novelist, and that, if Chamerovzow's health allows, he is welcome to find someone more skilled to do the job in the next month for the five pounds Brown can pay.[68] However, the book was not advertised as "preparing for press" until a year later, and was eventually printed and published in London, not Edinburgh, in late January or early February 1855.

Chamerovzow's unwillingness to let Brown's narrative escape the BFASS's control likely caused this deviation from Wigham's plan. Many Black American abolitionists were reluctant to align with the BFASS, an allied organization of the Tappan brothers' American and Foreign Anti-Slavery Society, because they were usually more sympathetic to Garrison's American Anti-Slavery Society, and because they wanted to maximize audiences by remaining above factional splits in the movement. Keeping ties with Brown, who was a gifted lecturer, would have helped the BFASS maintain a higher profile in discussions of American slavery, now a more popular topic than ever following the success of *Uncle Tom's Cabin*. To maintain control of Brown's narrative, either the BFASS or Chamerovzow himself seems to have paid the costs of publishing. In late February 1855, Edward Wigham, writing on behalf of his cousin John who was then ill, suggests that Chamerovzow be "paid by John Brown *as* he receives the money . . . & only let him have what he can sell at one time, so as to let him repay thee by degrees. I hope thou wilt soon be relieved from the weight of the expenses—we shall do what we can to get it into notice."[69] The latent distrust that Brown would remit money for publication costs suggests that the BFASS did not view the partnership as one of equals, but one in which they needed to keep a tight hold on Brown by restricting his access to his books.

The BFASS's arrangement with Brown thus differs from both commission publishing, where the author paid costs up front, and trade agreements, in which publishers bore the risks and paid outright for copyright, shared profits with the author, or paid royalties. Unlike the former, the BFASS or Chamerovzow—and not Brown—paid the upfront costs, and unlike the latter, the author—and not the publisher—received payments from sales. In order to keep costs down, the Wighams "always hoped J. Brown would sell them himself & thus save the bookseller's percentage."[70] The BFASS themselves made the same point when advertising the second edition in the *Anti-Slavery Advocate*, observing that the work "was intended chiefly for circulation through private influence, and at the very low price at which it is sold will not bear trade discounts."[71] This created a scenario in which the publisher (in this case, an organization acting as the publisher) bore the risks, and the author, who was a direct recipient of monies from sales, was expected to pay the publisher back for expenses they had incurred producing the book by remitting a percentage of each sale.[72]

By suggesting that Brown would "repay" the BFASS or Chamerovzow, Edward Wigham renders the publication costs as debt owed by Brown, an association that stands in complex relation to slavery itself. Stephen Best has argued that antebellum figurations of the fugitive, most notably in the Dred Scott decision, positioned the enslaved person as a debtor in ways that require the enslaved to be both property and person. Despite the fact that the slave cannot incur debt "since there is no slave in advance of liability who can will a debt," "the figuration of the fugitive as debtor produces a willful subject against the express legal nullification of willfulness" and "it . . . fabulates a subject not owned when the owned escapes."[73] The financial arrangements for *Slave Life in Georgia* therefore both confirm Brown's freedom as a subject who can will a debt and also place him in a state of indebtedness that echoes slavery itself, in which he has to pay back the costs of his narrative of self-emancipation, if not the costs of freedom itself. While its aim was ostensibly to raise money to establish Brown as a cotton farmer in the West Indies or Africa, the socially embedded publication of *Slave Life in Georgia* seems instead to have indentured Brown to the BFASS.

However, not all sales were expected to come through Brown. Edward Wigham suggested that "we could take charge of distributing the copies already subscribed for," and while this "we" is ambiguous—does he mean the BFASS, or himself and his cousin?—correspondence suggests that Chamerovzow directed dissemination.[74] He sent copies of *Slave Life in Georgia* both to those who subscribed and to supporters of the BFASS whom he deemed likely to be able to sell copies or who would buy copies to give away. For example, he wrote to John Bishop Estlin in February 1855 that "Slave Life in Georgia is out. I feel desirous of getting it into good circulation, on account of the valuable information it contains, & the interior view it gives of Slavery. Can you do anything for it in Bristol, amongst your anti-slavery friends?"[75] Supporters who bought copies for or sold copies to friends and associates remitted the money to the BFASS, who (we hope) sent Brown his portion. This social dissemination via volunteer agents had disadvantages and advantages. It was slow, as copies had to travel from Chamerovzow to the agent, who would then take them to the subscribers that Brown had listed before the money flowed back along the same chain. If an antislavery lecture or meeting was taking place, copies might sell quickly, as happened in Southampton, where Joseph Clark requested more copies after having "an extraordinary sale"—thanks, it seems, to Brown's presence in the area.[76] Otherwise, the BFASS relied on the agent to make contact with fellow supporters.

Social dissemination thus required person-to-person networking, which could strengthen ties between abolitionists. As well as cutting out the booksellers' margins, circulating a narrative within one's personal networks enabled volunteer agents to show commitment to the antislavery cause and gave supporters an excuse to raise the topic of antislavery among potential sympathizers. The text of *Slave Life in Georgia* echoes this use of the material text as a nexus for social, ideological, and philanthropic networks. After explaining how John Glasgow was wrongfully enslaved in Georgia, Brown's narrative reaches out and asks any reader who knows the whereabouts of Glasgow's English wife to "write forthwith, to the Secretary of the *British and Foreign Anti-Slavery Society*, who will place the parties in communication with such friends as may be anxious to take steps in this distressing case."[77] Social dissemination also kept *Slave Life in Georgia* outside of the market and reduced the commodification of Brown that was such a feature of *Twelve Years a Slave*. In doing so, it reinforced the narrative's own contrast between slavery in the United States and laws against trading in humans in England. Brown gives the cost of commodities like corn and cotton in dollars and the equivalent in pounds sterling, but when describing his own sale for three hundred and ten dollars he does not translate the price into British currency—a subtle reminder that Black bodies could not be purchased in pounds.

The social distribution of *Slave Life in Georgia* was unevenly successful. Some volunteer agents sold books with gusto. Francis

Calder took over one hundred copies, despite his warning that his hometown, Belfast, was "practically a dreadful pro-slavery town."[78] Joseph Clark sent remittance for fifteen dozen copies sold in Southampton only a month after he requested them.[79] More often, however, agents wrote of difficulties selling copies, observing that the delay between Brown's visit and the publication had reduced interest in the text. While professing that he would "like to serve John Brown as well as possible," Thomas Owen of Bedfordshire, South East England noted that "it is so long since John Brown obtained the names of subscribers for his book that the interest felt in it is lost. Some of the parties are dead some removed and some are not known to me at all."[80] William Smeal in Glasgow, who authored one of the testimonies in *Slave Life in Georgia*, complained that "a number of those whose names were down for copies, either were not to be found or declined to pay for them when presented."[81] Miss S. Hilditch of Rothesay explained that her family no longer had the social connections to facilitate circulation: "We are strangers here & know of no channel through which they may be sent free of expense."[82] The "distance of time," as one Dalkeith stationer expressed it, between Brown's physical presence and his appearance in print hindered the ability to circulate his narrative.[83]

Complaints from agents frequently returned to the necessity of John Brown's body—or, at least, his recent appearance in the locality—for selling the *Narrative*. In Brown's prolonged absence, sales slowed or ceased altogether. Social dissemination, as well as market distribution, relied on placing the Black body under the white gaze. While the material text of *Slave Life in Georgia* did not objectify the Black body as immediately and visually as did the cover of *Twelve Years a Slave*, honorary agents knew that their purchasers wanted to speculate on Brown himself before they speculated financially on his narrative. The selling of *Slave Life in Georgia* thus echoes Brown's description of the slave pen in New Orleans in which the slave must be "looking bright" because the "price a slave fetches depends, in a great measure, upon the general appearance he or she presents to the intending buyer."[84]

While social dissemination of *Slave Life in Georgia* echoed the logic of slavery, becoming an object of speculation did not inevitably entail a loss of agency for Brown. In the slave pen at New

Orleans, Brown makes himself an object of visual and economic speculation at the same time as he challenges the idea of the Black body as straightforwardly legible or consumable. When he notes that a slave's price depends "upon the general appearance he or she presents to the intending buyer," the verb ambiguates whether this presentation is an ingenuous display or a carefully constructed performance, and whether a distinction between the two is even possible.[85] Brown himself makes the slave pen into a site for negotiation, "draw[ing] out the buyers, in order to learn what they wanted me for."[86] The slave pen thus emerges as a site of Black performance, some of which is enforced by enslavers and some of which is initiated by enslaved persons and is subversive in effect. It would be naïve, therefore, to think that Brown did not also seek to subvert the possessive white gaze in the British lecture halls to the same, potentially liberating, ends.

Reports of Brown's lectures in Britain suggest that he was aware of white viewers' desires to speculate on his body. Several describe Brown displaying himself in the "bells and horns," an instrument of torture that consisted of an iron headpiece with bells attached that weighed at least twelve to fourteen pounds, which an enslaved person was forced to wear day and night to prevent escape.[87] If the bells and horns originally prevented Brown from fleeing the white gaze, in the lecture hall it signified his ability to willingly command that gaze. Choosing to don this apparatus on stage, Brown transformed an object that had restricted his mobility into a performance that sustained his liberty in Britain. Moreover, even when his enslaver forced him to wear the bells and horns in Georgia, Brown claimed that he "thought more of John Glasgow, and getting off to England, that I had ever done all the time before, with such a firm purpose."[88] Enforced embodiment and the white gaze here engender a secret agential desire that conjures a transatlantic subjectivity. In returning to the bells and horns in the lecture hall—a space of performance and of bookselling—Brown may not have been reclaiming and subverting experiences of enslavement so much as reinhabiting ways in which he had accessed and nurtured his humanity within a dehumanizing system.

If Brown primarily achieved this subjectivity in the lecture hall, other African American abolitionists achieved it in the printed book and, in particular, in its paratexts. Turning first to Frederick Douglass and then to William Wells Brown, I argue that by controlling the reprinting of their narratives in Britain, these writers materialized the break between their enslaved life and their life thereafter and repositioned themselves as autobiographers, who construct narratives from experience, rather than simply as witnesses to slavery.

Subjectivity in the Margins: Print and the Paratexts of Frederick Douglass and William Wells Brown

When the *Narrative of the Life of Frederick Douglass* and the *Narrative of William W. Brown* were reprinted in Britain under the superintendence of their authors, both Douglass and Brown introduced paratextual changes. These changes have received relatively little attention despite extensive scholarship on both men and on the ways that the paratext's "marginal spaces and places have functioned centrally as a zone transacting ever-changing modes of white domination and resistance to that domination" in African American books, as Beth McCoy observes.[89] In part, this lack of attention stems from the hyper-canonization of the first US edition of Douglass's *Narrative*. Reflecting on the dominance of the 1845 *Narrative* in anthologies and scholarship, Rachel Blumenthal contends that fixing Douglass in this moment distorts understandings of his development as a writer and thinker and of the slave narrative genre in general.[90] Building on her arguments, I suggest that the hyper-canonicity of the 1845 text obscures how Douglass used the republication of his *Narrative* in Ireland and Britain to transform himself from a narrator, who locates his subjectivity in literacy and composition, to an author, who locates his subjectivity in print and publication. Silencing the transatlantic revisions to this most canonical of slave narratives also mutes the ways that William Wells Brown expanded on Douglass's use of reprinting. Brown experimented with recirculating his enslaved self in the paratexts of his later British publications to sustain multiple, co-existing authorial personas across and between his appearances in print. In doing so, Brown used reprinting and republishing to create a diffuse subjectivity and an authorial consciousness that resists capture, even by his readers.

Robert Levine and Fionnghuala Sweeney both suggest that Douglass's Dublin paratexts assert intellectual and political independence from Garrison and show Douglass reinventing himself as a cosmopolitan and Atlantic subject.[91] Douglass's first substantial change to the Dublin editions was to place his own preface ahead of the preface by Garrison that had opened the 1845 Boston edition. Garrison's preface presents Douglass as an unusually eloquent witness to the horrors of slavery, stressing that the *Narrative* was "essentially true" with "nothing drawn from the imagination."[92] In his own preface, Douglass presents himself as an author, not just a reporter, and focuses on his achievements in print after his self-emancipation, opening with the publication and sales of his narrative in the United States. He expands this material evidence of authorship in the preface to the second Dublin edition, adding a new paragraph in which he observes that "an edition of 2000 copies of my Narrative has been exhausted, and I am in great hopes that before my visit to Great Britain shall be completed, thousands and tens of thousands of the intelligent and philanthropic will be induced to cooperate with the noble band of American abolitionists."[93] While Garrison's preface explains how the AAS created a writer, Douglass's preface predicts that his authorship will create a transatlantic abolitionist fellowship.

Douglass's new preface and appendix shift the locus of subjectivity from writing to print and from composition to (re)circulation. The main text of Douglass's *Narrative* exhibits the generic commonplace identified by James Olney, among others, in which a slave narrator associates their (interior and geographic) journey to freedom with their acquisition of literacy.[94] The association between literary and subjectivity is then succinctly encapsulated in the title page formulas "Written by himself" or "Written by herself." Douglass famously describes literacy as a source of "the white man's power to enslave the black man" and as a necessary step on "the pathway from slavery to freedom," recounting how he paid local boys to teach him to read and write and how studying *The Columbian Orator* helped formulate his consciousness of the inequities of slavery.[95] However, in the second Dublin edition of

Narrative, Douglass directs readers not to his composition but to his editorial work of arranging the materials around the text: he "beg[s] to refer readers" to other paratexts and notes his addition of "an attempted refutation of my Narrative, lately published in the 'Delaware Republican' by Mr. A. C. C. Thompson" and his own reply.[96] Levine notes that Douglass's reprinting of Thompson's letter and his own reply from the *Liberator* shows "editorial mastery" in parodying "one of the key conventions of the antebellum slave narrative—the authenticating testimony of the white editor or publisher."[97] While Thompson's original aim was to discredit Douglass's account of the cruelties of white enslavers, Douglass repurposes the letter so that it supports his own *Narrative* by providing evidence that "Frederick Bailey" was enslaved by the people he describes.

Like Northup's citations of British poetry, Douglass's reprinting of the exchange with Thompson shows a Black American establishing himself as an author through the transatlantic circulation of texts. In the letter, Douglass makes clear that British print offers him space and rights that he is denied in the United States. "In any other country but America, I might hope to get a hearing through the columns of the paper in which I was attacked," Douglass professed; however, the *Delaware Republican* "might be willing to advertise me as a fugitive slave, but on no other condition" could Douglass appear in its pages.[98] American print confines Douglass to a state of fugitivity, and this is true even of the *Liberator*, where his reply to Thompson first appeared. Douglass made several changes to his own letter when he republished it in Dublin. The most prominent, Levine notes, is that he addresses Thompson directly rather than writing to Garrison, creating a print version of the face-to-face encounter that Douglass imagines "if I should meet you where I now am, amid the free hills of Old Scotland."[99] Smaller changes illustrate how recirculating his *Narrative* in Britain enabled Douglass to cast off the confining identity of fugitive witness. In both versions of the letter, Douglass establishes a break between his identities in slavery and in freedom. However, in the *Liberator* letter, Douglass's enslaved self still intrudes, and these intrusions are registered in the printed text. In the *Liberator*, Douglass observes (I preserve the line breaks in the column for clarity):

> Frederick
> Douglass, the *freeman*, is a very different person from
> Frederick Bailey,* the *slave*. I feel myself almost a
> *My former name.
> new man—freedom has given me new life.[100]

Douglass's "former name" physically interrupts the flow of print as a reminder that a former self haunts this confident authorial response, leaving Douglass "almost" a new man—but not quite. In the *Liberator*, the fugitive self, the version of Douglass in his *Narrative*, cannot be separated from the authorial subject Douglass was fashioning in Britain. In the Dublin edition, however, Douglass's former surname is dropped from the statement, which reads without interruption: "Frederick the Freeman is a very different person from Frederick the Slave. To judge me now by what I was then, is to do me great injustice. I feel myself a new man. Freedom has given me new life."[101] With no need any longer for the hedging "almost," the break that Douglass envisions between "Freeman" and "Slave" is echoed in the material form of the book, in which Frederick the Slave of the *Narrative* is separated from Frederick the Freeman of the paratext.

The Dublin edition, therefore, materially articulates a transitional moment in Douglass's sense of self and for his authorship: the moment in which he leaves behind the role of slave narrator and moves into the roles of public intellectual and autobiographer. Levine, Sweeney, and Tom Wright all argue that Douglass's first visit to Britain transformed his outlook and sense of purpose, so that he returned to the United States with new, broader ambitions: Wright notes that after returning in 1847, Douglass's lectures shifted from the antislavery circuit to "unsegregated northern lecture stages" where he spoke "on topics often at one remove from the constraints of a reformist script."[102] But Douglass registers this shift earlier, through the changes than he is able to make when publishing the second Dublin edition. The new preface and postscript depart from what Robert Stepto calls the slave narrative's characteristic "demands of audience and authenticity."[103] In the response to Thompson, published in the appendix, Douglass is aware that his body no longer testifies to his enslavement, but he cares little: "The change wrought in me is truly amazing. . . . I have really got out of my place."[104] If, as Rachel Blumenthal argues, the transition from slave narrative to autobiography takes place when the narrator's body is "no longer . . . a *text* available for the reading and editing pleasure of white abolition," then the Dublin *Narrative* exhibits a truly autobiographical voice.[105] Furthermore, in the paratexts Douglass both shifts the burden of testimony onto a white man—he thanks Thompson for "the testimony he bears to the substantial truth of my story"—and reframes his own authorial practice as a manipulation of existing print elements instead of the immediate witnessing for which the *Narrative* was valued by white US abolitionists.[106] Douglass does not simply recirculate his *Narrative* in Britain, he re-presents it, and, in doing so, remakes himself.

However, the interventions of Douglass's Dublin publisher, Richard Davis Webb, did not fully support Douglass's radical uses of print. On the title page verso of the first and second Dublin editions, Webb printed a resolution by the Hibernian Anti-Slavery Society, of which Webb is named as secretary, that recommends Douglass to "all abolitionists with whom he may meet," as he "has long been known to us by reputation, and is now introduced to us by letters from some of the most distinguished and faithful friends of the Anti-Slavery cause in the United States."[107] While the resolution contributes to Douglass's repositioning as an Atlantic figure, it also documents conversations between white men that validate Douglass's credentials, but in which Douglass himself remains silent. The positioning of the resolution is also significant. It occupies the space that in the US edition belonged to the copyright declaration that designated Douglass as the owner of his text, and through which he claimed rights of citizenship that his race and fugitive status meant that he was otherwise denied. This change thus replaces Douglass's self-declaration of personhood through the infrastructures of print, with a statement suggesting that a transatlantic network of Garrisonians was still attempting to control his circulation in print and in person.

If Douglass came to understand print as a tool for authorial self-fashioning while in Ireland, William Wells Brown arrived in

Britain aware that "producing oneself as a free subject in print and in life is embedded within a set of material textual practices—practices that are . . . also constitutive in processes of racialization."[108] Scholars of Brown's work have observed his creative play with the mechanisms of print.[109] Observing that Brown plagiarized at least 87,000 words from 282 texts across his authorial career, Geoffrey Sanborn argues that Brown embeds his writing within the broader print culture to demonstrate his "capacity to move between [subject positions]," taking "the very basis of identity and send[ing] it into promiscuous circulation."[110] In these uses of print, Brown reconfigures an incident that occurred while he was hired out to Elijah P. Lovejoy, the publisher and editor of the *St. Louis Times*. As he carried type from one newspaper office to another, Brown was attacked by "sons of slaveholders." Then, the type impeded Brown's mobility—"having the heavy form of type in my hands, I could not make my escape by running"—echoing how print objects, from fugitive slave advertisements to the printed page's visual and material enforcement of absolute divisions between Black and white confined African Americans.[111] In contrast, Brown's writings employ print circulation to explore liberating forms of his mobility as a free subject, and he pioneered these print experiments in Britain.

William Wells Brown arrived in Britain with the stereotype plates of his *Narrative*, illustrating his awareness of the importance of controlling his own print circulation. After docking in Liverpool in August 1849, Brown immediately took his plates to Webb in Dublin.[112] He contracted with Webb to print the text, but his book was then published by Charles Gilpin of London, Gilpin and Webb having agreed to market one another's works in 1846.[113] Because Brown financed the publication and sold copies at lecturers and meetings, he was, in a real sense, its author, publisher, and distributor. He, of course, had to pay Webb for the publication costs, but unlike the BFASS and John Brown, Webb does not seem to have restricted William Wells Brown's access to copies or figured the relationship in terms of an ongoing obligation even though he grumbled about what Brown owed. Reprinting his *Narrative* in Britain gave Brown control over his text and enabled him to fashion himself as a mobile subject, distinct from both the enslaved self that he describes within the *Narrative* and his fugitive status in the United States.

The paratext of the British edition of Brown's *Narrative* contrasts his mobility in Britain with his confinement in the United States. First, it replaced the copyright statement with a reference to the text's material transmission: "Printed, chiefly from the American Stereotype Plates, by Webb and Chapman, Great Brunswick Street, Dublin."[114] On the one hand, this substitution swapped Brown's declaration of authorship, property ownership, and citizenship in the US for a statement that situated Webb as the narrative's authorizing figure; printing from stereotype guarantees authenticity by suggesting direct transmission and fixes Brown in place as a fugitive slave. On the other hand, the reference to "American Stereotype Plates" locates the fixative print process on the opposite side of the Atlantic, a distancing reinforced by the change of title from *Narrative of William W. Brown, A Fugitive Slave* in the United States to *Narrative of William W. Brown, An American Slave* in Britain. Brown might be "fixed" as an enslaved person in the United States, but he can inscribe his own personal mobility and the printed circulations of his narrative in the paratexts of the British edition: the parts of the text not printed from the US plates. Brown's new "Note to the Present Edition" begins by observing that "the present narrative was first published in Boston (U.S.) in July, 1847, and eight thousand copies were sold in less than eighteen months from its time of publication."[115] Furthermore, between the first two British editions, Brown changes the location from which he signs the otherwise almost identical authorial "Notes," from "176, Great Brunswick-street Dublin, August 14th, 1849" to "Newcastle-upon-Tyne, January 1st, 1850."[116] The paratexts that differentiate the British edition from its "American Stereotype Plates" introduce textual fluidity and authorial mobility, reinforcing the transition from object to subject that Brown would later associate with coming to Britain: "I had been bought and sold as a slave, in the Southern States. In the so-called free States, I had been treated as one born to occupy an inferior position. . . . But no sooner was I on British soil, than I was recognized as a man, and an equal."[117] Importantly, this mobility emerges not simply from publication in Britain but from the narrative's republication, through which Brown locates himself in two distinct subject positions in order to illustrate his mobility between them.

Brown's next book, *Three Years in Europe; or, Places I Have Seen and People I Have Met*, published with Gilpin in 1852, narratively and materially expands on Brown's attempts to achieve new forms of mobility and subjectivity by (re)circulating his enslaved self in British print. In *Three Years in Europe*, the circulation of Brown's slave narrative enables him to adopt an authorial persona very different from the slave narrator: that of the urbane, genteel, and leisured travel writer. As Charles Baraw argues, the narrator of *Three Years in Europe* has a "mobility . . . that is profoundly different from the forced migrations of the middle passage and the domestic slave trade, and different too from the 'covert geographies' of flight and escape mapped by conventional slave narratives."[118] Brown, in fact, follows directly in the footsteps of Washington Irving in *The Sketch-Book of Geoffrey Crayon* (1819). Brown narrates his passage through the sights of London, beginning with a trip around the British Museum Library, the setting for Irving's sketch "The Art of Book-Making," where Brown, like Irving before him, watches the authors of the present "manufacturing books" (in Irving's words) as they sit under portraits of authors of the past.[119] Britain—and, more particular, a room full of British print objects—provide a space for Brown to insert himself into a national American genealogy of authorship. In borrowing so neatly from Irving (one of many sources Brown inserts into *Three Years*), Brown playfully enacts the plundering work of authorship skewered in "The Art of Book-Making," in which Irving daydreams of the authors of the present "decking [themselves] out piecemeal" in the cast-offs of the great authors of the past. Furthermore, Brown is more successful than Irving in inserting himself into this authorial milieu: while Irving's sketch ends with him being unceremoniously booted out of the library for lacking "a card of admission," Brown strolls out at his own leisure to view the rest of the museum.[120]

If Brown borrows this episode to model himself after Irving as a genteel author whose travels and success in Britain shaped his as a distinctly American voice, then he just as quickly punctures the image of himself as leisured traveler. Immediately upon leaving the museum, Brown reminds the reader, and perhaps himself, that he can only fund his stay in London because he has "published the narrative of my life and escape from slavery, and put it into the booksellers' hands." Brown the tourist only exists because Brown is circulating his enslaved self elsewhere, and the precarity of this balancing act is about to become apparent. Having an upcoming lecturing engagement in Worcester, which he believes is close to London and where he will "in all probability, sell a number of my books," Brown confidently sends almost all of his money to his daughters in the United States. He has, however, miscalculated. Worcester is more than a hundred miles away and he does not have enough to pay the rent due on his lodgings and the train fare. Instantly, his mobility and his gaze are transformed. Brown is no longer the perceptive tourist as he walks through fog-shrouded streets where his "sight could not penetrate through the dark veil." His movements seem newly enforced as he is left "wander[ing] from street to street, with the hope that I might meet some one who would lend me money enough to get to Worcester," and then "pacing my room."[121] As he walks the streets—ironically, those of London's bookselling district of Fleet Street and the Strand—Brown encounters a fellow Black American for whom travel to England has not proved a liberating experience. Brown summarizes the man's history in his text, offering what Baraw describes as "a story of unsuccessful mobility, an unwritten slave narrative translated across the Atlantic without success."[122] What Brown portrays is a version of his life in England if he had not written and circulated his narrative: what would have happened to him had he not been able to circulate himself in print. Emphasizing that this unnamed fugitive is an alter ego, Brown ends this encounter by having himself and the unnamed man part as doubles, each with 6d from Brown's last shilling in his pocket.

Separating Brown from the unnamed man are the sales of his printed narrative. In his Slough of Despond, Brown receives a surprise visit from a minister's son, who "had gone among his father's congregation, and sold a number of copies of my book, and had come to bring me money." These sales give Brown enough money to circulate himself to Worcester as an antislavery lecturer, but also to regain the genteel mobility of the traveling author. With the proceeds, he goes to "dinner at the Adelphi [hotel], with a good cut of roast beef before me, and felt myself once more at home."[123] Selling an account of himself in slavery allows Brown to perform an act of consumption that signifies his status as a travel writer: buying a typically English dinner at a middling hotel. Brown's authorial subjectivity thus relies on the publication and dissemination of his objectification under slavery and the transformation of his existence into a fungible commodity. In his own account, printing and selling his narrative redeems Brown from the unstable state of fugitivity, allowing him instead to feel "at home" in touristic mobility as long as he remains in two (printed) states at once.

These two printed states exist not only in the separate publications of Brown's *Narrative* and *Three Years in Europe*, but within the arrangement and the physical book of the travelogue alone. *Three Years in Europe* is prefaced by an extended "Memoir of the Author," by William Farmer, a British abolitionist and friend of Garrison. Farmer begins by reminding readers that "a narrative of the life of the author of the present work has been most extensively circulated in Britain and America." Brown is an author whose "narrative" must precede him, just as its sales facilitate his mobility in Britain. Farmer begins by rehearsing the slave narrative's standard opening, giving Brown's birth in a specific location but an uncertain time: "William Wells Brown was born at Lexington, in the state of Kentucky, as nearly as he can tell in the autumn of 1814."[124] This shift from first to third person diffuses the tension between author-as-enslaved and author-as-narrator-of-enslavement that traditionally structures a slave narrative; the enslaved Brown exists as a character in Farmer's text, while Brown can represent himself as a different kind of narrating subject in the travel narrative proper. Although these narrating subjects are separated by the division between text and paratext, by retaining his enslaved self in the paratext of *Three Years in Europe*, Brown shows that he understands the ways in which his enslaved self and slave narrative "ensure the text's presence in the world," as Gérard Genette argues of the paratext's function.[125] In his own preface to *Three Years in Europe*, Brown observed that its interest to British readers, familiar with the sites he described, would stem from his book "being the first production of a Fugitive Slave, as a history of travels."[126]

Gilpin's publication of the book reflected the dual identity that Brown describes. Writing to Wendell Phillips in September 1852, Brown explained that the book would be "published by subscription at ten and sixpence or about two dollars and a half. A high price this for a book from a fugitive. A cheap edition at five shillings is to be put out almost immediately."[127] Like commission publishing, subscription publishing was commonly used for texts with a discrete audience, suggesting that Gilpin thought Brown's book would appeal to a niche antislavery public. Gilpin's cover choice aligns with this sense of the book's market: he issued *Three Years in Europe* in a cloth binding with a stock antislavery image of a kneeling and chained enslaved man embossed on its cover and a title page that identified Brown as a "Fugitive Slave." Yet the book was also sufficiently distinct from Gilpin's other antislavery publications. The proposed prices of 10s 6d and 5s, and even the 3s 6d at which Gilpin ultimately advertised *Three Years in Europe*, were "high price[s]" for books by fugitives (*Twelve Years a Slave* at 6s would not be published until the following year). Moreover, the speed with which Brown's letter to Phillips moves from his own book to the multiple editions of *Uncle Tom's Cabin* that had sprung into circulation ("the dearest is 7/6 . . . the cheapest is 6d"), suggests that Brown envisioned his own text occupying a similar market to that of popular fiction. Equally, Brown appears to have imagined a shift in his own place in the literary field, from the position of political author outlined in Drescher's analysis of his relations with Gilpin to something more like Stowe's own complex position as an author whose Americanness enabled her to balance trade success and political convictions because copyright law (supposedly) prohibited her from achieving the economic returns that would have threatened to undermine the ideological purity of her work.

But it is not only Brown's location in the literary field that is contingent and conflicting, it is also his geographical location, which becomes hard to pin down between his distinct and yet interlinked circulations in Britain as travel writer and fugitive slave. Brown's Preface to *Three Years in Europe* begins by observing that the book's letters "will be interesting chiefly to American readers," even though the book was initially published in Britain. Underlying this statement might be a hope that Brown can, again, follow in the footsteps of Irving—and perhaps Melville and even Longfellow and Sigourney—and cultivate American readers through the transatlantic materials of his work. Yet Brown also admits that some of book's contents had already been published in "'Frederick Douglass's paper,' a journal published in the United States." Brown's curiously careful phrasing—"a journal published in the United States" rather than "an American journal"—suggests his consciousness that Douglass's paper was a transatlantic artifact. Arguing persuasively for both the influence of British activist Julia Griffith on *Frederick Douglass's Paper* and for the "transatlantic colloquy" of the periodical's political wielding of "gentlemanliness, civility, and descent," Sarah Meer positions the *Paper* as both "local and international."[128] In his preface, then, Brown locates his authorship not only in Britain and America, but also in a transatlantic space of abolition that existed across and between them, that encompassed both nations but was also distinct from them.

These multiple and multiply located versions of Brown further proliferated when he reprinted his slave narrative for a third time as a paratext for *Clotel; or, The President's Daughter: A Narrative of Slave Life in the United States*, published by Partridge & Oakey in 1853. *Clotel* opens with a preface in which Brown locates himself in the heart of literary London at "22, Cecil Street, Strand," also the location of the preface to *Three Years in Europe*, and makes no reference to having been enslaved. The preface is followed by a "Memoir of the Author" titled "Narrative of the Life and Escape of William Wells Brown," which, while narrated in the third person, was almost certainly written by Brown himself. Like Farmer's preface for *Three Years in Europe*, this memoir transforms Brown the author into a character. Its opening statement, "William Wells Brown, the subject of this narrative," briefly suggests that he will be a figure in the novel proper. Brown further fragments subjectivity in the memoir by inserting long quotations from the *Narrative of William W. Brown* and *Three Years in Europe*, so that "William" or "Brown" sometimes constructs his story and selfhood in his own words, and sometimes is himself constructed by the words of the anonymous narrator. The memoir further includes quotations from a series of transatlantic texts: a letter from Brown's enslaver Enoch Price (earlier reproduced in the preface to the *Narrative*), an address from the "ladies of Bolton," a notice from *Frederick Douglass's Paper*, and several reviews of *Three Years in Europe* from English periodicals. Far from being "written by himself," "Brown" emerges from a nexus of printed and reprinted texts from both sides of the Atlantic; he is a figure who does not so much exist in printed documents as amid and between their circulation and recirculation. Scholars like Laura Soderberg and Christopher Stampone have examined how Brown produces new models of sympathy and heroism adequate to the problem of slavery by constructing subjectivity and character across *Clotel*'s four editions rather than locating them in singular and stable individuals.[129] But if Brown developed the creative potential of recirculation across later editions of *Clotel*, he pioneered it with his own narrative in Britain as a way to ensure his mobility as an author while still trading on his enslavement.

At this point, we might ask if we can still call the fragmented selfhood that William Wells Brown fashions across reprints of his narrative but does not locate in any particular printed book "subjectivity." There is certainly no single subject position from which the author subverts a racialized gaze, as is the case in Northup's and John Brown's uses of transatlantic circulation. Nor is there even the binary division between "Frederick the Slave" and "Frederick the Freeman" that Douglass materializes in the Dublin editions' division between paratext and text. Emerging between texts in the same book but also between different printings of the same text, William Wells Brown cannot be pinned down. Is either the "Brown" that signs *Clotel*'s preface or the "Brown" of the memoir the same "Brown" who narrates the conclusion to *Clotel* and suddenly collapses divisions between authorial subject and narrative object by proclaiming that he "personally participated in many scenes"? This narrator of *Clotel* then seems to negate his subjectivity altogether when he explains that other stories in the book came from "fugitives" who "made me a depository of their sufferings and wrongs."[130] The recirculation of narratives across the Atlantic, initially orally but finally in print, results not in the fashioning of personhood but of its emptying out, so that subjects can become vessels for the stories of others. At the end of *Clotel*, circulating the self through reprinting produces a state of dislocation that resembles fugitivity even as it also offers an opportunity for almost limitless mobility that looks something like freedom.

Brown's extensive, if ultimately conflicting, (de)construction of self across his British books returns us to the question with which this chapter began: Did British print and transatlantic circulation facilitate and further Black abolitionists' articulations of subjectivity? The somewhat unsatisfactory answer seems to be sometimes, and in limited ways. Northup and John Brown imaginatively deployed transatlantic circulation to subvert the racialized gaze of slavery, yet were themselves located as objects of that gaze by both commercial and charitable British publishers. Douglass and Brown, who had connections to antislavery networks, relative financial stability, literacy, and sophisticated understandings of print, could harness the recirculation of their texts in Ireland and Britain to fashion themselves as transatlantic authors rather than "slave narrators." Douglass's and Brown's repositioning of themselves in the literary field through British print occurred in tandem with their intellectual and political relocation as Atlantic subjects, and a fuller investigation of the ways in which their uses of British print also invoked other locations in the Atlantic rim—Haiti, the West Indies, West Africa—is certainly necessary.[131]

Yet, as this chapter has shown, British publishers' participation in these print experiments was minimal; at worst, their framing of abolitionist texts actively undermined the politics of those texts. Some anti-slavery publishers, like Gilpin and Webb, succeeded in circulating slave narratives to abolitionist audiences through their embeddedness within those audiences. But British editions are absent the complex reception of American writers' ideas of authorship and visions of nationhood and national culture that we find in Bentley's covers, Bogue's illustrations, series architecture, gift book coteries, and even in the unsuccessful national polyphonies of American magazines. As their reviews and sales show, these narratives were nevertheless celebrated in Britain, and Britain's sense of itself as an antislavery nation meant that they were certainly received as emblems of a distinctly American problem—even as their authors located themselves at scales other than the nation. But, unlike in works by their white contemporaries, British publishers did not use the materials of these publications as opportunities for imagining possibilities for a new, distinct, and valuable American tradition.

Bridget Bennett has recently argued that British archives allow us "to reimagine the contours and climate of mid-century abolition, . . . revealing questions of visibility and invisibility and remind[ing] us of how much can still be found."[132] Recovering the British publication of US slave narratives reminds us that there is much yet to discover about their histories—discoveries that offer new examples of and models for Black authorship, like John Brown, or that challenge canons in the way that William Wells Brown's expansions of Douglass's experiments with reprinting encourage scholars to look beyond the 1845 Boston edition of Douglass's *Narrative*. If the twenty-first-century flourishing of Black book history has brought new information about the authorship, publishing, and reading of Black Americans and recovered important texts, books, and periodicals, we have barely scratched the surface of Black American engagements with print outside of the United States. The transatlantic materials of Black print are still largely invisible in scholarship on abolition literatures and early African American writing, and this chapter is only an initial step toward uncovering them.

CODA

Uncle Tom's Cabin, *Dred*, and the End of American Literature's Transatlantic Materials

This book has argued that British publishers and their material texts played a vital role in forming the field of American literature in the three decades before the Civil War. Through authorized and unauthorized editions, and through print objects that were neither authorized nor unauthorized or were both at once, British publishers materialized different versions of American literature and different models of US authorship. Rather than settling the question of what a national literature was and should be, the heterogeneity of publication in Britain allowed competing models of aesthetics and authorship to coexist. Through their publication in Britain and their imaginative engagements with transatlantic print circulation and print forms, US authors claimed various forms of authority and value. Publication in Britain could offer economic remuneration, but equally as important were British publishers' celebrations of their aesthetic skill, their arguments for the centrality of authorship to a national print culture, and the creation of transatlantic canons and coteries. All of these enabled US authors to claim particular positions within an emergent field, creating the struggle between producers that formed the field of American literature and gave it autonomy from its British counterpart.

Debates over the shape and future of American literature were political as well as aesthetic questions, as illustrated by Herman Melville's *The Whale* combining colonialism and copyright in a discussion that was most clearly materialized in Richard Bentley's 1851 London edition. The collections and series that were envisioned and compiled by British publishers echoed and then amplified the ways that Early American and antebellum writers penned consciously national works that nevertheless imagined the nation as a relational rather than essential space. Henry Wadsworth Longfellow and Lydia Huntley Sigourney found space in and through British print to expose the entanglement of racialized violence and national culture, although both retreated from the radical potential of such critiques and ultimately reaffirmed white nationhood. The editors of London's American magazines employed transatlantic reprinting to diffuse sectional tensions, but failed because of the unsustainability of their national polyphonies and because both the magazine form and transatlantic circulation were inherently unstable. British editions of slave narratives manifested tensions between their authors' claims to subjectivity at an Atlantic scale and the ways that their material texts and distribution processes made spectacles of Black bodies. When we examine the contradiction between the shared success of British publishers and Black abolitionists in circulating these texts to anti-slavery audiences, and the failure of the material texts to embody the anti-slavery politics of the literary texts, we are reminded that transatlantic circulation and US authorship could work at cross-purposes, and that British print mapped American authorship and the national literary field on to whiteness.

In seeking to illustrate the breadth and variety of American literature's transatlantic materials, I have given less attention to some landmark publications. Most notable for its relative absence is Harriet Beecher Stowe's *Uncle Tom's Cabin* (1852); by far the most successful US book in nineteenth-century Britain, it has only appeared fleetingly in this study thus far. Its extraordinary sales led contemporary commentators and later critics to view its reprinting as the moment when American literature truly arrived in Britain. By ending this study with *Uncle Tom's Cabin*, I want to suggest the opposite: that the mass republication and huge sales of Stowe's novel in Britain were the culmination of over two decades of publishing US texts in Britain. Furthermore, Stowe's novel arrived at a transitional moment in the transatlantic print marketplace. In 1852, developments in copyright law, infrastructure, communication, and the structure of the US print market were about to combine with seismic global events to remap what British print meant to US authors and to reduce its capacity to materialize and authorize divergent conceptions of American authorship, aesthetics, and print culture. Moving forward to Stowe's second novel, *Dred* (1856), demonstrates these changes and invites reflection on the legacy and the forgetting of American literature's transatlantic materials.

Uncle Tom's Cabin arrived in Britain through the back doors of the book trade.[1] The text's serialization in Washington, DC, abolitionist weekly the *National Era* would have made it very difficult for Stowe to secure an authorized British edition.[2] Her Boston publisher, John P. Jewett—who specialized in religious works and textbooks—gave no thought to British copyright, concentrating instead on energetically advertising in the United States. According to the reminiscences of Charles H. Clarke and Henry Vizetelly, who collaborated on the first British edition, a clerk in a US publishing house sent a copy to David Bogue (and possibly other British houses), suggesting that the book was worth reprinting and requesting a small sum for the intelligence.[3] Bogue was a sensible choice as his illustrated editions of Longfellow were proving successful on both sides of the Atlantic, but Vizetelly recalled Bogue "not caring to embark in cheap reprints of American authors."[4] Bogue's refusal illustrates that grouping together unauthorized editions obscures their differences in materiality and the forms of value they embody. There was a chasm between Bogue's elegant, illustrated *Evangeline* and a quick, cheap reprint of a popular novel, even if both occupied the same position under copyright law. Furthermore, after publishing *The Golden Legend* from advanced sheets in November 1851, Bogue had become Longfellow's authorized publisher and he may have wanted to avoid sullying his reputation with a prized US author by dabbling in a less legitimate trade.

According to Clarke, Bogue first offered Stowe's book to Charles Gilpin, who also refused it.[5] As I discussed in chapter 6, Gilpin was probably the most established London publisher of slave narratives before 1852, having recently published the narratives of William Wells Brown and James W. C. Pennington. The apparent plausibility of Gilpin's involvement with an edition of *Uncle Tom's Cabin*—more than whether or not he was actually offered the book—suggests that the British trade initially viewed Stowe's book as part of a burgeoning transatlantic antislavery print culture that was distinct from the literary trade. The story of Gilpin's refusal creates an alternative history for *Uncle Tom's Cabin* in which it did not become emblematic of American literature in Britain but instead arrived as a different type of text altogether: an antislavery work that sat within a transnational movement rather than a national literary field. Via Gilpin or not, Bogue's copy of Stowe's book ultimately reached Vizetelly, who had just commenced his shilling series, Readable Books, and thought *Uncle Tom's Cabin* would be an ideal addition. He arranged the first London edition with Clarke, another reprint publisher, in May 1852; accounts disagree about the edition's size, whose imprint it appeared under, and whether the two men partnered on the edition or Vizetelly sold the book to Clarke outright. Initially slow sales increased rapidly over summer, and by October, several other publishers had printed editions in an effort to capitalize on this literary sensation.

It was then that Clarke attempted to retrospectively authorize his edition in the hopes of persuading Stowe to supply future advanced sheets. Clarke published a 7s 6d edition of *Uncle Tom's Cabin* "with 40 illustrations" in September 1852, and sent his new junior partner, Samuel O. Beeton, across the Atlantic with the electrotype plates to convince Stowe to make their firm her authorized publisher. Stowe was not persuaded by Beeton's proposition. In one version of the story, Stowe strongly disliked the illustrations because they visualized the physical violence of slavery that she had deliberately refrained from describing. In another, she politely told Beeton she would prefer a cash sum. Clarke, Beeton & Co., along with Thomas Bosworth, Sampson Low, and Richard Bentley, did offer Stowe money from their sales in return for being able to advertise their editions as the author's, and the first three firms were rewarded with advanced sheets for *The Key to Uncle Tom's Cabin* in 1853.[6] In a third version of the story, another British firm got to Stowe first. When British sales of *Uncle Tom's Cabin* took off in autumn 1852, Sampson Low's son, Sampson Jr., was in the United States and so could meet with Stowe in person. Edward Marston, later a partner in Low's firm, tells a wonderful but likely apocryphal story of Low Jr. meeting Beeton walking toward Stowe's house as he himself was walking away, having already sealed the deal.[7] Whatever the truth, Sampson Low won Stowe's authorized business, beginning a business relationship and warm friendship that would last the rest of Stowe's life.[8]

British publishers' efforts to secure Stowe's British business recall Bentley's proactive courtships of Cooper and Melville, Bogue winning Longfellow's business through illustrated editions, and the *Forget Me Not*'s encouragement of Sigourney and Hannah Flagg Gould's sentimental nationalism. But they also illustrate power shifts in the transatlantic literary marketplace. While US authors had once come to Britain—in person, or in print—to make their names and reputations, now British publishers were crossing the Atlantic to secure the business of an American. Low Sr.'s agreement with Stowe also marks, even if it does not exactly coincide with, his shift from the Harper brothers' trusted agent to a leading transatlantic publisher. That trade was now established enough to support specialist firms like Low's, who replaced the various contingent and experimental practices for producing authorizing editions with well-oiled systems for navigating copyright law and balancing the competing imperatives of the US and British markets.

In his history of his family's firm, J. Henry Harper praised Low as a "warm friend" of Fletcher Harper, observing that "our interests in England were absolutely identified with his own."[9] Authors, as well as publishers, trusted Low's guidance. Stowe wrote that "Sampson Lowe [sic] has always done well and liberally by me as a publisher" in a letter to her then Boston publisher James Fields in 1867, and told Low that she felt assured he would show friends visiting London "all kindness . . . as you always are so ready to do to us Americans lost on your shores."[10] Maria Cummins, another bestselling American sentimentalist, seems to have taken Low's advice on the direction of her writing as well as the best way to publish her works. After the lackluster reception of her Oriental novel *El Fureidis* (1860), she welcomed Low's views on why the book failed: "I am also sufficiently convinced of the advisability of laying the scene of a future story on my native soil."[11] By sending circulars about developments in copyright law to leading US authors (one appears in Longfellow's correspondence) and to publications like the *Literary World*, Low positioned his firm as a successor to Richard Bentley & Sons as Britain's leading publisher of US texts, just as Bentley was prevented from taking on new works by his firm's financial crisis.

Low's agreement with Stowe could not prevent the unauthorized reprinting of *Uncle Tom's Cabin*, which was unprecedented in its scale. My previous chapters all examined how *individual* British books, series, and magazines materialized aesthetic and market value for their different US texts and authors. Their material variety allowed British print as a whole to fashion a terrain on which contrasting and sometimes competing visons of American literature were realized. Not every writer was given access to all positions in this literary field: Black writers are missing from lists of the literary publishers specializing in authorized and unauthorized editions who were most invested in forging American literature. But many white writers found forms of publication that supported their own conception of the values that defined the American literary field and their strategies for position-taking within it. Before *Uncle Tom's Cabin*, however, never had so many British publishers issued a single US text or had a single text appeared in almost every conceivable print format. In the twelve months following the first British edition, at least eighteen different publishers issued editions ranging from paperbacks priced below one shilling to ornate drawing room volumes. Rather than particular British editions making specific interventions in debates over what American literature should look like, the full spectrum of British print was placed in the service of a single text, author, and form of US writing. The British reprinting of *Uncle Tom's Cabin* promised to bury the question "Who reads an American book?" but it also threatened to define absolutely what an American book was.

For some in the United States, this made *Uncle Tom's Cabin*'s success in Britain a cause for concern rather than celebration because they opposed the book's antislavery politics or disliked its feminine aesthetic or because they believed its popularity stemmed from anti-American feeling rather than admiration for its literary merits. The influential *Democratic Review*, for example, connected Stowe's extraordinary sales to a British government campaign to secretly aid abolitionism in the hopes of undermining US prosperity and stability. The *Review* even began supporting an international copyright agreement with Britain, a reverse of its previous stance, for fear that transatlantic abolitionist organizations could manipulate a decentralized print culture.[12] In 1852, therefore, *Uncle Tom's Cabin* still testified to the power of transatlantic materials to shape American literature as a national field, albeit through fears that its mass reprinting might give a new fixity to the structure of the field, orienting it around the nationally divisive issue of slavery.

The *Review*'s fears of a second abolitionist bestseller were ultimately unfounded. There were other US hits in Britain in the years immediately after *Uncle Tom's Cabin*, such as Cummins's *The Lamplighter* (1854) and Longfellow's *Hiawatha* (1855), but their politics were less divisive and their sales did not reach Stowe's numbers. Furthermore, the mid-to-late 1850s also saw changes to Anglo-American print culture, some immediate and some more gradual, that altered the relationship between British print and US literature. The most immediate of these came in August 1854 when the House of Lords ruled, in *Jeffreys v. Boosey*, that prior publication in Britain had never conferred copyright on works by foreign authors, placing almost all US texts in the public domain. This must have been especially disappointing for Sampson Low, who had issued Stowe's travelogue *Sunny Memories of Foreign Lands* in June. The firm's adverts implored potential purchasers to "specify *the Author's Editions*," explaining that "the Author has no redress except such as is afforded by public discrimination," but by September, seven other publishers were selling *Sunny Memories*.[13]

Data from the *Publishers' Circular* suggests that reprint publishers initially took advantage of the Lords' decision, with a relatively high number of US works announced in autumn 1854 compared to the years before *Uncle Tom*. George Routledge likely enjoyed reprinting the works of Cooper, Bentley's prized American author, having been forced to destroy his editions of Irving's and Melville's works in 1851. Low put out works by Bayard Taylor, Mary Langdon, and Fanny Fern, for which he must have assumed he would have copyrights and which were swiftly reprinted by competitors. However, announcements for US literary works in the *Circular* fell in 1854 compared to 1853, which was still experiencing Uncle Tom mania, and they continued to fall through 1858 with only a small upturn in 1859.

It would be oversimplistic to suggest that *Jeffreys v. Boosey* alone ended the period in which British publishers and print were crucial vectors for authorizing US writers and projecting futures for American literature. But it did conclude three decades of debate over precisely what constituted an authorized edition, and that debate created space for publishers to experiment with conferring authority through prestige editions, cash payments, illustrations, and series and periodical formats, as well as through prior publication. In this period of generative ambiguity over copyright, a range of authorizing formats flourished, which made it possible for British publishers to champion competing visions for American literature, some more successfully than others. By codifying the law on copyright, the Lords curtailed the variety of British publishers' authorizing forms as much as the rights of US authors.

Jeffreys v. Boosey did, however, confirm that any author resident "within the Queen's dominions" at the time of publication could claim a British copyright, allowing US writers to protect their works by traveling to Britain for their publication.[14] This was only possible for writers without professional, domestic, or other obligations, and who were wealthy enough to pay travel costs or who had a publisher willing to pay them. Low's publication of Stowe's second novel, *Dred*, in August 1856 was one of the earliest attempts to establish copyright by residency. Stowe was an ideal author with whom to test this new system. Any new novel by Stowe was guaranteed to sell well, and so bringing her to England was worth Low's expense; he would later do the same for Cummins when she published *El Fureidis*. Stowe's Boston publisher was now Phillips, Sampson & Co., who were also practiced in transatlantic editions as the publisher of the historian William Hickling Prescott, whom Stowe consulted for advice on British copyright.[15] Perhaps most crucially, Stowe enjoyed transatlantic travel and required little persuading to make the trip. Nevertheless, *Dred*'s transatlantic publication was stressful. Stowe was still writing the book on the steamer to Liverpool, and she finished it in the rooms that Low rented for her family in London, with one of Low's daughters helping to copy the manuscript for the printers.[16] When Stowe sent proof sheets to Moses Phillips, she wrote in relief, "You may have it published as soon as you please—We shall have [?]n out within ten days from this 15th of August. Congratulate me!—I hardly thought I should do it—but its done. . . . I am worn to a rag—but shall mend now rapidly."[17]

The pressures of transatlantic publication drained Stowe, but writing from and for London gave her space to vehemently condemn slavery and its supporters. *Dred*'s US preface presents slavery as a "great moral problem" that God has given the United States so that its people can, inevitably, find a solution and fulfil the nation's providential destiny.[18] In contrast, *Dred*'s British preface boils over with Stowe's righteous anger, which Low materialized in his cheap edition's blood-red covers. This anger is directed at slavery (not a "moral problem" but a "tremendous evil"), at enslavers whose "every breath is an oath," at proslavery clergymen, and, most of all, at Preston Brooks for his "cowardly" beating of Charles Sumner with a gutta-percha cane on the floor of the Senate in May 1856.[19] The space Stowe gives to this incident reflects its proximity to *Dred*'s publication, Sumner's popularity in Britain, and the ways that the circumstances of and responses to the attack merged sectional conflict and transatlantic print culture. Seeking to justify Brooks's violence, his cousin, Senator Andrew Butler—whose honor Brooks claimed to have been defending—argued that Sumner had transmitted his speech on Kansas, which supposedly slandered Butler, to England, intending that it would be widely reprinted. As Christopher Hanlon notes, such accusations implicitly positioned Sumner's speech as a second *Uncle Tom's Cabin*: an antislavery fiction that could circulate in Britain without restriction (Butler had directly compared Sumner's oratory and Stowe's novel in 1854). For the proslavery faction, Brooks's gutta-percha cane was a justified and even eloquent retort to such uncircumscribed publication of falsehoods. Indeed, Hanlon argues that pro- and antislavery observers endowed the gutta-percha cane with the exciting, but potentially destabilizing communicative power of the new transatlantic telegraph that was wrapped in the same material.[20]

In the London preface, Stowe wrests Brooks's cane from his hands and renders it inarticulate. She warns that if Britain sacrifices its moral opposition to slavery for the economic gains of trading with the South, the nation will "be led in cotton bands by such hands as smote down Charles Sumner." Stowe's unusual focus on Brooks's hands rather than his weapon displaces the gutta-percha cane from the preface and prevents its proslavery eloquence from entering her denunciation of slavery. She then places the gutta-percha cane in the hands of Tom Gordon, the violent brother of her heroine and the villain of *Dred*. Gordon inflicts two beatings: one on his mixed-race half-brother Harry, and one on Edward Clayton, a planter who wants to gradually emancipate his slaves. The second of these is explicitly compared to Brooks's attack on Sumner: "[Gordon] proved his eligibility for Congress by beating his defenseless acquaintance on the head, after the fashion of the chivalry of South Carolina." When Dred interrupts this beating by breaking Gordon's arm, he emits "volumes of oaths, such as our readers have never heard, and the paper refuses to receive."[21] In the preface, the gutta-percha cane is removed from written denunciations of antislavery, and in the text the verbal manifestation of its violence cannot be translated into print. As well as failing to state the proslavery case, Gordon's beatings indirectly illustrate the necessity of immediate abolition. Dred's intervention in the beating precipitates an attack on his maroon enclave in which Dred himself is killed, and after which Clayton is driven out of North Carolina for educating his slaves for emancipation. *Dred* argues that any efforts toward gradual emancipation will be met with inarticulate yet effective violence, leaving immediate abolition as the only option.

Stowe's silencing of proslavery rhetoric and transmission of abolitionist arguments did not happen through the limitless, public domain circulation that Brooks and Butler feared. It took place through a copyrighted text and through the London-dated preface that registered and embodied that copyright. *Dred*'s negotiations of transatlantic authorization punctured the *Democratic Review*'s argument for international copyright as a defense against the unchecked spread of antislavery rhetoric by illustrating how regimes and materializations of intellectual property could be placed in the service of an antislavery politics. *Dred*'s transatlantic property is echoed in the book's London preface, which approaches slavery as a transatlantic problem. In contrast, the US preface presents slavery as an exceptional problem for an exceptional nation to solve by merging "two nations, the types of two exactly opposite styles of existence" into one "American people."[22] Unlike many of the texts discussed in this book, *Dred* and its subject are more national in its US edition than in its British. Still, it was writing and publishing in a transatlantic print market that allowed Stowe to temper her emotions and predict *future* national unity at home while also giving voice to her anger about slavery abroad, risking (or perhaps hoping to instigate) political instability in the United States by encouraging the British public to turn their antislavery sympathies into abolitionist action.

Stowe's conciliatory framing of slavery as a temporary impediment to the Union in *Dred*'s US preface speaks to the United States' shift from a set of regional print economies to a national print market after 1850. Increasingly, publishers in the Northeast shipped their editions to customers across the United States rather than publishers in each city reprinting a text for their local market. The expansion of the railways and development of express companies enabled the reliable shipping of books across the nation, and from 1850 onward "jobbing firms" began to manage distribution, acting as middlemen between publishers and booksellers.[23] September 1855 saw the first edition of the *American Publishers' Circular and Literary Gazette*, the first enduring trade publication connecting booksellers and publishers across the nation through the sharing of trade intelligence.[24] This shift from regional markets to a national one was entangled with the politics of slavery and abolition. Trish Loughran argues that antislavery organizations pioneered national communication infrastructures for their printed materials, and, as texts began to circulate nationally, their reception brought to the fore sectional differences over slavery.[25] Similarly, Meredith McGill observes that it is a "constitutive irony of the period of American literary emergence" that "a national market for literary works becomes possible at a moment in which the nation is on the verge of disintegration."[26]

The 1850s also saw US publishers increasingly taking on the work of defining a national tradition and celebrating national authorship that critics like Lewis Gaylord Clark had claimed was performed by the British trade. As percentages of the total numbers of books published in the United States each year, reprints of English authors decreased and original works by US authors increased. Celebrated children's author Samuel Griswold Goodrich estimated that by 1856, three-quarters of literary and popular reading in the United States was by Americans.[27] In 1853, George Palmer Putnam founded *Putnam's Monthly Magazine*, which only printed original articles by Americans, in contrast to *Harper's Monthly*, which then still largely reprinted from English titles. Furthermore, after Sampson Low successfully defended the principle that a US work could be copyrighted in Britain if the author was resident in Canada when it was published, US publishers took on more of the logistical work in a transatlantic edition.[28] For the publication of Stowe's *Oldtown Folks* in 1869, James Fields had to print proofs speedily, exchange telegraphs with Low about sending those sheets, and appease Stowe, who was unhappy about having to travel to Montreal in winter: "I don't see, why the old poke should insist upon it that I should wait to have a preface dated in Canada get to him and I <u>won't</u> either—I can't spend so much time there in this cold weather."[29] Such letters show Fields's increasing importance in Stowe's professional and personal life. Indeed, Jennifer Harris suggests that Stowe found her ideal author-publisher relationship with Fields and his wife, Annie, that extended "beyond material concerns and marketplace transactions to include spouses, homes, and—in Stowe's case—children."[30] These qualities of Stowe's relationship with the Fields replicated her earlier relationship with the Lows, suggesting the increased power and autonomy of US publishers in the American literary field.

Simultaneously, there was a decline in the number of US texts being published in Britain, caused by a combination of national and transnational factors within and outside the book trade. British publishing stagnated in the mid-1850s. Britain's expensive and increasingly unpopular participation in the Crimean War drew attention away from literature and required income tax hikes that reduced spending on discretionary goods like books, as Bentley explained to Prescott when he tried—and failed—to persuade him to come to England to secure his copyright.[31] The Crimean War ended in February 1856, but the following year a financial crisis that started in August in the US spread to Britain by autumn. That panic exacerbated a decline in the number of US titles published after the print frenzy around *Uncle Tom's Cabin*. Wright's *American Fiction* lists 172 titles for 1853, but only 146 for 1856 and 82 for 1858. In late 1858, the *Publisher's Circular* seemed hopeful the transatlantic trade would pick up: "A London publisher put into our hands the other day three letters he had received from different correspondents, by *the same mail*, each offering him the simultaneous publication in England. Their estimation of their respective books is rather good."[32] But recovery was jettisoned by the Civil War, which severely impacted American publishing and bookselling. In late 1861, the British trade periodical *The Bookseller* observed that "the state of the book trade in and with America is such that we cannot recommend any houses in England to extend their business in that direction"; while the writer was primarily discussing sales of English texts in the United States, the same sentiment applied to publishing American books in Britain.[33] By the time the trade in American books picked up, "Canadian copyright" was established and many publishers had branch houses that standardized and smoothed arrangements for Anglo-American publishing. The multifarious and vitally material authorizing practices of the 1830s, 1840s, and early 1850s were a thing of the past.

Still, as late as 1869, the American novelist and first editor of *Scribner's Monthly* Josiah Gilbert (J. G.) Holland wrote to Sampson Low about his proposed republication of Holland's novel *Kathrina* (1867) in terms that recall letters between US authors and British publishers of thirty years before. Holland observes that "the presentation of my book to the British public is to <u>me</u> a matter of more than ordinary moment." He claims never to have written with the British public in mind, a claim of US authors now positioning themselves in the field of American literature by publishing at home. Yet he "know[s] there is no reason why an American book, provided it is good, should not find an appreciation in England, even beyond that which it receives in the country of its birth," so long as it is properly presented. Like his predecessors writing to John Murray and Richard Bentley, Holland focuses on the print materiality of his British editions:

> It is a great deal more important that you present the book to your public in the right way than that you pay me anything.

> What I mean by "the right way" is, that wisdom be exercised as to the time of its appearance, the garb in which it shall appear, the price at which it shall be sold, &c &c.[34]

Holland's discussion of "garb" suggests that even after the Civil War, US authors still saw British print as a means of materializing various forms of capital that gave their writings value and situated them in the field. Nevertheless, his brisk and business-like tone and his sense that publishing in Britain is an experiment rather than a necessity demonstrate a decline in the power and importance of British print for US authors.

If the heyday of American literature's transatlantic materials ended quickly, then the forgetting of British publishers' contribution to the invention and development of an American national tradition was even quicker. In the decades after the Civil War, descriptions of British publishers as champions of US writing and of British editions as apt celebrations of American literary prowess were replaced by stories of British publishers exploiting copyright law and American authors for their own gain. In part, such narratives arose from a new, sustained push for an Anglo-American copyright agreement, as a speech by James Russell Lowell demonstrates. In 1888, on his last visit to England, Lowell spoke to the Society of Authors about literary relations between Britain and the United States and his hopes that international copyright might finally be in sight. Suggesting that American reprinters were not "so much more wicked than their English brethren," Lowell compared books and game birds, in that both were, legally, "feræ naturæ": "when they fly over your neighbours' boundaries he may take a pot shot at them."

Lowell perhaps intended the metaphor to evoke Washington Irving's description of the British Museum Library as a literary "preserve" subject to game laws in the episode from *The Sketch-Book* that William Wells Brown echoed in *Three Years in Europe*. It also resonates with Herman Melville's analogy between "Loose-Fish" and public domain works in *The Whale*. But Lowell's ornithological analogy was most likely chosen because it fed neatly into an anecdote:

> More than thirty years ago it must have been, that Longfellow, my friend and neighbour, asked me to come and eat a game-pie with him. Now Longfellow's books had been sold in England by tens of thousands, and that game-pie—and you will observe the felicity of it being a game-pie, *feræ naturæ* always, you see—that game-pie was the only honorarium which he had ever received from this country for reprinting his books.[35]

Lowell's tale must have amused the assembled British writers, and it is all the better for being at least partly true. John Walker's letters to Longfellow, discussed in chapter 1, show that he sent the poet a game pie for Christmas in 1850, and another seems to have arrived from Britain for the Christmas of 1853. But pies were far from the "only honorarium" Longfellow received from the British trade. His earnings from Britain were small in comparison to his large sales overall, but Bogue and Routledge paid him for advanced sheets, and Ticknor and Fields paid him royalties on American sales of Bogue's illustrated editions distributed under their imprint. Furthermore, the pie from Walker was part of a series of non-financial and extra-legal authorizing arrangements around Longfellow's British editions, with which Longfellow was satisfied. Lowell, however, ignores all of this to figure the pie as a poor substitute for cash payments and an emblem of US authors' powerlessness and deprivation in a west-east transatlantic book trade shaped by the absence of international copyright law.

This book has told a new story about the importance of British publishers and their material texts to antebellum US authors and to the emergence of a national American literature and print culture in the mid-nineteenth century, and so I want to conclude with a new history of Longfellow's game pies to counterbalance Lowell's. Joining Lowell at a New Year's Day party in 1853 to eat "a Yorkshire pie . . . sent out to Longfellow from England" was English poet Arthur Hugh Clough, who had been inspired to try life in New England by his reading of and friendship with Emerson.[36] Nervously inviting Emerson to visit him in Oxford in November 1847, Clough wrote that "amongst the juniors there are many that have read and studied your books." By the time that

Clough extended this invitation, at least five editions of Emerson's essays circulated alongside the edition of *Essays and Other Works* distributed by Wiley & Putnam in 1843 via their London branch house. Emerson and Clough's correspondence further illustrates the circulation of US texts in Britain via private gifts and in the literary marketplace. Emerson passed on Longfellow's praises for Clough's pastoral *The Bothie of Toper-na-fuosich* (1848), and Clough replied that its hexameters were inspired by *Evangeline*, which he read aloud to his mother and sister and "is very popular here." In 1856, Clough thanked Emerson for a US edition of his *English Traits*, a "far prettier book" than an unauthorized reprint by Routledge that he had already bought.[37] In both Walker's letters to Longfellow and Clough's letters, game pies are one of the many transatlantic exchanges that produced a national American literature in the mid-nineteenth century, but they are exchanges that exemplify the dense materiality of American literature in Britain and the pleasures of that materiality for US authors and British publishers.

In this history of Longfellow's pies and in this book as a whole, I have sought to reach back before Lowell's—I think, willful—forgetting of American literature's transatlantic materials, and recover how antebellum authors understood British publishers and print as vital participants in the production and authorization of American literature. British editions of US texts were complex acts of reception that engaged with the cultural work and aesthetic goals of the texts they published and with the forms of capital and value their authors sought. Too long confined to footnotes or excluded from scholarly editions and literary histories, these print objects and their material and imaginative circulations back into the United States deserve our attention. British editions of US texts are not merely supplements to histories of American literature, they are integral to that history. Antebellum American literature is sometimes hopeful and sometimes hate-filled; it welcomes some and excludes others. It is beautiful and violent, inspiring and disappointing, and, as scholars and readers, we are continually examining anew its material and linguistic surfaces, depths, and limits. As we confront its complexities and explore its resonances in the world, then and now, we do so more completely when we comprehend how British print shaped its emergence.

NOTES

Introduction: The Transatlantic Materials of American Literature

1 Timothy Hampton, *Literature and Nation in the Sixteenth Century: Inventing Renaissance France* (Ithaca, NY: Cornell University Press, 2001), 19; Homi K. Bhabha, "Introduction: Narrating the Nation," in *Nation and Narration* (London: Routledge, 1990), 1–7.

2 Here, I draw on Charles Withers and Miles Ogborn's argument that one book can have "many possible geographies. The material conditions of the production and circulation of books take place on every scale from that of the printed page itself to the global networks of trade and empire." Miles Ogborn and Charles W. J. Withers, "Introduction: Book Geography, Book History," in *Geographies of the Book* (Farnham: Surrey, 2010), 12.

3 Pierre Bourdieu, *The Field of Cultural Production: Essays on Art and Literature*, ed. Randall Johnson (Cambridge: Polity Press, 1993), 34, 75.

4 Gisèle Sapiro, "Field Theory from a Transnational Perspective," in *The Oxford Handbook of Pierre Bourdieu*, ed. Thomas Medvetz and Jeffrey J. Sallas, (Oxford: Oxford University Press, 2018), 176.

5 Pascale Casanova, *The World Republic of Letters*, trans. M. B. DeBevoise (Cambridge, MA: Harvard University Press, 2004), 39.

6 Joseph Rezek, *London and the Making of Provincial Literature: Aesthetics and the Transatlantic Book Trade, 1800–1850* (Philadelphia: University of Pennsylvania Press, 2015), 3.

7 Hampton, *Literature and Nation in the Sixteenth Century*, 9.

8 Edgar Allan Poe, "Editorial Miscellany," *Broadway Journal*, October 4, 1845, 199.

9 Benedict Anderson, *Imagined Communities: Reflections on the Origin and Spread of Nationalism*, rev. ed. (London: Verso, 1991), 44.

10 *Leaves of Grass* and *Walden* were not published in Britain until 1868, and 1884 respectively, although both circulated in imported editions. British poet Arthur Hugh Clough described extracts of *Walden* being reprinted in the *Athenaeum* and being shown an imported copy of *Leaves of Grass* by Charles Eliot Norton when he visited Britain. Arthur Hugh Clough, letter to William Allingham, January 14, [1856]; Arthur Hugh Clough, letter to Ralph Waldo Emerson, September 12, 1856, in *The Correspondence of Arthur Hugh Clough*, ed. F. L. Mulhauser, vol. 2 (Oxford: Oxford University Press, 1957). Oxford Scholarly Editions Online (2018), https://www.oxfordscholarlyeditions.com/view/10.1093/actrade/9780198778059.book.1/actrade-9780198778059-work-1.

11 See W. W. Greg, "The Rationale of Copy-Text," *Studies in Bibliography* 3 (1950/51): 19–36. This method is required by the Center for Scholarly Editions and has been used to edit the vast majority of antebellum texts for which there are scholarly editions.

12 Meredith L. McGill, "Echocriticism: Repetition and the Order of Texts," *American Literature* 88, no. 1 (2016): 21.

13 Caroline Levine, "From Nation to Network," *Victorian Studies* 55, no. 4 (2013): 653.

14 For these studies, see Amanda Claybaugh, *The Novel of Purpose: Literature and Social Reform in the Anglo-American World* (Ithaca: Cornell University Press, 2007); Leslie Elizabeth Eckel, *Atlantic Citizens: Nineteenth-Century American Writers at Work in the World* (Edinburgh: Edinburgh University Press, 2013); Paul

Giles, *Transatlantic Insurrections: British Culture and the Formation of American Literature, 1730–1860* (Philadelphia: University of Pennsylvania Press, 2001); Paul Giles, *Virtual Americas: Transnational Fictions and the Transatlantic Imaginary* (Durham, NC: Duke University Press, 2002); Richard Gravil, *Romantic Dialogues: Anglo-American Continuities, 1776–1862*, 2nd ed. (Turril: Humanities-Ebooks, 2015); Christopher Hanlon, *America's England: Antebellum Literature and Atlantic Sectionalism* (New York: Oxford University Press, 2013); Susan Manning, *The Puritan-Provincial Vision: Scottish and American Literature in the Nineteenth Century* (Cambridge: Cambridge University Press, 1990); Joseph Roach, *Cities of the Dead: Circum-Atlantic Performance* (New York: Columbia University Press, 1996); Juliet Shields, *Nation and Migration: The Making of British Atlantic Literature, 1765–1835* (Oxford: Oxford University Press, 2016); Elisa Tamarkin, *Anglophilia: Deference, Devotion, and Antebellum America* (Chicago: University of Chicago Press, 2008); Leonard Tennenhouse, *The Importance of Feeling English: American Literature and the British Diaspora, 1750–1850* (Princeton: Princeton University Press, 2007); Robert Weisbuch, *Atlantic Double-Cross: American Literature and British Influence in the Age of Emerson* (Chicago: University of Chicago Press, 1986). Such studies acknowledge the material circulation of books and texts between Britain and the United States insofar as they underpinned imaginative exchanges between writers, but rarely do they address these material circulations as objects of analysis in their own right.

15 Clarence Gohdes, *American Literature in Nineteenth-Century England* (New York: Columbia University Press, 1944).

16 Paul Gilroy, *The Black Atlantic: Modernity and Double Consciousness* (London: Verso, 1993), 16.

17 Aileen Fyfe, *Steam-Powered Knowledge: William Chambers and the Business of Publishing, 1820–1860* (Chicago: University of Chicago Press, 2012), 126–28, 216–19.

18 Jessica DeSpain, *Nineteenth-Century Transatlantic Reprinting and the Embodied Book* (Farnham: Ashgate, 2014); Rezek, *London and the Making of Provincial Literature.*

19 Stephanie Palmer, *Transatlantic Footholds: Turn-of-the-Century American Women Writers and British Reviewers* (Abingdon: Routledge, 2019), 1–5.

20 "Nathaniel Hawthorne," *New Monthly Magazine and Humorist*, February 1852, 202; Frederick Law Olmsted, *Walks and Talks of an American Farmer in England* (New York: George Palmer Putnam & Co., 1852), 163.

21 "The Emerson Mania," *English Review*, September 1849, 139.

22 "Longfellow," *National Review*, January 1859, 198.

23 Henry Howard Paul, *Dashes of American Humour* (London: Piper Brothers and Co., 1852), 237.

24 Alexis Weedon, *Victorian Publishing: The Economics of Book Production for a Mass Market* (Aldershot: Ashgate, 2003), 51. Weedon estimates these percentages of fluent readers from the proportions of the population who were able to sign the marriage register.

25 Richard D. Altick, *The English Common Reader: A Social History of the Mass Reading Public, 1800–1900* (Chicago: University of Chicago Press, 1957), 277–78.

26 For the effect of events and social, religious, and political crises on publishing, see Simon Eliot, "Some Trends in British Book Production, 1800–1919," in *Literature in the Marketplace: Nineteenth-Century British Publishing and Reading Practices*, ed. John O. Jordan and Robert L. Patten (Cambridge: Cambridge University Press, 1995), 28.

27 Simon Eliot, *Some Patterns and Trends in British Publishing, 1800–1919*, Occasional Papers of the Bibliographical Society 8 (London: Bibliographical Society, 1994), 8–12. Eliot takes his statistics from Stationers' Company records, British Library

deposits, and trade publications, including *Bent's Monthly Literary Advertiser* (1802–1860) and *Publishers' Circular* (1837–1959).

28 Eliot, "Some Trends in British Book Production," 39, 41. Eliot categorizes publications in *Bent's Literary Advertiser* as high (over 10s), medium (between 10s and 3s 6d) and low (below 3s 6d). It is worth observing that these are very broad pricing categories, that the price a book was advertised at could differ substantially from the price for which any one copy eventually sold, and that the publishers of higher-priced books were more likely to announce their volumes in *Bent's*.

29 Altick, *The English Common Reader*, 286.

30 Lee Erickson argues that after the 1820s, "The annuals effectively divided poetry into one kind for a limited audience made up largely of gentlemen and scholars, and another for a much larger audience composed primarily of women and children." Lee Erickson, *The Economy of Literary Form: English Literature and the Industrialization of Publishing, 1800–1850* (Baltimore: Johns Hopkins University Press, 1996), 33.

31 Michael Twyman, "The Illustration Revolution," in *The Cambridge History of the Book in Britain, Vol. 6: 1830–1914*, ed. David McKitterick (Cambridge: Cambridge University Press, 2009), 123, 117–27.

32 William St Clair calls this practice, in which a publisher would issue a text at a cheaper price having first exhausted the market at the higher price point, "tranching down." William St Clair, *The Reading Nation in the Romantic Period* (Cambridge: Cambridge University Press, 2004), 32–34. During the mid-century, the time between "tranches" decreased so that cheap editions of current popular fiction were available more quickly.

33 James Raven, *The Business of Books: Booksellers and the English Book Trade, 1450–1850* (New Haven: Yale University Press, 2007), 324.

34 This figure does not represent the total number of American books noticed in the *Circular*, as it does not include schoolbooks, medical books, geographies, political writings, useful knowledge, and technical publications, among other categories. These fall outside the scope of this study, which focuses on the relationship between US literary texts and British print. American periodicals were sometimes noticed in the *Circular*, especially by booksellers and publishers advertising imported US titles, but as these notices were irregular and as this study focuses on US writing published in Britain, I have excluded these.

35 George Palmer Putnam, *American Facts: Notes and Statistics Relevant to the Government, Resources, Engagements, Manufactures, Commerce, Religion, Education, Literature, Fine Arts, Manners, and Customs* (London: Wiley & Putnam, 1845), 82.

36 Robert A. Gross, "Building a National Literature: The United States 1800–1890," in *A Companion to the History of the Book*, ed. Simon Eliot and Jonathan Rose (Oxford: Wiley-Blackwell, 2009), 322.

37 Anon, "American Literature," *Cleave's Penny Gazette of Variety and Entertainment*, May 20, 1843, 2.

38 For a list of American fiction published in Britain before 1832, see Rezek, *London and the Making of Provincial Literature*, 200–206.

39 Nassau William Senior, *American Slavery: A Reprint of an Article on "Uncle Tom's Cabin" of Which A Portion Was Inserted in the 206th Number of the "Edinburgh Review"* (London: Longmans, 1856), 50.

40 "The Emerson Mania," *The English Review*, September 1849, 139. For Emerson's cross-class appeal in England, see W. H. G. Armytage, *American Influence on English Education* (Abingdon: Routledge, 1967), 9–10; Daniel Koch, *Ralph Waldo Emerson in Europe: Class, Race and Revolution in the Making of an American Thinker* (London: I. B. Tauris, 2012), 124.

41 "Subscription Lists for the *Literary World*," c. 1847–55, Duyckinck Family Papers, MssCol 873, Box 59, Manuscripts and Archives Division, New York Public Library.

42 Charles Sedgwick, letter to Wiley & Putnam, January 15, 1839, George Palmer Putnam Collection, C0685, Box 3 Folder 41, Subseries 1A: "Private,"Manuscripts Division, Department of Special Collections, Princeton University Library .

43 Leon Jackson, *The Business of Letters: Authorial Economies in Antebellum America* (Stanford: Stanford University Press, 2008), 29.

44 Michael J. Everton, *The Grand Chorus of Complaint: Authors and the Business Ethics of American Publishing* (Oxford: Oxford University Press, 2011), 13–15.

45 Lydia Huntley Sigourney, letter to John Murray II, February 24, 1834, John Murray Archive, MS41090, National Library of Scotland.

46 Harriet Beecher Stowe, letter to Sampson Low, September 13, 1858, facsimile, Kirkham Database, Harriet Beecher Stowe Center, Hartford CT. Original in Harriet Beecher Stowe Center. Harriet Beecher Stowe, letter to Clarke Beeton & Co., February 19, 1859, Papers of Harriet Beecher Stowe, 6318, Clifton Waller Barrett Library, Special Collections, University of Virginia Library.

47 Charles Dickens and James Fenimore Cooper were writers who successfully obtained both forms of value in their respective fields. David Bogue's editions of Longfellow's poetry, discussed in chapter 1, materialize the aesthetic value of his verse and transform his poetry into a heavily commodified object for the Christmas trade.

48 Foreign works were also protected under the International Copyright Acts of 1844 and 1852, if foreign states made bilateral treaties with Britain that gave authors mutual protection. The United States, however, did not make international copyright treaties until 1891. US authors seeking British copyrights therefore had to rely on arguments that the Statute of Anne (1710) applied to foreign authors.

49 Melissa J. Homestead argues that while Cooper's exceptional popularity led to unauthorized reprints of his novels, most American authors could feel secure that if their work appeared in a British edition printed from advanced sheets and published before the American edition, it would not be widely reprinted. "American Novelist Catharine Sedgwick Negotiates British Copyright, 1822–57," *Yearbook of English Studies* 45 (2015): 200.

50 For a full account of the cases through which the English courts established and then dismissed prior publication as a route to copyright for foreign authors, see James J. Barnes, *Authors, Publishers and Politicians: The Quest for An Anglo-American Copyright Agreement, 1815–1854* (London: Routledge and Kegan Paul, 1974), 153–76. Chapters 1 and 2 give more detail on individual court decisions.

51 Tim Sommer, "Embedded Authorship: Thomas Carlyle, Ralph Waldo Emerson, and Nineteenth-Century "Transatlantic Bibliopoly," *Book History* 24, no. 2 (2021): 356–57.

52 McGill, "Echocriticism," 21.

53 For Dana and Moxon's trade relations, see Jeffrey L. Amestoy, *Slavish Shore: The Odyssey of Richard Henry Dana Jr.* (Cambridge: Harvard University Press, 2015), 66.

54 Claire Parfait, *The Publishing History of "Uncle Tom's Cabin," 1852–2002* (Basingstoke: Ashgate, 2007), 106–7.

55 As Will Slauter observes in a recent study of copyright and newspapers, "copyright law was designed for books," and therefore has historically neglected, or has proved a poor fit for multi-authored or serial publications. Will Slauter, *Who Owns the News?: A History of Copyright* (Stanford: Stanford University Press, 2019), 12. See also, Will Slauter, "Toward a History of Copyright for Periodical Writings: Examples from Nineteenth-Century America," in *Book Practices & Textual*

Itineraries: From Text(s) to Book(s): Studies in Production and Editorial Processes, ed. Nathalie Collé, Monica Latham, and David Ten Eyck (Nancy: PUN-Éditions universitaires de Lorraine, 2014), 65–84.

56 Meredith L. McGill, *American Literature and the Culture of Reprinting* (Philadelphia: University of Pennsylvania Press, 2003), 19, 7–8.

57 There are no statistics that allow a comparison of the numbers of British-published editions of US texts with editions published in other nations. However, Michael Winship has shown that the United States imported more British books than those of the ten other leading nations combined between 1828 and 1848, while British imports of US books increased more than twenty-fold in the same period, growing more rapidly than those from any other nation. "The Transatlantic Book Trade and Anglo-American Literary Culture in the Nineteenth-Century," in *Reciprocal Influences: Literary Production, Distribution, and Consumption in America*, ed. Steven Fink and Susan Williams (Columbus: Ohio State University Press, 1999), 118–19. Antebellum American texts were also reprinted in continental Europe, and the British-American print market was entangled with this trade, but mapping those entanglements is beyond the scope of this study and beyond my linguistic capabilities. Other scholars are pursuing these histories; see the chapters on France, Germany, and Spain in Tracy C. Davis and Stefka Mihaylova, eds., *"Uncle Tom's Cabin"s: The Transnational History of America's Most Mutable Book* (Ann Arbor: University of Michigan Press, 2018); Charles Johanningsmeier, "Exporting America via Leipzig, Germany: Tauchnitz Editions and the International Popularization of American Literature," *Papers of the Bibliographical Society of America* 112, no. 2 (2018): 201–29.

58 For the place of these US texts in mid-Victorian working class culture, see Marianne Holohan, "British Editions of *Uncle Tom's Cabin*: Race, Working-Class Literacy and Transatlantic Reprinting," *Resources for American Literary Study* 36 (2011); Jonathan Rose, *The Intellectual Life of the English Working Classes* (New Haven: Yale University Press, 2001), 354.

59 Rose, *Intellectual Life*, 355.

60 Giles, *Virtual Americas*, 164–84; Julia Sun-Joo Lee, *The American Slave Narrative and the Victorian Novel* (Oxford: Oxford University Press, 2010).

61 Levine, "From Nation to Network," 649, 657.

62 For studies of US literary development that privilege the novel, see, for example Jonathan Arac, *The Emergence of American Literary Narrative, 1820–1860* (Cambridge, MA: Harvard University Press, 2005); Cathy N. Davidson, *Revolution and the Word: The Rise of the Novel in America* (New York: Oxford University Press, 1986); Jason Richards, *Imitation Nation: Red, White, and Blackface in Early and Antebellum US Literature* (Charlottesville: University of Virginia Press, 2017). McGill documents and critiques the dominance of the novel in transatlantic studies in Meredith L. McGill, "Introduction: The Traffic in Poems," in *The Traffic in Poems: Nineteenth-Century Poetry and Transatlantic Exchange*, ed. Meredith L. McGill (New Brunswick: Rutgers University Press, 2008), 1–14.

63 Histories of these transatlantic bestsellers already exist. For *The Sketch-Book* in Britain, see Rezek, *London and the Making of Provincial Literature*, 100–12; Ben Harris McClary, ed., *Washington Irving and the House of Murray: Geoffrey Crayon Charms the British: 1817–1856* (Knoxville: University of Tennessee Press, 1969). For *Uncle Tom's Cabin*, see Sarah Meer, *Uncle Tom Mania: Slavery, Minstrelsy, and Transatlantic Culture in the 1850s* (University of Georgia Press, 2005); Parfait, *Publishing History of "Uncle Tom's Cabin."* For *The Lamplighter*, see Susan S. Williams, "'Promoting an Extensive Sale': The Production and Reception of *The Lamplighter*," *New England Quarterly* 69, no. 2 (1996): 179–200.

Chapter 1: Illustration as Authorization in Longfellow's Reprints

1 "Summary Accounts Ledger," British Library MS46676A, *The Archives of Richard Bentley & Son, 1829–1898*, microfilm edition (British Library holdings), 55 reels (Cambridge: Chadwyck-Healey, 1977), reel 54, vol. 117 A, image 28.

2 Leon Jackson, *The Business of Letters: Authorial Economies in Antebellum America* (Stanford, CA: Stanford University Press, 2008), 2–6.

3 Clarence Gohdes, *American Literature in Nineteenth-Century England* (New York: Columbia University Press, 1944), 22.

4 John Greenleaf Whittier, letter to Elizur Wright, February 24, 1844. John Greenleaf Whittier, *The Letters of John Greenleaf Whittier*, ed. John B. Pickard, vol. 1 (Cambridge: Belknap Press, 1975), 628.

5 Elizur Wright, "Preface," in John Greenleaf Whittier, *Ballads, and other Poems* (London: H. G. Clarke, 1844), viii.

6 In 1845, George Palmer Putnam placed Whittier below national bards like Richard A. Dana Sr., James G. Percival, and William Cullen Bryant, and observed that he "has written much on behalf of the colored race, and against the wrongs of slavery"; *American Facts: Notes and Statistics Relevant to the Government, Resources, Engagements, Manufactures, Commerce, Religion, Education, Literature, Fine Arts, Manners, and Customs* (London: Wiley & Putnam, 1845), 100. Michael C. Cohen argues that the "invention of Whittier as a national figure" did not take place until the 1860s, when popular focus shifted from his anti-slavery poetry to his New England ballads following the success of *Snow-Bound* (1866), which could evoke nostalgic feelings in audiences in the North and South: *The Social Lives of Poems in Nineteenth-Century America* (Philadelphia: University of Pennsylvania Press, 2015), 165.

7 Henry Wadsworth Longfellow, *The Letters of Henry Wadsworth Longfellow, Volume III: 1844–1856*, ed. Andrew Hilen (Cambridge, MA: Belknap Press of Harvard University Press, 1972), 27.

8 Ibid., 212.

9 William Charvat, *The Profession of Authorship in America, 1800–1870*, ed. Matthew Bruccoli (Columbus: Ohio State University Press, 1968), 159–63.

10 Clarence Gohdes, "Longfellow and His Authorized British Publishers," *PMLA* 55, no. 4 (December 1940): 1178.

11 Advert for John Walker's edition of *Hyperion*, *Publishers' Circular*, November 15, 1848.

12 The letter that accompanied the parcel is lost, but Longfellow's response is dated April 17, 1849, suggesting that they must have been posted sometime between November 1848 and the end of March 1849. Longfellow, *Letters*, 3:195.

13 Jackson, *Business of Letters*, 95–96.

14 Longfellow, *Letters*, 3:195.

15 Henry Wadsworth Longfellow, *The Letters of Henry Wadsworth Longfellow, Volume V: 1866–1874*, ed. Andrew Hilen (Cambridge, MA: Belknap Press of Harvard University Press, 1982), 127.

16 Longfellow, *Letters*, 3:195.

17 John Walker, letter to Henry Wadsworth Longfellow (*hereafter* HWL), May 5, 1849. MS Am 1340.2, folder 5789, Letters to Henry Wadsworth Longfellow, Houghton Library, Harvard University.

18 The Maine reprinter, Thomas Bird Mosher, sent George Meredith a copy of his fine press (but unauthorized) reprint of *Modern Love* (pub. 1862, repr. 1892): Adela Pinch, "Transatlantic Modern Love," in *The Traffic in Poems: Nineteenth-Century Poetry and Transatlantic Exchange*, ed. Meredith L. McGill (New Brunswick: Rutgers University Press, 2008), 164. Other US publishers

used similar methods to attract the business of British authors later in the nineteenth century.

19 MS Am 1340.2, folder 4813, Letters to Henry Wadsworth Longfellow (*hereafter* LHWL). Routledge announced five different reprints of Longfellow's work in the *Publishers' Circular* between January 1850 and September 1851, making it difficult to know which one he sent to Longfellow, but it may have been an edition of *Hyperion and Kavanagh* he published in July 1851, which retailed at 2s 6d in cloth.

20 George Routledge, letter to HWL, March 23, 1855, MS Am 1340.2, folder 4813, LHWL.

21 Routledge, letter to HWL, December 28, 1855, MS Am 1340.2, folder 4813, LHWL.

22 Longfellow, *Letters*, 3:226.

23 John Walker, letter to HWL, February 9, 1850, MS Am 1340.2, folder 5789, LHWL.

24 Longfellow, *Letters*, 3:57.

25 Samuel Longfellow, *Life of Henry Wadsworth Longfellow, with Extracts from His Journals and Correspondence*, vol. 2 (London: Kegan Paul, Trench & Co, 1886), 158. The discrepancy between the date of the journal and the date of Walker's letter suggests either that Walker wrote to Longfellow after sending the book (which agrees with his use of "sent"), or that someone else also sent Longfellow Bogue's edition.

26 Longfellow, *Letters*, 3:253.

27 This letter is lost; the date of Longfellow's letter is established from Bogue's reply.

28 David Bogue, letter to HWL, February 22, 1850, MS Am 1340.2, folder 596, LHWL.

29 Gohdes, "Longfellow and His Authorized British Publishers," 1168–70.

30 Bogue, letter to HWL, December 23, 1851, October 8, 1852, MS Am 1340.2, folder 596, LHWL.

31 Longfellow's papers contain receipts for "$100.00, in September 1850, for an English illustrated edition of *Evangeline* (500 copies); $480.10 on December 13, 1851 for a London edition of *The Golden Legend*; and $200.00 on December 15, 1851 for a London edition of *Poems* illustrated," Charvat, *Profession of Authorship*, 165. The first of these is likely to be Ticknor, Reed and Fields's royalty payment for the 500 copies ordered from Bogue in June 1850: Warren S. Tryon and William Charvat, eds., *The Cost Books of Ticknor and Fields and Their Predecessors, 1832–1858* (New York: Bibliographical Society of America, 1949), 167. The second is probably Bogue's payment for his authorized edition of *The Golden Legend*, being roughly equivalent to the £100 Bogue offered, with some reimbursement for the cost of shipping sheets. The date of the final payment matches Ticknor's purchase of 350 copies of Bogue's illustrated *Voices* and 250 copies of his illustrated *Poems*, but the royalty payment would have been $145 rather than $200. Bogue explained to Longfellow that "in supplying these books to Ticknor I always counted on them paying you copyright," suggesting that he did not pay Longfellow. Bogue, letter to HWL, May 23, 1853, MS Am 1340.2, folder 596, LHWL.

32 Hugh Amory, "'Proprietary Illustration': The Case of Cooke's *Tom Jones*," in *An Index of Civilization: Studies in Printing and Publishing History in Honour of Keith Maslen*, ed. D. R. Harvey, Wallace Kirsop, and B. J. McMullin (Clayton, AU: Centre for Bibliographical and Textual Studies, Monash University, 1993), 139.

33 In *Bogue v. Houlston* (1852) Chancery judge Sir James Parker concluded that if a book had been properly registered under the requirements of the Copyright Act of 1842, "such copyright extends to the illustrations and designs of the book,

equally as to the letterpress." *Bogue v. Houlston* (1852), 5 De Gex & Smale 267, 64 E.R. 1111.

34 Meredith L. McGill observes that the *Southern Literary Messenger*'s use of woodcut signatures in Poe's "Autography" (1836) "disrupt[ed] the process of reprinting," because other magazines could not afford to rent or reproduce them: *American Literature and the Culture of Reprinting, 1834–1853* (Philadelphia: University of Pennsylvania Press, 2003), 183. Illustrations did not always disrupt reprinting, especially for British reprints of US texts that contained fewer and less skillfully executed illustrations than Bogue's. In her discussion of British reprints of *The Wide, Wide World*, Jessica DeSpain demonstrates that some publishers of cheap editions illustrated the same episodes with very similar images, even as she traces differences in the way those images frame the text. *Nineteenth-Century Transatlantic Reprinting and the Embodied Book* (Farnham: Ashgate, 2014), 71–76.

35 Tryon and Charvat, *Cost Books*, 167.

36 "Literature," *John Bull*, March 2, 1850, 139.

37 "Summary," *Literary Gazette*, January 12, 1850, 30.

38 Advertisement for "Books in Press," *Literary World*, June 8, 1850, 576.

39 "Correspondence," *The Literary World*, March 9, 1850, 236.

40 John Reuben Thompson, "Notice of New Works," *Southern Literary Messenger*, December 1850, 761.

41 "Fine Arts," *Republic*, November 16, 1850, 3.

42 "Review of New Books," *Graham's Magazine*, September 1850, 199.

43 "Notices of New Books," *The Examiner*, February 16, 1850.

44 Paul Goldman and Simon Cooke argue that "Sixties" illustration is characterized by intense and detailed visual interpretation of the written word. This style reached its height in the 1860s, but is also found in the decades before and after. "Introduction," in *Reading Victorian Illustration, 1855–1875: Spoils of the Cutting Room*, ed. Paul Goldman and Simon Cooke (Farnham: Ashgate, 2012), 3–5.

45 Henry Wadsworth Longfellow, *Evangeline: A Tale of Acadie* (London: David Bogue, 1850), 1.

46 Julia Thomas, *Pictorial Victorians: The Inscription of Values on Word and Page* (Athens: Ohio University Press, 2004), 38.

47 Longfellow, *Evangeline*, 52, 53.

48 Longfellow, *Letters*, 3:41.

49 S. Longfellow, *Life of Henry Wadsworth Longfellow*, 2:73–74.

50 Leslie Elizabeth Eckel, *Atlantic Citizens: Nineteenth-Century American Writers at Work in the World* (Edinburgh: Edinburgh University Press, 2013), 45.

51 Longfellow, *Evangeline*, 53.

52 Ibid., 51, 68, 84, 88–89.

53 Henry Wadsworth Longfellow, *Hyperion: A Romance. Illustrated with Nearly One Hundred Engravings on Wood from Drawings by Birket Foster* (London: David Bogue, 1853), 282.

54 Charvat, *Profession of Authorship*, 121.

55 Matthew Gartner, "Becoming Longfellow: Work, Manhood, and Poetry," *American Literature* 72, no. 1 (2000): 72.

56 Ticknor and Fields also ordered copies of *Hyperion* with their imprint from Bogue as they had with *Evangeline*, although Bogue's letters to Longfellow show that their order was not as large as Bogue had hoped. Bogue, letter to HWL, May 27, 1853, MS Am 1340.2, folder 596, LHWL.

57 Longfellow, *Letters*, 3:329.

58 Longfellow, *Hyperion*, v.

59 Bogue, letter to HWL, January 9, 1852, MS Am 1340.2, folder 596, LHWL.

60 Henry Vizetelly, *Glances Back through Seventy Years: Autobiographical and Other Reminiscences*, vol. 1 (London: Kegan Paul, Trench, and Trubner, 1893), 366.

61 Richard Maxwell, "Walter Scott, Historical Fiction, and the Genesis of the Victorian Illustrated Book," in *The Victorian Illustrated Book*, by Richard Maxwell (Charlottesville: University of Virginia Press, 2002), 2, 42.

62 Longfellow, *Hyperion*, v.

63 Henry Vizetelly, "Notes of a Tour in the Footsteps of Paul Flemming," in Longfellow, *Hyperion*, 293.

64 Ibid., 294, 295.

65 Longfellow, *Hyperion*, 46.

66 "Notices," *Literary Gazette*, February 26, 1853, 203.

67 Longfellow, *Hyperion*, 189.

68 Ibid., 220, 219, 281.

69 Svetlana Boym, *The Future of Nostalgia* (New York: Basic Books, 2001), 41, 53.

70 Jennifer K. Ladino, *Reclaiming Nostalgia: Longing for Nature in American Literature* (Charlottesville: University of Virginia Press, 2012), 13.

71 Henry Wadsworth Longfellow, "The Courtship of Miles Standish," in *Poems and Other Writings*, ed. J. D. McClatchy (New York: Library of America, 2000), 294, 320.

72 Ibid., 283.

73 Robert A. Ferguson, "Longfellow's Political Fears: Civic Authority and the Role of the Artist in Hiawatha and Miles Standish," *American Literature* 50, no. 2 (1978): 204.

74 Longfellow, "Courtship of Miles Standish," 287, 283.

75 Ibid., 308, 317.

76 Ibid., 238, 313, 314.

77 Ibid., 323.

78 Henry Wadsworth Longfellow, *The Letters of Henry Wadsworth Longfellow, Volume IV: 1857–65*, ed. Andrew Hilen (Cambridge, MA: Belknap Press of Harvard University Press, 1972), 11.

79 Advertisement for Illustrated Presentation Volumes, *Publishers' Circular*, July 16, 1857, 301.

80 Ibid.

81 "Literature," *Lloyd's Weekly Newspaper*, December 20, 1857, 8; "Notices of New Works," *Southern Literary Messenger* (October 1858): 313–20, 318.

82 Quoted in Advert for *Poe's Poetical Works*, *The Daily Dispatch*, December 24, 1858, 2.

83 William Cullen Bryant, letter to Richard Henry Dana Sr., May 26, 1854, and William Cullen Bryant, letter to Frances Fairchild Bryant, November 6, 1856, in William Cullen Bryant, *The Letters of William Cullen Bryant*, ed. William Cullen Bryant II and Thomas G. Vos, vol. 1 (New York: Fordham University Press, 1981), 334, 597.

84 McGill, *Culture of Reprinting*, 173.

85 Edgar Allan Poe, "The Literarti of New York City. No. IV," *Godey's Lady's Book*, August 1846, 72–78, 72.

86 Poe complained to his friend writer Frederick W. Thomas that *Graham's Magazine* had a "namby-pamby character" as a result of its "contemptible pictures, fashion plates, music and love tales," May 25, 1842, in Edgar Allan Poe, *The Letters of Edgar Allan Poe, Volume I: 1824–1845*, ed. John Ward Ostrom (New York: Gordion Press, 1966), 197.

87 Michael Von Cannon, "A Tale of Optics: Poe, Visual Culture, and Antebellum Literary Celebrity," *Poe Studies* 47, no. 1 (2014): 43. The focus of Von Cannon's essay is daguerreotypes and engraved portraits.

88 Wood engraving, like letter press, uses a relief printing method, meaning that the text and image can be printed side-by-side and at the same time; steel engraving is an intaglio method (ink is deposited in grooves on a plate rather than sitting on top of relief sections) and requires a much heavier press, meaning that steel engravings had to be printed separately.

89 Poe, letter to James Russell Lowell, March 30,1844, in Poe, *Letters*, 247.

90 Edgar Allan Poe, *The Poetical Works of Edgar Allan Poe* (London: Sampson Low & Co., 1858), 24, 26.

91 "Ulalume" was first published in the *American Review* in December 1847. Poe asked Nathaniel Parker Willis to reprint the text in his *Home Journal*, with an inquiry as to its author as part of Poe's efforts at "re-establishing myself in the literary world"; "Ulalume" was later reprinted in the *Providence Journal* and Poe sent a copy of this text to the *Literary World* so that magazine could also reprint it. The long and complex textual and publication history of "Ulalume" is explained at "Edgar Allan Poe Society of Baltimore—Works—Poems—Ulalume," Edgar Allan Poe Society of Baltimore, January 21, 2019, https://www.eapoe.org/works/info/pp087.htm.

92 Poe, *Poetical Works*, 24.

93 For the identification of these two allusions, now largely accepted by Poe scholars, see Lewis Leary, "Poe's 'Ulalume,'" *Explicator* 6 (January 1947): item 25; T. O. Mabbott, "Poe's 'Ulalume,'" *Explicator* 1 (February 1943): item 60.

94 Poe, *Poetical Works*, 28. Redfield and Low's edition follows the text of "Ulalume" in Griswold's 1850 edition of Poe's complete works, which omits the final stanza of the poem that appears in many other printings.

95 Cropsey's illustrations for "The City in the Sea" also draw on an American landscape tradition, echoing the composition of the doomed city in the last two paintings in Thomas Cole's "The Course of Empire" series.

Chapter 2: Authorized Editions and the Materials of American Authorship

1 "American Authors and English Piracy," *New York Herald*, November 18, 1854.

2 "Our London Correspondence: American Authors and English Piracy," *New York Herald*, November 16, 1854.

3 Geoffrey Sanborn, *The Value of Herman Melville* (Cambridge: Cambridge University Press, 2018), 21.

4 Meredith L. McGill, *American Literature and The Culture of Reprinting, 1834–1853* (Philadelphia: University of Pennsylvania Press, 2003), 90.

5 For a list of London editions of US fiction from 1797 to 1832, see Joseph Rezek, *London and the Making of Provincial Literature: Aesthetics and the Transatlantic Book Trade, 1800–1850* (Philadelphia: University of Pennsylvania Press, 2015), 199–206.

6 For further information on Miller, see: James J. Barnes, "John Miller: First Transatlantic Publisher's Agent," *Studies in Bibliography* 29 (1976): 373–79; Melissa J. Homestead, "American Novelist Catharine Sedgwick Negotiates British Copyright, 1822–57," *The Yearbook of English Studies* 45 (2015), 200–202; Joseph Rezek, "Furious Booksellers: The 'American Copy' of the Waverley Novels and the Language of the Book Trade," *Early American Studies* 11, no. 3 (2013): 563; Emily B. Todd, "Establishing Routes for Fiction in the United States: Walter Scott's Novels and the Early Nineteenth-Century American Publishing Industry," *Book History* 12, no. 1 (2009): 116.

7 Quoted in Ben Harris McClary, ed., *Washington Irving and the House of Murray: Geoffrey Crayon Charms the British: 1817–1856* (Knoxville: University of Tennessee Press, 1969), 18.

8 For accounts of the transatlantic publication of *The Sketch-Book*, see McClary, *Washington Irving*, 18–20; Rezek, *London and the Making of Provincial Literature*,

99–101. Exceptions to Murray's exclusive publication of Irving's authorized editions were *Astoria* (1836) and its sequel, *The Adventures of Captain Bonneville* (1837), which Bentley published.

9 For histories of the House of Murray, see Humphrey Carpenter, *The Seven Lives of John Murray: The Story of a Publishing Dynasty* (London: John Murray, 2009); George Paston, *At John Murray's: Records of a Literary Circle, 1843–1892* (London: John Murray, 1932).

10 Manuscript Book, September 1831–August 2, 1855, MS 42633, John Murray Archive, National Library of Scotland (*hereafter* JMA).

11 For an account of the London publication of *The Pioneers*, see Wayne Franklin, *James Fenimore Cooper: The Early Years* (New Haven: Yale University Press, 2007), 353–57.

12 For Bentley's partnership with Colburn and its demise, see Royal A. Gettmann, *A Victorian Publisher: A Study of the Bentley Papers* (Cambridge: Cambridge University Press, 1960), 18–22.

13 Charles Fenno Hoffman, letter to [?], January 12, 1838, MSS 7706, Papers of Charles Fenno Hoffman, Special Collections, University of Virginia Library. The recipient was probably Thomas Aspinwall, an American diplomat who acted as an agent for several American writers and arranged the publication of Hoffman's *Wild Scenes* with Bentley.

14 To Hart, Bentley proposed "a mutual understanding to be entered into between us to forward to each other early copies of the respective works we may undertake; and guaranteeing each other in all cases against loss in each individual book, the net profits arising out of each to be equally divided between us." Richard Bentley (*hereafter* RB), letter to Abraham Hart, February 22, 1850, British Library MS46641, *The Archives of Richard Bentley & Son, 1829–1898* (*hereafter* ARBS), microfilm edition (British Library holdings), 55 reels (Cambridge: Chadwyck-Healey, 1977), reel 40, vol. 82, image 64. He made similar offers to the other firms listed.

15 To Scribner and Baker, Bentley complained that "Battle Summer [by Donald Grant Mitchell] is only half a book & sold as half a book," the implication being that it was ill suited to the multivolume format on which the British book trade, and Bentley's business model in particular, relied. RB, letter to Scribner and Baker, May 30, 1850, British Library MS46641, ARBS, reel 53, vol. 82, image 89.

16 Copies Leger C, MS42728, 121, JMA; Agreement for *The Pathfinder*, British Library MS46613, ARBS, reel 27, vol. 54, image 252. Cooper's payment was, however, reduced by £200 to offset Bentley's losses on Cooper's unsuccessful *The History of the Navy of the United States of America* (1839).

17 Homestead, "Catharine Sedgwick Negotiates British Copyright," 197.

18 Summary Accounts Ledger, British Library MS46676A, ARBS, reel 54, vol. 117A, image 24.

19 George Palmer Putnam, *American Facts: Notes and Statistics Relevant to the Government, Resources, Engagements, Manufactures, Commerce, Religion, Education, Literature, Fine Arts, Manners, and Customs* (London: Wiley & Putnam, 1845), 85.

20 Rezek, *London and the Making of Provincial Literature*, 90.

21 "Diedrich Knickerbocker's History of New York," *Blackwood's Edinburgh Magazine*, July 1820, 369.

22 John Murray II (*hereafter* JMII), letter to Edward Everett, March 3, 1843, Murray Letterbook, 1839–1846, MS. 41911, 107–8, JMA. *The Conquest of Mexico* was actually published by Bentley, who offered £650 for a sale of copyright outright. While Prescott had concerns that Bentley's advertising ate into his profits on *Ferdinand and Isabella* (1838) and about Bentley being difficult to deal with, the larger offer won over Prescott and Aspinwall, who was acting on his behalf.

23 JMII, letter to Rev. T. Hartwell Horne, March 3, 1843, Murray Letterbook, 1839–1846, JMA.

24 William Hickling Prescott, *The Correspondence of William Hickling Prescott, 1833–1847*, ed. Roger Wolcott (Boston: Houghton Mifflin, 1925), 12, 535.

25 Thomas Aspinwall, letter to JMII, June 30, 1835, and July 9, 1835, MS 40027, JMA.

26 Richard Burleigh Kimball, letter to RB, November 20, 1849, MSS 7813, Papers of Richard Burleigh Kimball, Clifton Waller Barrett Library, Albert and Shirley Small Special Collections Library, University of Virginia Library. It is difficult to know whether Kimball's ruse worked. *Saint Leger* received some very positive reviews, none of which identify the author as an American. However, by August 1850, Bentley was using Kimball's name to advertise the work, suggesting its American origins did not stay secret for long.

27 RB, letter to John Pendleton Kennedy, May 14, 1834, British Library MS46640, ARBS, reel 39, vol. 81, image 115.

28 RB, letter to Baker & Scribner, February 22, 1850, British Library MS46641, ARBS, reel 40, vol. 82, image 64.

29 For an outline of Sampson Low's work as a transatlantic agent and publisher, see James J. Barnes and Patience P. Barnes, "Sampson Low: Organizer of the Victorian Book Trade," *Papers of the Bibliographical Society of America* 105, no. 1 (2011): 69–89.

30 Robert Cooke, letter to George Palmer Putnam, November 23, 1849, George Palmer Putnam Scrapbook, Manuscripts Division, Department of Special Collections, Princeton University Library.

31 "Give me a long month clear from the time you send me the last sheets for their transmission to London, and then Twenty days more as time to compleat the printing here, we should be quite safe." JMII to Mrs. Pierce Butler (Fanny Kemble), August 16, 1834, Murray Letterbook, November 2, 1823–March 2, 1839, MS 41910, JMA.

32 Innes Keighren, Charles W. J. Withers, and Bill Bell observe that "the vast majority of Murray's authors were men, and British men of a certain social status and position, often within the British Admiralty, or associated with the diplomatic service or Britain's overseas trade, or, simply, possessed of independent means and with the desire to travel." We can assume that most of these men were also white. *Travels into Print: Exploration, Writing, and Publishing with John Murray, 1773–1859* (University of Chicago Press, 2015), 25.

33 British women writers that Bentley published between 1830 and 1854 include: Letitia Elizabeth Landon, Anna Maria Hall, the Countess of Blessington, Frances Trollope, Mary Howitt, Catherine Gore, Ellen Wallace Grace Webster, Katherine Thomson, and Anna Eliza Bray. He published more than one novel for all of these writers, except for Mary Howitt, who moved away from the three-volume form.

34 Writers of serials would often be finishing the work after the first instalment was published, making it impossible for the whole text to be published in London before any of it was published in the US. Bentley altered his plans for Stephens's *Fashion and Famine* (1854) when he discovered that it was serialized in the London weekly *The Family Herald*, putting it out in a cheap edition that sold for 3s 6d, rather than a prestige three-volume novel: RB, letter to Ann Sophia Stephens, July 28, 1854, British Library MS46642, ARBS, reel 40, vol. 83, image 48.

35 Joanna Brooks, "The Unfortunates: What the Life Spans of Early Black Books Tells Us About Book History," in *Early African American Print Culture*, ed. Jordan Alexander Stein and Lara Langer Cohen (Philadelphia: University of Pennsylvania Press, 2012), 40, 50.

36 Eric Gardner, *Unexpected Places: Relocating Nineteenth-Century African American Literature* (University Press of Mississippi, 2010), 10.

37 "Our London Correspondence: American Authors and English Piracy."

38 Quoted in Leon Howard, "Historical Note," in Herman Melville, *Typee: A Peep at Polynesian Life* (Evanston: Northwestern University Press; Newberry Library, 1966), 278.

39 Quoted in Hershel Parker, *Herman Melville: A Biography*, vol. 1 (Baltimore: Johns Hopkins University Press, 1996), 378.

40 Geoffrey Sanborn, "Purple Haze: Making Sense of Uncertainty (and Uncertainty of Sense) in *Typee*," *ESQ: A Journal of the American Renaissance* 51, no. 1–3 (2005): 132.

41 For readings of *Typee* as a critique of travel narratives, see Alex Calder, "Mapping *Typee*: Space and the Games of Truth," *ESQ: A Journal of the American Renaissance* 51, no. 1 (2005): 115–20; Douglas Ivison, "'I Saw Everything but Could Comprehend Nothing': Melville's *Typee*, Travel Narrative, and Colonial Discourse," *ATQ* 16, no. 2 (2002): 115–30; Robert T. Tally, "'Spaces That before Were Blank': Truth and Narrative Form in Melville's South Seas Cartography," *Pacific Coast Philology* 42, no. 2 (2007): 181–98.

42 Keighren, Withers, and Bell, *Travels into Print*, 222–23, 14.

43 For a more expansive discussion of Murray's use of paratexts when publishing travel writing, see Keighren, Withers, and Bell, 132–45.

44 John Murray III (*hereafter* JMIII), letter to Herman Melville (*hereafter* HM), December 3, 1845, Murray Letterbook, 1839–1846, MS. 41911, JMA.

45 Herman Melville, *Narrative of a Four Months' Residence among the Natives of a Valley of the Marquesas Islands; or, a Peep at Polynesian Life* (London: John Murray, 1846), 25.

46 Bryant explores changes, largely between the thirty leaves of the *Typee* manuscript and the published editions, to attempt to reconstruct Melville's processes of thought in composition and revision, and how Melville transformed experience into narrative. He observes that his revision narratives, though based in variants between the manuscript and published texts, are "speculative." Moreover, Bryant is concerned with tracing Melville's "motivation, direction and rhetorical strategy" rather than intersections between textual revision and material publication. John Bryant, *Melville Unfolding: Sexuality, Politics, and The Versions of Typee* (Ann Arbor: University of Michigan Press, 2008), 283–84.

47 Gansevoort Melville, letter to JMIII, December 6, 1845, MS 42478, JMA.

48 Hershel Parker, "Evidence for 'Late Insertions' in Melville's Works," *Studies in the Novel* 7, no. 3 (1975): 411–13. For Leon Howard's contrasting argument, with which Parker takes issue, see "Historical Note," 282.

49 The Melville brothers' correspondence does not survive, making it impossible to know precisely what Melville knew about *Typee*'s transatlantic publication once Gansevoort was in London.

50 Gansevoort Melville, letter to Maria Melville, September 16, 1845, in Gansevoort Melville, *Gansevoort Melville's 1846 London Journal and Letters from England*, ed. Hershel Parker (New York: New York Public Library, 1966), 62.

51 Rezek, *London and the Making of Provincial Literature*, 102–10, 124–31.

52 Melville, *Narrative of a Four Months' Residence*, 172–73.

53 Ibid., 173.

54 Darwin's theory contradicted Charles Lyell's earlier suggestion that coral grew on volcanos that were always below sea level; Darwin noted that coral only grow in certain depths and that it would be strange if all volcanoes reached that height. Lyell came to accept Darwin's theory, although debates over the formation of coral islands would continue throughout the century. Melville bought a copy of the Harper Brothers' edition of Darwin's *Journal of Researches* (the book in which he expands on the coral insect theory) in 1847, after he composed *Typee*, but

the coral insect debate was common knowledge in the mid-nineteenth century. For the place of the coral insect debate in nineteenth-century discourses of religion and science, see David Armitage and Alison Bashford, *Pacific Histories: Ocean, Land, People* (Basingstoke: Macmillan, 2014), 251–53; David Dobbs, *Reef Madness: Charles Darwin, Alexander Agassiz, and the Meaning of Coral* (New York: Pantheon, 2005), 3–6.

55 Michelle Elleray, "Little Builders: Coral Insects, Missionary Culture, and the Victorian Child," *Victorian Literature and Culture* 39, no. 1 (2011): 225.

56 See, for example, John Evelev, who suggests that "though Melville's first novel was a narrative written for the purposes of satisfying a perceived community of readers, the energies of rejection and the anxieties about entering a system of exchange are bound into the text, written in as repressed and refracted contexts." "'Made in the Marquesas': *Typee*, Tattooing and Melville's Critique of the Literary Marketplace," *Arizona Quarterly* 48, no. 4 (1992): 41.

57 Marovtiz suggests that Melville's training as a surveyor would have enabled him to copy a detail from a map he owned, but he does not explain how Melville came to possess a copy of the *Typee* map in the first place. Indeed, Melville's ownership of the copy Marovitz examines is uncertain; it was housed in a map case that Melville is believed to have owned, but it is unclear when or how the map was put there. Sanford Marovitz, "Mapping the Marquesas for *Typee*," in *Whole Oceans Away: Melville and the Pacific*, ed. Jill Barnum, Wyn Kelley, and Christopher Sten (Kent, OH: Kent State University Press, 2007), 121.

58 Family Library Ledger, MS 42769, 170, JMA.

59 Melville, *Narrative of a Four Months' Residence*, 22–23.

60 As Robert Tally observes, Melville criticized cartography's claim to make space legible, and yet, "for Melville, *truth* is always related to *space*, and consequently, the ascertaining of truth, and truth-telling or narrative, are imagined as geographic or cartographic enterprises." "'Spaces That before Were Blank,'" 191.

61 "Advert for Library of American Books," *Wiley and Putnam's Literary Newsletter*, April 1846, 26.

62 HM, letter to JMIII, January 28, 1849, in Herman Melville, *Correspondence*, ed. Lynn Horth (Evanston: Northwestern University Press; Newberry Library, 1993), 114.

63 HM, letter to RB, June 19, [1847?], in Melville, *Correspondence*, 94. Bentley's letter is unlocated, hence the tentative dating.

64 "No American Copyright in England," *Literary World*, November 3, 1849, 373.

65 Hershel Parker discusses various iterations of the story of Melville "hawking" his book in London in *Melville Biography: An Inside Narrative* (Northwestern University Press, 2012), 376–82. He quotes the *Literary World* articles below but does not identify "K."

66 "International Copyright," *Literary World*, February 23, 1850, 179.

67 "Mr Melville and Copyright in England," *Literary World*, March 2, 1850, 205.

68 HM, letter to RB, June 27, 1850, in Melville, *Correspondence*, 163–64.

69 RB, letter to HM, July 3, 1851, in Melville, *Correspondence*, 614. Melville's letter offering the book for a second time is lost.

70 Judgement in *Boosey v. Jeffreys* came down in May 1851. The *Literary World* for June 14, 1851, carried a report on the case ("American Copyright in England," 480–81). Melville was in New York on June 14 so could have read about the decision in the *World*, or discussed it with Evert Duyckinck, whom he was very likely to have seen.

71 Adam Gordon, *Prophets, Publicists, and Parasites: Antebellum Print Culture and the Rise of the Critic* (Amherst: University of Massachusetts Press, 2020), 3.

72 [Lewis Gaylord Clark], "Editor's Table," *Knickerbocker Magazine*, March 1850, 277.

73 [Lewis Gaylord Clark], "Editor's Table," *Knickerbocker Magazine*, July 1851, 87–88.

74 Michael J. Everton, *The Grand Chorus of Complaint: Authors and the Business Ethics of American Publishing* (Oxford: Oxford University Press, 2011), 92.

75 Herman Melville, *The Whale; or, Moby-Dick*, vol. 3 (London: Richard Bentley, 1851), 29. Chapters 3 and 4 of volume 3 of *The Whale* became chapters 89 and 90 of the US one-volume *Moby-Dick*; modern editions of the text follow the US numbering.

76 Melville, *The Whale*, 3:33.

77 Ibid., 3:33.

78 Ida Rothschild, "Reframing Melville's 'Manifesto' 'Hawthorne and His Mosses' and the Culture of Reprinting," *The Cambridge Quarterly* 41, no. 3 (2012): 340.

79 Melville, *The Whale*, 3:34–36.

80 James Barbour, "The Composition of Moby-Dick," *American Literature* 47, no. 3 (1975): 347.

81 RB, letter to George Palmer Putnam, August 15, 1850, George Palmer Putnam Correspondence, 1843–71, MssCol 4589, Folder 2, Manuscripts and Archives Division, New York Public Library.

82 Everton, *Grand Chorus of Complaint*, 110.

83 "Our Weekly Gossip," *Athenaeum*, January 26, 1850, 102; "Facts and Opinions," *Literary World*, March 9, 1850, 237.

84 Bentley also makes no mention of the binding in his advertisements for the volume, or the review in his magazine, *Bentley's Miscellany*, which suggests that it did not form a central part of his publicity for the book.

85 Melville, *The Whale*, 1:220.

86 Even when refusing to publish *Pierre* without substantial amendment, Bentley told Melville that "everybody must admit the genius displayed in your writings:" RB, letter to HM, May 5, 1852, in Melville, *Correspondence*, 620.

87 McGill, *Culture of Reprinting*, 87, 94.

88 Melville's reception history in Britain is somewhat different, with *Moby-Dick* finding an audience among left-wing intellectuals who did situate the book as distinctively American. See Maki Sadahiro, "Fin-de-Siècle British Socialism and a Prelude to the Melville Revival," *Leviathan* 22, no. 2 (2020): 38–53.

89 Review of *The Whale*, *John Bull*, October 25, 1851.

90 Hershel Parker, *Herman Melville: A Biography*, vol. 2 (Baltimore: Johns Hopkins University Press, 1996), 20.

91 RB, letter to HM, May 6, 1852, in Melville, *Correspondence*, 620.

92 Ticknor, Reed and Fields, letter to RB, February 28, 1850, Houghton Mifflin Company Records, MS Am 2030.2, (52)—(63), book 58, Houghton Library, Harvard University. The sheets were sent "through the kindness of our friend Capt. Harrison," likely William Harrison, a noted and popular captain on the Cunard line.

93 RB, letter to Ticknor, Reed and Fields, April 5, 1850, British Library MS46641, ARBS, reel 40, vol. 82, image 79. Bentley claimed that Ticknor, Reed and Fields published the book on March 16 and did not send the second half of the sheets until March 18.

94 Nathaniel Hawthorne, *The Scarlet Letter*, ed. Brian Harding (Oxford: Oxford University Press, 2007), 10, 6, 32.

95 Lauren Berlant, *The Anatomy of National Fantasy: Hawthorne, Utopia, and Everyday Life* (Chicago: University of Chicago Press, 1991), 184–89.

96 Hawthorne, *Scarlet Letter*, 37.

97 James T. Fields, letter to Nathaniel Hawthorne, May 21, 1852 in Nathaniel Hawthorne Collection of Papers, Henry W. and Albert A. Berg Collection of

English and American Literature, the New York Public Library, *New York Public Library Digital Collections*, accessed November 23, 2018, http://digitalcollections.nypl.org/items/8e4c5ca0-cbc7-0130-c18a-58d385a7b928. Fields explains that this Chapman is not John Chapman, publisher of the *Westminster Review* who had both distributed and published American writers including Ralph Waldo Emerson.

98 RB, letter to George Bancroft, September 5, 1854, British Library MS46642, ARBS, reel 40, vol. 83, image 51.

99 Hawthorne turned down Bentley's offer of an "agreement" for a new work, while Warner used Bentley for the British edition of *Say and Seal* (1860), co-written with her sister. RB, letter to Nathaniel Hawthorne, February 16, 1857, in Nathaniel Hawthorne Collection of Papers, Henry W. and Albert A. Berg Collection of English and American Literature, the New York Public Library, *New York Public Library Digital Collections*, accessed November 23, 2018, http://digitalcollections.nypl.org/items/186b7b80-e358-0130-f372-58d385a7b928; RB, letters to Susan Warner, February 8, 1857, and September 3, 1859, British Library MS46642, ARBS, reel 40, vol. 83, images 138, 195.

Chapter 3: The Transatlantic Architecture of the Publisher's Series

1 "Introductory," *Publishers' Circular*, May 1, 1852.

2 Laura Doyle, "Toward a Philosophy of Transnationalism," *Journal of Transnational American Studies* 1, no. 1 (2009): unpaginated.

3 Gérard Genette, *Paratexts: Thresholds of Interpretation*, trans. Jane E. Lewin (Cambridge: Cambridge University Press, 1987), 2.

4 Richard D. Altick, "From Aldine to Everyman: Cheap Reprint Series of English Classics," *Studies in Bibliography* 11 (1958): 11.

5 Leslie Howsam, "Sustained Literary Ventures: The Series in Victorian Book Publishing," *Publishing History* 31 (1992): 5, 13.

6 For accounts of individual nineteenth-century series, see Aileen Fyfe, "Periodicals and Book Series: Complimentary Aspects of a Publisher's Mission," in *Culture and Science in Nineteenth-Century Media*, ed. Louise Henson, et al. (Aldershot: Ashgate, 2004); Howsam, "Sustained Literary Ventures"; Paul Raphael Rooney, *Railway Reading and Late-Victorian Literary Series* (Basingstoke: Routledge, 2018); Barbara Schaff, "'Sound Information and Innocent Amusement': John Murray's Books on the Move," in *The Culture of the Publisher's Series, Volume One: Authors, Publishers and the Shaping of Taste*, ed. John Spiers (New York: Palgrave Macmillan, 2011), 219–36.

7 Also popular were series of self-improvement and useful knowledge books. Successful examples of this type of series included *Lardner's Cabinet Cyclopaedia* (1830–1841) and John Murray's *Family Library* (1829–1834), the latter of which featured an abridged version of Washington Irving's *Life of Columbus* as its eleventh volume. School books, religious books, and society and government publications were also issued in series; the former two categories very often included American books but are beyond the scope of this study of literary publishing.

8 John Spiers, "Introduction. Wondering about 'the Causes of Causes': The Publisher's Series, Its Cultural Work and Meanings," in *Culture of the Publisher's Series*, ed. Spiers, 28.

9 *The Pilot* was originally published in Britain by John Miller, who arranged with Cooper for advanced sheets. For its publication history, see Kay Seymour House, "Textual Commentary," in James Fenimore Cooper, *The Pilot: A Tale of the Sea*, ed. Kay Seymour House (Albany: State University of New York Press, 1986), 435–48. For an account of the partnership between Bentley and Colburn and its acrimonious breakdown, see chapter 2. Bentley took over the Standard

Novels after the break from Colburn in 1832, and it is therefore often referred to under his name alone.

10 Advert for the Standard Novels, *John Bull*, March 14, 1831.

11 William St Clair observes that Colburn and Bentley overstated the cheapness of their series, noting that at 6s per volume, "within his chosen market, Bentley positioned himself as far upmarket as he could go." *The Reading Nation in the Romantic Period* (Cambridge: Cambridge University Press, 2004), 362.

12 Copies of the advert listing *Caleb Williams* as the first number appeared in *The Edinburgh Literary Journal; or, Weekly Register of Literature and Belles Lettres*, February 12, 1831; *The Standard*, February 15, 1831; *Times*, February 16, 1831 (altered by February 19); *Scotsman*, February 19, 1831.

13 List of New Books, *Literary Gazette*, February 12, 1831.

14 Prospectus of the Novelist's Miscellany, in James Fenimore Cooper, *The Spy* (Liverpool: A. C. Baynes, 1831).

15 For details of Cooper's revisions to the Standard Novels editions of his texts, see Joseph Rezek, *London and the Making of Provincial Literature: Aesthetics and the Transatlantic Book Trade, 1800–1850* (Philadelphia: University of Pennsylvania Press, 2015), 124–30, 141–48.

16 Cooper only received the copies of the American editions of *The Spy* he had requested on April 5, and the volume was due to be published in early May. He managed to correct the whole novel by April 15, and Colburn and Bentley published the revised edition on May 2. For letters describing the revision process, see James Fenimore Cooper, *Letters and Journals of James Fenimore Cooper*, ed. James Franklin Beard, vol. 2 (Cambridge, MA: Belknap Press of Harvard University Press, 1960), 63–69.

17 Joseph Rezek, "Bentley's Standard Novelist: James Fenimore Cooper," in *Transatlantic Literature and Author Love*, ed. Paul Westover and Ann Werida Rowland (Basingstoke: Palgrave Macmillan, 2016), 59, 70.

18 Cooper, *Letters and Journals*, 2:61. Beard further suggests that Cooper may have informed Colburn and Bentley of the competition from Baynes on February 24, demonstrating Cooper's awareness of his value and willingness to play publishers against one another. Ibid., 56.

19 Royal A. Gettmann, *A Victorian Publisher: A Study of the Bentley Papers* (Cambridge: Cambridge University Press, 1960), 21. This figure is slightly skewed by Cooper's novels being published earlier in the series, but, for example, *Last of the Mohicans* made £160 more than William Godwin's *St Leon* published one month earlier.

20 Clarence Gohdes, *American Literature in Nineteenth-Century England* (New York: Columbia University Press, 1944), 32, see also 20–33.

21 One example is Henry Bohn's Extra Volumes, which included translations of important works that he deemed too salacious to include in his family-friendly Standard Library; these volumes were of a uniform size but had a differently colored binding. Carol O'Sullivan, "Translation within the Margin: The 'Libraries' of Henry Bohn," in *Agents of Translation*, ed. John Milton and Paul Bandia (Amsterdam: John Benjamins, 2009), 115–16.

22 The major bibliographic catalogues of nineteenth-century fiction that include series publications are: Michael Sadleir, *XIX Century Fiction: A Bibliographical Record Based on His Own Collection*, 2 vols. (London: Constable & Co, 1951); Chester W. Topp, *Victorian Yellowbacks & Paperbacks, 1849–1905*, 9 vols. (Denver: Hermitage Antiquarian Bookshop, 1993); Robert Lee Wolff, *Nineteenth-Century Fiction: A Bibliographical Catalogue Based on the Collection Formed by Robert Lee Wolff* (New York: Garland Pub., 1984).

23 Clarke sold the printed sheets of at least some of his library volumes to fellow London reprinter George Slater, who rebranded them in his own Shilling Library.

Sadleir, *XIX Century Fiction*, II:26. Slater's Shilling Library is not catalogued by Low.

24 Marie Leger-St-Jean, "Mid-Nineteenth-Century Cheap Novels: Speeding Towards Global Mass Transmedia Culture" (paper presented at the European Social Science History Conference, April 11, 2012).

25 Charles Knight, *The Old Printer and the Modern Press* (London: John Murray, 1854), 265, 67.

26 "Review of Literature," *Monthly Chronicle*, July 1839, 192.

27 Advert for Smith's Standard Library, in George Colton, *Tecumseh; or, the West Thirty Years Since. A Poem* (London: William Smith, 1843), back cover.

28 "Notices of New Works, and Literary Intelligence," *Southern Literary Messenger*, November 1841, 816. No editions of either the poems of Longfellow or Dana Sr. appeared in Smith's Standard Library. The *Messenger* may be confusing the series with Clarke's Home Library, which published both writers at around the same time.

29 Contemporary lists of the Railway Library give *The Pilot* as the first title as does Sadleir, but this numbering was applied retrospectively. Chester Topp's catalogue of the Routledge libraries lists *The Red Rover* first, as it was published in December 1848, and *The Pilot* fifth, published in July 1849. Judgement in *Boosey v. Purday* was handed down on June 5, 1849. For further discussion, see chapter 2.

30 Knight, *Old Printer and the Modern Press*, 269.

31 Henry Vizetelly, "Preface," in Edgar Allan Poe, *Tales of Mystery, Imagination and Humour; and Poems*, Readable Books (London: Henry Vizetelly, 1852), vii.

32 Rezek, *London and the Making of Provincial Literature*, 144.

33 Advert for Cheap and Uniform Edition of Cooper's Novels, *Morning Post*, September 24, 1832.

34 Charles Lock, "Book History and the Metonymies of Text," in *Moveable Type, Mobile Nations: Interactions in Transnational Book History*, ed. Simon Frost and Robert W. Rix, Angles on the English-Speaking World, vol. 10 (Copenhagen: Museum Tusculanum Press, 2010), 141.

35 William H. Sherman, "On the Threshold: Architecture, Paratext, and Early Print Culture," in *Agent of Change: Print Culture Studies after Elizabeth L. Eisenstein*, ed. Sabrina Alcorn Baron, Eric N. Lindquist, and Eleanor F. Shevlin (Amherst: University of Massachusetts Press, 2007), 79, 72.

36 Oliver Wendell Holmes, letter to Sampson Low, September 26, 1867, Sampson Low Collection, Open University.

37 Genette, *Paratexts*, 1.

38 Quoted in Sadleir, *XIX Century Fiction*, II:167–68.

39 Ralph Waldo Emerson, *Emerson's Essays and Orations* (London: Ingram, Cooke & Co, 1853), back cover.

40 Melissa J. Homestead, *American Women Authors and Literary Property, 1822–1869* (Cambridge: Cambridge University Press, 2005), 91.

41 Catharine Maria Sedgwick, *Home* (Boston: James Munroe and Company, 1850), 4.

42 Amy Kaplan, *The Anarchy of Empire in the Making of U.S. Culture* (Cambridge, MA: Harvard University Press, 2005), 25.

43 Sedgwick, *Home*, 8.

44 Homestead, *American Women Authors*, 94–96.

45 Sedgwick, *Home*, 139, 140.

46 "Notice: By the Publisher," in Fredrika Bremer, *The H—Family* (London: William Smith, 184[?]), iv.

47 Advert for "American Poets," in Oliver Wendell Holmes, *Poems: New Complete and Uniform Edition* (London: George Routledge & Co., 1853), back cover.

48 Thomas Campbell [William Collins, and Thomas Gray], *The Pleasures of Hope, Gertrude of Wyoming, and Other Poems* (London: George Routledge & Co., 1852), 44. Campbell's father had emigrated to Virginia, although the family returned to Scotland before Campbell's birth in 1777 after their fortunes fell following the Revolutionary War.

49 Mitford's *Recollections* included Longfellow, Whittier, and Holmes, all of whom were published in Routledge's American Poets. Josephine McDonagh, *Literature in a Time of Migration: British Fiction and the Movement of People, 1815–1876* (Oxford: Oxford University Press, 2021), 179.

50 For further information about Ticknor and Fields' brown covers and their connotations of cultural prestige, see Jeffrey D. Groves, "Judging Literary Books by Their Covers: House Styles, Ticknor and Fields, and Literary Promotion," in *Reading Books: Essays on the Material Text and Literature in America*, ed. Michelle Moylan and Lane Stiles (Boston: University of Massachusetts Press, 1996), 77–84.

51 Advert for the American Poets, Holmes, *Poems*, rear cover.

52 Lydia Huntley Sigourney was the only woman to feature in the series.

53 James Fenimore Cooper, *The Pilot* (London: Henry Colburn and Richard Bentley, 1831), 1.

54 Sydney Smith, "Review of *Statistical Annals of the United States* by Adam Seybert," *Edinburgh Review* 33, no. 65 (January 1820): 69–80.

55 Cooper, *The Pilot*, 59.

56 Jason Berger, "Killing Tom Coffin: Rethinking the Nationalist Narrative in James Fenimore Cooper's 'The Pilot,'" *Early American Literature* 43, no. 3 (2008): 647; Cynthia Schoolar Williams, *Hospitality and the Transatlantic Imagination, 1815–1835* (Basingstoke: Palgrave Macmillan, 2014), 98.

57 Cooper, *The Pilot*, 134, 405, 418, 305, 419. Cooper's previous novels, *Precaution*, *The Spy*, and *The Pioneers* had all been reprinted. Even before Cooper arranged to sell early sheets of *The Pilot* to John Walker, he had good reason to expect that *The Pilot* would have a transatlantic circulation.

58 Cooper, *The Pilot*, 1, 375.

59 Charles Brockden Brown, *Edgar Huntly; or, Memoirs of a Sleep-Walker*, ed. Philip Barnard and Stephen Shapiro (Indianapolis: Hackett, 2006), 3–4.

60 O.C., "Introduction," in *The Ghost-Seer and Edgar Huntly*, by Friedrich Schiller and Charles Brockden Brown (London: Colburn and Bentley, 1831), v.

61 Ibid., vi, xiii.

62 Ibid., vi. Christopher Apap argues, in relation in *Wieland* in particular, that Brown is building upon how German pre-Romantics, such as Schiller, transformed the British Gothic tradition exemplified by Godwin and his followers. Christopher Apap, "Irresponsible Acts: The Transatlantic Dialogues of William Godwin and Charles Brockden Brown," in *Transatlantic Sensations*, ed. Jennifer Phegley, John Cyril Barton, and Kristin N. Huston (Farnham: Ashgate, 2012), 26.

63 Brown, *Edgar Huntly; or, Memoirs of a Sleep-Walker*, 3.

64 Charles Brockden Brown, "Edgar Huntly; or, The Sleep Walker," in *The Ghost-Seer and Edgar Huntly*, 158–59, 147. Philip Barnard and Stephen Shapiro read this comparison as part of the novel's critique of imperialism, connecting "two Indian frontiers—one in North America, the other in South Asia," both of which "belong to the same environment of conflicts between imperial powers mediated through native populations." "Introduction," in Brown, *Edgar Huntly*, xxxi.

65 Brown, "Edgar Huntly," 183.

66 Advert for the Universal Library, Emerson, *Emerson's Essays and Orations*, back cover.

67 Comparing him to Coleridge, who frequently wrote of being surrounded by children in the domestic sphere despite living apart from his family for extended

periods, Julie Ellison notes that "Emerson, who did most of his writing at home, rarely refers to this fact." Julie Ellison, "Tears for Emerson: *Essays, Second Series*," in *The Cambridge Companion to Ralph Waldo Emerson*, ed. Joel Porte and Saundra Morris (Cambridge: Cambridge University Press, 1999), 146. Although Emerson wrote a lecture on "Home" in 1838, this concluded that "home" was less a specific architectural space than a mobile concept.

68 Emerson, *Emerson's Essays and Orations*, 15.

69 To generate the illustrations for his volume, Putnam either requested illustrations of homes from the writers or sent artists to sketch them, just as he also sent writers to produce written sketches.

70 *Homes of American Authors; Comprising Anecdotal, Personal, and Descriptive Sketches by Various Writers* (New York: G. P. Putnam and Co., 1853), iv.

71 Ibid., 254.

72 Ibid., 243.

73 Emerson, *Emerson's Essays and Orations*, 53, 55.

Chapter 4: The *Forget Me Not*, the American Poetess, and Sentimental Nationalisms

1 Frederic Shoberl, "Preface," in *Forget Me Not: A Christmas, New Year's and Birthday Present, for 1838*, ed. Frederic Shoberl (London: Ackermann and Co., 1837), 3.

2 "Literary Notices," *Knickerbocker Magazine*, June 1834, 457.

3 Jane P. Tompkins, *Sensational Designs: The Cultural Work of American Fiction, 1790–1860* (Oxford: Oxford University Press, 1986). I discuss scholarship that explores the public and national work of sentimental writing in more detail below.

4 See, for example Mary Louise Kete, who attributes this regression to Sigourney's growing anxieties over sectional tensions over slavery; she compares poems from 1837 and 1847 to suggest that Sigourney's interrogation of the violence of national fashioning disappears so that she can "pay more attention to modeling a means by which the North/South divisions could be healed." *Sentimental Collaborations: Mourning and Middle-Class Identity in Nineteenth-Century America* (Durham, NC: Duke University Press, 2000), 128.

5 Other British gift books contained some Americans contributions. For example, *Heath's Book of Beauty* published three pieces by Nathaniel Parker Willis and one by Washington Irving between 1834 and 1836. But none had the *Forget Me Not*'s consistent US contributions. It was more common for British writers to appear in gift books and anthologies published in the United States, as Páraic Finnerty argues. "Women's Transatlantic Poetic Networks," in *A History of Nineteenth-Century American Women's Poetry*, ed. Jennifer Putzi and Alexandra Socarides (Cambridge: Cambridge University Press, 2016), 170–85.

6 This note in another hand, written on Lydia Huntley Sigourney (*hereafter* LHS), letter to John Murray III, December 8, 1843, MS41909, John Murray Archive, National Library of Scotland (*hereafter* JMA).

7 Gary Kelly, "Gendered Atlantic: Lydia Sigourney and Felicia Hemans," in *A History of Nineteenth-Century American Women's Poetry*, ed. Jennifer Putzi and Alexandra Socarides (Cambridge: Cambridge University Press, 2017), 126. Kelly's argument focuses on single-author volumes rather than anthologies.

8 Lorraine Janzen Kooistra, *Poetry, Pictures, and Popular Publishing: The Illustrated Gift Book and Victorian Visual Culture, 1855–1875* (Athens: Ohio University Press, 2014), 5.

9 Margaret Linley, "A Centre That Would Not Hold: Annuals and Cultural Democracy," in *Nineteenth-Century Media and the Construction of Identities*, ed. Laurel Brake, Bill Bell, and David Finkelstein (London: Palgrave Macmillan UK, 2000), 56.

10 Katherine D. Harris, *Forget Me Not: The Rise of the British Literary Annual, 1823–1835* (Athens: Ohio University Press, 2015), 84.

11 Elizabeth A. Petrino, "Presents of Mind: Lydia Sigourney, Gift Book Culture, and the Commodification of Poetry," in *A History of Nineteenth-Century American Women's Poetry*, ed. Putzi and Socarides, 88–93.

12 *Selections from the American Poets: With Some Introductory Remarks* (London: Simpkin and Marshall, 1834); "Mrs. Sigourney and Miss Gould," *North American Review*, October 1835, 430–54.

13 Hannah Flagg Gould (*hereafter* HFG), letter to Robert Shelton Mackenzie (*hereafter* RSM), February 9, 1835. Simon Gratz autograph collection (Collection 0250A) (*hereafter* SGAC), Case 6 Box 30 Folder 36, Historical Society of Pennsylvania (*hereafter* HSP).

14 Frederic Shoberl, "Preface," in *Forget Me Not: A Christmas, New Year's and Birthday Present, for 1842*, ed. Frederic Shoberl (London: Ackermann and Co, 1841), 3.

15 Shoberl, "Preface," *Forget Me Not . . . for 1838*, ed. Shoberl, 4.

16 Editions of the *Forget Me Not* from the late 1830s and early 1840s feature Appleton's imprint on their title pages.

17 Harris observes that American publishers "claim[ed] British volumes as their own, cancelling title pages and tipping in others that altered the year and the publisher—all without indicating that these were reissues." Harris, *Forget Me Not*, 146.

18 Later in the century, some British periodical publishers did attempt to protect their publications by including American texts within them. In 1848 *Blackwood*'s magazine secured an authorized US publisher by secretly inserting articles by Americans and then threatening the American reprinter, Leonard Scott, for breach of copyright. Scott and *Blackwood*'s agreed that Scott would pay for advanced sheets. For an account of this episode in copyright history, see James J. Barnes, *Authors, Publishers and Politicians: The Quest for An Anglo-American Copyright Agreement, 1815–1854* (London: Routledge and Kegan Paul, 1974), 37–48.

19 HFG, letter to RSM, March 21, 1838, SGAC, Case 6 Box 30, HSP.

20 HFG, letter to RSM, April 15, 1840, SGAC, Case 6, Box 30, HSP.

21 Frederic Shoberl, letter to LHS, April 25, 1839, Hoadley Collection, Box 6 Folder 1, Connecticut Historical Society (*hereafter* CHS).

22 Teed argues that "[Sigourney] understood the literary marketplace to be both impersonal and competitive, and she was convinced that she could negotiate it successfully only if she mastered the contractual rules of business" and that she had "by the 1840s, essentially abandoned her attempt to couch her interest in moral and noncommerical terms when dealing with publishers." Melissa Ladd Teed, "A Passion for Distinction: Lydia Huntley Sigourney and the Creation of a Literary Reputation," *New England Quarterly* 77, no. 1 (2004): 61, 64. However, she only considers Sigourney's letters to US publishers.

23 LHS, letter to RSM, April 27, 1837, Watson Autograph Collection, MS 594, National Library of Scotland.

24 LHS, letter to RSM, August 11, 1837, SGAC, Case 6, Box 35, HSP.

25 Shoberl, "Preface," in *Forget Me Not . . . for 1838*, ed. Shoberl, 4.

26 RSM, letter to LHS, May 30, 1837, Hoadly Collection, Box 5, Folder 17, CHS; LHS, letter to RSM, August 11, 1837, SGAC, Case 6, Box 5, HSP.

27 Frederic Shoberl and Charles Swain, "Preface," in *Forget Me Not: A Christmas, New Year's, and Birthday Present for 1840*, ed. Frederic Shoberl (London: Ackerman & Co., 1839), iv.

28 James Montgomery, "To Her Majesty, Queen Victoria," in *Forget Me Not . . . for 1840*, ed. Shoberl (1839), 9.

29 Edward Quillinan, "Funeral of Robert Southey," in *Forget Me Not: A Christmas, New Year's, and Birthday Present for 1845*, ed. Frederic Shoberl (London: Ackerman & Co., 1844), 19.
30 Shoberl, "Preface," in *Forget Me Not... for 1838*, ed. Shoberl , 3–4.
31 Lydia Huntley Sigourney, "The Constant Friends," in *Forget Me Not... for 1845*, ed. Shoberl, 172.
32 Hannah Flagg Gould, "American Wild Flowers, for Queen Victoria," in *Forget Me Not... for 1842*, ed. Shoberl, 13.
33 Hannah Flagg Gould, "American Wild Flowers, for Queen Victoria," in Hannah Flagg Gould, *New Poems* (Boston: William J. Reynolds & Co., 1850), 94.
34 Finnerty, "Women's Transatlantic Poetic Networks," 176.
35 Rufus Wilmot Griswold, "Preface," in *The Female Poets of America*, ed. Rufus Wilmot Griswold (Philadelphia: Carey and Hart, 1849), 8.
36 Lydia Huntley Sigourney, "The Benefactress," in *Forget Me Not: A Christmas, New Year's and Birthday Present for 1841*, ed. Frederic Shoberl (London: Ackermann and Co., 1840), 220.
37 Glenn Hendler, *Public Sentiments: Structures of Feeling in Nineteenth-Century American Literature* (Chapel Hill: University of North Carolina Press, 2003), 22.
38 Mary Louise Kete, *Sentimental Collaborations*, 105; Shirley Samuels, "Introduction," in *The Culture of Sentiment: Race, Gender, and Sentimentality in Nineteenth-Century America*, ed. Shirley Samuels (Oxford: Oxford University Press, 1992), 3.
39 For competing views, see Tricia Lootens, who argues that the poetess's performance of privacy also "perform[s] . . . service to the state," and John O'Leary, who suggests that sentimentalism was a "strategic discourse" that humanized marginalized groups like Indigenous peoples "in a ways that was both novel and effective." Tricia Lootens, *The Political Poetess: Victorian Femininity, Race, and the Legacy of Separate Spheres* (Princeton: Princeton University Press, 2017), 14; John O'Leary, "'Unlocking the Fountains of the Heart': Settler Verse and the Politics of Sympathy," *Postcolonial Studies* 13, no. 1 (2010): 68.
40 Lootens, *Political Poetess*, 9.
41 Elizabeth Maddock Dillon, "Sentimental Aesthetics," *American Literature* 76, no. 3 (2004): 506.
42 Gould, "American Wild Flowers, for Queen Victoria," in *Forget Me Not... for 1842*, ed. Shoberl, 10, 11.
43 Ibid., 9, 13, 12.
44 Elisa Tamarkin, *Anglophilia: Deference, Devotion, and Antebellum America* (Chicago: University of Chicago Press, 2008), 37. Tamarkin here builds on arguments by historians David Cannadine and Margaret Homans that Victoria's symbolic power and popularity among her British subjects increased as her political power declined throughout the nineteenth century.
45 Gould, "American Wild Flowers, for Queen Victoria," in *Forget Me Not... for 1842*, ed. Shoberl, 12.
46 LHS, letter to RSM, November 12, 1841, SGAC, Case 6 Box 35, HSP.
47 Nina Baym, *Feminism and American Literary History: Essays* (New Brunswick: Rutgers University Press, 1992), 154, see also 155–56.
48 Petrino, "Presents of Mind," 98.
49 Tricia Lootens, "States of Exile," in *The Traffic in Poems: Nineteenth-Century Poetry and Transatlantic Exchange*, ed. Meredith L. McGill (New Brunswick, NJ: Rutgers University Press, 2008), 28.
50 Lydia Huntley Sigourney, "The American Indians," in *Forget Me Not... 1838*, ed. Shoberl, 70.
51 RSM, letter to LHS, March 6, 1838, Hoadley Collection, Box 5, Folder 17, CHS.
52 For example, the *Arkansas Intelligencer*, March 22, 1845, which attributed the poem to *Neal's Saturday Gazette*, a weekly magazine published in Philadelphia.

53 "Osceola's Grave" was published in the *Biblical Recorder*, out of Raleigh, NC, on June 19, 1847, and the *Tiogo Eagle*, out of Wellsboro, PA, on June 23, 1847; both of these publications credited the *Philadelphia Saturday Courier*.

54 Kate Flint, *The Transatlantic Indian, 1776–1930* (Princeton: Princeton University Press, 2009), 38.

55 Lydia Huntley Sigourney, "The Grave of Osceola," in *Forget Me Not . . . for 1845*, ed. Shoberl, 51–52.

56 Ibid., 51.

57 Lydia Huntley Sigourney, "Osceola's Grave," *Biblical Recorder*, June 19, 1847.

58 Sigourney, "The Grave of Osceola," 53.

59 Lydia Huntley Sigourney, "Death of a Father," in *Pocahontas, and Other Poems* (New York: Harper and Brothers, 1841), 125.

60 Kete observes a similar pairing of a familial metaphor for the nation with a critique of the violence and the power of economic capital involved in nation-building in Sigourney's earlier "On the Admission of Michigan into the Union" in *Sentimental Collaborations*, 125–28.

61 Lydia Huntley Sigourney, "Welcome to Wisconsin," Lydia Huntley Sigourney Papers (*hereafter* LHSP). Literary Papers, Folder 31, CHS. The version in the *Courant* was reprinted in the (Milwaukee) *Evening Courier* on March 19, 1847, and the *Brooklyn Daily Eagle* on May 28, 1847. "Welcome to Wisconsin" also appears under "'Forget Me Not'—London" on a list of contributions to various periodicals for 1847 in Sigourney's hand: LHSP, Literary Papers, Folder 31, CHS.

62 Additionally, both print and manuscript versions of the poem have postscripts that explains the accession of Wisconsin to statehood, but this is simplified in the manuscript version, which omits any mention of the State Constitutional Convention at Madison and carefully notes that Wisconsin "alone, the last admitted of the thirty United States, has extended the elective franchise to the civilized Indians within her bounds." This suggests that Sigourney had British readers, less familiar with US government, in mind. The manuscript seems to have been revised when Sigourney sent a copy to Judge James D. Doty, one of the politicians responsible for guiding Wisconsin toward statehood, whose name appears at the top of the manuscript in variant ink that matches a set of revisions. Because this name appears above Sigourney's note "Forget Me Not, London, March 27," these revisions are likely to have been included in the version she sent to Britain, and so I have included them in quotations from the manuscript. Ibid.

63 Ibid.; Lydia Huntley Sigourney, "Welcome to Wisconsin," *Hartford Courant*, January 14, 1847.

64 Sigourney, "Welcome to Wisconsin," LHSP.

65 Ibid.

66 Lydia Huntley Sigourney, "Indian Names," in Lydia Huntley Sigourney, *Poems* (Philadelphia: Key & Biddle, 1834), 165–66.

67 Sigourney, "Welcome to Wisconsin," *Hartford Courant*; Sigourney, "Welcome to Wisconsin," LHSP. The word "Ontario" is thought to be derived from a Wyandotte (Huron) word, and "Wyalusing" comes from a Lenape word, and while the etymology of "Oregon" is disputed, a popular theory in the nineteenth century and beyond was that it was a corruption of Indigenous American words for "river."

68 Sigourney, "Welcome to Wisconsin," LHSP.

69 Observing that these editions exclude much of Sigourney's earlier historical and political verse, Baym warns they over-represent her domestic elegies and are "directed to the preferences of audience rather than author": *Feminism and American Literary History*, 152.

70 Flint, *Transatlantic Indian*, 41.
71 Lydia Huntley Sigourney, *Pleasant Memories of Pleasant Lands* (Boston: J. Munroe and Company, 1842), iii–iv, v.
72 LHS, letter to James Munroe and Co., January 16, 1843, MSS 892, Box 1, Folder 44, Lydia Howard Sigourney Collection, 1811–1864, Beinecke Library, Yale University (*hereafter* LHSC).
73 LHS, letter to James Munroe and Co., November 3, 1843, MSS 892, Box 1, Folder 45, LHSC.
74 Gordon S. Haight, *Mrs. Sigourney: The Sweet Singer of Hartford* (New Haven: Yale University Press, 1930), 52.
75 RSM, letter to LHS, March 6, 1838, Hoadley Collection, Box 5, Folder 17, CHS.
76 Samantha Matthews, "'O All Pervading Album!': Place and Displacement in Romantic Albums and Album Poetry," in *Romantic Localities: Europe Writes Place*, ed. Christopher Bode and Jacqueline Labbe (London: Pickering & Chatto, 2010), 103. See also Saeko Yoshikawa, who notes that at least one guidebook of the period suggested that parts of Wordsworth's house were open to the public: *William Wordsworth and the Invention of Tourism, 1820–1900* (Farnham: Routledge, 2014), 54, 58.
77 Sigourney, *Pleasant Memories*, 49, 281.
78 Ibid., 54–55. Southey was not actually a doctor, but Sigourney is perhaps confused by Southey's semi-autobiographical seven-volume work *The Doctor* (published 1834–38).
79 Sigourney, *Pleasant Memories*, 55, 51.
80 Lauren Berlant, *The Female Complaint: The Unfinished Business of Sentimentality in American Culture* (Durham, NC: Duke University Press, 2008), 5.
81 Sigourney, *Pleasant Memories*, 54, 118, 199.
82 Ibid., 360–61.
83 Berlant, *Female Complaint*, 35.
84 Sigourney, *Pleasant Memories*, 6.
85 Robert Bell, "Festival of the Story-Tellers: Gathering the First," *The Story-Teller; or, Table-Book of Popular Literature*, May 1843, 7.
86 "Mrs. Sigourney, Mrs. Southey and the British Press," *Brother Jonathan*, May 20, 1843, 77.
87 John Gibson Lockhart, "Pencillings by the Way," *Quarterly Review*, September 1835, 469.
88 "Our Weekly Gossip," *Athenaeum*, April 29, 1843, 418.
89 Hendler, *Public Sentiments*, 160.
90 Kate Thomas, *Postal Pleasures: Sex, Scandal, and Victorian Letters* (Oxford: Oxford University Press, 2012), 31; Matthew Pethers, "Dead Letters and the Secret Life of the State in Nineteenth-Century America," in *The Edinburgh Companion to Nineteenth-Century American Letters and Letter-Writing*, ed. Celeste-Marie Bernier, Judie Newman, and Matthew Pethers, Edinburgh Companions to Literature (Edinburgh: Edinburgh University Press, 2016), 136–51.
91 Elizabeth A. Petrino, "A Chain of Correspondence: Social Activism and Civic Value in the Letters of Lydia Huntley Sigourney," in *Edinburgh Companion*, ed. Bernier, Newman, and Pethers, 450.
92 Maria Edgeworth, letter to LHS, September 4, 1843, Hoadley Collection, Box 6, Folder 7, CHS.
93 Bell, "Festival of the Story-Tellers," 7–8.
94 "Our Weekly Gossip," *Athenaeum*, April 15, 1843, 369.
95 LHS, letter to James Monroe, July 24, 1843, Lydia Howard Huntley Sigourney letters, poems, and other material, 1829–1864, MS 4632, New York Public Library.

96 LHS, letter to Mrs. S. C. Hall [Anna Maria Hall], December 28, 1843, MSS 892, Box 1, Folder 70, LHSC.

97 "Mrs. Sigourney, Mrs. Southey and the British Press," 78.

Chapter 5: "American" Magazines and the Failures of Transatlantic Reprinting

1 These magazines were distinct from three other types of "American" periodicals that circulated in mid-century Britain. Those three types were, first, newspapers that contained intelligence about Anglo-American trade, like *Charles Wilmer's American News Letter* (1843–45). Second, magazines aimed at Americans resident in Europe, like the *American Register and Morning News* (1868–1914). Third, periodicals primarily published in America that were also circulated in Britain or had British editions, including *Putnam's Monthly Magazine* (1853–57), *Godey's Lady's Book* (1830–98), and the *North American Review* (1815–1939). British periodicals also featured pieces by American writers. Some, like *Bentley's Miscellany* (1837–68) paid their American contributors, whereas others reprinted without permission or payment, like the weekly sensation magazine *Cleave's Penny Gazette of Variety and Entertainment* (1837–44).

2 Matthew Levay, "On the Uses of Seriality for Modern Periodical Studies: An Introduction," *Journal of Modern Periodical Studies* 9, no. 1 (2018): v.

3 James Mussell, "Repetition; or, In Our Last," *Victorian Periodicals Review* 48, no. 3 (2015): 350.

4 Periodicals scholars have argued that form is defined by its instability and fluidity. Kenneth M. Price and Susan Belasco Smith describe periodicals as "publications that are issued at intervals that are more or less regular. Such a definition points to the instability of the term *periodical* and of the form itself." "Introduction," in *Periodical Literature in Nineteenth-Century America*, ed. Kenneth M. Price and Susan Belasco Smith (Charlottesville: University of Virginia Press, 1995), 9.

5 Peter P. Reed, *Rogue Performances: Staging the Underclasses in Early American Theatre Culture* (Basingstoke: Palgrave Macmillan, 2009), 6.

6 Meredith L. McGill, *American Literature and the Culture of Reprinting, 1834–1853* (Philadelphia: University of Pennsylvania Press, 2003), 27.

7 Jeffrey H. Richards, "Print, Manuscript, and Staged Performance: Dramatic Authorship and Text Circulation in the New Republic," in *Cultural Narratives. Textuality and Performance in American Culture Before 1900*, ed. Sandra M. Gustafson and Caroline F. Sloat (Notre Dame, IN: University of Notre Dame Press, 2010), 77.

8 Michael J. Collins, *The Drama of the American Short Story, 1800–1865* (Ann Arbor: University of Michigan Press, 2016), 18–19.

9 Ibid., 19; Jenna M. Gibbs, *Performing the Temple of Liberty: Slavery, Theater, and Popular Culture in London and Philadelphia, 1760–1850* (Baltimore, MD: Johns Hopkins University Press, 2014); Amy Hughes, *Spectacles of Reform: Theater and Activism in Nineteenth-Century America* (Ann Arbor: University of Michigan Press, 2012).

10 The most famous example of mid-century dramatic spectacle is the fifth-act steamship fire in Dion Boucicault's *The Octoroon* (1859). Discussing British Victorian print, Lynn Voskuil notes that "books, newspapers, and illustrations frequently harnessed the scale, intensity, and excesses of the spectacle," often for didactic purpose. *Acting Naturally: Victorian Theatricality and Authenticity* (Charlottesville: University of Virginia Press, 2004), 17.

11 Isabelle Lehuu remarks that such papers were "antithetical to private reading," and were "conceived for display." *Carnival on the Page: Popular Print Media in Antebellum America* (Chapel Hill: University of North Carolina Press, 2000), 64.

12 Anne Horn, "Theatre, Journalism, and Thackeray's 'Man of the World Magazine,'" *Victorian Periodicals Review* 32, no. 3 (1999): 29.
13 Josette Féral and Ronald P. Bermingham, "Theatricality: The Specificity of Theatrical Language," *SubStance* 31, no. 2/3 (2002): 98, 105.
14 Monica F. Cohen, *Pirating Fictions: Ownership and Creativity in Nineteenth-Century Popular Culture* (Charlottesville: University of Virginia Press, 2017), 2, 9.
15 Adrian Johns, *Piracy: The Intellectual Property Wars from Gutenberg to Gates* (Chicago: University of Chicago Press, 2010), 306.
16 "The Quarter Deck," *Corsair*, March 16, 1839, 1.
17 "The Great Western," *Brother Jonathan*, June 11, 1842, 185.
18 The editor of the *American Miscellany* is unnamed and unknown. A reference to "the literary productions of our transatlantic brethren" suggests that he or she was British, or at least wanted to be read as British. "Preface," *American Miscellany*, vol. 1, unpaginated, (i).
19 Isaac C. Pray, obituary, *New York Times*, November 29, 1869, 5.
20 For information on Paul's life, see: "Paul, Howard," in *Appleton's Cyclopaedia of American Biography, 1888, Vol. 4—Facsimile Reprint* (Detroit: Gale Research Company, 1968), 678–79.
21 Isaac Clarke Pray, "Science and Art," *Great Western Magazine*, May 1842, 189.
22 See, for example: Rosemarie K. Bank, *Theatre Culture in America, 1825–1860* (Cambridge: Cambridge University Press, 1997); Jason Schaffer, *Performing Patriotism: National Identity in the Colonial and Revolutionary Americas* (Philadelphia: University of Pennsylvania Press, 2007); S. E. Wilmer, *Theatre, Society and the Nation: Staging American Identities* (Cambridge: Cambridge University Press, 2002).
23 Joseph Roach, *Cities of the Dead: Circum-Atlantic Performance* (New York: Columbia University Press, 1996), 3–5, 26–28.
24 For histories of the stage Yankee, his reception, and his transformations, see: Bank, *Theatre Culture in America*, 38–42; Francis Hodge, *Yankee Theatre: The Image of America on the Stage, 1825–1850* (Austin: University of Texas Press, 1964); Maura L. Jortner, "Playing 'America' on Nineteenth-Century Stages; or, Jonathan in England and Jonathan at Home," PhD dissertation, University of Pittsburgh, 2006; Winifred Morgan, *An American Icon: Brother Jonathan and America Identity* (Newark: University of Delaware Press, 1988).
25 Karen Halttunen, *Confidence Men and Painted Women: A Study of Middle-Class Culture in America, 1830–1870* (New Haven: Yale University Press, 1982); Stephen Mihm, *A Nation of Counterfeiters* (Cambridge, MA: Harvard University Press, 2009).
26 Heather S. Nathans, "Representing Ethnic Identity on the Antebellum Stage, 1825–61," *The Oxford Handbook of American Drama*, January 7, 2014, https://doi.org/10.1093/oxfordhb/9780199731497.013.021.
27 Matthew Pethers, "That Eternal Ghost of Trade: Anglo-American Market Culture and the Antebellum Stage Yankee," in *The Materials of Exchange between Britain and North East America, 1750–1800*, ed. Daniel Maudlin and Robin Peel (Farnham, UK: Ashgate, 2013), 98, 101.
28 George Handel Hill, *Scenes from the Life of an Actor . . . by a Celebrated Comedian*, ed. C. Hill (New York: Garrett & Co., 1853), 130.
29 All reviews quoted in W. K. Northall, ed., *The Life and Recollections of Yankee Hill: Together with Anecdotes and Incidents of His Travels* (New York: W. F. Burgess, 1850), 51, 52. Of the London reviews collected by Northall, only the *Sunday Times* identified the Yankee as a regional type rather than a national figure: 56.
30 Pethers notes that Mathews's trickster inspired James Henry Hackett, Hill's predecessor as America's leading Yankee comic, to add an edge of sharpness to his Yankee. Pethers, "That Eternal Ghost of Trade," 101.

31 Dale Cockrell, *Demons of Disorder: Early Blackface Minstrels and Their World* (Cambridge: Cambridge University Press, 1997), 24; Sean X. Goudie, "The West Indies, Commerce, and a Play for U.S. Empire: Recovering J. Robinson's 'The Yorker's Stratagem' (1792)," *Early American Literature* 40, no. 1 (2005): 7; Nathans, "Representing Ethnic Identity."

32 Jeffrey H. Richards, "Race and the Yankee: Woodworth's *Forest Rose*," *Comparative Drama* 34, no. 1 (2000): 40.

33 Review of *The Forest Rose* from the *Examiner*, in *The Living Age*, November 1851, 288.

34 For further information about Berger's activities, see: John Adcock, "Yesterday's Papers: George Berger and His Sons, 1796–1868," accessed May 25, 2016, http://john-adcock.blogspot.com/2014/08/george-berger-and-his-sons-1796-1868.html.

35 "Preface," *American Miscellany*, (i).

36 For histories of the *Corsair* and the *Mirror*, see Frank Luther Mott, *A History of American Magazines, 1741–1930* (Cambridge, MA: Harvard University Press, 1930), 356–58, 320–30.

37 For a history of the *Ladies' Companion*, see: Mott, *History of American Magazines*, 626–28.

38 Lehuu, *Carnival on the Page*, 11.

39 Bob Nicholson, "'You Kick the Bucket; We Do the Rest!': Jokes and the Culture of Reprinting in the Transatlantic Press," *Journal of Victorian Culture* 17, no. 3 (2012): 285, 274.

40 "Miscellany (From the American Papers)," *American Miscellany*, September 28, 1839, 32.

41 Nathaniel Parker Willis, "Jottings Down in London: Number Three," *Corsair*, August 17, 1839, 362.

42 Timothy Titterwell, *Yankee Notions: A Medley* (Boston: Otis, Broaders, and Company, 1838), xiv.

43 Ibid., vi.

44 As Loughran argues, "Rhetorical projections of nationalist sympathy among different regions preceded sustained material connections by many decades." Trish Loughran, *The Republic in Print: Print Culture in the Age of U.S. Nation Building, 1770–1870* (New York: Columbia University Press, 2007), 26.

45 "To Contributors and Well-Wishers," *American Miscellany*, April 11, 1840, 16.

46 John Neal, "Traits of the New-Englanders, Otherwise the Yankees," *American Miscellany*, February 15, 1840, 342.

47 "To Contributors and Well-Wishers," *American Miscellany*, 16.

48 Publisher's Note, *American Miscellany*, volume 2, n.d., (1).

49 *Blackwood's Magazine* published a poem that Pray sent from New York dated April 20, 1839. Isaac Clarke Pray, "Sonnet on the Death of a Lady," *Blackwood's Edinburgh Magazine*, June 1839, 830. Pray's residence in England in March 1843 is confirmed by his appearance as a witness in the trial of Chartist leader Feargus O'Connor for sedition, as the registered proprietor of the *Evening Star*, the paper that O'Connor edited. For Pray's testimony, see: *The Trial of Feargus O'Connor, Esq. (Barrister at Law) and Fifty-Eight Others at Lancaster on a Charge of Sedition, Conspiracy, Tumult and Riot* (Manchester: A. Heywood, 1843), 318–19.

50 Isaac Clarke Pray, "The Editor's Study: Introduction," *Great Western Magazine*, April 1842, 99.

51 Isaac Clarke Pray, "Will It Be Characteristic?," *Great Western Magazine*, April 1842, 100–101.

52 "War with America: An Examination of the Instigations and Probable Effects, by a Kentuckian," *Great Western Magazine*, April 1842, 97.

53 [Henry W. Bellows], "Moral and Political Freedom," *Great Western Magazine*, July 1842, 289–95; [Abel P. Upshur], "The Nature and Character of the Federal Government of the United States," *Great Western Magazine*, July 1842, 338–78, 385–438.

54 "War with America," 97.

55 Isaac Clarke Pray, "The North American Indians," *Great Western Magazine*, April 1842, 1.

56 Pray, "Will It Be Characteristic?," 100.

57 For a history of Arcturus, see Mott, *A History of American Magazines*, 711–12.

58 "The Drama at Tinnecum, or Mr. Chipp in the 'Provinces,'" *Great Western Magazine*, May 1842, 166, 167, 171, 175.

59 Mott, *A History of American Magazines*, 607–14.

60 Karl M. Kippola, *Acts of Manhood: The Performance of Masculinity on the American Stage* (New York: Palgrave Macmillan, 2012), 11.

61 "The United States and England," *Great Western*, September 1842, 5, 78.

62 "Introduction," *Great Western*, April 1842, 99.

63 "The United States and England," 75.

64 Henry Howard Paul, "Introductory," *American Magazine*, October 1851, 51, 52.

65 "What the Press of the United Kingdom Say of Us," *American Magazine*, December 1851, 170.

66 Henry Howard Paul, "Kossuth and American Literature," *American Magazine*, December 1851, 166.

67 Henry Howard Paul, Chit Chat, *American Magazine*, October 1851, 53.

68 Henry Howard Paul, Chit Chat, *American Magazine*, January 1852, 225–26.

69 "A Chunk of Fun from the 'New York Dutchman,'" *American Magazine*, February 1852, 281.

70 In the version of *The Forest Rose* published in 1855 (cited by most scholars of the play), Bellamy is a British tourist who declares that he will "not fail to notice you all when I publish my Three Months in America." Samuel Woodworth, *The Forest Rose, or, American Farmers: A Drama, in Two Acts.* (Boston: William V. Spencer, 1855), 31. In the version submitted for licensing in London in 1851, Bellamy vows to "go back to New York and put you all in the Herald." Samuel Woodworth, "The Forest Rose: A Yankee Comedy in Two Acts," 1851, Add. MSS 43037 ff. 60–94b, f. 94., Lord Chamberlain's Plays, British Library.

71 William Bayle Bernard, "The Yankee Pedlar," n.d., Add. MSS 42944, ff. 514–526b, f. 526., Lord Chamberlain's Plays, British Library.

72 Cynthia Lee Patterson, *Art for the Middle Classes: America's Illustrated Magazines of the 1840s* (Jackson: University Press of Mississippi, 2010), 11,15. For histories of these magazines, see Mott, *A History of American Magazines*, 580–94, 544–55, 769–72.

73 Clara Moreton, "The Estranged Hearts. An American Prize Tale," *American Magazine*, October 1851, 12.

74 Anne Norton, *Alternative Americas: A Reading of Antebellum Political Culture* (Chicago: University of Chicago Press, 1986), 167.

75 Caroline Lee Hentz, "The Pedlar. The Sequel to the Mob Cap," *American Magazine*, December 1852, 118, 119, 117. In this reading, "The Pedlar" becomes a trying out of Hentz's later anti-Tom novel, *The Planter's Northern Bride* (1854), in which a marriage between a Northern woman and a Southern man quietens abolitionist sentiments among Northerners and creates a unifying national feeling. That novel—which depicts Southern enslavers as beneficent patriarchs, abolitionists as base agitators, and enslaved people as happy and well-treated—ends with a warning against sectional conflict, arguing that "the North and the South are branches of the same parent tree, and the lightning bolt that shivers the one,

must scorch and wither the other." Caroline Lee Hentz, *The Planter's Northern Bride* (Philadelphia: T. B. Peterson and Brothers, 1854), 579.

76 Hentz, "Pedlar," 120, 121, 123.

77 Robert C. Winthrop, "Washington and the Union," *American Magazine*, February 1852, 275.

78 "Merry Graphs," *American Magazine*, October 1851, 56; Henry M. Klapp, "The Whale Fishery on the Brazil Coast," *American Magazine*, January 1852, 196–206.

79 "Periodicals for the People," *Dundee, Perth and Cupar Advertiser*, March 16, 1852, 3.

80 "Chit Chat," *American Magazine*, December 1851, 169. For further discussion of the reprinting and adaptation of American fiction by British periodicals, see Stephan Pigeon, "Steal It, Change It, Print It: Transatlantic Scissors-and-Paste Journalism in the Ladies' Treasury, 1857–1895," *Journal of Victorian Culture* 22, no. 1 (2017): 24–39.

81 Margaret Beetham, *A Magazine of Her Own: Desire and Domesticity in the Woman's Magazine, 1800–1914*, electronic edition (Abingdon: Routledge, 2003), 73.

82 As Thomas E. Sebrell explains in his history of the *London American*, the paper evolved from a gazette aimed at Americans and those with American interests into an organ of Northern propaganda at the outbreak of the Civil War. Thomas E. Sebrell, *Persuading John Bull: Union and Confederate Propaganda in Britain, 1860–1865* (Lanham, MA: Lexington Books, 2014), 23–28. Sebrell's book does not mention the *American Scrap Book*.

83 *American Scrap Book*, December 28, 1861, 156; November 16, 1861, 60. Such attacks on the Confederacy did not stop the *Scrap Book* printing derogatory jokes about African Americans, or reprinting fiction that portrayed slavery as an essentially benevolent institution. It would be more accurate to describe the *Scrap Book* as anti-secession than anti-slavery.

Chapter 6: The Transatlantic Slave Narrative Trade

1 George Thompson, letter to William Lloyd Garrison, September 24, 1852, Anti-Slavery Collection, Boston Public Library, https://www.digitalcommonwealth.org/search/commonwealth:2v23xk13n.

2 Hannah-Rose Murray, *Advocates of Freedom: African American Transatlantic Abolitionism in the British Isles* (Cambridge: Cambridge University Press, 2020), 10,18.

3 This number comes from William L. Andrews's annotated bibliography of slave narratives, *To Tell a Free Story: The First Century of Afro-American Autobiography, 1760–1865* (Chicago: University of Illinois Press, 1986), 333–42, and searching the *Publishers' Circular* and union library catalogues. It does not include narratives published in Britain after 1860 (for example, the 1862 London edition of Harriet Jacobs's *The Deeper Wrong; Or, Incidents in the Life of a Slave Girl*) or autobiographical narratives by African Americans who were not enslaved (for example, Zilpha Elaw's *Memoirs of the Life, Religious Experience, Ministerial Travels and Labours of Mrs Zilpha Elaw*, published in London by the author in 1846).

4 John Passmore Edwards, *Uncle Tom's Companions; Or, Facts Stranger than Fiction. A Supplement to "Uncle Tom's Cabin": Being Startling Incidents in the Lives of Celebrated Fugitive Slaves* (London: Edwards and Co., 1852).

5 Moses Roper, letter to BFASS Committee, May 9, 1844, in C. Peter Riley, ed., *The Black Abolitionist Papers, vol. 1: The British Isles, 1830–1865* (Chapel Hill: University of North Carolina Press, 1985), 134.

6 Frederick Douglass, *The Frederick Douglass Papers, Series Three: Correspondence, Volume 1: 1842–1852*, ed. John R. Kaufman-McKivigan (New Haven: Yale University Press, 2009), 59.

7 In 2010, Leon Jackson argued that scholars were reaching a "tipping point," at which "scholars of African American studies and scholars of print culture will

learn to share their secrets." "The Talking Book and the Talking Book Historian: African American Cultures of Print—The State of the Discipline," *Book History* 13 (2010): 254. Important early examples of such work include Lois Brown, "Memorial Narratives of African Women in Antebellum New England," *Legacy* 21, no 1–2 (2003): 38–61; Frances Smith Foster, "A Narrative of the Interesting Origins and (Somewhat) Surprising Developments of African-American Print Culture," *American Literary History* 17, no. 4 (2005): 714–40; Jocelyn Moody, "Silenced Women and Silent Language in Early African- and Anglo-American Newspapers," in *Cultural Narratives: Textuality and Performance in American Culture before 1900*, ed. Sandra Gustafson and Caroline Sloat (Notre Dame, IN: University of Notre Dame Press, 2010), 220–39.

8 Paul Gilroy, *The Black Atlantic: Modernity and Double Consciousness* (London: Verso, 1993), 111.

9 Fionnghuala Sweeney, *Frederick Douglass and the Atlantic World* (Oxford: Oxford University Press, 2007), 2.

10 Michaël Roy, "Cheap Editions, Little Books, and Handsome Duodecimos: A Book History Approach to Antebellum Slave Narratives," *MELUS: Multi-Ethnic Literature of the United States* 40, no. 4 (2015): 70.

11 Leon Jackson, *The Business of Letters: Authorial Economies in Antebellum America* (Stanford: Stanford University Press, 2008), 2–6.

12 See, for example Eric Gardner, *Unexpected Places: Relocating Nineteenth-Century African American Literature* (Jackson: University Press of Mississippi, 2009); Derrick Spires, *The Practice of Citizenship: Black Politics and Print Culture in the Early United States* (Philadelphia: University of Pennsylvania Press, 2019).

13 Brigitte Fielder and Jonathan Senchyne, "Introduction: Infrastructures of African American Print," in *Against a Sharp White Background: Infrastructures of African American Print*, ed. Brigitte Fielder and Jonathan Senchyne (Madison: University of Wisconsin Press, 2019), 14.

14 For examples of material histories of slave narratives, see Teresa A. Goddu, "The Slave Narrative as Material Text," in *The Oxford Handbook of the African American Slave Narrative*, ed. John Ernest (Oxford: Oxford University Press, 2014), 149–64; Teresa A. Goddu, *Selling Anti-Slavery: Aboliton and Mass Media in Antebellum America* (Philadelphia: University of Pennsylvania Press, 2020), especially 55–82; Michaël Roy, "Cheap Editions," 69–93; Michaël Roy, "The Vanishing Slave Narrative: Publishing the Narrative of Charles Ball, from *Slavery in the United States* (1836) to *Fifty Years in Chains* (1858)," *Papers of the Bibliographical Society of America* 111, no. 4 (2017): 513–45; Samantha M. Sommers, "Harriet Jacobs and the Recirculation of Print Culture," *MELUS: Multi-Ethnic Literature of the United States* 40, no. 3 (2015): 134–49.

15 Examining the British reception of slave narratives, Audrey Fisch notes the "widespread circulation of [those] narratives in the literary marketplace," and historian R. J. M. Blackett, in a study of Black Americans in Atlantic abolitionism, quotes sales in the tens of thousands for narratives by Douglass and Northup. Audrey A. Fisch, *American Slaves in Victorian England: Abolitionist Politics in Popular Literature and Culture* (Cambridge: Cambridge University Press, 2000), 8; R. J. M. Blackett, *Building an Antislavery Wall: Black Americans in the Atlantic Abolitionist Movement, 1830–1860* (Baton Rouge: Louisiana State University Press, 2002), 26. For other scholarship on the influence of slave narratives on British literature, see Julia Sun-Joo Lee, *The American Slave Narrative and the Victorian Novel* (Oxford: Oxford University Press, 2010); Helen Thomas, *Romanticism and Slave Narratives: Transatlantic Testimonies* (Cambridge: Cambridge University Press, 2000).

16 Wilson Armistead, letter to Louis Alexander Chamerovzow (*hereafter* LAC), June[?] 15, 1854, Archive of the Anti-Slavery Society (*hereafter* ArcA-SS), MSS. Brit. Emp. s. 18/C27, fol. 57, Bodleian Library, Oxford University.

17 Michaël Roy, "'Printers Were Almost Afraid to Set Up the Types': Publishing and Circulating Antislavery Literature in Antebellum America," in *Undoing Slavery: American Abolitionism in Transnational Perspective (1776–1865)*, ed. Michaël Roy, Marie-Jeanne Rossignol, Claire Parfait (Paris: Éditions Rue d'Ulm, 2018), 95–96.

18 Roy, "'Printers Were Almost Afraid,'" 111.

19 For the expansion of US abolitionist societies and their print infrastructures, see Trish Loughran, *The Republic in Print: Print Culture in the Age of U.S. Nation Building, 1770–1870* (New York: Columbia University Press, 2007), 303–62. For the decline of organized abolitionism as a political force in Britain and the rise of a popular and malleable anti-slavery sentiment, see Richard Huzzey, *Freedom Burning: Anti-Slavery and Empire in Victorian Britain* (Ithaca, NY: Cornell University Press, 2012), 17–21. The first time the BFASS appeared on the title page of a US slave narrative was in the 1855 publication of *Slave Life in Georgia*.

20 "Obituary," *Publishers' Circular* 37, no. 188, September 16, 1874, 622.

21 Douglass, *The Frederick Douglass Papers*, ed. Kaufman-McKivigan, 69.

22 Roy, "Cheap Editions," 77–79.

23 Reviews of *The Fugitive Blacksmith* appeared in the *Christian Witness*, *Nonconformist*, *Teetotal Times*, *British Friend*, and *Anti-Slavery Reporter* in 1849.

24 James W. C. Pennington, "Mr. Charles Gilpin," in *The Fugitive Blacksmith; Or, Events in the History of James W. C. Pennington, Pastor of a Presbyterian Church, New York, Formerly a Slave in the State of Maryland, United States*, 2nd ed. (London: Charles Gilpin, 1849), iii.

25 Ronald J. Zboray and Mary Saracino Zboray, *Literary Dollars and Social Sense: A People's History of the Mass Market Book* (New York: Routledge, 2013), 127.

26 James W. C. Pennington, "Preface to the Third Edition," *The Fugitive Blacksmith; Or, Events in the History of James W. C. Pennington, Pastor of a Presbyterian Church, New York, Formerly a Slave in the State of Maryland, United States*, 3rd ed. (London: Charles Gilpin, 1850), xvi–xvii.

27 Josiah Henson, *The Life of Josiah Henson: Formerly A Slave* (London: Charles Gilpin, 1852), back cover.

28 Hannah Webb, letter to Maria Weston Chapman, November 17, 1845, Anti-Slavery Collection, Boston Public Library, https://ark.digitalcommonwealth.org/ark:/50959/7s75ds99q.

29 Michael Rodegang Drescher, "The Publishing of Protest: Brown, Pennington, and Gilpin's Network of Dissent," in *Racial and Ethnic Identities in the Media*, ed. Eleftheria Arapoglou, Yiorgos Kalogeras, and Jopi Nyman (London: Palgrave Macmillan, 2016), 68.

30 The publication statement on the title page of the 1846 edition reads, "Published for the author." Moses Roper, *Narrative of the Adventures and Escape of Moses Roper, from American Slavery* (Berwick-upon-Tweed: Published for the author, and printed at the Warder Office, 1846). Martha Cutter suggests that before these self-published editions, Roper still "had a large degree of control over the successive versions of his text, adding material about his own life after slavery deleting an 'authenticating' letter from one of his sponsors, and expanding the amount of visual content." *The Illustrated Slave: Empathy, Graphic Narrative, and the Visual Culture of the Transatlantic Abolition Movement* (Athens: University of Georgia Press, 2017), 109–10.

31 On December 11, 1849, Webb wrote to antislavery activist Caroline Weston that Brown "owes us nearly 200 dollars for an edition of his book." Anti-Slavery

Collection, Boston Public Library, https://ark.digitalcommonwealth.org/ark:/50959/qz20tn351.

32 See Patrick Scott, "The Business of Belief: The Emergence of 'Religious' Publishing," in *Sanctity and Secularity: The Church and the World*, vol. 10, Studies in Church History (Oxford: Blackwell, 1973), 216, 222; Michael Winship, *American Literary Publishing in the Mid-Nineteenth Century: The Business of Ticknor and Fields* (Cambridge: Cambridge University Press, 1995), 44–45, 50.

33 Winship, *American Literary Publishing*, 53.

34 Patrick Scott observes that for religious texts, a publisher's imprint often suggested the theological leanings of the text and this information was part of the reason for the increasing separation of religious publishing from the rest of the trade over the century. "The Business of Belief," 221. It is possible that keeping slave narratives out of the commercial market allowed antislavery supporters to make similar associations with certain firms.

35 "The Life of Frederick Douglass," *Spectator*, November 29, 1845, 1145.

36 "Twelve Years a Slave," *Athenaeum*, June 25, 1853, 761.

37 Roy, "Cheap Editions," 80.

38 James Cephas Derby, *Fifty Years among Authors, Books and Publishers* (New York: G. W. Carleton & Company, 1884), 108; "English and American Agencies," *Literary World*, October 30, 1852.

39 "Advertisement for *Twelve Years a Slave*," *Norton's Literary Gazette*, April 15, 1853, 71.

40 "Our Weekly Gossip," *Athenaeum*, January 21, 1854, 90.

41 *Twelve Years* was dictated to and edited by white Auburn lawyer David Wilson, so it is difficult to attribute the presence of these quotations to Northup with any certainty. Nevertheless, Northup describes how as a young man he spent much time "employed over my books," and the frequent reprinting of British poetry in American periodicals means that Northup may have read these texts after he was rescued from slavery, or surreptitiously during his enslavement: Solomon Northup, *Twelve Years a Slave. Narrative of Solomon Northup, A Citizen of New-York, Kidnapped in Washington City in 1841, and Rescued in 1853, from a Cotton Plantation near the Red River, in Louisiana* (London and New York: Sampson Low, Son & Co., 1853), 20. Moreover, for my argument, the question of who is responsible for the quotations matters less than the way in which they contribute to the presentation of "Solomon Northup" as a narrating subject.

42 Daniel Hack, *Reaping Something: New African American Transformations of Victorian Literature* (Princeton: Princeton University Press, 2017), 181.

43 Northup, *Twelve Years a Slave*, 259–60. Northup slightly varies the second line of the quotation from its original, which reads: "With being's strife on earth opprest." John Malcolm, "Byron's Prayer," *Edinburgh Literary Review*, March 28, 1831, 339.

44 "Introductory," *Publishers' Circular*, June 16, 1853, 222.

45 "List for July: Sampson Low, Son, And Co.," *Literary Gazette*, July 2, 1853, 222.

46 John Sekora, "Black Message/White Envelope: Genre, Authenticity, and Authority in the Antebellum Slave Narrative," *Callaloo* no. 32 (1987): 502.

47 Solomon Northup, *Twelve Years a Slave.* British Library 10881.b.38.

48 For further discussion of the illustrations, see Elizabeth Pope, "Twelve Years a Slave, the Book: Dramatizations, Illustrations, & Editions," Past Is Present: The American Antiquarian Society Blog, February 28, 2014, https://pastispresent.org/2014/good-sources/twelve-years-a-slave-the-book-dramatizations-illustrations-editions/.

49 Cutter, *The Illustrated Slave*, 10–11.

50 This image also appears on the cover of at least one later American edition of *Twelve Years a Slave*. It bears close resemblance to an image used on the cover of an 1853 London edition of *Uncle Tom's Cabin* by Clarke Beeton, in which a chained enslaved woman is kneeling beneath a man who is raising a whip over his shoulder, about to beat her.

51 Cutter, *The Illustrated Slave*, 10.

52 Andrew Piper, *Book Was There: Reading in Electronic Times* (Chicago: University of Chicago Press, 2012), 2.

53 Northup, *Twelve Years a Slave*, 80.

54 "Brief Notices," *Eclectic Review*, April 1854, 496.

55 Advertisement for *Twelve Years a Slave*, *Athenaeum*, August 13, 1853, 956; Advertisement for *Twelve Years a Slave*, *Literary Gazette*, August 13, 1853, 780.

56 Northup, *Twelve Years a Slave*, 64.

57 Saidiya Hartman, *Scenes of Subjection: Terror, Slavery, and Self-Making in Nineteenth-Century America* (New York: Oxford University Press, 1997), 21.

58 Edward Marston, *After Work: Fragments from the Workshop of an Old Publisher* (London: Heinemann, 1904), 41.

59 A testimonial from John Scoble, then Secretary of the BFASS, included as an appendix to *Slave Life in Georgia*, is dated June 20, 1851: John Brown, *Slave Life in Georgia: A Narrative of the Life, Sufferings, and Escape of John Brown, a Fugitive Slave, Now in England*, ed. Louis Alexis Chamerovzow (London: [British and Foreign Anti-Slavery Society], 1855), 243.

60 For more information on the Negro Seamen Acts, see Philip M. Hamer, "Great Britain, the United States, and the Negro Seamen Acts, 1822–1848," *Journal of Southern History* 1, no. 1 (1935): 3–28.

61 Brown, *Slave Life in Georgia*, 36.

62 Ibid., 24.

63 Fisch, *American Slaves in Victorian England*, 64–68.

64 Ikuko Asaka, "Different Tales of John Glasgow: John Brown's Evolution to *Slave Life in Georgia*," *Black Studies* 49, no. 3 (2018): 215.

65 Brown, *Slave Life in Georgia*, 103–4, 106–7.

66 No letters survive between Brown and the BFASS, nor do any of the BFASS's financial records for the years either side of the book's publication.

67 John Wigham (*hereafter* JW), letter to LAC, October 26, 1853, ArcA-SS, MSS. Brit. Emp. s. 18, C37/82.

68 JW, letter to LAC, October 31, 1853, ArcA-SS, MSS. Brit. Emp. s. 18, C39/83.

69 Edward Wigham (*hereafter* EW), letter to LAC, February 27, 1855, ArcA-SS, MSS. Brit. Emp. s. 18, C37/64.

70 Ibid. Booksellers who stocked the narrative would have taken a percentage of the purchase price on each sale, eating into either Brown's 3d share from each copy or the BFASS's attempts to recoup expenses.

71 *Anti-Slavery Advocate*, June 1, 1855, 8.

72 Unlike half-profits contracts, there is no suggestion that the BFASS had to be paid before Brown took his cut.

73 Stephen M. Best, *The Fugitive's Properties: Law and the Poetics of Possession* (Chicago: University of Chicago Press, 2004), 81.

74 EW, letter to LAC, February 27, 1855, ArcA-SS, MSS. Brit. Emp. s. 18, C37/67.

75 LAC, letter to John Bishop Estlin, February 6, 1855, MS A.9.2 v.28, p.39, Boston Public Library. https://ark.digitalcommonwealth.org/ark:/50959/2z10zr730

76 Joseph Clark, letter to LAC, March 21, 1855, ArcA-SS, MSS. Brit. Emp. s. 18, C29/131.

77 Brown, *Slave Life in Georgia*, 44.

78 Francis A. Calder, letter to LAC, April 16, 1855, ArcA-SS, MSS. Brit. Emp. s. 18, C29/26.
79 Joseph Clark, letter to LAC, March 21, 1855, ArcA-SS, MSS. Brit. Emp. s. 18, C29/131.
80 Thomas Owen, letter to LAC, February 26, 1855, ArcA-SS, MSS. Brit. Emp. s. 18, C34/153.
81 William Smeal, letter to LAC, April 12, 1855, ArcA-SS, MSS. Brit. Emp. s. 18, C36/57.
82 S. Hilditch, letter to LAC, February 19, 1855, ArcA-SS, MSS. Brit. Emp. s. S.22, G84.
83 David Jerdan, letter to LAC, March 6, 1855, ArcA-SS, MSS. Brit. Emp. s. 18, C32/145.
84 Brown, *Slave Life in Georgia*, 115.
85 Brown encapsulates the difficulty, identified by Hartman, of distinguishing agency from subjection in a system of absolute dominion: "Is it possible to consider, let alone imagine, the agency of the performative when the black performative is inextricably linked with the specter of contented subjection, the tortuous display of the captive body, and the ravishing of the body that is the condition of the other's pleasure?" Hartman, *Scenes of Subjection*, 52.
86 Brown, *Slave Life in Georgia*, 125.
87 Ibid., 89. Accounts in the *Worcestershire Chronicle* (July 28, 1852), London *Morning Advertiser* (September 8, 1851), and *Bristol Times and Mirror* (May 17, 1851) mention Brown wearing the bells and horns.
88 Brown, *Slave Life in Georgia*, 89.
89 Beth A. McCoy, "Race and the (Para)Textual Condition," *PMLA* 121, no. 1 (2006): 156. For the classic reading of how white-authored paratexts confine Black experience even as they enable that experience to circulate in the world, see Sekora, "Black Message/White Envelope," 497.
90 Rachel A. Blumenthal, "Canonicity, Genre, and the Politics of Editing: How We Read Frederick Douglass," *Callaloo* 36, no. 1 (2013): 178–90.
91 Robert S. Levine, *The Lives of Frederick Douglass* (Cambridge: Harvard University Press, 2016), 91; Sweeney, *Frederick Douglass and the Atlantic World*, 19–36.
92 William Lloyd Garrison, "Preface," in *Narrative of the Life of Frederick Douglass, an American Slave*, by Frederick Douglass (Boston: Anti-Slavery Office, No. 25 Cornhill, 1845), viii.
93 Frederick Douglass, "Preface to the Second Dublin Edition," in *Narrative of the Life of Frederick Douglass; an American Slave*, by Frederick Douglass (Dublin: Webb and Chapman, 1846), iv.
94 James Olney argues that in many slave narratives, the "subthemes of literacy, identity, and freedom . . . lead into one another in such a way as they end up being altogether interdependent and virtually indistinguishable as thematic strands." "'I Was Born': Slave Narratives, Their Status as Autobiography and as Literature," *Callaloo* 7, no. 1 (1984): 53–54.
95 Frederick Douglass, *Narrative of Life of Frederick Douglass; an American Slave* (Dublin: Webb and Chapman, 1846), 33.
96 Douglass, "Preface to the Second Dublin Edition," iv, v–vi.
97 Levine, *The Lives of Frederick Douglass*, 101.
98 Douglass, *Narrative*, (1846), cxxvi.
99 Douglass, *Narrative* (1846), cxxvii. For Levine's discussion of changes to the *Liberator* letter, see *The Lives of Frederick Douglass*, 104–7.
100 Frederick Douglass, "Letter from Frederick Douglass," *Liberator*, February 27, 1846.
101 Douglass, *Narrative* (1846), cxxvii.

102 Tom F. Wright, *Lecturing the Atlantic: Speech, Print, and an Anglo-American Commons, 1830–1870* (Oxford: Oxford University Press, 2017), 56–57.
103 Robert B. Stepto, *From Behind the Veil: A Study of Afro-American Narrative* (Chicago: University of Illinois Press, 1991), 25.
104 Douglass, *Narrative* (1846), cxxvii.
105 Blumenthal, "Canonicity, Genre, and the Politics of Editing," 187.
106 Douglass, "Preface to the Second Dublin Edition," vi.
107 Resolution of the Hibernian Anti-Slavery Society, in Frederick Douglass, *Narrative of the Life of Frederick Douglass, an American Slave* (Dublin: Webb and Chapman, 1846), title page verso.
108 Jonathan Senchyne, "Bottles of Ink and Reams of Paper: *Clotel*, Racialization, and the Material Cultures of Print," in *Early African American Print Culture*, ed. Lara Langer Cohen and Jordan Alexander Stein (Philadelphia: University of Pennsylvania Press, 2012), 141.
109 For some examples of work on Brown's engagement with print culture, which usually focus on *Clotel*, see Lara Langer Cohen, "Notes from the State of Saint Domingue: The Practice of Citation in *Clotel*," in *Early African American Print Culture*, ed. Lara Langer Cohen and Jordan Alexander Stein (Philadelphia: University of Pennsylvania Press, 2012), 161–77; Mary Gangster, "Fact, Fiction and the Industry of Violence: Newspapers and Advertisements in *Clotel*," *African American Review* 48, no. 4 (2015): 431–44; Christopher Stampone, "'[H]Eroic Bravery in More than One Battle': The Creation of Heroes in William Wells Brown's Multi-Edition *Clotel*," *African American Review* 49, no. 2 (2016): 75–91.
110 Geoffrey Sanborn, *Plagiarama! William Wells Brown and the Aesthetics of Attractions* (New York: Columbia University Press, 2016), 11, 34.
111 William Wells Brown, *Narrative of William W. Brown, A Fugitive Slave* (Boston: Anti-Slavery Office, No. 21 Cornhill, 1848), 28.
112 For the publication history of Brown's *Narrative* in the United States, see Ezra Greenspan, *William Wells Brown: An African American Life* (New York: W. W. Norton & Company, 2014), 150–53, 167–69.
113 Richard S. Harrison, *Richard Davis Webb: Dublin Quaker Printer, 1805–72* (Cork: Red Barn Publishing, 1993), 54.
114 William Wells Brown, *Narrative of William W. Brown, an American Slave* (London: Charles Gilpin, 1849), title page verso.
115 William Wells Brown, "Note to the Present Edition," in *Narrative of William W. Brown, an American Slave*, iii.
116 Ibid., iv; William Wells Brown, "Note to the Present Edition," in *Narrative of William W. Brown, an American Slave* (London: Charles Gilpin, 1850), iv.
117 William Wells Brown, *Three Years in Europe; or, Places I Have Seen and People I Have Met* (London: Charles Gilpin, 1852), 7–8.
118 Charles Baraw, "William Wells Brown, *Three Years in Europe*, and Fugitive Tourism," *African American Review* 44, no. 3 (2011): 454.
119 Washington Irving, *The Sketch-Book of Geoffrey Crayon, Gent.*, vol.1 (London: John Murray, 1821), 122.
120 Ibid., 126, 129.
121 Brown, *Three Years in Europe*, 110, 111, 113, 114.
122 Baraw, "*Three Years in Europe*, and Fugitive Tourism," 462.
123 Brown, *Three Years in Europe*, 115, 116.
124 William Farmer, "Memoir of the Author," in *Three Years in Europe*, by Brown, ix.
125 Gérard Genette, *Paratexts: Thresholds of Interpretation*, trans. Jane E. Lewin (Cambridge: Cambridge University Press, 1987), 1.
126 Brown, *Three Years in Europe*, xxxi.

127 William Wells Brown, letter to Wendell Phillips, September 1, 1852, Wendell Phillips Papers, MS Am 1953, (327), Box 9, Houghton Library, Harvard University. Digital copy accessed December 11, 2019, http://nrs.harvard.edu/urn-3:FHCL.HOUGH:11816329. George Thompson also described it as "an expensive volume when compared with the others," presumably referring to narratives by formerly enslaved Americans, in his letter to William Garrison of September 24, 1852, cited above.

128 Sarah Meer, *American Claimants: The Transatlantic Romance, c. 1820–1920* (Oxford: Oxford University Press, 2020), 97, 86.

129 Laura Soderberg, "One More Time with Feeling: Repetition, Reparation, and the Sentimental Subject in William Wells Brown's Rewritings of *Clotel*," *American Literature* 88, no. 2 (2016): 241–67; Stampone, "[H]Eroic Bravery," 75–91.

130 William Wells Brown, *Clotel; or, the President's Daughter* (London: Partridge & Oakey, 1853), 244.

131 For explorations of Douglass's and Brown's textual engagements with these locations, see Martha Schoolman, "Violent Places: *Three Years in Europe* and the Question of William Wells Brown's Cosmopolitanism," *ESQ: A Journal of the American Renaissance* 58, no. 1 (2012): 25–28.

132 Bridget Bennett, "Guerrilla Inscription: Transatlantic Abolition and the 1851 Census," *Atlantic Studies* 17, no. 3 (2020): 378.

Coda: *Uncle Tom's Cabin*, *Dred*, and the End of American Literature's Transatlantic Materials

1 There is not space here for a full account of the publication of *Uncle Tom's Cabin* in the United States and Britain, and its reception, cultural impact and remediations. For publication history, see Barbara Hochman, "*Uncle Tom's Cabin* in the National Era: An Essay in Generic Norms and the Contexts of Reading," *Book History* 7, no. 1 (2004): 143–69; Claire Parfait, *The Publishing History of "Uncle Tom's Cabin," 1852–2002* (Aldershot: Ashgate, 2007); Michael Winship, "'The Greatest Book of Its Kind': A Publishing History of 'Uncle Tom's Cabin,'" *Proceedings of the American Antiquarian Society* 109, no. 2 (October 1999): 309–32. For its cultural impact in the nineteenth century and beyond, see Sarah Meer, *Uncle Tom Mania: Slavery, Minstrelsy, and Transatlantic Culture in the 1850s* (Athens: University of Georgia Press, 2005); Adena Spingarn, *Uncle Tom: From Martyr to Traitor* (Stanford: Stanford University Press, 2018).

2 *Uncle Tom's Cabin* was serialized between June 5, 1851, and April 1, 1852, and while book publication had been planned since September 1851, this was still too late to secure a British copyright for the entire text. The first edition of *Uncle Tom's Cabin* was published on March 20, 1852, twelve days before the serialization concluded. Winship, "The Greatest Book of Its Kind," 313.

3 John Adcock provides a detailed comparison between various accounts of the first English edition of *Uncle Tom's Cabin*, including those by Clarke and Vizetelly, which differ on the details of their arrangement for publishing the first edition (discussed below). John Adcock, "Yesterday's Papers: The Clarkes of Paternoster Row—Part 1," *Yesterday's Papers* (blog), June 26, 2013, http://john-adcock.blogspot.com/2013/06/the-clarkes-of-paternoster-row-part-1.html. I have drawn upon this information across the following paragraphs.

4 Henry Vizetelly, *Glances Back through Seventy Years: Autobiographical and Other Reminiscences*, (London: Kegan Paul, Trench, and Trubner, 1893), 1:358.

5 Clarke's account of the publication of *Uncle Tom's Cabin* is quoted in Harriet Beecher Stowe and Charles Edward Stowe, *Life of Harriet Beecher Stowe: Compiled from Her Letters and Journals* (Boston: Houghton Mifflin, 1889), 191.

6 Writing to Bentley in December, Stowe explained that "had I at the time received your letter, I should have included you also in this arrangement, but now

the thing has gone out of my power." She offered to write to Clarke to ask if Bentley might be included in the authorized edition of the *Key*, but this did not happen. December 1, 1852, Papers of Harriet Beecher Stowe, MS 6318, Special Collections, University of Virginia Library. Bentley may have been relieved as the *Key* sold poorly.

7 Edward Marston, *After Work: Fragments from the Workshop of an Old Publisher* (London: Heinemann, 1904), 60. Other sources have Low arriving after Beeton.

8 The Low and Stowe families shared strong Christian faiths, and the Lows hosted the Stowes personally on their visits to London, with the Stowes extending hospitality to Low's son. Mary Beecher Perkins, letter to Thomas Clapp Perkins, August 17–20, 1856, Harriet Beecher Stowe Center. Low offered handsome payments for Stowe's business, proposing to match the Edinburgh firm Constable and Co.'s offer of £2000 up front plus half profits for a temperance novel in 1856. "He wants to be Hatty's sole publisher. He will do all she asks," her brother, Charles, wrote in his journals. Charles Beecher, *Harriet Beecher Stowe in Europe: The Journal of Charles Beecher*, ed. Joseph S. Van Why and Earl French (Hartford: Stowe Day Foundation, 1986), 87.

9 J. Henry Harper, *The House of Harper: A Century of Publishing in Franklin Square* (New York: Harper and Brothers, 1912), 560.

10 Harriet Beecher Stowe (*hereafter* HBS), letter to James Fields, September 3, 1867, facsimile, Kirkham Database, Harriet Beecher Stowe Center. Original in Huntington Library, California; HBS, letter to Sampson Low, July 27, 18??, Sampson Low Collection, Open University.

11 Maria Cummins, letter to Sampson Low, Low & Co., December 17, 1860, Sampson Low Collection, Open University.

12 Meredith L. McGill, *American Literature and the Culture of Reprinting, 1834–1853* (Philadelphia: University of Pennsylvania Press, 2003), 254–56.

13 Advert for Mrs. Stowe's New Work, *Publishers' Circular*, August 16, 1854, 376.

14 *Jeffreys v. Boosey*, (1854) 4 HLC 815.

15 HBS, letter to William Hickling Prescott, before April 27, 1855, facsimile, Kirkham Database, Harriet Beecher Stowe Center. Original in Massachusetts Historical Society.

16 Mary Beecher Perkins, letter to Thomas Clapp Perkins, August 13, 1856, Letters of Mary Beecher Perkins—Mrs. Thomas Clapp, Harriet Beecher Stowe Center.

17 HBS, letter to Moses Dresser Phillips, August 15, 1856, facsimile, Kirkham Database, Harriet Beecher Stowe Center. Original in Boston Public Library.

18 Harriet Beecher Stowe, *Dred; a Tale of the Great Dismal Swamp* (Boston: Phillips, Sampson, 1856), iv.

19 Harriet Beecher Stowe, *Dred: A Tale of the Great Dismal Swamp* (London: Sampson Low, Son & Co., 1856), vi, v.

20 Christopher Hanlon, *America's England: Antebellum Literature and Atlantic Sectionalism* (New York: Oxford University Press, 2013), 125–47.

21 Stowe, *Dred* (London), vi, 448.

22 Stowe, *Dred* (Boston), iii–iv.

23 Michael Winship, "Distribution and the Trade," in *The Industrial Book, 1840–1880*, ed. Scott E. Casper, et al., vol. 3, A History of the Book in America (Chapel Hill: University of North Carolina Press, 2007), 120–21.

24 Jeffrey D. Groves, "Trade Communication," in *The Industrial Book*, ed. Casper, 131.

25 Trish Loughran, *The Republic in Print: Print Culture in the Age of U.S. Nation Building, 1770–1870* (New York: Columbia University Press, 2007), 26.

26 McGill, *Culture of Reprinting*, 276.

27 Michael Winship, *American Literary Publishing in the Mid-Nineteenth Century: The Business of Ticknor and Fields* (Cambridge: Cambridge University Press, 1995), 11.

28 Sampson Low published a 16s edition of Maria Cummins's *Haunted Hearts* (1864) while Cummins temporarily resided in Montreal, and Cummins assigned her copyright to Sampson Low. Routledge then published a 2s reprint. Low won an injunction against Routledge for breach of copyright, arguing that Cummins was resident in "British dominion" at the time of his publication, and he could therefore have copyright under the principles established in *Jeffreys v. Boosey* (1854). Routledge appealed the injunction all the way to the House of Lords, who, in 1868, upheld Low's copyright. *Routledge v. Low and Cummins* (1868) L.R. 3 H.L. 100. For an account of the case and its implications, see Catherine Seville, *The Internationalisation of Copyright Law: Books, Buccaneers and the Black Flag in the Nineteenth Century* (Cambridge: Cambridge University Press, 2006), 90–94.

29 HBS, letter to James T. Fields, February 3, 1869, facsimile, Kirkham Database, Harriet Beecher Stowe Centre. Original in Huntington Library, California.

30 Jennifer Harris, "It's a Family Affair: Harriet Beecher Stowe and Annie and James T. Fields," in *Popular Nineteenth-Century American Women Writers and the Literary Marketplace*, ed. Earl F. Yarington and Mary De Jong (Newcastle: Cambridge Scholars, 2007), 319.

31 Richard Bentley, letter to William Hickling Prescott, February 9, 1855, British Library MS46642, *The Archives of Richard Bentley & Son, 1829–1898,* microfilm edition (British Library holdings), 55 reels (Cambridge: Chadwyck-Healey, 1977), reel 40, vol. 83, image 64.

32 Introductory, *Publisher's Circular*, December 1, 1858, 524.

33 "America," *Bookseller*, December 30, 1861, 873.

34 Josiah Gilbert Holland, letter to Sampson Low, February 5, 1869, Sampson Low Collection, Open University.

35 *Report of the Proceedings at the Dinner Given by the Society of Authors to American Men and Women of Letters* (London: Society of Authors, 1888), 22.

36 Clough recounted the occasion in a letter to his future wife, Blanche Smith, and lists the guests as "Mr. N. Appleton [Longfellow's father-in-law], [Charles Conway] Felton, Lowell, Mrs. Mackintosh [Longfellow's sister-in-law], and a Yorkshire pie." December 29, 1852–January 4, 1853, *The Correspondence of Arthur Hugh Clough*, ed. F. L. Mulhauser, vol. 2 (Oxford: Oxford University Press), Oxford Scholarly Editions Online (2018), https://www.oxfordscholarlyeditions.com/view/10.1093/actrade/9780198778059.book.1/actrade-9780198778059-work-1.

37 Arthur Hugh Clough, letter to Ralph Waldo Emerson, November 26, 1847; Ralph Waldo Emerson, letter to Arthur Hugh Clough, January 16, 1849; Arthur Hugh Clough, letter to Ralph Waldo Emerson, February 20, 1849; Arthur Hugh Clough, letter to Ralph Waldo Emerson, September 12, 1856, *Correspondence of Arthur Hugh Clough*, ed. Mulhauser, vol. 2.

INDEX

KATIE MCGETTIGAN (BA University of Oxford; MSt University of Oxford; PhD Keele University) is senior lecturer of American literature at Royal Holloway, University of London. Her first book, *Herman Melville: Modernity and the Material Text*, was published in 2017 by the University of New Hampshire Press, and her essays have appeared in *American Literature*, the *Journal of American Studies*, *Leviathan: A Journal of Melville Studies*, *Symbiosis: A Journal of Transatlantic Literary and Cultural Relations*, and *Journal of Victorian Culture*. She has previously served on the executive committees of the British Association for American Studies and the British Association of Nineteenth-Century Americanists.